Georgina

David Munro

This is a work of fiction. Names, characters, organisations and incidents are products of the author's imagination or are used fictitiously. Any resemblance to actual persons living or dead, or actual incidents, is coincidental.

ISBN: 978-1-8381687-1-1

DEDICATION

This book is dedicated to Bob Scott, taken before his time.

ACKNOWLEDGMENTS

Editor Pat Watts
Proofreader Elaine Stone
Design Ewan Crawford
Cover art Christian Holzinger

CHAPTER 1

HEARTACHE

One evening in an elegant Californian mansion, Georgina sat alone and miserable with a glass of wine to comfort her. She picked up a magazine, started to read, then laid it on the white wooden kitchen table. Another glance at the wall clock as ten drew closer. Eddie had promised to return home three hours ago, so what would be his excuse this time? Georgina sighed, lifted her half-empty glass and then took a large swallow. She had answered the telephone earlier and hoped to hear Eddie's voice, but the line went dead. An occurrence that Georgina had experienced on several occasions in the past week.

The first six months with Eddie had been amongst her happiest, however, sadness now prevailed. No welcome look appeared in Eddies' eyes and little or no tenderness in his touch. The tall handsome jovial individual, who stole Georgina's heart less than two years ago, had become a stranger. The charm, generosity and compassion had gone. Also, Eddie's drinking had become excessive and his well-groomed appearance now a memory. What would the rest of 1931 have in store? Georgina recalled rumours that Eddie's wife had died from a sleeping tablet overdose. Could she have suffered from the same insecurity and unhappiness? If so, Georgina sympathised. After she met Eddie, Georgina wanted to settle into a carefree and lavish Los Angeles lifestyle. Financial problems and a drunken partner had beset her marriage, a secret kept from Eddie. Also, Georgina did not tell Eddie that her husband had been shot. Leaving New York for Los Angeles and a different name had eluded the NYPD. However, it now appeared Georgina had fallen foul of the same intolerable circumstances. As she filled her empty glass, an automobile came up the driveway. Georgina rushed to greet Eddie at the front door. However, after she opened it, different headlights shone towards her. Shielding her eyes, Georgina observed two dark-uniformed men get out. They approached the entrance with grim expressions. Georgina stared.

"Ma'am, there's been an accident," said one of the police officers. "Eddie's okay, just a bit shaken."

Georgina sighed. "Thank goodness."

"We'll give you a lift to the hospital," said the second officer.

Whilst Georgina dashed inside for a coat, the two officers returned to their black-coloured vehicle. Moments later, Georgina closed the door behind her, walked to the police vehicle and got in. After it exited the trimmed tree-lined driveway, she gathered her thoughts. "What happened?"

An officer in the front passenger seat turned round. "Eddie's automobile skidded off the road, ma'am."

"Was anybody else hurt?" Georgina sniffed.

The office looked at his colleague, then glanced round. "A young woman, but she has only a few cuts and bruises."

"A passer-by?"

The officer hesitated. "A passenger."

Georgina contemplated. As I suspected. That's why he spruced himself up this evening.

The vehicle travelled through quiet dark Los Angeles suburbs and soon arrived at the hospital. A police officer got out, opened the passenger door and Georgina stepped out. "Thanks for the lift," she said gratefully.

"When Eddie appeared in films, both of us were fans," said the officer, as he glanced at his colleague, who gave a slight grin.

After the officer got back into the vehicle, it sped off. Georgina took a deep breath, then went through the glass double-door entrance. When she approached reception, a woman with short dark hair looked up from her seated position. "Yes, madam, can I help you?"

"My partner was admitted earlier tonight."

"Eddie Arnott?"

Georgina nodded.

"Ward B." The woman pointed. "Straight along the corridor, turn left and then second right."

Georgina walked along the pristine white walled corridor with a marble floor. As she arrived at Eddie's private ward, he awaited her. "I heard your footsteps," said Eddie, as he gave a slight grin.

Georgina gave Eddie a hug. "How do you feel?" She sat on a wooden chair next to his bed.

"My neck and back ache. How did you get here?"

"In a police vehicle. They came to the mansion and explained what had happened."

"That was considerate of them," said Eddie. "Did you get their names?"

"They're fans," said Georgina, as she gave a slight smile.

"How much did they tell you?"

"Not much." Should I ask about his passenger? I'll wait in the meantime.

"The doctor said I've to stay here for a few days. He wants to run a few tests."

"On your neck?"

Eddie hesitated. "My heart." He sighed. "Before the accident, I suffered pains in my chest."

"Did you lose control of the automobile?"

Eddie nodded. Seconds later, his eyes started to close and then open. Following an extended yawn, Georgina got up from her chair. "I'll come back tomorrow."

"Can you make it in the afternoon?"

"Yes, okay." Is someone else due in the evening?

"See you tomorrow afternoon."

Georgina gave Eddie a hug, then left the ward. She walked back to reception, approached the desk and the woman looked up. "Yes, madam?"

"Can you call me a cab, please."

"It'll be around ten minutes, have a seat."

As the receptionist made a call, Georgina sat in a nearby waiting area, looked at her watch and yawned.

After a light lunch, Georgina gazed out the kitchen window, which looked onto the large rear garden. The trees had no leaves and flowers were devoid of any colour. Spring would be here in several weeks, however, could the same be said for Georgina? Persistent rumours of an affair between Eddie and a young vibrant raven-haired actress of beauty had been rife in Whitley Height's Hollywood community. For the first time, Georgina experienced the discomfort of being isolated and it put a dent in her self-esteem. At least in New York, if she fell out of favour with her husband, a wide circle of friends would lend their support. Then, Georgina heard a familiar noise come from the front entrance. Walking through the hall, she approached the mailbox and then opened it. As she took out three letters marked URGENT, Georgina observed their financial institution logos. After she laid them on an oak table, Georgina returned to the kitchen for another cup of coffee to comfort her. Whilst she waited for a kettle to boil, the telephone started to ring. Georgina sighed, went into the hall and picked up the receiver.

"Is Eddie there?" asked a gruff male voice.

"No, he isn't."

"When will he be back?"

"Who is this?" asked Georgina sharply.

"When he returns, tell him Marco Bellini called."

As the line went dead, Georgina replaced the receiver, shook her head and returned to the kitchen.

Not long after, a taxicab appeared at the front entrance. Georgina looked out the nearest window. Good, he's on time. She put on a pale blue coat to match her hat, grabbed her black leather handbag and then closed the main door. After Georgina stepped into the shiny white automobile, she sat in the rear passenger seat. Its driver looked over his shoulder at Georgina. "Where to, lady?"

"The hospital, please." Georgina flicked a blonde hair off her coat.

As it left the mansion, the driver looked at Georgina's reflection in his front mirror. "I hear your neighbour's new movie is forecast to be a huge hit."

"John hosted a party two weeks ago for the cast and crew."

"Was the top guy in MGM there?"

"No, they don't see eye to eye."

The driver grinned. "Hollywood's worst kept secret."

Whilst the taxicab headed towards its destination, Georgina reminisced about her introduction to Hollywood society. Visiting a restaurant, which included none other than Charlie Chaplin at a nearby table. Then, her first celebrity party at John Gilbert's mansion with a host of famous film stars. Indeed, the majority were likeable natural people. Although Mary Pickford could be a tad feisty.

"What's Eddie up to these days, lady?" asked the driver, as again he looked into his front mirror.

"Up to!" said Georgina, as she stared at the driver.

"Is there a comeback role in a 'talkie' on the cards? Not many silent films are made nowadays."

"He's been sent scripts from several movie companies." Georgina looked out the window. I wish.

"Weighing up his options?"

"Yes." A young actress, or me.

A short while later, Georgina arrived at the hospital. She paid the driver, and approached the light-coloured building, which caught the bright Los Angeles sunshine. Shading her eyes, Georgina walked through the doors to a reception desk. A different receptionist looked up. "Yes, can I help you?"

"I'm here to visit Eddie Arnott."

"Miss Harte is it?"

Georgina stared. "No, Miss Arnott!"

The receptionist hesitated. "Do you know where the ward is located, ma'am?"

Georgina stormed off towards Eddie's private ward, and when she got there, he had his nose in the Los Angeles Times. Eddie glanced up, then laid the newspaper on his lap. Georgina hugged Eddie and then sat down. "How are you today?" She unbuttoned her dark coat.

"My neck isn't as stiff."

"What about the tests on your heart?"

"No word as yet."

"Was the Hotrod damaged?"

Eddie sighed. "Afraid so."

"When I get home, I'll contact the insurance company."

Eddie paused. "I didn't pay the premium, Georgina."

"Why not?" she asked in amazement.

"I forgot."

"Forgot!" said Georgina sharply. "How bad is the damage?"

"A wing will have to be replaced. It could have been worse," said Eddie, as he attempted to quell Georgina's anger.

"To repair the damage will cost a small fortune!" Exasperated, Georgina blew between her teeth.

Eddie remained silent in the knowledge he had put himself and Georgina further in debt. The extent of which Georgina was unaware.

"A Marco Bellini called."

Eddie hesitated. "What did he say?"

"Just to tell you he called."

"That's all?" asked Eddie, surprised, but relieved.

Georgina gave a slight nod. "Who is he?"

"A friend of a friend."

At that moment, a tall slim fair-skinned young woman in a white uniform and cap to match entered and approached Eddie. "Time for a few more tests, Mr Arnott." She glanced at Georgina.

"I'll come back tomorrow," said Georgina, as she got up.

"Okay, see you then."

When Georgina departed the ward, Eddie gave a warm smile to the nurse, who reciprocated.

Whilst Georgina prepared dinner in the kitchen, Eddie sat in the front lounge and read a film magazine. Discharged two days ago from hospital after making a good recovery, he had been advised to change his lifestyle, or face the consequences. Hearing the sound of an automobile come up the driveway, Eddie laid his magazine on the beige couch and went to the front entrance. As he opened the door, three men in dark pinstripe suits and fedora hats got out and one approached Eddie. "Good to see you," said a stocky man with a dark moustache.

"Hi Marco. What do you want?" Eddie chewed his lip.

Flanked by a tall well-built individual with a grim expression, Marco faced Eddie and glared. "You know only too well what I want."

Eddie looked over his shoulder and not wanting Georgina to hear the conversation, closed the door. Marco gave a sly grin. "Does your dame know how much you owe?"

"I'll get you the money by next week, Marco."

"You said that last week, pal," said Marco, as he looked at Eddie's bulging eyes. "Do you take me for a fool!"

"I had an accident." Eddie stammered.

"Yeah, I heard. Is one dame not enough?" said Marco, as he glanced at the two accomplices who laughed.

"Please, Marco, keep your voice down," said Eddie, as he glanced behind. "I'll get you the cash." He stammered.

"If I don't get the money I loaned you by next week, that young dish of an actress won't recognise you!"

Georgina walked to the door, looked out and observed three men get into a flashy white automobile. After it moved off, Eddie took a couple of deep breaths.

"Who was that all about?" asked Georgina sharply.

"Someone lookin' for John," said Eddie, as he glanced down the bottom of the driveway, relieved.

"He's on location filming his next movie."

"That's what I told them, but they didn't believe me." Once more, Eddie glanced towards the bottom of the driveway. "Must get the automatic gate fixed, anyone can enter."

"The Hotrod is a priority."

Eddie mulled his thoughts. That's the least of my worries. Georgina noticed Eddie's hand had a slight shake. "Let's go inside, dinner is almost ready."

"I'm not hungry, Georgina," said Eddie, dejected.

"You look as if you've got the weight of the world on your shoulders," said Georgina, as she held his arm.

Eddie gave a forced smile. "It's all those tests that the medical staff carried out."

"They would insist you still have to eat."

Eddie agreed, however, he had a strong drink to calm his nerves. Not because of Marco's demand, also if Georgina found out about his 'other' life.

Unknown to Georgina, Marco Bellini was one of the city's most notorious thugs with a reputation for violence and illicit dealing. Anyone who landed on his wrong side ended up lifeless in a back alley or a river.

As Marco sat in the rear seat with a large cigar in his mouth, both men in the front remained silent. Moments later, one glanced over his shoulder. "Straight to the club, boss?"

Marco removed his cigar. "No, to Don's place. It won't be raided tonight."

The driver and front passenger looked at each other and Marco puffed on his cigar. "Keep your eyes on the road, I want to get there in one piece."

"Sure, boss," said both men in unison.

"What time is the liquor delivery tomorrow night?"

The accomplice in the front passenger seat looked round. "About midnight, boss."

"Before, or after?" Marco said sharply.

"Before, I think."

"I don't pay you to think, I pay you to know!"

"I'll find out."

"I don't want any problems this time," said Marco, as he looked out the side window.

"The Feds must have been tipped off," said the driver, as he glanced at Marco's reflection in the front mirror.

"If I find out who, they'll be attached to a meat hook." Marco wound down the window and flicked out his cigar.

A short while later, the automobile drew up alongside a row of shiny black Cadillacs. One accomplice got out, went to the rear door and then opened it. After Marco stepped out, he made his way to the club's entrance. As he walked in, a well-groomed dark-haired man in a dinner suit approached. "Good evening, Mr Bellini."

"Is Don around?" asked Marco, as he took off his coat and hat, then handed them to the man.

"I'll see if he is available, Mr Bellini."

The two men joined their boss and soon a tall well-dressed clean-shaven middle-aged man appeared. "Marco, good to see you." He held out his hand and after Marco shook it, Don glanced around the vicinity. "Let us talk in private."

"Get a drink, I'll see you later, said Marco, as he looked at his two men."

When both headed off, Don led Marco into a room with a small bar, where two voluptuous young women waited. Both stood at the bar with a drink and cigarette holder. Don looked their way. "Beat it, ladies, Marco and I have important business to discuss."

"Can we come back later?" asked the blonde."

"Maybe," said Don.

After both blonde and brunette left, Don poured two glasses of whisky. Taking a swig from one, he handed the other to Marco. "I hear Eddie's in trouble," said Don.

"You bet he is." Marco took a sip of his drink. "If he doesn't pay me soon, his broad will be on her own."

"One of my contacts spotted him with the Chief of Police. He had been involved in a serious accident, but the police hushed it up."

"In return for a favour, no doubt," said Marco, staring.

"They knew about your recent delivery."

"I'm goin' to kill that son of a bitch!"

"Not so fast, we can use him to our advantage."

Marco considered. "Let him have information about the next delivery."

"Of the false kind." Don grinned, then finished his drink. "We'll discredit him."

"And if he disappears, the law won't dig too deep."

"It's a win-win situation for us," said Don, as a grin flickered over his face.

"What if he doesn't pay me the money owed?"

"You'll make it up on bootlegging."

At that moment, the two young women returned and approached Don, who turned to face them and gave a slight nod.

Next morning, Georgina read a newspaper at the breakfast table. Eddie sipped a cup of coffee, then stared into it. Georgina looked up. "How do you feel, today?"

"Still a bit groggy." He paused. "Anythin' of interest?"

"They've legalised gambling in Nevada, therefore, Las Vegas will be popular for a vacation," said Georgina, as she looked up.

"Due to the 'crash', only movie chiefs and actors can afford to take a trip."

Georgina turned a page. "A lot of automobile manufacturers have gone bust over the past two years," she said gravely.

Eddie took another sip. "A replacement wing for the Hotrod is $340."

Georgina glanced at Eddie. "You'll have to dip into your savings."

Eddie stared at his cup. I'm overdrawn $30,000, what am I going to do? He looked at Georgina as she turned another page, then smiled at him.

"You can now dispose of razor blades, a company has produced an electric razor." Georgina sipped her coffee. "This article says that California can expect an influx of people from the Mid-West."

Eddie raised his head. "Last year's bad drought would have hit farms and many people will be on the lookout for work. Any good news?"

Georgina gave an enthusiastic smile. "Eddie, this article mentions that the Empire State building opens next month."

"Do you miss New York?"

"Sometimes." Most times.

When Eddie looked towards the door, Georgina put aside her newspaper and looked his way. "I'll get the mail." She went to the front door and picked up several letters, but before she returned to the kitchen, went through them. She laid the letters in front of Eddie and then sat down. As he observed them, Georgina stared. "Are you not going to open your mail?"

"No point," said Eddie, as he leaned back and sighed, fearing only bad news.

Georgina remained silent.

"Institutions who want their money back," said Eddie gravely.

"But why do you have to borrow, Eddie? You have plenty of capital, do you not?"

He started to sweat and took deep breaths. Then, Eddie's heart thudded in his chest and when both hands shook, Georgina stared. As his vision became clouded, he felt light-headed and slumped into the chair. Georgina rushed to him. "I'll call an ambulance!" She dashed into the hall, made a call, then returned and knelt beside Eddie. "An ambulance is on its way." Georgina held his hand.

Eddie whispered, "I'm sorry, Georgina, I've let you down."

"No, you haven't," said Georgina, as she gripped his hand. Seeing that Eddie was sweating, Georgina got up and returned with a wet cloth and dabbed his forehead.

"I'm on fire!" He blinked, repeatedly.

Georgina sniffed. "The ambulance won't be long."

One soon arrived and the crew attended to Eddie. Georgina made herself respectable and accompanied him to Los Angeles Hospital. As Eddie's condition worsened, the ambulance reached its destination. The crew took him inside and then into theatre. Georgina composed herself, then went into the main entrance. Sitting in the waiting area, Georgina wiped her eyes with a handkerchief. The receptionist stared, left her desk and approached Georgina. "Would you like a coffee?"

Georgina looked up. "Yes, yes, thanks." She sniffed.

A few moments later, the receptionist returned with a cup and handed it to Georgina. "I hope it's not too strong."

Georgina gave a faint smile. I hope it is.

A tiresome stressful period had passed when a white-coated gentleman approached the reception desk. He spoke with the receptionist, then looked towards Georgina. As the doctor walked towards her, she stared. "How is Eddie?"

"I'm afraid we couldn't save him," said the doctor in a sombre voice. When Georgina started to sob, the doctor sat beside her. "Before going to theatre, Eddie's condition deteriorated."

Georgina's voice grew raspy. "He was okay this morning."

"Heart failure can be swift," said the doctor gravely, as he stood.

"Can I see him?" Georgina sniffed.

"Do you feel up to it?"

Georgina hesitated. "Yes."

"Come this way." The doctor led Georgina to the theatre, where several medical staff could be seen. Eddie lay covered by a white sheet and the doctor pulled it back to reveal his face. Georgina glanced at the doctor. "He looks peaceful."

After reflection, a female nurse led Georgina away from the theatre and then accompanied her to reception. "Can we call you a cab?"

As Georgina nodded and dabbed her eyes, the nurse spoke to the receptionist and then walked back along the corridor. Georgina took a seat, however, several people appeared minutes later. Feeling uncomfortable, she got up and went to the desk.

"Would you like another coffee?" asked the receptionist.

"No, thanks, I'm going to wait for the cab outside."

"I understand," said the receptionist, as she gave a sympathetic smile.

Leaving the building, Georgina took a deep breath. She gazed upwards at the sun against a blue cloudless sky, then at people who strolled past her with carefree expressions. Once more, she wiped her eyes. Why is life so cruel? As Georgina reflected, a cab came to a halt outside the hospital entrance. Getting out, its driver looked at Georgina. "Waiting for a cab, ma'am?"

"Yes." Georgina walked towards it and the tall dark driver opened a door. "Thanks."

After Georgina got in, the driver closed the door and then returned to his seat. As he checked the controls, Georgina looked out the window, staring into space. The driver glanced round. "Apologies, ma'am, I'm new to this." He fidgeted with a knob.

"How long have you been a cab driver?"

"Not long enough." He tried another knob, then released the handbrake and the cab moved off. "Where to, ma'am?"

Georgina hesitated.

"Ma'am!" said the driver, as he glanced over his shoulder.

She looked at him. "Whitley Heights, please."

The driver glanced at Georgina's reflection in his front mirror. "Not many people say "please" to me. You're not from here, are you?"

"Originally, New York."

"I'm off to New York in September. I'm due to appear on Broadway."

Georgina looked at the driver. "So why drive a cab?"

"To pay my rent until I start work in New York."

"Is there no acting work here?"

The driver shook his head. "The effects of 1929 still linger, I'm afraid."

When the cab came to a halt at a set of traffic lights, the driver turned round and gave a broad smile. "You don't remember me, do you?"

Georgina stared.

"Our paths crossed in St Louis and also at a Hollywood party."

"It's Archie, isn't it?"

"Not anymore, I've changed it to Cary."

"Will it help?"

"It's got me into a play on Broadway," the driver said cheerily.

As the lights changed, the cab moved off and soon reached affluent Whitley Heights. Minutes later, it approached John Gilbert's mansion. Georgina moved forward. "This is fine."

The cab stopped and its driver got out. He opened the passenger door and smiled. "Having been here before, I managed not to get lost."

"Does it happen often?"

"Frequently, I've a terrible sense of direction."

"How much do I owe you?"

"Two dollars will cover the fare."

Georgina brought notes out of her coat pocket and gave them to the driver waiting in anticipation. "Here's four."

"Thank you, ma'am." As the driver was about to get into his cab, he looked at Georgina. "Oh, how is Eddie?"

"He passed away just before lunchtime," she said in a solemn voice.

"I'm terribly sorry."

Georgina gave a forced smile, then walked up the driveway. After she opened the main door and then closed it, burst into tears. Wiping her eyes, she went into the kitchen and poured herself a drink. Sitting down still wearing her coat, Georgina brooded over the past.

The funeral of Eddie Arnott had been well attended by close friends and members of Hollywood's acting fraternity. However, Georgina found herself not only alone, but unsure of what the future held. She sat in the kitchen with a glass of wine for company, a normal daily routine going back several months. Once more, she contemplated the future. Should she return to New York, or perhaps, Scotland? Georgina sat back, and reminisced about her early life in Argyll. Its rural cold blustery countryside being a far cry from busy cosmopolitan New York, or warm sunny Los Angeles. Solace for Georgina in her depressed state came in the form of a gorgeous mansion, plus, Eddie's life insurance payout. Just as Georgina considered a refill, the telephone rang. She put down the glass, went into the hall and answered the call. A well-educated voice could be heard. "Georgina, it is Henry Hicks."

"Thanks for attending Eddie's funeral, Henry," said Georgina gravely.

"It's about the estate."

"What about it?" asked Georgina sharply.

"It would be easier if we spoke face to face."

"Tomorrow afternoon?"

"Two o'clock?"
"See you then."
"Bye."
As Georgina replaced the receiver, she deliberated. The mansion, what about it? Since Eddie has no dependents, I'm the sole beneficiary. Not long after I moved in, he made a will. Georgina returned to her glass of wine. For a distraction, she went into the lounge and turned on the radio. Through the speaker came a musical rendition of Gershwin's An American in Paris. Sipping her wine, Georgina tried to forget about recent adversity. After the programme finished, the male host announced a romantic play would follow the sponsor's advertisement. Georgina got up, turned the radio off and went into the kitchen. Following another glass, she felt drowsy and went upstairs to her bedroom. Passing a mirror, Georgina glanced, then stopped. That wasn't me! She stared at her reflection. One glass too many.

Hearing an automobile come up the driveway, Georgina went to the front entrance. Dark-suited lawyer Henry Hicks had arrived and on time. A friend to every client who hired him and paid their fees on time. As he approached the door, Georgina welcomed him. "Good to see you again, Henry."

"And you, Georgina," said Henry, as he removed his dark fedora.

Georgina led her guest into the front lounge and as Henry rested himself on the soft couch, Georgina asked, "Something to drink, Henry?"

"No thanks, it's too early for me," he said with a slight grin.

As Georgina sat opposite, she observed Henry. He looks glum.

"A good turnout at the funeral, Eddie was a popular guy."

"Indeed, he was."

Henry stared at his host. "I've bad news, Georgina. You'll have to sell the mansion."

"Sell!"

Henry sighed. "I'm afraid so, my dear."

"Why?" Georgina asked in amazement.

"Over the last nine months, Eddie has run up a mountain of debt. Were you aware of this?""

"No." Georgina paused. "How did he get into debt?" she asked sharply.

Henry sighed. "He'd a gambling addiction and took out loans to compensate for his losses."

Georgina lowered her head, and after several seconds, raised it. "I had planned to sell the mansion and start a new life in another city."

"I have to say that you may not make any money on the sale," said Henry gravely.

"Of course, I will! It's an elegant property in a desirable area."

"Eddie ran up debts which could exceed the value."

Georgina sighed. "Surely, not."

"I've checked everything out."

"I need a drink." Georgina rose. "Sure you don't want one?"

"No, thanks."

After Georgina left the room, Henry took out a letter from his inside jacket pocket, and laid it on the table. Minutes later, Georgina returned with a glass of wine. When she sat down, Henry handed her the letter. "What's this?" Georgina set her glass on the table.

"I was asked to give it to you personally."

Georgina opened the letter, read it and looked at Henry, who had a blank expression. "I had my suspicions."

Henry got up. "A representative will call to value the property within the next few days."

Georgina put the letter aside, rose, and accompanied her guest to the front entrance. As Henry replaced his hat, she frowned.

"What will you do?"

Georgina shrugged her shoulders. "I don't know."

"At least Eddie got rid of his shares before the stock market crashed. A lot of people have been ruined." Henry shook Georgina's hand.

"If you need anything, give me a call."

"I will do."

As Henry got into his shiny black German-made Whittell Coupe and drove down the driveway, Georgina closed the door. Brushing a blonde hair off her navy-blue dress, she returned to the lounge, lifted her glass and took a large swallow of wine. After another, Georgina stared at the letter. Her promising career as a movie star will have to be put on hold. Serves her right. As Georgina mulled her thoughts, the telephone started to ring. As she went into the hall, it stopped. Georgina considered. Bet it's the cleaner with an explanation why she didn't turn up this morning. Moments later, the telephone rang again and after Georgina answered it, only a crackle could be heard.

CHAPTER 2

From Los Angeles to New York

On a dull wet New York Monday morning, Detective McAndrew stood in his office and gazed at the completed prestigious Empire State building. A knock on the door broke his train of thought. "Yeah, what is it?"

A tall slim man with brown swished-back hair who wore a sober grey suit entered and looked towards the window. Detective McAndrew turned around and gave a faint smile. "A lot of rooms to fill, Sam."

He nodded. "And in the midst of a depression."

"Some bureaucratic officials still can't understand the link with increased crime in the city." Detective McAndrew shook his grey head of hair, then stared at Sam. "Is that last week's figures?"

Sergeant Rodgers handed over a printed sheet of paper and Detective McAndrew read it, then looked up.

"We set free the ten vagrants arrested last week in 'Hooverville'."

"Why?"

"The judge blamed the depression," said Sergeant Rodgers, as he gave a faint smile. "He also gave each of them two dollars to buy a meal."

"From public funds, no doubt."

Sergeant Rodgers shook his head. "I'm told out of his own pocket."

"Next, robbers will be granted a reprieve." Detective McAndrew received a second sheet and after a few moments, raised his grey eyebrows. "Is it her?"

"I'm positive."

"This has brightened up the day." Detective McAndrew continued to read. "Living in Los Angeles, a district called Whitley Heights."

"Where the movie stars stay."

"Indeed."

"A neighbour is John Gilbert."

"She's done well for herself," said Detective McAndrew, as he glanced at his colleague. "In New York, she didn't have two dimes to rub together."

"The boyfriend she lived with died last month."

Detective McAndrew looked up. "Oh?"

"Going by the coroner's report, a heart attack."

"There's still the unfinished case here from two years ago." Detective McAndrew went on. "We'll pull her in for questioning."

"It'll take a week to LA and back."

"Our public duty, Sam." Detective McAndrew gave a wry smile. "Look on it as a working vacation."

"I'll get onto it right away."

As Sergeant Rodgers headed for the door, Detective McAndrew looked towards his junior colleague. "Sam," he said sharply.

Sergeant Rodgers looked round. "Yes, Detective?"

"How did you manage to trace her?"

"The LAPD conducted an investigation after the recent boyfriend's death and in an interview, she gave them her real name." Sergeant Rodgers went on. "She was known to outsiders as Jean Arnott."

Detective McAndrew deliberated. "Concealin' her identity for a good reason, no doubt."

Sergeant Rodgers nodded, then left. When the door closed, Detective McAndrew sat down behind his desk, opened a drawer and took out a file. After he browsed through it, reflected. Three men who have been involved with Georgina Rhodes in the last three years are now dead. The husband, a New York banker and now an ex-movie star. This isn't a coincidence.

Awaiting a cab to take her into the centre of LA, Georgina thought about the two years spent with Eddie. Emotions of joy, heartache and sadness filled her head. In the mansion's reception, she cast her gaze around it for the last time. Eddie's debts had been paid off, however, Georgina had become homeless and broke. Henry Hicks had fixed her up with a job waiting on tables and a small rented apartment. Life had once more dealt a harsh blow to Georgina. Her recent lavish lifestyle would be a memory to mull over. Hearing an automobile enter the driveway, Georgina checked herself in the hall mirror, picked up a suitcase and went to the front door. As she opened it, two police officers and a man in a dark suit stood with stern expressions. Georgina stared.

"Georgina Rhodes?" said one of the officers.

Georgina hesitated. "Yes."

"Can we speak inside?"

Georgina let them in, put down her suitcase and closed the door. As the man in a suit removed his dark fedora, the same officer spoke, "This is Sergeant Rodgers from NYPD, who has a warrant for your arrest."

"Arrest!" cried Georgina. "What for?" she asked in amazement.

"In connection with the death of your husband, almost two years ago," said Sergeant Rodgers sharply.

"He was shot by a robber," replied Georgina.

"I have to take you back to New York for questioning, ma'am," said Sergeant Rodgers, as he glanced at Georgina's suitcase. "It appears I got here just in time."

"Were you going on vacation?" asked the police officer.

"No, I'm off to the centre of LA."

"With a suitcase?" Sergeant Rodgers frowned.

"The property has been sold and I have to vacate it today, I'm moving into a shoe-box of an apartment."

"Not today," said Sergeant Rodgers, "you're off to New York with me."

"But I start a new job in two days," said Georgina, staring at him.

"Sorry, ma'am," said Sergeant Rodgers, replacing his hat

As the three officers returned to the vehicle, Georgina slammed the door behind her, then locked it. Picking up her suitcase, she walked to the vehicle, entered and sat in the rear seat beside Sergeant Rodgers.

After leaving the property, Georgina looked behind, then at Sergeant Rodgers. "The cab driver won't be pleased."

"What's his number?" An officer in the front passenger seat glanced round.

Georgina produced a card out of her pale blue jacket pocket. "Here."

The officer took the card. "We'll call him and explain the situation."

"That I have been arrested," said Georgina, as she glanced at Sergeant Rodgers, who gave a slight smile.

The officer looked round. "We'll think of something."

"I have to hand in the keys to a selling agency," said Georgina, as she looked at Sergeant Rodgers.

"In the city centre?" he asked.

Georgina nodded.

"We'll drop you there," said the same officer.

"Only if you promise not to run off," added Sergeant Rodgers.

"I'm wearing high heels," quipped Georgina.

Whilst Sergeant Rodgers remained stone-faced, the driver glanced at his colleague and both grinned.

Following a stop at the agency, Sergeant Rodgers and his fellow traveller arrived at La Grande Station for the sleeper service bound for New York. The sergeant looked at Georgina. "Wait here."

After he visited the booking office, Sergeant Rodgers returned with tickets and then checked his watch. Georgina gave a faint smile. "I could have tried to escape."

"Do you want us to be handcuffed for the next three days?"

Georgina hesitated. "I'll behave myself." Mind you, he is attractive.

"Did you say something?"

Georgina shook her head.

The two passengers boarded a ten-car passenger train and then went to their designated double compartment. As Sergeant Rodgers tipped up his hat and sat down, there came a knock on the adjoining compartment door. He got up and slid it open.

"Could we go to the dining car, Sergeant? I've not eaten since breakfast."

The sergeant looked at his watch. "Okay."

When they reached the dining car, a man in a white jacket, white collared shirt, black tie and trousers came forward. "A table for two, sir?"

Sergeant Rodgers nodded.

"This way, please."

The dark-haired waiter led Sergeant Rodgers and Georgina to a table with a crisp white hanging cloth and shiny silver cutlery. Taking their order, he scribbled it down on a pad, smiled and departed. Sergeant Rodgers and Georgina removed their hats and placed them on a spare chair next to them. Georgina looked across the table. "You don't strike me as being just a sergeant."

"Add detective."

"Since we're going to share a table for the next three days, do I get to know your first name? After all, you know mine."

"Sam, but you will refer to me as Detective Sergeant, or Sergeant."

"Have you been in the force long?" Georgina paused. "Sergeant?"

"Sixteen years. I joined NYPD six months ago."

"And before that?"

"Based in Chicago." She's a curious one.

"It must have been interesting."

"That's the polite term."

Georgina smiled. "Did you work with Elliot Ness?"

As Sergeant Rodgers nodded, the waiter returned with a silver tray, which contained a jug of water and two empty glasses. After he filled both, departed. Georgina picked up her glass and whilst she looked at Sergeant Rodgers, took a sip. "I didn't kill my husband."

"My boss wants to question you, it's routine." Sergeant Rodgers lifted his glass. "No more discussion on the case," he said sharply, then took a sip.

Georgina considered. If I step out of line, it could be a long three days.

Sergeant Rodgers sipped his water. If she steps out of line, this is going to be an arduous journey.

Georgina looked over his shoulder. "Good, here comes lunch."

Whilst Sergeant Rodgers and Georgina had their evening meal, the train pulled into Chicago's Union Station. A large number of passengers got off, whereas not many boarded. As both diners looked out the window, Georgina glanced at Sergeant Rodgers. "It would appear Los Angeles is more popular than New York."

"There is less crime and more sunshine in Los Angeles."

"Are you from Chicago, Sergeant?"

"No, New York. At the age of nine, my parents moved to Chicago."

"Why?"

"My father had been transferred there."

"Also in the force?"

Sergeant Rodgers nodded. "During the latter half of the last century, my grandfather worked as a beat policeman."

"New York must have been tough in those days." Georgina sipped her glass of water. I could do with a real drink.

"My grandfather told me stories of police riots, let alone criminal goings-on."

"Really?" Georgina raised her eyebrows.

"I believe it had to do with reorganisation of the force and as a consequence, many officers rebelled."

"My goodness!"

"Also, due to mass immigration, Lower Manhattan became a 'hotbed'. As the city grew, so did corruption."

"With the depression, there will be a lot of it now."

When Sergeant Rodgers gave a rare smile, Georgina stared. Heavens, he managed one. Sergeant Rodgers considered. Don't get close, remember, she's a murder suspect.

"When I stayed in New York, older people would tell me horror stories about mass bereavements."

"In the 1880's, epidemics were rife. Overcrowding due to immigrant families in small apartments and grime on the streets, made worse by horse manure."

"No motorised vehicles in that era."

"Just horses to pull carts and coaches."

"What will it be like in fifty years?" Georgina gazed out the carriage window.

"Faster trains, air travel and hopefully, a better standard of living."

"Air travel?"

"People will travel by airplane to destinations all over." Sergeant Rodgers paused. "It will be quicker."

"In America?"

"The world." Sergeant Rodgers lifted his glass. "Charles Lindbergh flew to France. In the future, trains could be obsolete." Sergeant Rodgers took a swig.

As the train moved off, two men in dark pinstripe suits entered the dining car, then sat at an empty table. A waiter approached them, chatted and took their order. Georgina stood, then looked at Sergeant Rodgers. "Before coffee arrives, I'm going to the powder room."

After Georgina departed, the two men in pinstripe suits left their table and then sat opposite Sergeant Rodgers. One of them spoke, "Evenin', Sergeant, we'd like a word."

"And who may you two gentlemen be?" Their faces are familiar.

"You're soon to testify in a court case."

"I don't discuss cases," said Sergeant Rodgers sharply.

"It relates to a raid in Chicago last year."

"Chicago? I work in New York."

"But you were drafted in for a particular raid."

"How do you know this?" asked Sergeant Rodgers, staring.

"We know a lot of things," said the man, as he moved forward. "Even who you
tipped off in the Chicago PD."

"You have me mixed up with someone else."

The other man with a cheek scar went into his inside jacket pocket and took out a white envelope. "Don't play hard to get, Sergeant, police officers tend to come around." He laid the envelope in front of Sergeant Rodgers. "The contents will cover your salary for five years."

"I get paid well enough, thanks."

"Take the money, Sergeant, and you'll live to spend it."

"I don't want your money, I'd rather have a clear conscience." Sergeant Rodgers stared at both men. "Money can't buy the satisfaction I get from being able to put your type behind bars."

"You're a fool," said the man, as he replaced the envelope into his pocket.

Returning from the powder room, Georgina noticed two men sitting opposite Sergeant Rodgers and sighed. Not more police officers. Sergeant Rodgers spotted her, then glanced at both men. "Here comes my associate."

They looked round, got to their feet and departed with stern expressions. Staring at them walking off, Georgina sat down. "Colleagues of yours, Sergeant?"

"Sort of."

"They didn't look pleased."

"Pressure of work," said Sergeant Rodgers with a slight smile.

A waiter appeared with two coffees on a tray and set them on the table.

Georgina lifted her cup, then looked at the sergeant. "Will alcohol ever be sold again?"

"I believe the ban will end soon." Sergeant Rodgers lifted his cup and took a sip.

"When?"

"Maybe in the next few years." The sergeant went on. "Prohibition has increased crime." He set his white cup down. "Ironically, it had been brought in to lower crime, but organised gangs have sprung up all over the country. Also, prohibition has hit the economy."

"In what way?"

"Less liquor tax revenues and bars forced to close their doors, which means people out of work. Besides, I like to go out for a beer."

As Georgina smiled, Sergeant Rodgers checked his watch, then looked across the table.

"That time already?"

"I'm afraid so."

"Hopefully, I'll sleep okay," said Georgina as she set her cup on the saucer. "The train rocks to and fro. If I had several gins, it would help."

"There's no law against the consumption of alcohol."

"Someone has to sell it to you first, and that's illegal, said Georgina with a wry smile."

A short time later, he and Georgina departed the dining car and headed to their carriage. Meanwhile, the two men discussed their next move. One took out a hand revolver from an inside jacket pocket, inserted six bullets, then replaced it. "Looks like this is the only way to silence him."

"What about the blonde broad, Joe?"

"She'll also have to be silenced."

The accomplice surveyed the long narrow carriage passageway, then looked at Joe. "Another passenger may intrude, we need somewhere private."

"We'll force them into his compartment." Joe pointed.

As they waited, Sergeant Rodgers entered the carriage and then stood back.

"What's wrong?" asked Georgina.

"Return to the dining car and ask a waiter to get the on-board security guard."

"What for?"

Sergeant Rodgers glanced back at Georgina. "Those two you thought were colleagues are goons after me."

Georgina stared. "The enemy of my enemy is my friend."

Sergeant Rodgers grinned. "When we reach New York, I'll get you a bottle of gin."

"Promise, Sergeant?"

"Yes!" He peeked round the corner.

"No need to be abrupt."

Sergeant Rodgers glanced at Georgina. "Apologies, I'll make it two bottles."

Georgina smiled.

"Now go to the dining car."

"What if they don't believe me?"

"Convince them, use your charm."

After Georgina left, Sergeant Rodgers took another peek, then checked the gun holster hidden under his jacket. The two men stood, waiting. "They should've been here by now," said Joe.

Georgina returned to the dining car and approached a waiter going about his duties. He turned to face her.

"The man I'm with requires the assistance of a security guard."

"Why, ma'am?" he asked, staring.

"Two goons are out to kill him.

The waiter looked towards a nearby table, where a bald man sat with a cup of coffee. Given the width of his grey jacket, he appeared to be a lover of hearty meals. When the waiter caught his attention, the man acknowledged. Georgina stared. "Him!" She glanced at the waiter.

He nodded, and as Georgina went over to the security guard, he got to his feet in a slow movement. "I know what you're going to say. Ever since they boarded, I've been expectin' trouble."

"They're at the end of our carriage."

"How far?"

"Three down."

Georgina followed the security guard and upon their arrival at the carriage, Sergeant Rodgers turned around. "Thanks for being prompt." He showed the guard his police badge. "They're at the end of the carriage."

"They don't know me, therefore, I'll walk to the other end and pull my gun when I'm behind them."

"What will you do with them?" asked Georgina.

"Take whatever weapons they have and lock them in a cell."

Georgina raised her blonde eyebrows. "You've one on the train?"

"Oh yes, ma'am."

When Sergeant Rodgers gave Georgina a bemused stare, she tilted her head. "Just curious, Sergeant."

"You can ask questions later, we have an urgent issue to deal with." Sergeant Rodgers rolled his eyes.

Meanwhile, both men looked at each other and then Joe stared up the corridor. After a moment's reflection, he did it again. "Let's go find the sergeant."

Whilst he walked along the narrow corridor, the security guard confronted both men. Due to a large waistline, they had to manoeuvre past him. The security guard gave a slight grin. "Sorry, guys."

"You need to go on a diet," said Joe.

After they edged past each other, the guard brought out a gun from his inside jacket pocket and pointed it at them. "Hey, guys, I don't like insults."

As they looked round, Sergeant Rodgers appeared with his gun also pointed at them. "Hands up."

Both men stared each way at a gun aimed in their direction and did as ordered. Following a search, the security guard removed their weapons, then led them away.

Whistling as he got dressed, Sergeant Rodgers looked forward to a delicious breakfast, albeit, a late one. Whilst Georgina could not embrace overnight rail travel, the sergeant had slept like a log. He knocked on Georgina's door, and waited. She opened it, and peeked out. "Won't be long."

Then, came two knocks on the main compartment door. When Sergeant Rodgers answered, a middle-aged man pointed a gun at his chest. He entered and ushered Sergeant Rodgers back. "I boarded at the last stop." The man closed the door. "To make sure the job got done."

"That's efficient."

"Nothin' personal, Sergeant, but you have to be taken care of."

Sergeant Rodgers raised his voice. "Can't we come to an agreement?"

The man shook his head. "I have my instructions."

Behind the door, Georgina listened. The sergeant needed help, but what could she do? An idea came to her, and she shouted. "Sam?"

"Who's that?" The man glanced sideways.

"Let's just say I hope my wife doesn't find out, replied Sergeant Rodgers, smiling."

"Come out." The man clicked his gun. "No funny business, or I shoot."

Georgina appeared with the top buttons of her lilac blouse undone, holding a black leather handbag. The man grinned, then looked at Sergeant Rodgers. "How could you, so much for bein' trustworthy."

Whilst he spoke, Georgina took out a small bottle from her bag. "Excuse me," she said in a seductive voice."

As the man looked at her, Georgina sprayed perfume into his eyes and when Sergeant Rodgers grabbed him, the gun fell onto the floor. Picking it up, the sergeant pointed it at a confused individual.

Georgina returned with the security guard and a third hood was cuffed, then led away. Sergeant Rodgers gave a slight smile. "You can button up your blouse now."

Georgina did so. "My apologies."

"No need to, you saved my life."

"And mine!"

"The spray?"

"It's just come onto the market," said Georgina, as she showed it to Sergeant Rodgers. He took the spray and examined it. "My thanks to the inventor," said Sergeant Rodgers gratefully.

Prior to mid-day, the train arrived at its New York destination. As passengers piled off, others waited to board for the return journey westward.

Leaving the station, Sergeant Rodgers took Georgina via the subway to his NYPD office located in Lower Manhattan. Once there, they went to the third floor then to the waiting area. "Do you want a coffee?" he asked.

"No, thanks." I need something stronger.

The sergeant put down Georgina's suitcase, went to a nearby door and knocked three times. Hearing a reply, he entered, then closed the door. Georgina took a mirror out of her small black leather handbag and looked into it. After she applied red lipstick, replaced both items into the bag. Georgina cast her gaze around the vicinity and sighed. No magazine or newspaper lay on a table to pass the time. A young well-built dark uniformed officer noticed Georgina, then approached her. "Are you being attended to, ma'am?"

"Yes, thanks." Georgina glanced at the table. "Do you have a newspaper I could read?"

"Only a police journal I'm afraid, ma'am."

After the officer departed, Georgina mulled over the previous two years with Eddie and warm sunny Los Angeles. A far cry from when the train approached New York and the heavens opened. The dismal weather now mirrored Georgina's frame of mind. In the office, Detective McAndrew listened to Sergeant Rodgers and then finished his cup of black coffee. "Just because she may have saved your life, Sam, it doesn't get her off the hook," he said sharply.

"She isn't the type to commit a murder, sir."

Detective McAndrew looked out the window, then at Sergeant Rodgers. "If I got ten dollars for every time I've heard that, I could buy a new Ford."

"My gut instinct, sir. Also, she didn't attempt to escape."

"Let's get her in."

Georgina would confront one of New York's toughest police officers, John McAndrew. Born and raised in the district of Queens, he was streetwise and did not suffer fools, especially those of the crooked kind. In the force all his working life, he wanted justice to prevail at all costs.

Sergeant Rodgers left the office, then went over to Georgina. As she looked up, he gave her a faint smile. "Detective McAndrew will see you now."

Georgina rose. About time.

Sergeant Rodgers lifted Georgina's suitcase, then led her into a compact room. She sniffed the air and noticed a nicotine-stained ceiling. After Sergeant Rodgers closed the door, he laid Georgina's suitcase in a corner. Detective McAndrew stared. "Have a seat."

Georgina sat and faced a wooden desk, whilst Sergeant Roberts sat alongside his boss. Detective McAndrew lit a cigarette. "First of all, thanks for your intervention, Sergeant Rodgers told me all about the incident."

Georgina glanced at the sergeant. "Just as well I had my perfume spray."

"Indeed, however, we've brought you here to discuss somethin' else."

"I didn't kill my husband," said Georgina sharply.

"Why did you leave New York soon after his death?"

"I met a nice guy, he stayed in LA and I wanted to be with him. Besides, as my late husband gambled away our apartment and savings, there was no reason to remain in New York."

"What about your sister who stayed in Manhattan?"

"Elizabeth became unhappy and planned to return home."

"I believe your late boyfriend also had a gamblin' problem."

"Do you think I killed him as well?"

"Did you?"

"No, Detective, I didn't. On both counts."

"Did you pay someone to kill your husband?"

Georgina's voice grew raspy. "I had no money."

"Therefore, you got the banker to put up the cash."

Georgina cleared her throat.

"Being an accessory to murder is a serious felony, Mrs Rhodes."

"He was also broke, his bank went bust." Georgina looked at Sergeant Roberts. "Can I have a glass of water?"

Sergeant Rodgers left the office, returned soon after and gave Georgina a glass. As she took a couple of sips, Detective McAndrew puffed on his cigarette.

"Am I not allowed a lawyer to be present, Detective?" Georgina took a large swallow.

"I'll take your empty glass," said Sergeant Rodgers, as he reached over.

"Thanks." Georgina handed the lipstick-stained glass to him.

Detective McAndrew fired questions at Georgina for a further twenty minutes, however, she kept her composure.

"After the murder, did you meet with the banker?"

"No."

"Why not?"

Georgina hesitated. "He was a lousy lover!"

As Sergeant Rodgers held back a smile, Georgina looked at Detective McAndrew, now on his third cigarette. "Any more personal questions,

Detective?"

He leaned back on his black leather chair. "You can go, we'll want to speak with you again."

"I can't stay in New York, I've no cash."

"My wife's sister owns a guest house, she'll put you up." Sergeant Rodgers stood.

Georgina looked across the desk. "How long do I have to remain in the city?"

"When I'm ready to let you leave, Mrs Rhodes." Detective McAndrew stubbed out his cigarette on a silver ashtray.

When Georgina rose, Sergeant Rodgers led her out of the office and into a corridor. He gave directions to the guest house. "Do you know the location?"

Georgina nodded.

"Tell Nancy I sent you, here's money for a cab." He handed over several dollars.

"Thank you, Sergeant," said Georgina gratefully.

"I'll be in touch."

After he walked Georgina to the elevator, Sergeant Rodgers returned to Detective McAndrew's office, and took a seat. The chain-smoking detective considered. "Just the one uneasy moment." He reached for his packet of Craven A cigarettes. "When interviewed soon after her husband's murder, she kept her cool then as well." Detective McAndrew lit a cigarette.

"If she wasn't that type, I wouldn't be here."

"Killers can be cool customers, Sam."

"I've been in her company for almost four days, my instinct says she's innocent. Besides, we've no hard evidence to link her with the crime."

Detective McAndrew puffed on his cigarette. "I suppose what we don't need in a depression is to waste taxpayers' cash on a dubious court case."

"At least we know why she had no further contact with the banker," said Sergeant Rodgers, as a smile flickered over his face.

Detective McAndrew grinned. "I had to keep my face straight."

"What do you want to do, sir?"

"Let her sweat for a day, or so, then she can return to LA."

Following her best sleep for several nights, Georgina went into Midtown to look up several old friends. Since she moved to California, Georgina had lost touch with them. Being back in New York presented her with an opportunity to reacquaint. However, as she travelled on the subway, it did not reignite her past fondness for the city. Whilst Georgina entered the station, she witnessed another woman's handbag being taken off her by a youth. Also, as she waited for the train, a scuffle broke out between two men and was stopped by the intervention of a well-built railway worker.

When the train reached Broad Street station, Georgina got off and then walked up the concrete staircase. An unshaven man, who wore grey cap, frayed jacket and baggy trousers, approached. "Spare a dime lady?" he asked humbly.

"I just managed to pay my fare."

"Please, just a dime." He stammered.

"Sorry," said Georgina, as she noticed the man stare at her handbag. Clutching it, she walked away with quick footsteps.

When Georgina reached a friend's apartment, she pressed the appropriate button. Moments later, an unshaven man in a white vest and dark trousers opened the door. "Yeah?"

"Is Ethel in?" asked Georgina, staring at the tall individual, who appeared worse for wear.

"Ethel?" He sneezed.

"Yes."

"She moved out eight months ago."

"Thanks."

"No, problem, lady," said the man, as he once more sneezed and closed the door.

Georgina looked up another two friends, however, they also had moved on. Before she got the subway train back to the guest house, Georgina spotted a coffee shop. She checked her purse and gave a relieved sigh. Enough for one cup. As she entered, a young dark-haired waitress soon approached. "A glass of watta?"

"No, a coffee."

"Take a seat," she said cheerily, "there's plenty to choose from."

After Georgina sat down and took off her hat, the waitress came over. "Meant to ask, sometin' to eat?"

"No, thanks," said Georgina, as she unbuttoned her jacket.

The waitress went to the counter and prepared a single coffee. Georgina cast her gaze around the white painted walls and discoloured ceiling. When the waitress returned with a white cup and saucer, Georgina looked up. "Why did you ask if I wanted a glass of water?"

"That's what most people do."

Georgina frowned.

"They've no cash to buy anythin' else."

As the waitress left, Georgina lifted her cup and took a couple of sips. She set her cup down, sat back and contemplated her future. The other customer got up, put on a mint green hat over her long dark hair and then came across. "Can I join you? I don't like to sit on my own."

"Of course." She's Irish.

"Are you a visitor to New York?"

"For the time being."

"Where are you from?"
"Originally, Scotland. I moved to New York, then Los Angeles."
"You're much travelled," said the lady, as she smiled.
"Are you a visitor, too?"
"I've lived here for a number of years."
"When did you leave Ireland?"
"Fourteen years ago, just after my twenty-first birthday."
"Have you noticed many changes?"
"Oh, yes." The lady paused. "Before I came over, you appeared deep in thought."
Georgina sighed. "My boyfriend in Los Angeles passed away and left me with nothing. He gambled everything away, even my own money." Georgina went on. "I'm not sure whether to return there, or stay here."
"What about Scotland?"
"My sister, who once stayed in New York, returned to Scotland two years ago."
"Do you keep in touch?"
"We write to each other."
"How is she?"
"She's bought a hotel and plans to expand. Lucky her."
The lady smiled. "Has your sister remarried?"
"An ex-boyfriend, it must have been fate that brought them together."
"It can happen." With a helping hand.
At that moment, the waitress reappeared with a broad smile and looked at both customers. "Another, ladies?"
"Two, please," said the Irish lady.
"Could you make mine stronger this time?" asked Georgina, as she looked at the waitress.
"Will do." The waitress departed.
"Did you enjoy the warm sunny climate of Los Angeles."
"Loved it."
"A friend of mine moved to Greece, it has a similar climate. She lives in Crete, it's full of history."
"I adore old historic places," said Georgina, as she beamed.
"Crete would suit you."
"But it costs money to get there, and I'm broke."
"Find a job to pay for the trip."
"Due to the depression, that will be difficult." Georgina looked around the shop. "Businesses are not doing well, besides, I'm no longer a spring chicken."
"You're not old."
Georgina considered. "I'll teach music, as I did before leaving New York.

The waitress returned with two coffees and both ladies continued to chat. A short time later, they set their cups down. The Irish lady picked up Georgina's bag off the floor, and handed it to her.

After she paid for both coffees, the Irish lady joined Georgina, as she waited outside and adjusted her hat. "What will you do?"

"I'll try and find work here and use the money for passage to Crete. I feel a fresh start would be beneficial."

"Go with your instinct."

"I forgot to ask, what's your name?"

"Lori."

"I'm Georgina."

"Good luck."

"Thanks."

"Bye," Lori said, smiling.

Whilst Georgina walked back to the subway station, she recollected her conversation with the Irish lady. How did she know Elizabeth had been married? Georgina entered the station, went down a stairway and as it arrived, caught the train. When a ticket inspector appeared, Georgina went into her handbag. She found an envelope, which contained a bundle of dollars and a hand-written note. *Enjoy Crete, embrace a new beginning.*

Sergeant Rodgers and Detective McAndrew discussed issues within Central Park. With many of the 'Hooverville' residents being former construction workers, their accommodation had been put together with the use of 'acquired' stone. Other residents with no construction skills had to settle for used crates and cardboard boxes. Most homes had a stove, of some kind, but depended on charities for essentials.

"How long before the government does something, sir?" asked Sergeant Rodgers.

Detective McAndrew shrugged his shoulders.

"The kids there will soon evolve into criminals."

"I've heard discussions about a programme of work-related projects to ease unemployment."

"Soon?"

Detective McAndrew remained silent.

"The government will have to act now."

"I know, Sam," said Detective McAndrew, as he reached for his packet of cigarettes.

About to leave, Sergeant Rodgers stopped and then faced Detective McAndrew. "Sir, did Bill Johnston get in touch?"

"About the Rhodes case?"

"One of Bill's informers made the revelation."

"I heard." Detective McAndrew sat back on his chair and lit a cigarette.

"The person who paid the killer turned out to be Johnny Vincent."

"Who Dale Rhodes owed a large amount of cash."

"He must have ignored threats from Johnny."

"To his peril," said Sergeant Rodgers gravely.

"Given that Johnny was killed in a shoot-out last year, we can't prosecute." Detective McAndrew gave a slight grin. "At least tax-payers' cash has been saved."

Sergeant Rodgers nodded.

"Is the Rhodes broad still in the city?

"As soon as we gave her the all-clear, she left."

"No doubt back to the sunshine and heat of LA." Whilst he puffed on his cigarette, Detective McAndrew glanced at the rain batter against his window.

"She's gone to Greece."

"Greece!"

"It's cheaper than New York and has the climate of LA."

"Where did she get the cash for a ticket?"

"Perhaps from one of her old friends she visited."

"She struck me as a shrewd one," said Detective McAndrew, as he stubbed out his cigarette.

"And cool."

"Bein' a looker, she'll no doubt attract another sucker."

Smiling, Sergeant Rodgers left his boss's office, reflecting as he walked along the corridor. A compelling lady.

CHAPTER 3

A NEW BEGINNING

As she stood on the deck, Georgina admired a deep blue sea and cloudless sky. She experienced a faint gust of wind on her face and then a seagull landed close by. Minutes later, Georgina spotted a coastline and turned to a member of the ship's crew. "Is that Heraklion?"

"Yes, we will soon reach the port."

Georgina stared ahead. And I thought New York to Los Angeles had been a long journey.

"Have you enjoyed the voyage?" asked the tanned grey-bearded crewman.

"Smoother than I had anticipated," said Georgina gratefully.

The crewman grinned. "Not in the winter months."

Georgina laughed.

"Have you come to Heraklion for a vacation?"

"To live."

"And work?"

Georgina nodded. "This is a new chapter for me and I'm going to embrace it."

"What is it you do?"

"I visit people in their home and give music lessons."

"What instrument do you teach?"

"The piano."

"We Greeks embrace music, it inspires us to dance and drink till we drop, said the crewman, cheerily."

"Your English is good," said Georgina, as she looked at the jovial individual.

"Thank you," he said politely.

"Did they teach English at your school?"

The crewman shook his head. "The teachers only taught certain subjects.

Intrigued by his reply, Georgina asked, "How did you learn to speak English?"

"From my grandmother. She came from Bristol in England."

"She taught you well."

"Being able to speak English benefited my uncle's business."

"Oh?"

"He traded with merchants from other countries, but only spoke Greek."

"Did you negotiate on his behalf?"

The crewman gave a slight nod and revealed to Georgina that he started his working life a few months after his twelfth birthday. She raised her blonde eyebrows. The crewman continued, "I worked with him for twenty-two years and then began a career on ships."

"You must enjoy being at sea."

"Since I was brought up on an island, it is essential," the crewman said, grinning.

Georgina considered. True.

"Our supply of farm stock and agricultural goods to other countries is essential for the Cretan economy."

Georgina gave a slight smile. "Are you ever home?"

"I am only there for a few months of the year, I think my wife likes it that way," he said with a wry grin. "I drink too much ouzo."

"A popular Cretan drink?"

"The only one." The crewman looked behind Georgina. "I have to go and prepare the ship for our arrival."

"Nice to chat with you, what's your name?"

"Mitsos, he said humbly."

As the crewman returned to duty, Georgina watched as the ship headed for Heraklion's port. A strong breeze meant she had to hold onto her hat, but with the temperature being high, Georgina welcomed wind on her face.

After it put into port, Georgina left the ship with a solitary suitcase. When a man with a long white beard and crooked back approached, she stared. His grey shirt and patched dark trousers had seen better days. Georgina sighed. Please, not a beggar, I've just got here. The old man tipped his grey cap and showed his faded white teeth. "Can I take you to where you are headed?" He stammered.

"Do you know of somewhere central where I can stay," said Georgina, as the old man moved closer and pointed to his ear. "Do you know where I can rent a room?" cried Georgina, as several locals glanced towards her.

"This way." Accompanied by a groan, the old man lifted Georgina's suitcase, then walked to a brown and white donkey strapped to a small wooden cart. Inside lay a crumpled cream-coloured sheet, which the old man unfolded and then spread out for Georgina to sit on. As he placed the suitcase beside her, she gave a faint smile.

The old man led his donkey along a narrow dusty road, where locals made polite gestures to an unfamiliar face. Georgina reflected. New York is a long way off.

Following an uncomfortable journey for its passenger, the donkey stopped outside a cottage-style white-stoned building. The old man looked at Georgina and pointed. "Accommodation to rent," he said, cheerily.

Georgina got off the cart, removed her hat, then shook her blonde shoulder-length hair. "How much do I owe you?" She considered. My goodness, I've no Greek money. Georgina put her hat back on.

"Five drachmas, please."

"I've only American money."

"That is fine."

Georgina gave him a note. "There's a dollar."

"Thank you," he said gratefully.

After he handed Georgina her case, she approached the wooden door and gave it three knocks. Georgina laid her suitcase on the ground, tried again, then sighed. Don't say nobody's home! Then, a woman with long dark hair and a slim waistline answered. "Can I help you?"

"Do you have a room for rent?"

"How did you know?"

"An old man who dropped me off mentioned it."

"Dropped you off?" Unaware of that particular term, the woman frowned.

"He had a donkey and cart."

"Ah, Sandros," said the woman, smiling. "Please, come inside."

Georgina lifted her suitcase, then entered a bright interior with white walls and minimal wooden furniture. The woman held out her hand. "I am Elena."

"Georgina." She shook it, then put down her suitcase.

"You are American?"

Georgina removed her hat. "I'm from Scotland, but have stayed in America for a number of years."

"Please, have a seat." The woman glanced towards a couch.

As Georgina made herself comfortable, the woman sat opposite on a chair, which matched. "There are two families in Heraklion who have come over from America. They came here to escape the hardship of the depression, although, Greece has also suffered."

"Which part of America are the families from?"
"East coast."
"New York?"
"One family is from there, I am not sure about the other."
"Some New Yorkers live in shacks in a park."
"Shacks? What are they?"
"A makeshift hut."
The woman hesitated. "It must be cold in winter."
"New York winters can be severe."
The woman smiled. "Is that why you have come to Crete?"
"I want to make a fresh start."
"I understand," said the woman, as she gave a wry smile.
"Can I see the room you have available?"
The woman rose. "This way."
Georgina accompanied her host through a narrow hallway with drab-coloured walls and a scratched wooden floor. The woman opened a door, and as Georgina entered, she looked around with curiosity. "Is it suitable?" asked the woman.
"How much?"
"Two hundred drachmas per month. In American currency, two dollars." As the woman observed Georgina considering the price, she added, "Plus breakfast."
Georgina gave a slight smile. "I'll take it."
"To toast our agreement, would you like a glass of wine?"
"Coffee?" I've had enough wine on my voyage to last a week.
"Hot or cold?"
"Hot, please."
"Do you want to unpack first?"
"Yes, thanks."
After she crammed clothes into a wooden wardrobe, Georgina stared at her half-full suitcase. Hope there is a spare wardrobe. As Georgina entered the main room and took a seat, her host appeared with a cup and saucer.
"Thanks." Georgina took a sip. That's strong.
"Is the coffee suitable?"
Georgina nodded.
"Greek coffee can be strong," said the woman, as she took a seat. "Is there a job for you in Heraklion?"
I wish. "I'll have to find one."
"That may be difficult, our economy is not in good shape. What is it you do?"
"I teach music."
"How wonderful!" said the woman, smiling.
"Where is the main school in Heraklion?"

"Close to the centre."

"Is that where you learned to speak English?" She's competent.

The woman shook her head. "I went to a private school."

"In Heraklion?"

"Yes."

Georgina considered. Her family must be wealthy.

"My father wanted me to work in London."

"Why there?"

"He told me it is the financial centre of Europe."

"Does he work in finance?"

"A bank in Heraklion. He is the owner, however, it is a difficult time, hence why I have to rent out a room." The woman gave a faint smile. "Income from my father is not as I would want it to be."

"Why did you not go to London?"

"The war with Germany began, therefore, I remained here and worked for my father."

"You may not have enjoyed London, it rains a lot and is colder than here," said Georgina with a slight smile. "Also, there has been political unrest with strikes and changes of government."

"There is unrest in Crete from various political groups."

Georgina took a large swallow.

"The Greek communist party has expanded in Athens and some industrial cities." The woman paused. "Other parties are therefore concerned."

"Revolution?"

"This is not Russia, and we will keep our monarch," said the woman sharply. "Do you have any plans for this evening?"

"I'm going to take a stroll around the town to familiarise myself."

"Before that, you can sample my moussaka."

"It will be my pleasure," said Georgina, smiling. I'm famished.

"Plus, Cretan wine."

Next morning, Georgina woke with a dry throat and a sore head. She sat up in her single bed and attempted to gather her thoughts. How many glasses of red wine did I have? As Georgina's head fell back onto the white pillow, there came a knock on the door. Georgina cleared her throat. "Come in."

Elena entered with a cup and laid it on the wooden bedside cabinet. Georgina lifted the cup, took a sip, and sighed.

"Better?" asked Elena, as she smiled.

Georgina nodded, then took another sip.

"Breakfast in about fifteen minutes."

"Can you make it nearer thirty," said a fragile Georgina, not used to a hangover in recent times.

Elena nodded.

"Thanks, said Georgina gratefully."

After Elena opened the two window shutters, she left the room, Georgina continued to sip her coffee and gaze around the sun-filled room. As I've lost my pair of sunglasses, a replacement is a priority.

Following her much-needed injection of caffeine, Georgina got dressed and then joined Elena in the kitchen, as she prepared breakfast.

"Can I help?"

"Almost finished, have a seat," said Elena, as she glanced at the table.

Moments later, Elena laid bread, cheese, buns, and yoghurt on the wooden table. Georgina sat and stared at the food, then at her host. "Is this your usual breakfast, Elena?"

"Yes." She placed a cup of coffee in front of Georgina.

Over breakfast, the two women chatted about places to visit in Heraklion, as well as those to avoid.

"Is there much crime?" Georgina held her cup.

"In the last two years it has got worse, more so in the centre of Heraklion."

"Because it's busier?"

Elena gave a slight nod. "Bars, restaurants and shops. Do not worry, it is only in the evening you have to be wary of thieves."

Georgina sipped her coffee. That's a comfort.

"What are your plans for today?"

"As it's daytime, I'll visit the centre of Heraklion."

Elena laughed.

Smiling, Georgina added, "I'll have to buy a pair of dark glasses."

"You could also visit the school, they may require someone to teach music."

Georgina raised her eyebrows. Good idea.

Following breakfast, Georgina got ready for her visit into Heraklion's commercial centre. As she stepped outside, the bright summer sun shone down. Dazzled, Georgina put a hand above her forehead to protect a pair of fragile blue eyes.

After a stroll through streets of Venetian architecture, Georgina arrived at a market. Rugs, clothes, trinkets and a selection of other household items lay on an assortment of displays for prospective buyers to view. When Georgina approached a stall that sold carved wooden figures, the male trader picked up one and showed it to her. "You like?" he asked cheerily.

"I'm just having a look, thanks," said Georgina politely.

"You buy tomorrow?"

"Perhaps." I doubt it.

"You are American are you not?"

When Georgina nodded, the trader grinned. Being American meant affluence, therefore, cash to spend. "See you tomorrow."

Georgina walked on and at another stall, a woman showed hats to a customer, who tried one on. Georgina stopped, then looked at the selection on offer. As the customer departed, the trader approached. "You like?"

"Yes, but I can't afford one."

"Maybe next week?"

"It's a pair of dark glasses I need."

"For drinking?"

When Georgina glanced upwards and shaded her eye, the grey-haired trader clasped her wrinkled hands. "Ah, sunglasses! Five stalls from here," she said, pointing.

"Thanks."

"You are welcome, madam."

Complete with a pair, Georgina arrived at the town's port and gazed out to sea. She walked along the breakwater and enjoyed a cool breeze off the Aegean. Noticing an ancient fort nearby, Georgina approached it, and took time to admire the formidable stonework. As she retraced her steps, Georgina came across a church and a clergyman in black attire that stood outside. She removed her sunglasses and stared at his cylinder-like black hat.

"Would you care to come inside for prayer? Visitors are welcome."

Peering into the sun-filled interior, Georgina observed rows of dark wooden chairs and a stained-glass window. "Later, perhaps."

"Are you a tourist?"

Georgina shook her head. "I've just arrived from New York."

"Your accent is not of a New Yorker."

"I'm originally from Scotland and spent time in Los Angeles."

"What brings you to our beautiful island?"

Following a glance upward, the clergyman acknowledged. "I understand."

"Bye," said Georgina, as she replaced her sunglasses.

"Hope to see you again."

Soon, Georgina came across an abundance of places to eat and drink. Feeling thirsty, she entered one with a colourful blue and yellow facade. A waiter spotted her, and came over.

"I'd like a nice cool drink, please."

"A glass of wine perhaps, madam?"

"A glass of lemonade would be good."

"Certainly, please have a seat."

Georgina sat down beside a window, took off her cream hat and removed the sunglasses. Laying both on an empty chair, she observed cheerful passers-by. The waiter returned with her drink, smiled, then tended to another customer.

As she sipped her drink, Georgina spotted Elena with a man of mature years going into a restaurant. That must be her father.

CHAPTER 4

THE WEDDING

Whilst they had an early morning cup of coffee, Georgina and Elena chatted. Since Georgina's arrival, four years had passed, and the two women now shared a close friendship. Elena had introduced Georgina to a professional gentleman, Stelios Balaskas. He taught mathematics at a local school and a relationship with Georgina had ensued. Also, Georgina now gave piano lessons to pupils at the same school, courtesy of a recommendation from Stelios to the Principal.

"What are your plans for today?" asked Elena, as she set her cup on the table.

"As there's no class, I'll go to the library."

"In the school?"

"The town centre. Our school library has only academic books and I'm not that type. Besides, almost every book in the school library is in Greek."

"It is not an easy language to learn."

"Fortunately, my pupils speak better English than I do Greek. During my schooldays, I had difficulty with Latin and had to drop out of the class."

"At least you play the piano in a competent manner."

"And, it has given me a regular income."

Elena got up, then laid her empty plate and cup beside the white ceramic sink. Georgina finished her coffee and then sat back on the wooden chair. "Have you arranged to meet Thamos at lunchtime?"

Elena looked round. "I will see him tonight."

As Elena turned on a tap, Georgina got up and assisted her to wash the crockery, then left for Heraklion's Municipal Library.

After a stroll through sun-kissed streets, Georgina arrived at the library.

Inside, more people than usual had appeared, therefore, only a few vacant chairs remained. Georgina went to the History section, took out a book and sat down. Since she arrived in Crete, Georgina liked to read about the island's turbulent and cultural past. Several moments later, a man leaned over. "Excuse me."

Georgina looked at the tall, tanned individual with dark wavy hair and a short moustache.

"Do you have a pencil I can borrow?"

"Sorry, no."

The man got up, went to the reception desk and spoke to an assistant. He returned with a pencil, sat down and then smiled at Georgina. "She saved the day."

"Are you carrying out research?"

"I have an idea for a book."

As the man scribbled on a piece of paper, Georgina looked on with interest. He stopped, leaned back and observed Georgina. "I forgot to bring one today."

"What is the book about?"

"A man returns to Greece from Russia, opens a disused mine and gives work to unemployed people in a nearby village."

"A Cretan village?"

The man hesitated. "In one of the smaller islands."

"At this moment, any Greek island would welcome employment," commented Georgina.

As the man laughed, Georgina returned to her book and turned a page. Once more, the man leaned over. "Excuse me for asking, I do not recognise your accent. Where are you from?"

Georgina put down her book. "Scotland, then I moved to America."

"Why did you come to Crete?"

"It's a lovely tranquil place to live and warmer than New York, where I stayed."

"I feel that the new American President's economic policies will be beneficial for the country. Projects will be implemented to get the unemployed back into work." He went on, "The American government will not let the economy remain as it is." The man gave a slight smile. "You will have to excuse me, I have to be somewhere else."

"Good luck with the book."

After the man left, Georgina once more returned to her book and then reflected. Strikes me as the knowledgeable type.

A short while later, Georgina left the library and ventured to a nearby museum. Due to its selection of ancient Cretan artefacts, Georgina found the museum fascinating. Whilst she studied an ancient scroll, a member of staff came over. Georgina turned round and gave him a smile. "I never tire of this place."

"I am happy you enjoy it here."

"It's not as busy today," said Georgina, as she cast her gaze around the room.

"After the last earthquake, people are apprehensive." He looked upwards. "Part of the ceiling came down."

"How many have you experienced?"

"1929, 1930 and the recent one."

Georgina considered. No wonder visitors are scarce.

"I have asked the government to build a solid safer structure."

"It would reassure the public and increase visitor numbers."

The member of staff gave a slight nod. "That is what I stated to them. Also, we want to keep our heritage intact."

"Absolutely."

"I will continue to persevere," he said, as a smile crept across his face.

Following a browse, Georgina left the museum, and headed for the outdoor market. After she purchased a couple of essential items, a midday coffee at a local establishment would beckon.

Next day at breakfast, Elena yawned, sipped her coffee and then yawned again. Holding her cup, Georgina gave a wry smile. The consequence of arriving home at three in the morning easy to spot. Elena set her cup on the kitchen table. "We have been invited to a wedding."

"In Heraklion?"

"Arhames. It is an idyllic village on a hillside."

Georgina raised her eyebrows. "When?"

"In two weeks," said Elena, as she yawned.

"That's short notice," said Georgina, as he took a sip of her coffee.

"There is a good reason," said Elena, as she looked at Georgina, who gave a slight nod. "You will find it different from a Scottish or American wedding."

"In what way?"

"The intended couple host a party prior to their wedding and much food and drink is consumed. The next day, men from the nearest village ride out to the bride's house and the first one to arrive, takes her to the reception."

"How many will be at the wedding?" asked Georgina, as she sipped her coffee.

"Between seven and eight hundred."

Georgina choked.

"People come from all over," said Elena, smiling.

Georgina coughed. "That will be a high cost."

"In Crete, we give money as a present instead of a gift."

Just as well. "Can Stelios come as my partner?"

"Of course. He will be acquainted with many of the guests. Crete is not a large island." Elena paused. "How serious is your relationship with him?"

"He wants us to get married."

"And will you?"

"No chance," said Georgina sharply.

Elena laughed.

"I've had my fair share of serious relationships."

Elena gave a wry smile. "The wedding may advance Stelios's proposal."

"I'll let him down gently."

Elena smiled, then glanced at the clock and finished her coffee. Laying the empty cup aside, she said, "I better get dressed, I have to go into the town centre."

"Me too, I have a class at nine o'clock."

Rushing out the door amidst a hot August sun, Georgina walked at a normal pace to the school. As she glanced at her watch, footsteps became more frequent and ten minutes later, the school came into view.

As she entered the building, Georgina once more glanced at her watch and sighed. She walked into the class, sat at her desk and waited for pupils to arrive for their Tuesday morning music lesson.

After an enjoyable session with her pupils and with no afternoon class, Georgina headed for the town centre. Stopping at an open-air restaurant, she removed her sunglasses, ordered a coffee and took a seat. Casting her gaze around the establishment, she observed only positive expressions. The Cretan economy had started to stabilise, which resulted in less unemployment and happier retailers. Heraklion, Crete's largest concentration of population, enjoyed a welcome economic resurgence. As Georgina soaked up the town centre atmosphere and sunshine, she spotted Stelios. His tall slim build and dark blue jacket, a contrast to other non-coloured attire within the vicinity. Georgina called to him whilst she stood and waved. He looked her way, acknowledged and then came across.

"No class this afternoon?" Georgina sat down.

Stelios sat opposite. "My next class is a late start."

"Lucky you."

He tilted his head. "Not really, I finish later."

Georgina laughed.

"How was your morning?" asked Stelios. As he attempted to attract a waiter's attention.

"Good. The pupils are attentive and well-behaved."

At that moment, a stocky white-shirted waiter appeared at the table, then looked at Stelios in a cheery manner. "Something to drink, sir?"

"A black coffee, please."

The waiter turned to face Georgina and gave the same cheerful expression. "And for the lovely lady?"

"Another white coffee, please," said Georgina, as she looked up at the waiter. At least this one smiles.

"Are you going to have lunch?" asked Stelios.

Georgina shook her head. "I like to remain thin."

As the waiter departed with a slight grin, Stelios cast his gaze around the area, then leaned back on his chair. "It is good to see smiling faces, there has been much hardship in Crete."

"Due to the recession?"

"Not only that, Georgina, a war with Turkey for several years." Stelios sighed.

Georgina could see from Stelios's body language that bitterness towards the Turks ran deep. "Was it a brutal conflict?"

"Atrocities carried out will never be forgotten."

"Why commit them?"

Stelios hesitated. "One side carries them out, then the other retaliates."

"Who started it?"

Stelios shrugged his shoulders. "Each side blames the other."

"Does a volatile situation between both countries still exist?"

"Especially, as the coastlines face each other."

"Thank goodness for the Aegean," said Georgina, as she looked at Stelios who gave a slight grin.

The waiter returned with two coffees on a wooden tray and set them down in front of both customers. Before he departed, looked at Stelios. "Will you be there tonight?"

"Yes," said Stelios, nodding.

Intrigued by the conversation, Georgina watched the waiter leave, then looked at Stelios. "A school meeting?"

Stelios lifted his and took a sip. "A gathering."

Georgina lifted hers and pondered.

Following a traditional Cretan wedding ritual prior to the reception, family and guests of the bride and groom celebrated in and around their local village taverna. As Georgina cast her gaze around the packed outlet, a fellow guest who enjoyed hearty meals squeezed past her on his way to the bar. Stelios returned to where Georgina stood with two glasses of wine. Taking her glass, Georgina smiled. "I trust the cellar is well stocked?"

"If not, there will be a riot."

Georgina laughed.

A fellow guest commented, "Do not laugh, it will happen," he said, walking past Georgina with a drink in each hand.

"Let us go outside," said Stelios, as he took a deep breath. "It is stuffy in here."

In the fresh air, Georgina and Stelios took a deep breath, then joined a group of the groom's friends. One of them, with a long dark beard, led a discussion. "Mussolini is a ruthless dictator on a quest for power." The man took a swig from his tankard of beer. "He will not stop until his army is all-powerful."

"Who do you think will be attacked?" asked a male guest.

"I believe a weaker nation, such as Abyssinia."

"And then?" asked another guest.

"Albania, then the Aegean islands."

"If Albania is invaded, we will be next," added Stelios.

The bearded man looked at him, nodding. "You are correct, my friend."

Georgina sipped her wine. Nice cheery chat. As the conversation attracted several guests, a woman spoke out sharply, "We now have the League of Nations to stop such acts." She flicked back her long black hair.

"And the British will intervene on our behalf," added Stelios.

The bearded man gave a slight grin. "Let us hope so, my friend."

"What are your views on Germany?" asked the woman.

"Like Mussolini, Hitler is a Fascist and a megalomaniac." He took a swig. "Europe is not safe."

As people started to mutter, the bearded man finished his drink, burped, and went to get a refill. Georgina shook her head. "Politics. Do you know him?"

"Yes," said Stelios, as he sipped his wine.

"Who is he?"

"A Government Diplomat."

Georgina laughed.

"He likes to air his views in public."

Georgina looked sideways. "Elena is in deep conversation with her father."

Stelios stared. "She is similar in appearance to her mother."

"Elena doesn't mention her."

"She now lives in Italy."

Georgina stared. "Italy?"

"Her mother met an Italian businessman who visited Heraklion and a relationship began." Stelios finished his drink. "Not long after, Elena's mother left Crete."

Georgina shook her head. "Poor Elena."

"And her father." Stelios paused. "He buried himself in his work. Another drink?" Stelios glanced at Georgina's near-empty glass and she nodded. After Stelios departed, Georgina finished her wine. Minutes later, Stelios returned and handed her a full glass.

"I'll take your empty glass," said a young man, as he approached with a tray.

As Georgina thanked him, he took it and gathered other empty glasses. Stelios glanced his way. "A nephew of the groom. His father was killed in the war with Turkey."

"Volatility appears to surround Greece."

"The recent threat of a military coup is another example." As Stelios took a swig, Georgina reflected. America didn't have that to contend with.

"We require a monarch to give Greece stability."

"Let's hope so."

Stelios looked towards a group of men. "Excuse me for a moment." He walked towards them.

Whilst Georgina waited, a grey-haired man with a beard approached her and then grinned. "What do you think of our island now? We last spoke about five years ago."

Georgina smiled. "I remember, you are Manos."

"Mitsos," he said humbly.

"I was close."

Grinning, the man held out his hand and Georgina shook it. "I believe you are now a teacher of music."

"Yes, I managed to find a job."

"I hear good things about you. I have many contacts in Heraklion."

"I hope they're dependable."

Mitsos laughed, then glanced sideways. "Goodbye."

After he left, Stelios returned, glanced towards Mitsos and then looked at Georgina. "Do you know him?"

"I know of him. He is a communist, I do not trust any of them."

A couple came over to Stelios and he introduced them to Georgina. Then, they looked towards the taverna entrance, where male voices became louder. Two men confronted each other and as one threw a punch, more men joined in. When a man fired a pistol into the air, men separated. Georgina stared at Stelios, then shook her head.

"A contrast of ideologies," said Stelios, with a slight grin.

"Indeed." The Wild West exists on Crete also.

"Aris to the rescue again," said a woman. "Kostas should keep his views private."

"As should Dimitris," added Stelios.

The woman gave a slight nod and Georgina began to mull over the past months. Her life in Crete so far had been positive and fruitful. However, given the volatile political situation in Greece and Europe, an uncertain, as well as unpredictable future lay ahead for all.

CHAPTER 5

INVASION

Following their evening meal, Georgina and Elena listened to the evening international news broadcast. With the Second World War in progress, everyone in Europe had become glued to a radio. The Axis countries of Germany, Italy and Japan appeared unstoppable with swift victories against traditional established powers. After only six weeks, France had suffered a defeat, which humiliated the whole country. The Axis juggernaut rolled on and the question on everyone's lips was who would be next?

The announcer finished with details of British cities being attacked by German bombers, which caused many innocent civilian casualties. With a shake of the head, Georgina looked at Elena. "Hitler is doing his utmost to bomb Britain into submission."

"The country will not surrender?"

"Not with Winston Churchill as Prime Minister. Also, the British people have a formidable spirit and will not give up without a fight."

"Winston Churchill's speeches will no doubt inspire them."

Georgina nodded. "However, Britain stands alone against the Nazi threat and will somehow have to hold out."

"And if they do not?"

Georgina sighed. "Then we're all done for."

"Could America not intervene?"

"Many Americans feel it's Europe's war and should not get involved."

"With Italy on the side of Germany, it is a dilemma for the American President."

"A large Italian population exists in New York and other large American cities."

"I overheard father in conversation with my aunt about Mussolini and it was not favourable."

"Mussolini is a dictator, similar to Hitler and hell bent on expansion."

"With the annexation of Albania, father said Greece would be next."

"As what happened to Czechoslovakia after the annexation of Austria by Germany."

"Father also mentioned that a Greek cruiser had been torpedoed and the incident hushed up by our government."

"An Italian submarine?"

Elena shrugged her shoulders. "Father feels war with Italy is inevitable."

Georgina stared out the living room window. To think I came here for a better life. She turned to face Elena. "What're your plans for this evening?"

"I will not be going out. Thamos has arranged to meet up with a group of friends." Elena went on. "What about you?"

"Stelios is doing the same."

"Since the end of last year, meetings have become regular."

Georgina reflected. Not long after Germany defeated Poland.

Unknown to Elena and Georgina, Stelios and Thamos were members of rival undercover movements based in Crete. One non-communist, and the other communist, with a huge distrust for one another. However, they had Crete's best interests at heart and both groups prepared for a possible war against Italy.

Elena clasped her hands. "Since we are on our own, let us open a bottle of wine."

"Good idea." Another hangover ensues, and I've a class tomorrow morning.

As Elena went into the kitchen, Georgina listened to the radio and soon up-tempo Greek folk music came through the airwaves. Moments later, Elena popped her head into the living room and Georgina commented. "No doubt to boost morale."

There was a knock and Elena looked towards the front entrance. "Who can that be?" As Elena went to open the door, Georgina turned down the volume. A petite grey-haired woman stood with a worried expression.

"Alexa, what is wrong?"

"You have a radio, Elena, what is the latest?"

"Come in."

"Thank you," said Alexa gratefully.

When Elena closed the door, Alexa looked towards Georgina and a sideboard, which hosted the radio.

"It's not good," said Georgina.

"The music sounds fine to me," said Alexa, as she glanced at Elena who gave a warm smile. "Have a seat. Coffee?"

Alexa looked up. "Yes, please, Elena, she said politely."

As Elena went into the kitchen, Alexa looked at Georgina, as she turned up the volume. Georgina sighed. "The broadcast only gave bad news."

"My son is based in London, I pray each night for him."

Georgina sat down opposite Alexa. "What does he do?" she asked with interest.

"He works in the Foreign Office."

"A spy!" said Georgina, as she raised her eyebrows.

"I am unsure. In his letters, he does not discuss his work."

"The British Government will check his letters to ensure no information is disclosed."

"It makes me feel uneasy that someone has read my son's letters," said Alexa sharply. "They are personal."

"I agree, but the British will view security as an important issue."

"I hate war! The conflict with Turkey took its toll on Greece from which it has never recovered." After a short reflection, Alexa looked at Georgina and gave a slight smile. "America is not my enemy."

"I'm from Scotland, I moved to New York years ago."

"Why did you come to Crete?"

Georgina hesitated. "For a better life."

Elena entered and handed her neighbour a welcome cup of hot coffee. As Alexa took a sip, Elena sat down next to her. "Is Theo kept busy?"

"Yes, Elena. I hope he is safe in London and away from the bombing."

"Government buildings will be protected," said Georgina, doing her best to console the frail woman.

"I hope so," said Alexa gravely.

Even though she was many miles from London, war had once more affected Alexa.

On the final Monday of October, Georgina locked the classroom door and then went to the administrator's office to hand in her key. When she arrived, a group of schoolteachers huddled round a radio. One of them turned to Georgina with an expression of sorrow. "Italy has invaded us, they came through Albania," the schoolteacher said gravely.

For the remainder of the impromptu broadcast, a dejected group listened. Although a foreigner, Georgina could feel their pain. Yet another country had been invaded at the command of a heartless and ruthless dictator. The administrator glanced around the group. "What happens now?"

"We fight them!" said a male schoolteacher.

"At least we are not on the mainland, where they have invaded," said the administrator.

A female schoolteacher sighed. "The Italians will be here soon enough."

"Crete is a strategic base for North Africa, which will strengthen their hold on the region," said the male schoolteacher. When another female schoolteacher started to sob, a colleague comforted her. Saddened, Georgina left the building, then made for home. On her journey, apart from the occasional group of men in deep conversation, she observed deserted streets.

When Georgina arrived home, Elena met her, and the two women hugged each other. Elena stared. "I have just heard the news on Athens Radio." Elena wiped her eyes.

"Greece will not be dictated to, Elena," said Georgina sharply.

"What right do those thugs have to march into our country." Elena sniffed.

"I heard a broadcast in school which mentioned the invasion, but not much else."

"The attack happened at 05.30, and our army has confronted the Italians at the border." Elena took a deep breath.

"I'm sure an attack would have been expected."

"Since August, my source has told me."

"That's when the army would have mobilised."

Exasperated, Elena blew between her teeth. "I need a drink."

"Me too," said Georgina, as she sighed.

After Georgina hung up her hat and jacket, she joined Elena in the kitchen. The two friends sat at the table and proceeded to have several glasses of wine. Elena left the kitchen and minutes later returned. As Georgina held her glass, Elena placed a photograph in front of her. She picked it up and looked at Elena. "Your father?"

"My uncle, when he served in the army."

"When was it taken?"

"1920."

"Does he stay in Crete?"

"He died in the war with Turkey."

After Georgina returned the photograph to Elena, she looked at it for several moments, then sighed. "I was his favourite niece."

"Who won the war?"

"A stalemate. Many people died for no reason." Elena took a large swallow of her wine. "Not to mention atrocities carried out by the Turks."

Georgina reflected. Stelios admitted both sides had been guilty. "What happened?"

The Turks massacred all the Greek Christians in the western part of Turkey. Each village was set on fire until none remained." Elena took another large swallow. "In one village, a mob, which consisted of Muslim civilians and soldiers hanged a Greek clergyman." Elena paused. "Why are soldiers not held accountable?"

"That is war," said Georgina gravely.

"If such actions occur this time, I hope someone will be held responsible." Elena finished her large glass of wine. "Another?" She looked across the table.

Georgina handed her empty glass to Elena, and as she filled both glasses, glanced at her uncle's photograph.

"What caused the war between Greece and Turkey?"

Elena handed over a full glass. "Following Turkey's defeat in 1918, Britain promised to give Greece a region of Turkish territory. When this did not happen, we attempted to take it."

Georgina sipped her wine. An invasion, similar to what's happening now.

"But we underestimated the Turks."

"Because they had surrendered in 1918 to Britain and France?"

Elena nodded. "Their morale had remained intact."

"They had not been the aggressor and would therefore fight with fortitude to preserve their land."

"As Greece will do against Italy." Elena took a large swallow, then another.

Georgina left a subdued classroom, handed in her room key and walked towards the town centre. Not in a good frame of mind, she had arranged to meet Stelios for lunch. Even though the conflict with Italy had begun, people went about their business as best they could. In Lions Square, a rally against Italian oppression took place daily. As she approached a cafe, Georgina heard loud cheers and being curious, popped her head inside. An elderly man with a broad grin came forward and gave her a hug. "The Italians are in retreat."

"Retreat!" That's been a quick war.

The man took off his grey cap, held it against his chest and looked upwards. Georgina entered the establishment and observed excited customers clap to the frantic up and down movement of a violinist's elbow. A waiter, who served drinks to customers at a nearby table, handed one to Georgina. He beamed. "Athens Radio announced that the Italians have fallen back and our troops are in pursuit." The dark-moustached waiter had a tear in his eye. "We kicked their fascist backsides."

Whilst Georgina drank a glass of ouzo, she overheard two middle-aged men discuss the battle. They stated that the mountainous terrain and cold wet November weather had no doubt hindered the Italian Army. Poor visibility meant that the Italian Air Force could not support its ground troops. The Greek Army knew the terrain and used it to their advantage for intermittent strategic assaults. Also, villagers assisted their army in the transportation of guns, food and other essential supplies in barrows and carts to the front. Drinking their glass of ouzo, both men had smug expressions. Georgina finished her glass and then departed the boisterous establishment. As people filled the streets around the centre of Heraklion, the inclement November weather did little to diminish the joyous celebrations. Georgina watched as people danced and sang in and around the iconic Morosini Fountain. Then, she spotted Stelios on his feet wave to her from a restaurant. After she squeezed past a group of men who wanted to hug and kiss her, Georgina joined him. "Phew!" She drew breath.

"Let us go inside."

The couple entered, managed to find a table and then took a welcome seat. Stelios glanced outside. "Since the radio announcement, people have gone wild! I witnessed them pour out of the nearby church cheering." Stelios shook his head. "What an experience!"

"No doubt all the Greek churches had been full."

"When the country is in danger, we rally and show a collective fortitude. The sturdiness of our soldiers stopped the Italian advance."

"With hearts of iron."

Stelios stared. "Exactly, Georgina."

"Were the Bulgarian Army in collaboration the Italians?"

Stelios shook his head. "They did not join the invasion."

Wearing a white shirt, dark trousers and a wide grin, a waiter appeared and looked at the couple. "What can I get you on this special day?" he asked, smiling.

"An ouzo for me," said Stelios.

"A coffee, please."

"No ouzo?" asked the waiter.

Georgina shook her head. As he departed, Georgina looked across the dark wooden table. "On my way here, I was handed a glass by an elated waiter at a nearby cafe."

Stelios grinned, looked at a clock on the wall and then Georgina. "I have to go soon."

"Why?"

"A meeting."

"In the town?"

"Hersonissos."

Moments later when a muddy black Ford Sedan drew up outside the restaurant, Stelios looked out the window. He got up, left the table and paid the waiter. Returning to Georgina, Stelios bent down and kissed her on the cheek. "See you tomorrow evening."

"Bye," said Georgina, as a smile flickered over her face.

With the Italian Army in full retreat, Heraklion's thirty-five thousand inhabitants could relax and start to enjoy life again. Georgina looked on as the crowd continued their celebrations in and around the fountain. Tonight, there would be many sore heads and wet shoes. Georgina finished her coffee and as she approached the exit, noticed a calendar behind the counter. Georgina moved closer. Wednesday, 13 November had been highlighted. She smiled. Not unlucky for Greece.

At the end of a torturous six-mile drive over narrow makeshift tracks, Stelios and his fearless driver, Dimitris, arrived at an apartment in the small town of Hersonissos. Getting out the vehicle, they could hear cheers and laughter emanate from a nearby taverna. Both men looked at each other and grinned. A stocky man with a grey beard greeted them at the door and then led them into a small furnished room. Moments later, a tall bald individual with a grin entered. "Hello, my friends." He shook hands with Stelios, and then Dimitris.

"It is good to see you again, Alexandros," said Stelios, grinning.

"You look well," added Dimitris.

"Thank you both, please, sit down," said Alexandros, as he took a seat.

"Where is Spiros?" asked Dimitris.

"He had urgent business to attend to."

Dimitris grinned. "No doubt his young wife."

Alexandros and Stelios laughed.

"How is Manilos?" asked Stelios.

"He is well," said Alexandros.

As the stocky man departed, Alexandros went to a cupboard, and brought out a bottle. "Let us drink a welcome toast." He filled three glasses, then handed one to each guest. "To victory."

All three men threw back their ouzo, and after a refill, repeated the act. Dimitris burped, then excused himself.

"No need to my friend, especially, on this day," said Alexandros. "However, my contact in Athens has told me that if Italy does not take Greece, then Germany will intervene." Alexandros stared at Stelios, then Dimitris.

"We have the Italians on the run," said Dimitris, "they are finished."

"Hence, why it is inevitable Germany will join them," said Alexandros. "Due to its location, Crete is of strategic importance to Germany."

"And Britain," added Stelios.

Alexandros gave a slight nod. "Greece cannot compete against Italy and Germany."

"The British will assist us," stated Dimitris.

"They will," said Alexandros. "But Germany is far stronger." Alexandros leaned back on his chair. "We will have to form an effective resistance movement."

"Along with the communists!" said Stelios."

"To be a strong unit we have to work together," said Alexandros.

"But they do not trust us," said Dimitris.

"As we do not trust them," replied Alexandros. "We have to put our differences aside."

"This war will be more difficult than we imagined," said Dimitris.

As all three men laughed, the stocky man reappeared with another bottle of the country's favourite drink.

"But for now, let us all get drunk." Alexandros laughed.

Both guests gave their approval.

On 14 November, the Greek Army launched a counter-offensive against the Italian Army. Consequently, areas that had been captured were soon back in Greek hands. Then, due to bad weather and Italian reinforcements, the offensive stalled in January 1941. When British reinforcements arrived to bolster their only ally in Europe, Germany intervened to assist the Italians in April. The name given to this particular campaign became known as Operation Marita. After a month, the formidable German Army had overrun mainland Greece, and the demoralised Greek Army surrendered.

The Italian offensive had highlighted major deficiencies within their army. They had over 154,000 casualties, whereas Greece suffered around 90,000. It was the first setback for Axis Forces and although defeated, a morale booster for Greece.

With mainland Greece secure, the German military plotted to take Crete. Having two airfields, the island could act as a launch pad for air attacks on British troops in North Africa. However, as Britain's Royal Navy guarded the coastline around Crete, the Germans decided on an airborne assault. Thus, on 20 May, 10,000 paratroopers fell close to Maleme Airport and the town of Chania in western Crete. Unknown to the German High Command, British codebreakers had cracked Enigma and decoded a message that revealed the date and time. British Commonwealth and Greek troops, plus members of the public waited, and before paratroopers reached the ground, they were shot at. Ferocious islanders attacked those who survived with knives and axes. Paratroopers, who survived, formed effective units and took control of the airfield. As reinforcements and supplies flew in, it became only a matter of time until the island was under German control. British Commonwealth troops were evacuated by ship on 28 May, and Greek troops surrendered three days later.

Before mainland Greece fell, its monarch and government left Athens for the safe haven of Crete. However, soon after it, too, came under attack and the government relocated to Egypt. Meanwhile, German, Italian and Bulgarian armies carved up Greece and the Aegean islands between them. Also, Hitler made sure his forces got the largest and strategic regions. Next, a puppet collaborative government known as the Hellenic State was put in place by the Axis powers.

At a secluded cottage within a forest on the outskirts of Hersonissos, Stelios and Dimitris once more met with Alexandros. He had vacated his apartment in the town for a discreet location. The three resistance members of the newly established Organisation of Crete sat poker-faced round a table.

"Why would the Germans make General Tsolakolous, Prime Minister?" asked Dimitris. "After all, he led our army."

"The German High Command want us to fall into line," said Stelios.

"It will not be the General who makes any decision," said Alexandros.

"The mainland is in bad shape." Stelios stared at his two colleagues.

"In what way?" asked Dimitris.

"The infrastructure."

"Industry, ports and roads have been damaged," added Alexandros. "Our economy has been decimated." He shook his head. "The Germans also want Greece to pay for the occupation."

"Is it not enough that they have destroyed our country!" said Dimitris.

"They will bleed us dry," added Stelios.

"And not only the economy," said Alexandros.

"What do you mean?" Dimitris stared.

"Our Jewish population."

"In what way, Alexandros?" asked Stelios.

"I have heard from a reliable source in the French Resistance that Jews are being deported from occupied countries to work in German factories."

"Slave labour," said Stelios.

Alexandros gave a slight nod. "In Germany, they were forced out of their businesses, homes and then the country. Those who remained had to wear the Star of David, and ridiculed."

"The General will not allow it," said Dimitris.

Stelios stared at his friend. "His hands will be tied."

"If the General protests, he may be sent to a German factory," said Alexandros.

As the three men contemplated the future, Alexandros's stocky friend appeared with a half-empty bottle of ouzo and three glasses. After he departed, Alexandros filled the glasses. As Dimitris received his glass, he looked at Alexandros. "Your friend never speaks."

Alexandros took a swig." "That is because he cannot. During the war with Turkey, Christos went on a mission to spy, and after being caught, the Turks tortured him."

"His tongue was cut out!" said Stelios, staring.

Alexandros nodded then took another swig. "We will have to be careful and take no chances." He laid his empty glass aside. "There will be collaborators in Crete." He filled Dimitris's glass and then his. "In war, people become desperate, and sell their soul to the devil."

Stelios looked at Dimitris. "In our case, the Germans."

Dimitris gave a slight nod.

"Due to last year's poor harvest, there are many hungry mouths on our island and the Germans will prey on that." Alexandros took a swig.

"Where are the British agents who stayed behind after the evacuation?" asked Stelios.

Alexandros grinned. "In a safe house, not far from here."

"How many?" asked Dimitris.

"Enough to assist us I have been told."

"Are the communists to fight alongside us?"

"For the time being, Dimitris," said Alexandros gravely.

As Stelios finished his drink, Alexandros refilled it, then looked at the bottle. "More ouzo, Christos," he shouted.

In a southern mountain retreat, members of Crete's communist organisation, Liberation Front, met to discuss the current situation. The leader, Aris, and two deputy's, Manos and Kostas, studied a photograph taken a week earlier in Athens.

"Surely it has not come to this," said Manos. "To wear an armband!"

"I am afraid it has," said Aris. "Similar to what happened in Germany, Austria and Poland."

"And we know what happened next," added Kostas.

"All Jews were imprisoned in camps," added Manos.

"Is it true that distinguished Jewish citizens are being forced to scrub pavements in public places?" asked Kostas, horrified.

"To humiliate them," said Manos, as he shook his head.

Kostas stared across the wooden table at Aris. "We cannot allow this to happen in our country."

Aris sighed. "It has, however, not on Crete."

"What about Rhodes?" asked Kostos. "They have a large Jewish contingent."

"As yet," said Aris, "I have not heard of any persecution."

Manos glanced at his two colleagues. "Give it time, the Wehrmacht will not alter their strategy of persecution."

Aris leaned back on his wooden chair. "I met with Alexandros Zervas for a discussion on the situation."

"And?" asked Manos.

"We will hold more talks in three days."

"I do not trust them," stated Kostas, "they are on good terms with the British."

"We need the British for weapons and food, therefore, cannot fall out with Zervas and his mob," said Aris.

"That is a complimentary term," quipped Kostas.

Manos laughed.

Aris grinned. "Katerina would agree with you."

"At least we have women in our organisation," said Kostas, "the other mob are not as patriotic as they would like us to believe."

Manos thumped the table. "Communist women have fortitude."

Once more, Aris grinned.

Kostos looked at him. "Is it true the government has to pay money to Germany for the occupation?"

"I believe so."

"That is ridiculous!" cried Manos.

Aris sighed. "Our economy is already in trouble."

"The fascists want to ruin us!" said Manos. Once more, he thumped the table.

"Our Russian comrades may be next," said Aris.

"What makes you say that?" asked Kostos. "They are in bed with the Germans."

Manos laughed.

"My contact in Athens believes Germany plans to invade Russia."

"Soon?" asked Manos.

Aris shrugged his broad shoulders. "They have moved troops near the border with Russia."

"Yugoslavia made a pact with Russia," said Manos.

"And then Germany attacked Yugoslavia," added Aris.

"Then us," said Kostos.

Manos considered. "If they attack Russia, their troops in Greece will be needed."

"The Germans will not relinquish control," said Kostos.

"Pity," added Manos, "we can handle the Italians."

Aris grinned, got up, went to a wall cupboard. Taking out a bottle of red wine and three glasses, he laid them on the table. "Let us drink to our comrades in Athens."

"And to the student who removed the swastika banner from the Acropolis," said Manos.

After the tall well-built Aris poured three large drinks, his two shorter comrades joined him in a series of toasts, which included their Russian comrades.

Now occupied by German and Italian troops, people on Crete would have to adhere to their rules and guidelines. Italian troops tended to be located in the east and south, whereas their German ally had troops in the west of the island. Due to Crete's mountainous northern region Axis troops remained non-existent. Crete's largest town, Heraklion, became a stronghold for

German troops, therefore, locals no doubt felt intimidated.

As Georgina arrived home from school, Elena greeted her with a slight smile. After she took off her hat and jacket, Georgina sat down then gave a long sigh.

"What is wrong?"

"I saw a German patrol approach a young man and moments later, led him away"

"Did he protest?"

"Yes, and then hit with a baton."

Elena remained tight-lipped.

Georgina shook her head. "Terrible."

"Where did they take him?"

"I'm not sure. They dragged him down an alleyway."

"German thugs! Because they lost many soldiers in the battle for Crete, patrols will extract revenge whenever and wherever possible."

"A woman who stood next to me mentioned that yesterday the young man had removed a swastika banner from outside the Town Hall."

"Someone must have told the patrol."

Georgina stared.

"Collaborators, Georgina."

"Betray fellow Cretans!"

Elena nodded. "For food and luxuries."

"I'm aware there are shortages, but find it difficult to believe people would go to that extreme."

"It is war, desperate people will do anything." Elena paused.

"Did you spot any Jewish citizens?"

Georgina nodded. "With those armbands, they must feel humiliated."

"My father revealed to me that the Germans are systematically working their way around the islands."

"What about mainland Greece?"

"Affluent Jews are allowed to leave the country to locate elsewhere."

"They have to pay."

"Yes, or face persecution."

Georgina shook her head.

"As we now have a 'puppet government', no minister will speak out."

"The Germans just bulldoze their way across Europe."

Elena frowned. "Bulldoze?"

"They walk over countries." Georgina went on. "Stamp would be more applicable."

Elena gave a slight smile. "A glass of wine?"

Georgina nodded.

"Due to a shortage in my supply, it will have to be a small glass."

"Better than no glass at all."

As Elena went into the kitchen, Georgina glanced at a clock, then turned on the radio to find out the latest news from Britain. When a bulletin interrupted the broadcast, she stared at the radio. Elena entered the living room and then handed a glass to a joyful Georgina. "Why the wide smile?"

"The announcer mention tensions between Germany and Russia."

"Is that not bad news?"

"If Germany invades Russia, then they will have bitten off more than they can chew," said Georgina, as a smile crept across her face.

"Let us hope they do."

"A toast to the Russian Army." Georgina raised her glass. "Let's hope the two countries fall out."

Elena followed.

That evening, Georgina and Stelios arrived at their favourite restaurant in the centre of Heraklion. On this occasion, three grey-uniformed German officers occupied a nearby table in the small establishment. As Georgina and Stelios sat down, the officers glanced in Georgina's direction and then continued to talk amongst themselves. Stelios looked across the table. "Do you understand German?"

"I learned the language at school, however, I'm a bit rusty."

"Rusty?"

"Not proficient." Georgina gave a faint smile.

"What are they talking about?"

Georgina listened. "Russia."

Stelios moved his head forward. "What about it?"

"How weak the Russian Army is. Obsolete tanks and planes. Also, a lack of leadership in the military."

"The German military?"

Georgina shook her head. "The Russian military."

"Pity." Stelios sighed.

"It doesn't portray the Russian Army in a good light."

"A good light? What do you mean?"

"They're not much of a threat.

As Stelios acknowledged, the waiter appeared and handed each of his guests a menu. "Good evening, how are you both?"

Downbeat, Stelios looked at the menu, therefore, pleasantries were left to Georgina. "Fine, thanks." She read the menu.

Stelios glanced behind, then whispered to the waiter. "How are they?"

"Polite. Would you like a bottle of your favourite wine?" The waiter glanced at his two regulars.

"Yes, thank you, said Stelios."

When the waiter departed, Georgia looked out a window, and watched a patrol of German soldiers march past. After he glanced out the window, Stelios sighed.

"Everyone will have to get used to it," said Georgina, as she looked across the table.

Whilst Stelios mulled his bitter thoughts, Georgina glanced at the three German officers. "They have a swagger about them."

"Since Germany invaded Poland, no battle has been lost. However, we Cretans put up a good fight."

"Men and women." Georgina read her menu.

"Hitler will not use paratroopers again, that is for sure." Stelios put his menu aside.

"How many casualties?" Georgina put down her menu.

"Thousands. The British Secret Service knew when the invasion would take place and alerted us."

Elena told me that people with no weapons killed paratroopers with their bare hands!" Georgina put her menu aside.

Stelios grinned. "Women and men."

"Will there be reprisals?"

Stelios gave a slight nod. "It is war."

After they paid for their meal, the German officers vacated their table. As one walked past Georgina, he stopped, then picked up a silver brooch. "Does this belong to you, madam?" The officer showed it to Georgina and she looked down her light blue dress, then at the officer. He gave the brooch to Georgina, then a slight smile.

"Thanks."

Moments later, Georgina looked across the table at a disenchanted Stelios. "Maybe some are not so bad."

"They are all Nazis, Georgina. Also, some Greeks."

"What do you mean?"

"There is a group of National Socialists based in Athens, a small party who will no doubt collaborate with their German brothers."

Then, the waiter brought a bottle of wine, poured two glasses and then departed. Stelios picked up his glass and took a swig. "Some may even side with the Germans in order to avoid a communist regime."

Georgina picked up her glass, took a sip and observed Stelios deep in thought. "What's on your mind?"

"I hope no German representative will turn up at the school."

"Why would they?"

Stelios lifted the bottle of wine, and filled his glass. "To re-educate young Greeks in the National Socialism philosophy. It would not surprise me, the Nazis are fanatics."

The waiter returned, took Stelios and Georgina's order, and departed. Then, four young German officers entered and sat down. Stelios stared, along with the restaurants six other customers. One German officer looked around the tables. "Have you not seen soldiers of the Wehrmacht before," he shouted.

Stelios looked at Georgina and whispered, "Not so nice."

The waiter approached the officers and then gave them a forced smile. "Gentlemen, what can I get you?"

"To begin with, four schnapps," said one.

"I am sorry, we do not sell schnapps."

"Why not?" asked another.

"We have no demand for it."

"You do now," said a third officer."

"I will order a bottle from my supplier tomorrow, gentlemen." The waiter looked at the four officers.

"You will need more than a bottle, make it a case," he cried, as his three colleagues laughed. "I trust you have cognac?"

The waiter gave a slight nod.

"Then four large ones, and be quick about it!"

When the waiter left their table, Georgina moved her head forward. "I agree."

"It is enough to put me off my food." Stelios glanced towards the four officers.

One of them spotted Stelios and then chatted to his companions, who all glanced his way.

Two days later, Stelios and Dimitris visited Alexandros at his discreet location. With a drink in their hands and contempt for the Germans, they discussed the current situation.

"The Germans have started to round up Jewish citizens in the Aegean," Alexandros revealed.

"Rhodes has the largest population," said Dimitris.

"How many?" asked Stelios.

"Around 70,000."

Alexandros drank his ouzo. "They are being taken to Germany and then put in camps."

"Labour camps?" Stelios took a swig.

"I believe that is the case."

"What about the mainland?" asked Dimitris.

"From my information, no Jew has been sent to Germany." Alexandros took a swig. "The Germans want to ridicule them first."

"Have you heard the latest rumours about tensions with Russia?" asked Stelios.

Alexandros finished his drink. "From my source in British Secret Service, the Germans plan to attack."

Stelios looked at Dimitris. "If true, the Ukraine could soon be in German hands."

"What makes you say that?" Dimitris stared.

"I overheard three German officers discuss Russian military weaknesses."

Alexandros looked at Stelios. "When did you learn to speak German?"

Stelios gave a slight grin. "Georgina does. We sat near them in a restaurant."

"If they take the Ukraine, Leningrad will be next," added Dimitris.

"And Moscow thereafter." Alexandros reached for the bottle of ouzo, and filled his glass. "The British want us to plan an attack on Heraklion Airport."

"To stop German reinforcements?" asked Stelios.

"And supplies."

"Will the British be involved?" asked Dimitris.

Alexandros nodded. "A team of agents." He took a swig. "Since we helped their army on Crete to escape, the British and us are best of friends."

"At present, Greece is their only friend," said Dimitris.

"And maybe Russia, Dimitris," said Alexandros, with a slight grin.

"Let us drink to Stalin," said Dimitris.

"And our communist colleagues on Crete?" added Stelios.

"Only for the time being," said Alexandros.

The three non-communist members clinked their glasses, emptied them and then had a refill.

With the Nazi swastika once more displayed outside Heraklion's prestigious Town Hall, Wehrmacht officials made it their 'seat of power' in Crete. At the helm as Military Governor was General Friedrich-Hans Muller, a middle-aged autocratic, power-driven individual. Having served as a soldier in WW1, he was battle-hardened and ready for the current conflict. Major Neuberger was a decade younger than his superior, but still as ruthless. He came from a military background and aspired to become a feared Nazi. Captain Hoeness on the other hand, had a university education and when war broke out with Britain and France, was conscripted into the army. Younger and unlike his fellow officers, he would rather settle a conflict through diplomatic means rather than fight. General Muller and his two colleagues discussed the occupation.

"As predicted, General, we have encountered hostility," said Captain Hoeness."

"In the towns?"

Major Neuberger shook his head. "In the villages, General."

"We believe there is now an organised resistance movement," said Captain Hoeness.

"From which part of the island?" asked General Muller.

"The south west, General."

General Muller leaned back on his black leather chair. "I have heard that there are two resistance movements. One is communist and the other has British contacts."

"Were all the British not evacuated, General?" asked Major Neuberger.

Captain Hoeness looked at Major Neuberger. "They hide in the southern mountains of Crete."

"Why have they not been rounded up?" asked General Muller sharply.

"They are always on the move, General," said Captain Hoeness. "But we have a source who will attempt to find out their present location."

"A local?" asked General Muller.

"This person was caught with stolen food, and in return for not being punished, will spy for us."

"I do not trust any native of Crete," stated General Muller. "During the invasion, they murdered four thousand of our paratroopers."

"For failure, their family will face a firing squad."

General Muller nodded in agreement. "Have the Jews in Crete adhered to our protocol?" He looked at Major Neuberger.

"So far, only several incidents, General."

"Where?"

"In nearby Hersonissos, however, the aggressors paid in blood."

"We have to be assertive," said General Muller.

"What of the Italians, General?" asked Captain Hoeness.

"They soak up the sun, drink wine and flirt with local women in the south of the island." General Muller shook his head of grey hair.

"What is the latest from Yugoslavia, General?" asked Captain Hoeness.

He grinned. "The uprising has been quashed and they have come into line."

"They concluded a pact with the Russians," said Major Neuberger. "Their army is in chaos."

"The result of purges by Stalin," said Captain Hoeness.

"An act of folly," added Major Neuberger.

General Muller got to his feet. "Gentlemen, let us celebrate the Russian disarray with a lavish lunch."

Captain Hoeness and Major Neuberger stood.

"All goes well for the Wehrmacht, and our Leader." General Muller addressed his two officers.

"He is a tactical genius," added Captain Hoeness.

"You will get the chance to meet him," said General Muller. "I am to attend a meeting on future Wehrmacht strategy and you will accompany me."

"Thank you, General." Captain Hoeness beamed.

General Muller looked at Major Neuberger. "Whilst I am gone, Major, you will be in command."

"For how long, General?"

"Several days." General Muller turned to Captain Hoeness. "We leave tomorrow morning."

CHAPTER 6

THE BERGHOF

As General Muller and Captain Hoeness sat in the rear of a chauffeur-driven limousine, they gazed at the scenic Bavarian countryside. The month of May had brought warm sunshine, plus colour to hills and valleys. The shiny black vehicle left a main road and then onto a minor one with a steep incline. A mile later, the driver brought the limousine to a halt on a concrete plateau. The grey-uniformed driver looked round at General Muller. "Sir, a guard will escort you from here."

"Thank you," said General Muller.

A black-uniformed SS guard, who stood at the entrance to a tunnel, approached, opened General Muller's door and then saluted, "Sir, this way, if you please."

General Muller got out and then the guard closed his door. After the driver showed a similar courtesy to Captain Hoeness, both officers followed the tall stone-faced guard along a narrow well-lit tunnel. Captain Hoeness admired the excellent workmanship of its smooth walls and walkway.

Two hundred metres later they arrived at a lift painted gold and with brown leather bench seats. When General Muller and Captain Hoeness entered, the guard closed the glass door and then pressed a button. As General Muller cast his gaze around the mirrored walls, Captain Hoeness brushed a brown hair of his uniform.

Moments later, the lift came to a halt and the guard opened its door. Both guests stepped out and then followed the guard to a reception area. He addressed General Muller. "Please wait here, someone will be with you shortly."

After the guard departed, Captain Hoeness looked out a wide

panoramic window and stared at the picturesque Bavarian peaks in the distance. General Muller joined him. "A sight to savour, is it not, Captain?"

"It is, indeed, General."

General Muller turned to face a wall. "A fine portrait of our host."

At that moment, a senior SS guard entered the reception area and led both officers into a large room full of uniformed officers and well-dressed women in conversation. Before he departed, the guard gave a courteous smile. Captain Hoeness glanced at the nearby, white-sheeted table stocked with a wide selection of bottled wine and spirits. Then, a middle-aged man who wore a white shirt, black tie and trousers approached. "Gentlemen, what can I get you?"

"Cognac, please," said General Muller. He looked at Captain Hoeness, who nodded. "Make it two glasses."

The drinks attendant poured with precision, handed a cognac to each officer, then departed. Whilst he took a sip, Captain Hoeness glanced at well-known guests, which included Albert Speer and Martin Bormann. A well-decorated Wehrmacht senior officer came up to General Muller. "Hans, good to see you again, how are you?"

"I am fine, thank you, General Bodell."

"The Cretan climate appears to agree with you." He grinned.

General Muller glanced sideways. "This is Captain Hoeness."

"A pleasure to meet you." Captain Hoeness shook General Bodell's hand. "Congratulations on your successful campaign in France."

"Thank you, Captain."

General Muller sipped his cognac. "The Berghof is a fine location."

"Let me introduce you to the architect."

General Muller looked at Captain Hoeness. "See you later."

Captain Hoeness nodded, then sipped his cognac. Several moments later, a well-groomed woman with short blonde hair who held a near-empty glass of champagne approached. "Could you fill my glass, please?" She glanced round the vicinity. "The attendant has vanished."

"Certainly." Captain Hoeness set his drink on the crisp, clean white tablecloth. "Same again?"

As the woman smiled, he gave her a full glass and she took a sip, then another. "I've not seen you here before."

"This is my first visit."

"Where are you based?"

"Crete."

The woman gave a wry smile. "Sun, sea and Cretan women."

Captain Hoeness gave a slight smile, then sipped his cognac.

"Better that than Poland," said the woman, as she took a large swallow of her champagne.

"The Poles have been defeated."

"There are issues in and around Warsaw, Captain, be glad you're not there. Are you married?"

"I was, but my wife and I have separated."

"At least you won't have a guilty conscience on your tour of duty."

"If married, I would remain faithful." Captain Hoeness sipped his cognac.

"Then you will find it difficult to fit in here," said the woman, as she cast her gaze around the room.

Captain Hoeness coughed.

"Enjoy the evening, Captain," said the woman, smiling.

When she departed and joined a group of men with distinguished uniforms, General Muller returned. "I noticed you in conversation with the good doctor's wife."

"The doctor, General?"

"Joseph Goebbels, that is his wife, Magda, watch what you say to her."

"She did most of the talking. Where is her husband?"

"No doubt in discussion with our Leader about certain matters of the utmost importance." General Muller glanced at a group of high-ranking Wehrmacht officers. "When the cat is away."

As Captain Hoeness gave a slight smile, General Muller finished his drink. "Another, General?"

Whilst Captain Hoeness stood at the drinks table and waited to be attended to, a fellow officer looked his way. He cut short a conversation with two colleagues, excused himself and then came over to the table. "Erich."

Captain Hoeness turned round, then paused. "Karl, is it you!"

"It is indeed my old friend." He beamed. "How are you?"

"I am well."

"Your tan confirms that," said Karl, grinning.

Erich laughed.

"How is Lisa?"

"We parted two years ago," said Erich gravely.

Karl hesitated. "We must chat later."

As his past acquaintance departed, Erich returned to General Muller, and handed him a cognac. "I just met an old friend from university." Captain Hoeness glanced towards Karl. "He could drink beer like no one else I have ever met."

General Muller looked towards the three men in conversation. "The other two are scientists."

"Scientists?" Erich raised his eyebrows.

"Based at a complex on the Baltic coast to develop rockets."

"Rockets!"

General Muller nodded, then took a sip of his cognac.

"The British still use biplanes on their aircraft carriers in the North Atlantic."

"Once the U-boats cut off their food and raw materials, Churchill will negotiate a surrender."

"When that happens, all Germany's goals will have been achieved."

"Not quite."

"To suppress the Poles in Warsaw?"

"You will learn of our new campaign at some point this evening," said General Muller with a wry smile.

At that moment, an SS guard entered the room and informed guests to make their way to another part of the building, where dinner would be served.

Captain Hoeness whispered, "Maybe you will be seated at the top table, General."

"I won't hold my breath, the inner circle will take precedence."

Murmurs between guests followed when they walked along a short corridor and into a bright long narrow room with a table set for a hundred guests.

Several hours after a lavish dinner and a speech from Germany's Leader, guests returned to the hospitality room, then mingled with friends and colleagues. Erich's friend from university approached. "Did you enjoy the speech?"

"I found it inspirational, Karl."

"Had he revealed the future plans for our complex on the Baltic, it would have taken your breath away."

"Can you tell me?"

Karl glanced around the vicinity and whispered, "In two years, we will have fighters with jet engines instead of propellers." He grinned. "The new fighters will smash the Spitfire out of the sky. Also, we won't have to fly bombers to British cities, rockets will be used."

"They would require a guidance system."

Karl nodded. "One that has to be 100% accurate." Karl sipped his drink. "At present, we are working on it."

Erich cast his gaze around the room. "Talking about an attack on Britain from the sky, where is the Head of the Luftwaffe?"

"He does not see eye to eye with Dr Goebbels."

A tall woman with long dark hair wearing a medium-length black dress confronted Karl. "That is not altogether true," she said, sipping her glass of wine. "Also, Dr Goebbels's wife."

Karl laughed, then looked at Erich. "This is Helga, one of the secretaries."

"Pleased to meet you, Fraulein." Erich shook her hand

"And you, Captain." Helga gave a faint smile.

Karl put a hand on Erich's shoulder. "See you later, I'll leave you in Helga's capable hands."

Whilst he watched Karl join a group of men, Erich turned to Helga. Sipping her wine she looked at the men. "The youngest is Von Braun. Our Leader believes he is a genius."

"To build a rocket is unbelievable! It is science-fiction."

Helga looked at Erich. "Not anymore."

Erich nodded, then sipped his cognac. "I haven't seen Von Ribbentrop this evening."

"He is at the Chancellery." Helga finished her wine. "He doesn't get on with Dr Goebbels, or Martin Bormann. Dr Goebbels stated he bought his name, married his money and swindled his way into office."

Erich smiled. "I can see why they do not get on."

"It is like a juggling act to keep the harmony." A smile flickered over Helga's powdered face.

Once more, Erich smiled. "Another glass of wine?"

Helga gave a slight nod and after Erich departed, a man with horn-rimmed spectacles and wearing a high-ranking SS uniform came over to where she stood. Whilst Erich made his way back, he noticed the officer leave. Helga took her glass. "Don't worry, I vouched for you."

Erich glanced at the officer. "Has any member of the Party replaced Deputy-Leader Hess?"

Helga shook her head. "Martin Bormann has now taken charge of all Party issues in the Chancellery." She took a large swallow. "He has begun to stamp his authority." Helga gave a slight smile. "Nice to meet you, I must go."

"And you, too."

Karl returned and the two ex-university friends began to chat. Moments later, Karl departed and then returned with two drinks. Sipping another cognac, Erich tried to spot Helga.

"An urgent withdrawal."

"Withdrawal?"

"Certain people don't like secretaries to talk for an extended time." Karl gave a wry smile. "They may disclose information of a sensitive nature."

"But I'm a Wehrmacht Captain."

"Doesn't matter, Erich. Since the Deputy-Leader flew to Scotland, security has been tightened."

"What will happen to him?"

"Interrogated by the British for information on German strategy."

"Does he know about the rocket experiments? That would prove vital for the British."

Karl shook his head. "It is top secret." He glanced at Himmler. "He is not even aware of the project." Karl faced his old friend. "And what of Crete?"

"The natives are fierce, it is not a good place to be most of the time."

"We have to bail out the Italians wherever they try to occupy a country," said Karl, shaking his head. "North Africa and now Greece."

"Our Leader's friendship with El Duce will be a factor. What is the latest on the campaign?"

"The British have suffered a series of setbacks and Rommel is on course to enter Egypt."

"No surprise that the Leader appeared buoyant with his speech."

"It goes well on all fronts." He whispered, "There is a new campaign on the horizon."

Erich raised his eyebrows. "Where?"

"First, I'll get us another drink."

Finishing his cognac, Erich observed guests in fine fettle. With a series of emphatic German victories across Europe, who could blame them? Battles that had been fought at great pace and ended without many casualties. Karl returned and handed Erich a cognac. After he disposed of his empty glass, Erich followed Karl out of the room and onto the balcony. "Have you heard anyone mention 'Barbarossa' this evening?"

Erich shook his head. "What is it?"

"It will begin soon."

"Where?"

"Russia."

"But we have a non-aggression pact with them. Erich whispered, "It doesn't make military sense."

"I agree. We have oil and military expertise agreements with the Russians."

"Russia is not France or Poland, it is vast."

"Living-space for Germans has been put forward as a reason."

"But not to start a war over." Erich sipped his cognac. "What about the Russian winter? It could begin around October."

"No doubt the Leader believes we will be in Moscow by then."

Erich looked into the distance and the range of picturesque Bavarian Alps. He considered the uncertain future.

"Do not worry, old friend, we will be victorious."

Erich turned to Karl. "What do your rocket colleagues think?"

He gave a slight grin. "They are too busy at work on a propulsion guidance system. We have had problems."

Erich laid his glass on a ledge. "If successful, will the rocket carry mustard gas?"

"No chemical weapons are to be used. Besides, due to our Treaty of Versailles restrictions, the British may have a larger stockpile and inflict more misery than we could."

"By order of the Leader?"

Karl nodded. "Because he experienced a gas attack in the last war."

At that moment, the host appeared, accompanied by three other members of the inner circle. Karl laid his glass on a ledge and like Erich, stood up straight.

"Good evening, a splendid view, is it not?" The host looked into the distance, then stared at Erich. "You are based in Crete?"

"Yes, My Leader."

"The casualties for an airborne invasion were high. We must contemplate another strategy for any future island assault." The host departed, followed by Party members.

Karl looked at Erich, took a deep breath, then Eric did likewise. Karl picked up his drink and finished it.

"Another?"

Karl nodded.

General Bodell and General Muller sat in a corner of the rear lounge. An opponent of Hitler's strategic aims, General Bodell had supporters who also kept opinions private for fear of being found dead. With no one around, General Bodell confessed his view on an imminent campaign. General Muller raised his grey eyebrows.

"I feel this is a gamble, which could have disastrous consequences," said General Bodell. "It does not make sense for us to launch an offensive fraught with danger."

"What is the reason being given for an assault on Russia?"

General Bodell sighed. "Hitler believes they will come to the aid of Britain."

"But we have a non-aggression pact in place."

"Hitler does not trust Stalin."

"I am sure Stalin has the same opinion, but it is not a reason to start a war!"

"Hitler believes the Russians are weak and we could overpower them in a matter of months. However, I have my doubts," said General Bodell, shaking his head.

"The Russians have the largest military force in Europe, however, a pre-empted strike could knock out their airfields and planes." General Muller went on. "When our troops met with Russian troops in Poland, a report was sent to Hitler. The Russian weaponry is obsolete, especially, their tanks. Our Panzers would trample over them."

General Bodell finished his drink and laid the empty glass on a table. "Indeed."

"Hitler states that you only have to kick in the door and the whole rotten structure will come crashing down."

"Do you believe it would?" General Bodell stared at his colleague.

"It does not matter what I believe, old friend." General Muller finished his drink. "Another cognac?"

General Bodell gave a slight nod and after General Muller departed, an elegant woman with bobbed brown hair and a pale blue dress appeared. "May I sit, General?"

General Bodell stood. "Please."

The woman smiled. "Thank you."

As she sat, General Bodell followed and gave the woman a courteous acknowledgement. She set her half-full glass of champagne on the table.

"Did you enjoy the Leader's after-dinner speech?"

"His speeches are uplifting. However, I would like to ask you about a rumour doing the rounds."

"About a future campaign? You have no reason to be concerned, the Leader requires your husband for other duties."

"He has been busy with various projects."

"Which includes a rebuild of Berlin from what I have heard."

At that moment, General Muller returned with two drinks and the woman looked up.

"This is Frau Speer, General."

General Muller placed both glasses on the table. "Can I get you something?"

Frau Speer rose and lifted her drink. "Thank you, but I must get back to Albert."

As she departed, General Muller sat down, lifted his cognac and took a sip. General Bodell watched Frau Speer depart the vicinity.

"The Russian campaign?" asked General Muller.

General Bodell nodded. "Concerned that her husband may be involved."

"No chance," said General Muller sharply.

"That is what I told her."

"His services are required elsewhere."

"The new 'Germania' being one of them." General Bodell picked up his glass, then took a swig.

"How long do you feel it will take us to reach Moscow?"

General Bodell finished his drink. "The 6th Army could do it in three months."

"This is not France, or Poland."

"The 6th Army is invincible, Hans."

"Let us hope our supply line is efficient, we don't want to get cut off." General Muller took a swig.

General Bodell grinned.

"What's amusing?"

"An imminent Russian campaign is the worst kept secret within the Berghof."

General Muller laughed.

In a discreet part of the Berghof, two high-ranking Wehrmacht officers discussed a delicate and dangerous subject. One of the officers, General Beck, had become a prominent member of German Intelligence. The other, Major Oster, of Prussian descent, believed the proposed assault on Russia could prove disastrous. Both officers stood and faced each other.

"I am glad that you share my view, General," said Major Oster.

"There are many of the same opinion."

"Has our military intelligence informed the Leader?"

General Beck nodded his bald head. "In great detail."

"Why take the chance?"

"He believes in destiny."

Major Oster paused. "His book."

General Beck nodded.

"The Russian campaign is not a fiction adventure," said Major Oster sharply. "Germany could lose everything it has gained."

"Take a seat, Major, I want to discuss a matter of secrecy."

As both officers sat, a man with a white jacket and shirt, black tie and trousers appeared. "Would you care for a glass of champagne, gentlemen?"

General Beck looked up. "I was not aware that drinks were served here?" he asked sharply.

"I have been told to serve guests wherever they are in the building, General."

"A glass of champagne," said Major Oster.

"Schnapps for me," said General Beck.

The drinks attendant returned soon after and from a silver tray, handed both officers a full glass of their chosen tipple. Following a courteous smile, the attendant departed. Once out of sight, Major Oster looked at General Beck. "Will having a conversation here not arouse suspicion?"

"If anyone should ask, I have a ready-made excuse."

"What is it you want to tell me, General?"

He paused. "Do you feel the war is being directed by the proper people?"

"Before I heard about the imminent campaign, yes."

"And now?"

"I have my doubts."

General Beck took a swig of his drink. "There is a movement who share your view and feel action may have to be taken at some point."

"But what can be done? He is in full command of the government and the Armed Forces."

"A Head of State can be removed."

Major Oster threw back his champagne. "Assassination?" He stared at General Beck.

"That would be one option."

"We took an oath to obey him. To participate in a murder plot is treason."

"Even to preserve Germany's future?"

"I am a Prussian, it would go against my family tradition."

"I understand," said General, nodding.

Major Oster set his glass down "Also, this conversation did not take place."

"I appreciate your discretion, Major."

"However, if the war in the east should prove disastrous, I may be in touch."

"And many others," said General Beck, as he stood. "Come, let us get back to the gathering, guests may think we are about to plot a coup."

Major Oster grinned and as both officers returned to the main room, the attendant stared at them, then carried on with his duties.

Whilst members of the 'inner circle' discussed important matters, their wives mingled with each other. Magda Goebbels looked at Margarete Speer and then Gerda Bormann. "Let us go outside."

"Yes, let's," added Margarete Speer. "I need fresh air."

The three women took themselves and their glasses of champagne onto the balcony and gazed at the Bavarian sunset. Magda Goebbels glanced at her half-full glass, then smiled. "One advantage of our French conquest."

"And their selection of fine wines," added Margarete Speer.

Magda Goebbels looked at Gerda Bormann. "What about you?"

"I have a French maid to clean the house and to cook."

"Me too," said Magda Goebbels. "What else?"

"An abundance of cognac," said Gerda Bormann, smiling.

"The French conflict has proved beneficial to us all." Magda Goebbels sipped her champagne.

"What say you, Margarete?" asked Gerda Bormann.

"Albert and I drink little in the way of alcohol."

"Is there anything from the occupied countries you have acquired?" asked Magda Goebbels.

"I am just grateful that the children are safe and well."

Magda Goebbels glanced at Gerda Bormann, as she finished her drink and set the glass on a table. "I understand, but we should take advantage of our victory."

"The spoils of war," stated Magda Goebbels.

As Margarete Speer remained silent and sipped her champagne, Gerda

Bormann looked her way. "What is on your mind?"

Margarete Speer set her glass on the table, then stared at both women. "Are you aware of the imminent invasion of Russia?"

"The Russians are sub-human and have to be eliminated," said Magda Goebbels sharply. "Also, their land will be necessary for German expansion."

"Do you not agree?" asked Gerda Bormann.

A drinks attendant appeared, picked up empty glass and then placed them on his tray. He looked at each of the well-dressed women. "Another glass of champagne?"

"One for me," said Magda Goebbels.

"I'll have another," said Gerda Bormann.

The attendant smiled at Margarete Speer and when she shook her head, he gave a courteous acknowledgement. After he left, Magda Goebbels looked towards Margarete Speer. "Do you enjoy this location?"

"Yes, the children adore the scenery."

"I have heard that our Leader is keen on regular walkabouts," said Gerda Bormann.

Margarete Speer nodded. "He pops in to see the children and Albert, if he is at home."

"What is he working on at present?" asked Magda Goebbels."

"A dome is to be built in the centre of Berlin."

"A dome?" Gerda Bormann frowned.

"To protect poor Berliners from the cold and snow in winter, of course," said Magda Goebbels.

Gerda Bormann laughed.

As all three women finished their drink, the attendant returned with two full glasses of champagne. After he departed, an officer appeared, and all three women stared.

"I enjoy the view," said the officer, as he looked into the distance."

"Where are you based?" asked a curious Gerda Bormann.

"Crete," said Magda Goebbels.

Gerda Bormann looked at her, then the officer. "How is the climate?"

"The weather is warm and sunny, but the natives are hostile."

"How hostile?" Gerda Bormann sipped her drink.

"The locals are driven by the devil himself!"

"The conquered should show respect for their masters," said Magda Goebbels.

"It would make life comfortable," said the officer.

Gerda Bormann giggled.

"I have heard the Cretans have formed a resistance," said Margarete Speer.

"There are two, one communist and the other non-communist."

"Have you sought them out?" asked Magda Goebbels.

The officer shook his head.

"Why not?" asked Gerda Bormann.

"Both groups are well-hidden in the mountains and when quizzed the locals are unaware of their whereabouts."

"Interrogate them, and use force," stated Magda Goebbels sharply."

"Our soldiers would face retribution."

"Round up suspects for a firing squad," added Gerda Bormann.

Margarete Speer looked at both women. "That would result in more revenge attacks against our soldiers."

The officer nodded. "We do not want a blood bath."

Magda Goebbels took a drink of champagne. "The SS will take care of the situation."

Margarete Speer glanced at the officer, who rolled his greyish blue eyes. Moments later, a high-ranking officer walked onto the balcony and glanced at each of the guests. He grinned at the officer. "You are a lucky man, Captain."

"The officer is a gentleman, General," said Margarete Speer.

"I know, Frau Speer."

"An easy campaign in Crete, General?"

"Not from the air, Frau Bormann. We lost many paratroopers." General Muller turned to Captain Hoeness. "Time to catch the flight back to Heraklion." He looked at the three women. "Excuse us."

"Nice to have met you, Captain," said Margarete Speer.

"The pleasure was all mine."

When General Muller and Captain Hoeness left, Magda Goebbels shook her blonde hair. "They did not appear interested," she remarked.

"In the war?" asked Margarete Speer.

"Us!"

"They are gentlemen officers," said Margarete Speer.

Moments later, the husband of each woman appeared with a glass of champagne for each spouse.

"Where is our Leader?" asked Magda Goebbels.

"He is bidding farewell to guests," said her husband.

A grey-haired woman approached with a tray of various delicacies, however, no one took advantage. Whilst about to leave, Gerda Bormann spoke, "Anna."

She turned round. "Yes, Frau Bormann?"

"You are a clairvoyant, are you not?"

"I dabble, Frau Bormann." Anna gave a slight smile.

"What does the future hold for Germany?"

"The long-term future?"

"The next two years."

Dr Goebbels sipped his cognac, then glanced at Martin Bormann, who stared at Anna. She set the tray on a table. "Last night, I had a vision about our army and saw dead soldiers in the snow." Anna paused. "Blood, blood and more blood."

"It would not be our soldiers," stated Dr Goebbels. As Anna remained silent, he stared at her. "Was it?"

"Yes, Herr Doctor." She picked up the tray, and made a quick exit.

"Rubbish!" Dr Goebbels finished his cognac.

"Fortune-tellers." Martin Bormann shook his head.

Margarete Speer looked at her pensive husband, who laid his glass of red wine on a nearby table. He, along with realists within the German Army, considered the forthcoming invasion of Russia as lunacy.

After she finished a drink, Helga headed for the bathroom to freshen up. On her way, she spotted a blonde-haired woman who wore an elegant lilac dress. Alone, she sat and stared out a window. Helga approached the woman and then sat down next to her. The woman gave a warm smile.

"Have you just arrived, Eva?"

She nodded.

"Does the Leader know you are here?"

"I did not want to disturb him, he is with a group of guests."

"Would you like a drink?"

"Adolf does not like to see me with a drink."

"He won't notice." Helga smiled. "I will get you a glass of champagne."

As Helga departed, the woman once more admired the view of the Bavarian mountain peaks. When Helga returned, the woman turned round.

"The Berghof has spectacular views from every room." Helga handed the woman a full glass.

"Thanks." She took a couple of sips.

"Better?"

The woman nodded.

"The Leader is still busy so you may have to wait a while."

"Perhaps time for more champagne?"

Helga laughed. "Albert and Margarete are outside on the balcony, I can let them know you have arrived."

"Are they with anyone?"

Helga nodded. "Why not join them?"

"Who are they with?"

"Dr Goebbels and his wife, plus the Bormanns."

"I'll stay here."

Helga gave a wry smile. "I understand."

As the woman finished her drink, Helga took the empty glass and moments later, returned. The woman took the glass and had a sip. Setting it on a side table, she faced Helga. "I have not seen much of Adolf."

"There have been frequent meetings with his generals."

"Is there a particular reason? I am the Leader's mistress, you can tell me."

Helga hesitated for a moment. "A new campaign is about to commence."

"In the east?"

When Helga nodded, the woman lifted her drink, took a sip and then reflected.

"What is wrong?"

"I have had hallucinations about death and destruction," the woman said gravely.

"Recently?"

"In the last month." She took another sip. "Our soldiers buried in the snow."

"Where?"

"I am not sure, but it made me shiver."

"Have you told anyone?"

"I dare not."

"As the campaign is soon to begin, winter is months from now. I have heard it should end in late September, or early October."

"Let us hope so."

Helga sat up and smiled. "Another?"

"Why not." The woman took a large swallow.

Taking the empty glass, Helga left the room. The woman went into a small bag, took out a packet of cigarettes and a lighter. When Helga returned, the woman sat with a cigarette in her hand. "I'm not allowed to do this either."

Helga set a glass on the side table. "None of us are."

The woman laughed.

"I have to leave, duty calls."

"Good to see you again."

After Helga left, the woman smoked her cigarette and then stubbed it out on a table ashtray. Then, an officer entered and looked towards the window. "Beautiful."

"Not for long, it will soon be dark. "I've not seen you before."

"This is my first visit here, I am based in Crete."

"A climate I adore."

"Not at present, the natives are spiteful."

"As with all our occupied territories. What is your name?"

"Captain Hoeness, Frau Braun."

"And your first name?"

"Erich."

"Have a seat, I feel like I'm being guarded," said the woman, as she smiled.

"I cannot stay, my commanding officer and I are about to leave."

"Is he with the Leader?"

Captain Hoeness nodded. "I had to make myself scarce for a short while."

The woman put her hand on a seat. "Come, sit down."

As Captain Hoeness did so, the woman stared at his uniform. "How long have you been a captain?"

"Two years."

"What did you do before that?"

"A schoolteacher."

"What did you teach?"

"Languages."

"I studied photography."

"You are in an ideal location."

The woman smiled.

At that moment, another officer appeared and Captain Hoeness stood. The officer looked at the woman. "Good evening, Frau Braun."

"Major Muller?"

The officer gave a faint smile. "General." He turned to his colleague. "Our taxi has arrived."

Captain Hoeness looked at the woman. "A pleasure to meet you." After he received a warm acknowledgement, Captain Hoeness followed General Muller out of the room. When they arrived at the lift, several guests stood waiting. One of them, an auburn-haired young woman, stared at General Muller. "You have a terrific suntan. Hic!"

"It is warm and sunny in Crete."

"And what of the women?"

General Muller stared at the woman. "I am married," he said sharply.

The woman's acquaintance looked at General Muller. "Apologies, the champagne flowed all evening."

Captain Hoeness gave a slight smile. When the lift arrived, guests entered and those who did not get a seat attempted to stand straight. Soon, the lift came to a halt at the lower level, last to get out was the auburn-haired woman. She adjusted her hat, then muttered to the acquaintance. "Who is he kidding, they're all the same."

General Muller and Captain Hoeness walked through the tunnel and got into their chauffeur-driven limousine. As it moved off, General Muller looked at Captain Hoeness. "The High Command wants Turkey brought into the war."

"That could allow our troops to vacate Crete and the rest of Greece, General."

"They will be needed elsewhere."

"East of Poland?"

General Muller nodded. "Upon our return, we can discuss the plan put forward."

"If the Turks enter, it will fuel an already volatile situation."

"Exactly."

An attendant who served guests with drinks the previous evening, made his way to an office situated in the basement. Herman Fergelein, one of Hitler's Adjutants, had requested that he report to him. Before he entered, the attendant paused, took a deep breath and then gave a faint knock on the door.

"Come," said an authoritative voice.

The attendant opened a thick wooden door, then entered. An officer who stood stared at him. "Close the door," he said sharply.

As the attendant did so, Herman Fergelein went behind his desk and sat on a brown leather chair. An officer with high ambitions, if anyone got in his way, they would suffer the consequences. The attendant faced him, hands sweating. Herman Fergelein glanced at a wooden chair opposite his desk. "Sit down."

"Thank you, sir, my feet still ache from yesterday evening." The attendant gave a forced smile.

"Indeed. Whilst you went about your duties, did you hear anything of interest?"

The attendant paused. "Interest, sir?"

"Come now, you know what I mean," said Herman Fergelein, as he gave a wry smile. "It will be to your advantage."

"I overhear conversations of interest at every official occasion, sir." The attendant stammered.

"That compromises security of The Reich," said Herman Fergelein sharply.

The attendant shook his head. "No, sir."

Herman Fergelein sat back on his char. "What do you hear?"

"It is officers who joke with each other about certain individuals."

"Who?"

The attendant hesitated. "How overweight someone is."

"I am aware of this individual. What else?"

"Disagreements over strategy."

"Strategy?"

The attendant wiped the palms of his hands.

"If you do not tell me, a transfer to an officer's club in Poland can be arranged. I do not need to tell you that it won't be as cushy as here."

"I may have overheard two officers discuss the Leader."

Herman Fegerlein stared. "What did they say?"

Once more, he attendant hesitated. "They believe we will soon be led into another conflict."

"With whom?"

"I could not hear who, sir."

"Anything else?"

"Both officers praised his leadership."

"Who were they?"

"General Beck and Major Oster, sir."

"You can go."

The attendant stood. "I can keep my job, sir?"

Herman Fergelein nodded.

The attendant departed, then closed the door behind him. As he walked along the corridor, a deep sigh of relief followed. A visit to the kitchen for a much-needed cup of coffee deemed necessary.

Hitler's chauffeur, Max, and his cook, Anna, sat in the kitchen with a morning cup of coffee. They discussed the previous evening's dinner for invited guests, then Anna looked at the wall clock.

"It is still too early," said Max.

"Normally, I prepare for eleven o'clock." Anna took another look. "Today, after twelve."

"He didn't go to bed until four, the last guests left in the early hours."

"Dr Goebbels and his wife?"

"The Bormanns."

"She enjoys a good time."

Max grinned.

"I expected to see Mussolini and his wife."

"With dissent in Italy over the war, he will be preoccupied." Karl drank his coffee. "The Greeks and now the British have shown how weak Italian troops can be."

"Why did Eva's sister, Gretel, not appear last night?"

As Max shrugged his broad shoulders, Anna poured coffee from a metal pot into his white cup. "Whenever Fritz is here, she is around." Anna laid the pot on the stove.

"He has a habit of talking out of turn." Max shook his head. "Not advisable for an SS officer when the Leader is around

"Is he moving to a new residence?"

"Residence?"

"I overheard Herr Speer mention it to a guest."

"There are new headquarters being built in East Prussia. A single rail track is being constructed from the main line."

"To his new headquarters?"

Max nodded. "It may now be complete."

Anna stared at him.

"What is wrong?"

"I've had visions of our soldiers lying motionless in the snow. Masses of German soldiers killed."

Max set his cup on the pine table. "Do not concern yourself, Anna. Our army has yet to experience defeat."

As she sipped her coffee and mulled her thoughts, Max gave her a reassuring smile. "It must have been the enemy."

Anna glanced at the clock.

"What film will he watch tonight in his private cinema?"

"Does Dr Goebbels hand-pick them?"

"Adventure films, but not American."

"What is the latest news of Deputy-Leader Hess?"

"He is being held in captivity by the British." Karl paused. "He sent a letter to Hitler."

"From Britain!"

"I'm not sure."

"It could be an apology for his sudden departure."

Once more, Anna glanced at the clock, then got up. "I better start to prepare breakfast."

"Time to wash the limousine, it has to look as good as new."

"It will sparkle in the early morning sunshine."

At that moment, a blonde-haired woman came into the kitchen. Turning round, Anna smiled. "Good morning."

She gave a forced smile. "I feel half-dead."

"Would you care for a cup of mint tea? I am about to prepare a pot."

The woman groaned. "Any kind of drink will do. I'm glad Gretel didn't turn up."

Grinning, Max got up from his chair. "Excuse me, have to wash the limousine." He left the kitchen.

Anna looked at the woman. "Would you like a cup of coffee instead?"

The woman nodded.

As she poured a cup, the woman yawned and covered her mouth. She leaned back on the chair, then yawned again.

"The fresh alpine air will help."

"Unlike too much champagne." The woman lifted her cup, took a sip and then another.

Anna gave a faint smile. "Do you have any plans for today?"

"I'll go for a walk and take some photographs of the countryside."

"It's a perfect day for it." Anna continued to prepare a breakfast.

"Anna?"

She turned round.

"You can tell the future?"

"Some of the time."

"Will I ever get married?"

"I would expect a fun-loving person such as yourself to be in demand."

"You didn't answer my question."

"I have had a vision of you going through a marriage ceremony."

"When?" The woman beamed.

Anna hesitated. "I'm not sure of the date."

"Did it take place in Berlin?"

"I believe so."

"In a grand historic church with a choir of children," the woman said, smiling.

"My vision appeared to be a room full of people."

"A large room, perhaps a hall?"

Not being able to look at the woman due to negative vibes, Anna shrugged her shoulders. The woman finished her coffee and smiled. "At least I am to be an honest woman," she said, as a smile flickered over her ashen face.

Anna remained silent, and suspected that the future for Germany and those associated with its leader could be bleak.

CHAPTER 7

ASSERTION

Five months after its troops invaded Crete, Germany's military authority in Heraklion held a meeting to assess the situation. General Muller, Major Neuberger and Captain Hoeness sat with a prefect of Chania. As with Heraklion, it had also been occupied by German troops for its strategic location in terms of a supply route.

"Instruct the resistance to hand over all their weapons," declared General Muller. "Otherwise, face the consequences." He went on, "Our assault on their hideout in Hora Sfakio is evidence of what we are capable of," he said sharply.

"Did you have to close the Monasteries?" stated the prefect.

"They have become a refuge for the resistance," said Captain Hoeness.

"It made the situation worse," said the prefect sharply.

General Muller thumped his desk. "Next time, it won't be twenty-six who are taken out and shot."

Major Neuberger stared at the prefect. "How did the resistance acquire their weapons?"

"They stole them from under the noses of British troops." The prefect gave a faint smile.

General Muller shook his head, then looked at his fellow officers. "Given the fiasco at Dunkirk, this is not a surprise."

Captain Hoeness grinned.

The prefect looked at General Muller. "I have been told by villagers that German troops steal food from them."

"That is nonsense," said Captain Hoeness. "Besides, our troops are well-catered for."

"A made-up story by villagers to cause friction between our soldiers and the Cretan population," added Major Neuberger.

As the prefect stayed tight-lipped, General Muller glared at him. "If attacks on our troops continue, for each German soldier shot, ten Cretans will face a firing squad."

The prefect stared. "That will escalate tensions, General."

"So be it."

Captain Hoeness moved towards the prefect. "We have heard that British agents train and work alongside the resistance."

"I have no knowledge of this." The prefect looked at General Muller. "Any member of the British Army who didn't evacuate, were taken prisoner by your forces."

"Not all," said Captain Hoeness. "We understand that some were given refuge by villagers."

"And we also want them rounded-up," stated General Muller. Then he gave a slight smile. "Come now, we only want what is best for the islanders." He glanced at his two officers.

"It is in everyone's best interest to work in harmony," added Captain Hoeness.

The prefect glanced at each officer, then wiped his sweaty hands underneath the table.

General Muller stared. "We will see you here in a month's time."

The prefect stood, and after he left the room, General Muller looked at Major Neuberger. "Have him followed."

Major Neuberger got up, went to a nearby table and then lifted the telephone. Seconds later, he spoke to a soldier. "The man who has just left."

"Yes, Major?"

"Have someone track his movements."

"Anything else, Major?"

"No." Major Neuberger replaced the telephone and then returned to his seat. General Muller addressed the two officers. "Who is in charge of the resistance?"

"He goes by the name of Manilos, General," said Captain Hoeness. "His whereabouts are unknown."

"I want him found, and dealt with." General Muller leaned back. "We'll hand him over to the Gestapo." He grinned. "They will extract information about British agents and then we can capture them."

Major Neuberger and Captain Hoeness nodded.

"Has there been dissent amongst the Heraklion community?"

Captain Hoeness remained silent.

"A few skirmishes, General," said Major Neuberger."

"How have you dealt with them?"
"Beatings."
The General scowled. "Be ruthless, shoot some of them if you feel it is necessary."
Captain Hoeness looked at his senior colleague, Major Neuberger, in the hope that he would mention such an act could fuel the current situation. However, no reaction followed.
"Gentlemen, we must be assertive and if so, any person on the island will think twice." General Muller looked at Captain Hoeness. "Do you agree, Captain?
"Yes, sir."
"Good."
"General?"
"Yes, Major?"
"With recent attacks by the resistance near Heraklion, why not declare the area to Lassithi a no-man's-land?"
"Why to Lassithi?"
"We believe it could be a base for the resistance to launch guerrilla attacks."
"Do you have evidence?"
"No conclusive proof, yet, General."
"When you do, let me know."
Captain Hoeness looked at General Muller. "Sir, that may lead to more dissent amongst locals."
Major Neuberger stared at him. "Then, they will be punished," he said sharply.
"I will consider your tactic, Major." General Muller stood. "Let us have some lunch."
The three Wehrmacht officers vacated the room, left the building and then walked to a nearby restaurant. As they entered, conversations amongst customers stopped. Sitting down, General Muller glanced at his two colleagues. "We have their attention."
A waiter approached. "Good afternoon," he said politely.
"Three schnapps," said General Muller."
When the waiter departed, a group of customers got up and left their table. Whilst they passed the three officers, a glare from each customer followed. General Muller commented, "Occupation of this island will not be without its problems."
The waiter returned, then set a drink in front of each officer. "Would you like to order something to eat?"
General Muller stared at him. "Later."
The waiter left, went to another table and then removed used plates and cutlery. Entering the kitchen, he shook his head.

"What is wrong?" asked the chef.

The waiter dumped plates into the sink. "Their arrogance is unbearable!" He blew between his teeth, exasperated.

"Do not let them get to you."

"That is easy for you to say, I have to serve them."

As the chef remained silent, his fellow worker returned to the dining area. A group of locals entered, spotted the German officers, then did an about turn. Major Neuberger spoke to the waiter. "Is the food not up to scratch?"

"We have had no complaints about the food, only other matters."

Major Neuberger glared. "Such as?" He stood.

"Waiter," shouted a man at another table. "Have you forgotten my order?"

"Be with you soon, sir." When the waiter left, Major Neuberger sat down. Moments later, the waiter laid a glass in front of the customer. "On the house," he said gratefully.

Outside the restaurant, raised voices could be heard and customers stared towards the window. Two German soldiers dragged a youth away, amidst disbelief from others within the vicinity. General Muller shook his head. "These Cretans never learn."

"They will have to," added Major Neuberger. "Fall into line, or else."

The waiter went to another table, removed empty plates and then entered the kitchen. His fellow worker looked at him. "What happened outside?"

"They arrested a Jew."

"What for?"

"Being Jewish."

"I heard that after dark they pick on people and arrest them for no reason. If they object, a squad arrives and they are dragged away."

"Where to?"

The chef shrugged his shoulders.

The waiter whispered, "What are the resistance doing about this?"

"They can't venture into the towns, it's too dangerous." The chef sighed. "Besides, if a German is killed, Cretans are shot." He stirred a pot of stew.

The waiter stared at it. "If any of the Germans order stew, let's make sure they won't be back."

The chef grinned. "I'll do my best."

After lunch, the three officers returned to their headquarters in the Town Hall. A corporal entered the room and approached General Muller. "This just arrived for you, sir."

When General Muller took the document, the corporal departed. He had a read, then handed it to Major Neuberger. Moments later, he passed the document to Captain Hoeness.

"There will be a backlash, General," said Major Neuberger.

"We have to achieve our quota, orders from Berlin."

"For our factories?" asked Major Neuberger.

General Muller sat back and remained silent. He was aware of what fate would fall on Crete's Jewish population.

"Factories in the Ruhr Valley, General," said Captain Hoeness.

General Muller paused. "More armaments are needed for the Russian offensive." He went on, "French, Belgian and Czech labour is still not enough."

"What about the Poles?" asked Major Neuberger.

"The Russians got half of their workforce," said Captain Hoeness.

"At present, there is much internal conflict within Poland, said General Muller."

"The Polish resistance?" asked Captain Hoeness.

General Muller nodded. "Our troops are bogged down in Warsaw."

"General," said Captain Hoeness, "is it true a mass grave of Polish officers has been discovered?"

"Thousands butchered by the Russians."

"What is the latest in Russia, General?" asked Major Neuberger.

"The Ukraine is ours, Moscow will soon follow." General Muller grinned. "All is going to plan."

"Another victory parade." Major Neuberger beamed.

General Muller looked at his two officers. "We must meet with our Italian counterparts in Agios Nikolaos, perhaps next week."

Major Neuberger turned to Captain Hoeness. "I hope you enjoy red wine," he said, grinning.

In the early hours of Sunday morning, Stelios heard a bang on his front door, followed by shouts. He got up, made himself decent and then went to investigate.

"Open up," a male voice shouted.

When Stelios opened the door, four armed German soldiers entered, then looked around the immediate vicinity. A sergeant stared at him. "Is anyone else here?"

"Do you always barge in?"

The sergeant moved closer to Stelios. "I will ask the questions," he said sharply.

"I am alone."

The sergeant turned to his fellow soldiers. "Search the property."

As two soldiers went to investigate, Stelios watched and drew breath. The sergeant stared at him. "Be thankful you're not a Jew."

"Why do you say that?"

Whilst the sergeant continued to stare, the two soldiers returned and one looked towards his superior. "Clear."

The sergeant turned to Stelios. "Where can we find the person called Manilos?"

Stelios frowned. "Who is he?"

"You know only too well."

"I've never heard of him. Manilosh you say?"

"Manilos." The sergeant gripped his rifle. "Where can we find him?"

"I've told you, I don't know him." Stelios blinked like an owl.

One of the soldiers came forward and thumped Stelios in the stomach with his rifle butt. He groaned, then buckled up. As the soldiers looked on, Stelios held his stomach and stared at the sergeant. "I, I don't know who he is." Stelios coughed.

"You visited a house near Hersonissos recently."

"That person is a friend." Once more, Stelios coughed.

"His name?"

Stelios remained silent.

"His name!"

"Alexandros." Stelios took a deep breath. "We have known each other for a long time."

"And the other man who accompanied you?"

Once more, Stelios remained silent then the same soldier butted him with his rifle and he slumped onto the wooden floor. The sergeant bent down. "I won't ask again."

Stelios got to his feet, groaning. "Dimitris, another friend."

The sergeant stared. "Where can we find him?"

Stelios scowled at him. "Why don't you ask your informer."

Following a beating, the soldiers got into their jeep and then headed back to Heraklion, leaving Stelios flat out on the floor.

After the German soldiers reached Heraklion, their jeep stopped outside a small house in a narrow street. As they left their jeep, a dog started to bark in a nearby property, which broke the night silence. Following repeated loud bangs on his door, Dimitris awoke, then gathered his thoughts. "Who can that be?"

The women beside him mumbled. "Go back to sleep."

When more bangs followed, Dimitris got up, put on a pair of trousers and then answered the door. As he opened it, Dimitris gave an extended yawn, then stared.

"Where is Manilos?" snarled the sergeant.

Dimitris hesitated. "Who?"

The sergeant grabbed him by the throat. "I am not going to ask again."

"I don't know, it's the truth." He stammered and his eyes became glazed.

As the sergeant let go, the three other soldiers brushed Dimitris aside and entered his house. Moments later, he heard a woman scream. Rushing into the bedroom, a woman held a sheet around her naked body. Dimitris bared his teeth at the three soldiers. "Get out of my bedroom." He clenched his fists.

All grinned, walked past Dimitris and then approached the sergeant. After one shook his head, the four intruders returned to their jeep. Dimitris slammed the door, and returned to the bedroom.

"Pigs!" said the woman.

Dimitris wiped his eyes, then comforted her.

On a warm sunny afternoon, Captain Hoeness relaxed in a restaurant on the outskirts of Heraklion. Off-duty and in uncharacteristic casual attire, he sipped a cup of coffee. As he gazed out the window, a lady entered and then sat in close proximity. The waiter arrived at her table with a courteous smile.

"A white coffee, please," she said.

"Anything to eat, madam?"

The lady shook her head. When the waiter departed, she removed her beige hat, then laid it on the wooden table. Captain Hoeness sipped his coffee and began to speculate. The lady sat back and cast her gaze around the restaurant. Captain Hoeness set his cup down. "A lovely day."

The lady looked his way, then gave a slight nod.

"You are American?"

"You are German?"

Captain Hoeness nodded. "My grandfather emigrated to America."

"When?"

"1870. However, my father brought us back to Germany."

"Why?"

"America declared war on Germany."

The lady gave a slight smile.

"With my father being a patriot, we had to return."

"It must have been a difficult period after the war ended."

"Food shortages, high unemployment and political unrest followed."

"You should have stayed in America."

Captain Hoeness smiled.

"In which part of America did your family stay?"

"Pennsylvania."

"Lots of mountains and valleys."

"Also, much farmland."

"You're English is very good, are you based here as a diplomat?"

Captain Hoeness shook his head. "I am an army officer, but off-duty. Before the war, I taught languages, which included English.""

"Are you not supposed to wear a uniform at all times?"

"Some uniform rules have been relaxed on Crete."

The waiter arrived with the lady's coffee, then departed. She lifted the cup, took a sip, and another.

"Does it disturb you that I am German?"

The lady set her cup on the saucer. "Let's put it this way, if I'm spotted with you, I will be in deep trouble."

Captain Hoeness laughed, lifted his cup, and then drank the contents. Standing up, he looked at the lady, who stared. "I was only joking."

"I have to go on duty soon."

The lady smiled, then began to blink. She took off her sunglasses and rubbed one of her eyes.

"An eyelash?"

"I'm not sure."

Again, the lady blinked, then Captain Hoeness approached her. "Let me have a look, please stand. It may be a bit of dust." Captain Hoeness examined the lady's eye.

"It feels like an eyelash."

Captain Hoeness picked up an unused napkin from the lady's table. "Please look up and then down."

As she did so, he used the napkin to remove an obstruction. The lady blinked and smiled.

"Better?" Captain Hoeness stood back.

She nodded, then sat down.

"May I ask your name?"

"Georgina. What's yours?"

"Erich."

Captain Hoeness paid for his coffee, then bid farewell to Georgina. Lifting her cup, she watched him walk away. When he tuned round and waved, Georgina did likewise. She sipped her coffee and reflected. Charming, as well as and gentle. I've seen him before, but where?

Major Neuberger and Captain Hoeness arrived at the Italian garrison in Agios Nikolaos at eleven o'clock prompt. As they got out of their jeep, two Italian officers saluted them.

"General Albaicci awaits you," said one of the officers, as he saluted.

The General, as with his German counterpart, fought in WW1, but was on opposite sides. In that war, Italy fought with Britain, France and America. Because of this, a division between Germany and Italy existed. Even the relationship between Mussolini and Hitler did not fill the cracks. Although well decorated, the general wanted an easy war with little casualties and plenty food and wine to consume.

After they entered the building, both German officers followed their Italian counterparts to a room, where a well-decorated soldier stood behind a large dark-wooden desk. Small in stature with a dark moustache, he walked towards Major Neuberger, who along with Captain Hoeness, saluted. General Albaicci returned the salute and showed his teeth.

"General Muller sends his apologies," said Major Neuberger.

"I hope we can meet in the near future," said the general, as a grin crept over his face.

Following officer introductions, General Albaicci asked his German guests to take a seat. Both officers removed their headwear and sat opposite General Albaicci's desk, flanked by an Italian counterpart. As the general sat behind his desk, a non-commissioned soldier entered the room with a tray of drinks and set them down. When he left, General Albaicci stood. "To celebrate our alliance."

The four officers got to their feet, then everyone lifted a glass of red wine from the silver tray and took a swig. When Captain Hoeness coughed, General Albaicci grinned. "Is Italian wine too strong, Captain?"

Captain Hoeness shook his head. "It is fine, General." He cleared his throat.

The other officers emptied their glasses and laid them on the tray. As the Italian officers stared at Captain Hoeness, he finished his drink. Major Neuberger looked at his fellow officer, then at General Albaicci. "Have you encountered much hostility on the island towards your troops, General?"

He shook his bald head. "However, on the mainland there are problems."

"In what way?"

"Constant attacks on our soldiers."

"If any German soldier encounters hostility, a number of Greeks are rounded up and shot." Major Neuberger glanced at Captain Hoeness. "On Crete, we adopt the same procedure."

"Has it solved the problem?" asked an Italian officer.

Major Neuberger nodded. "Force is necessary for obedience."

Both Italian officers looked across the desk.

"In the towns and villages within your sector, have you come across many Jews?" asked Major Neuberger.

"Jews?" General Albaicci stared. "Why do you ask?"

"General Muller wanted to know."

General Albaicci hesitated. "Then perhaps he should have made the effort to be here and ask me himself."

As the cordial atmosphere in the room changed to one of tension, Major Neuberger drew his breath and stared.

"We encounter enough difficulties without the need to round up Jews."

"Such as?"

"Food on the island is in short supply and our troops have to be fed."

"Take food from local families."

"We have, but shortages still exist."

Major Neuberger glanced at Captain Hoeness. As General Albaicci stood, so did his two officers, followed by his invited guests. "Pass on my best wishes to General Muller, Major," said General Albaicci. Both German officers replaced their headwear, and after being escorted to the exit, got into their jeep. The Italian officers returned to General Albaicci's office and then sat opposite him. He shook his head. "Nazis."

"Killing Greeks hasn't halted the resistance movement." stated an officer. "The situation has become worse."

General Albaicci looked at his two officers. "I agree." He leaned back on his brown leather chair.

"The British continue to supply arms," said the other officer.

General Albaicci considered. "If America enters the war, we may have to alter our future plans."

"The Americans, General?" asked the same officer.

He nodded. "Because of an oil embargo with Japan tensions exists. If a conflict begins, Hitler will no doubt involve Germany and us to escalate the situation." General Albaicci paused. "Give my regards to General Muller."

Both German officers replaced their headwear, got up and left the room. Leaving the building, Major Neuberger shook his head. "I've never understood them."

The two officers got into their vehicle and soon left the town. Whilst he drove, Captain Hoeness glanced at a subdued Major Neuberger. "They did not give me the impression of being allies."

He sighed. "To think we rescued them out of a situation that demoralised their so-called army."

"If we had attacked Russia in May instead of June, we would be in the Kremlin by now."

"The delay of a solitary month has proved decisive."

At that moment on a remote part of their journey, a gunshot could be heard and a bullet whizzed past Captain Hoeness, who skidded of the road. Another shot followed and both officers jumped out, then crouched behind the jeep. Major Neuberger looked up and then at Captain Hoeness. "The shots appeared to come from a hillside opposite."

"Only two shots, therefore, it is maybe a lone sniper."

Major Neuberger glanced up. "I spotted a rifle, the sun reflected onto it."

Captain Hoeness popped his head up. "I'll run along the road and you pick him off."

"Could be risky."

"We have no choice." Captain Hoeness paused. "Ready?"

Major Neuberger took out a pistol from his holder and then faced the hillside. "Ready."

As Captain Hoeness ran from the jeep towards bushes, a shot could be heard, then Major Neuberger looked up and fired several times. A figure fell to the ground and the two officers approached with caution. When they reached the sprawled-out body, Captain Hoeness shook his head. "A teenager, maybe only sixteen."

"He is still an assassin, let's go." Major Neuberger replaced the pistol in his holster.

Captain Hoeness stared. "We cannot leave him like this, Major."

"He is dead, let's go. The birds can have a feast."

Whilst Major Neuberger walked towards the jeep, his fellow officer, with reluctance, followed. Both officers got in, and the jeep sped off back to Heraklion.

"From now on, we must ensure that two guards accompany us," said Major Neuberger.

Captain Hoeness remained silent.

General Albaicci and his two officers sat and drank coffee on the balcony of their meeting room. Being an ally, the three Italians impression of General Neuberger had raised concerns.

"It is what I suspected, General." The officer set his cup on the saucer.

"What is that, Gianni?"

"The Germans will bully us around, as well as the Cretan population."

"We have to maintain a close-knit relationship." General Albaicci sipped his coffee. "Or, give that impression." He gave a wry smile.

"For how long, General?" asked the second officer.

General Albaicci set his cup down. "Until I receive further orders."

"Is it true that there has been unrest in Italy, General?" The second officer glanced at his colleague.

The general shook his head. At that moment, a junior soldier approached the balcony with a tray of drinks and General Albaicci looked his way. "Thank you."

"Anything else, sir?"

"Not for now."

After he departed, all three officers finished their cups of coffee, then lifted a glass of cognac.

"To Il Duce," said General Albaicci.

As his two officers followed in a toast, they glanced at each other, aware of severe food shortages back home. General Albaicci laid his empty glass on the table, sat back and grinned at both officers. "Cheer up, our country has grown stronger these past years."

"My brother is in Russia, General," said Gianni. "Is there a problem there?"

General Albaicci frowned. "Why do you say that?"

"Since June, he wrote every week, but our family has not heard from him for several weeks."

Jose looked at Gianni.

"It will no doubt be a transportation delay," said General Albaicci. "I am aware our army and the Germans are close to Moscow." He tilted his head. "It is a long distance from there to Italy." As General Albaicci looked round and raised his arm, the junior soldier came forthwith. "Another three cognacs."

"Yes, sir." He departed.

From the street below, a man stood and looked up at the balcony. He staggered, steadied himself and raised a clenched fist. "We defeated your army, go back to Italy where you belong," he shouted.

As General Albaicci and his two officers stared downwards, two locals grabbed the man and then led him away.

"When will they learn," said General Albaicci.

"They won't accept the occupation," said Gianni.

"They will have to," stated General Albaicci.

The junior soldier brought another tray of drinks and set them down. General Albaicci looked up. "Same again in fifteen minutes."

"There is a group of women downstairs, sir. One of them said they had been invited by you."

"What did she look like?"

"Around 25, slim and long dark hair."

"Ask them to come up."

"Will I offer them a drink, sir?"

General Albaicci nodded and the two officers grinned. Another session of entertaining guests would commence, much to everyone's delight.

CHAPTER 8

HINDRANCE

General Muller, Major Neuberger and Captain Hoeness sat round a table in an office of the Town Hall. Since the Wehrmacht took control of Crete, seventeen troublesome months had passed. Rather than suppress the resistance, they now endured a more powerful foe. A 'no-man's-land' area from Heraklion that stretched six kilometres to Laaithi had now been put into place. However, skirmishes still continued within the area much to the German High Command's annoyance. Looking at Major Neuberger, General Muller leaned forward on his chair. "Why does the problem still exist?"

"They just do not give up, General."

"Round up more locals and then shoot them," he said sharply.

"We have purged villages, but the resistance flee to the mountains."

"They blend in with the terrain," added Captain Hoeness. "Also, they are well-organised."

"With help from British agents on the island," said Major Neuberger.

As General Muller mulled his thoughts, a private appeared with a tray and then laid three cups of coffee on the table. General Muller acknowledged the soldier, and he departed. Sipping their coffee, the three officers relaxed.

"The Japanese will one day rule Asia, General," said Major Neuberger. But their navy suffered heavy losses from the Americans at Midway," added Captain Hoeness.

"A blip," said General Muller.

"What is the latest on the eastern front, General?" asked Captain Hoeness as he sipped his coffee.

"I have been told that we are on course to achieve all of our objectives and once we have the Russian oil fields, victory is ours."

"Will we join the Japanese in Asia?" asked Major Neuberger.

General Muller shook his head. "The next phase of our military strategy will be to enter Egypt." He went on, "Once we get rid of the British and Americans in North Africa."

Major Neuberger put down his cup. "The Field-Marshall has given them a host of problems."

"Rommel is an excellent tactician," added General Muller.

"How many times do we have to bail out the Italian Army," said Major Neuberger, shaking his head.

"Because our Leader is friends with Mussolini, we have no choice." General Muller finished his coffee, then pushed a photo towards Captain Hoeness. "This is a ringleader in the resistance, he will know where Manilos can be found."

Captain Hoeness glanced. "Does this person stay local?"

"You will find him at this address." General Muller handed over a written piece of paper. "I got this information from a reliable source."

"Interrogate him?"

"If no joy, pass him onto the Gestapo."

Captain Hoeness drank his coffee, got up and then left the room. Gathering a squad, he left the building, then headed towards a nearby property. Once there, he knocked on the door and a young woman answered.

"Is Spiro Drakos here?"

The young woman scowled.

"Is he in, or not?" asked Captain Hoeness sharply.

She remained silent.

"We know he lives here."

"What do you want with him?" She swallowed.

"Only to ask questions."

The young woman glanced at a squad of armed soldiers with stern expressions and bit her lip. A stocky middle-aged man came to the door, faced Captain Hoeness, then the young woman. "It is okay."

As she went inside, the man looked behind, his eyes fixed on her and then at Captain Hoeness.

"Please come with us," he said politely."

"You are a unique one, I'll get my jacket."

As the man went inside, Captain Hoeness signalled for two soldiers to guard the property's rear door. After several seconds, he heard a shot being fired. At gunpoint, the two soldiers escorted Spiro Drakos to where Captain Hoeness stood. He shook his head. "That was not clever."

The prisoner was taken to German HQ, where Captain Hoeness and two guards took him into a room with only two wooden chairs and a table. As Captain Hoeness sat, Spiro Drakos did likewise and glared at him. Captain Hoeness opened a file, read it and then viewed his prisoner. "Where is Manilos?"

"Who?"

"Manilos, leader of the resistance."

Whilst Spiro Drakos fidgeted with his hands underneath the table, an observant guard cried. "Hands on the table."

Spiro Drakos did as ordered and then Captain Hoeness made another attempt. "Where can we find him?"

"I do not know who he is."

"Oh, yes you do."

Spiro Drakos remained silent and then Captain Hoeness took a photograph out of the file. "This is your brother-in-law, he said holding it up."

Spiro Drakos glanced at the photograph.

"The woman in the house is his youngest sister." Captain Hoeness replaced the photograph. "You would not want her harmed, am I correct?"

Spiro Drakos gritted his teeth. "I do not know where he is."

Captain Hoeness leaned back on his chair, and sighed.

"He will be somewhere in the southern mountains."

"Yes, but at what precise location?"

Spiro Drakos shrugged his shoulders.

"If you don't reveal to me where he is, someone else will beat it out of you."

"The Gestapo is good at that, it is a popular pastime with them."

"If you don't want to protect yourself, what about your wife?"

"Leave her out of this!" His eyes bulged.

"Then tell me what I want to know."

Spiro Drakos leaned forward and sneered. "When this war ends and your filthy Reich disintegrates, I will be there to witness it."

Captain Hoeness stood, and stared downwards. "I doubt you will live long enough."

Both guards glared at the prisoner and after Captain Hoeness picked up his file and left, Spiro Dracos deliberated as to whom had betrayed him.

From October 1942, the German military position began to change in terms of invincibility and dominance. The Wehrmacht experienced a number of unexpected setbacks, which through time filtered down through their ranks. Whilst some senior officers elected to hide the truth from subordinates, others came clean in order to avoid false rumours being discussed.

Close to mid-day, a glum-faced General Muller walked into the meeting room where Major Neuberger and Captain Hones waited. "My apologies for being late, have a seat." General Muller sat down. "I have received a telephone call from Berlin."

Major Neuberger glanced at Captain Hoeness, who portrayed a negative expression. Both officers perceived bad news.

"Our forces are surrounded by the Red Army near Stalingrad." The General paused. "Almost three quarters of a million of our men are trapped," he said gravely.

"What about North Africa, General?" asked Major Neuberger.

"We have been pushed back to Tunisia, the end will come soon."

"The Italian Army is to blame, not Montgomery's tactical expertise, General," said the major sharply.

He sat back. "Our situation may get worse."

"In what way, General?" Major Neuberger asked in amazement.

"With North Africa taken care of, the British and Americans may invade southern Crete."

"Make the south coast a 'no-go' area, similar to the north."

General Muller considered. "There is the possibility of Italy also being invaded."

"Will the Italians not fight to protect their homeland?"

"If Italian cities are bombed similar to ours, their government will want an end to hostilities."

"Especially, if Rome is attacked," added Captain Hoeness. "The Italians will want to preserve their Holy City."

Major Neuberger looked at his colleague. "Our new jet fighters will shoot British and American bombers out of the sky."

"They won't be ready for at least another year," said General Muller. "Constant bombardment of our factories has delayed production."

Major Neuberger remained tight-lipped.

General Muller stood. "Gentlemen, let us forget the war for a short while and have lunch."

The three officers left their headquarters and then walked to a nearby restaurant. As they entered, the usual silence ensued and followed by icy stares. A waiter appeared at their table. "The usual drinks to start with?"

General Muller nodded.

The waiter went behind the counter, poured three schnapps, then returned to his glum-faced customers.

"For lunch, we will have the same as yesterday," said General Muller.

As the waiter acknowledged, Major Neuberger looked at him. "More salad this time."

When the waiter stormed into the kitchen, a woman who prepared several meals stopped, and looked up.

"Nazis!" The waiter shook his head.

"Did you hear what happened at Vorizia?"

The waiter stared at the woman with a solemn look on her wrinkled face. She gripped the knife in her hand. "They almost captured Manilos, but he escaped."

"What about his men?"

"Several were killed, but twice as many Germans suffered the same fate."

The waiter grinned.

"Do not rejoice. The pigs gathered men from the village, shot them and then set houses on fire."

The waiter scowled.

"A German officer made an accusation that villagers had sheltered members of the resistance."

"There's one in the restaurant capable of such acts."

"The previous waiter couldn't take their arrogance and left. He's now an active member of the resistance."

"We could poison their food," said the waiter, as he grinned.

"I am all for it but the owner relies on their custom."

"Pity." The waiter paused. "Three meat and cheese salads, small portions."

Georgina and Elena sat in the living room and listened to the evening news broadcast. The main headline being a possible surrender of Italian forces to the American and British armies. Georgina looked at a pensive Elena. "That would put the cat amongst the pigeons."

"What do you mean?"

"It's a British term, which means havoc could be on the horizon."

"The Germans would lose an important ally in the region."

"Not only that, the Italians may side with the Americans and British."

Elena stared. "Why would they do that?"

"To join the future victors." Georgina sipped her glass of wine. "The German armies have begun to stall, or retreat on all fronts." Georgina went on. "The Americans and British pound German cities from the air and the Red Army has started to advance towards Germany."

"If their cities continue to be bombed, the Germans may surrender. Factories which make weapons will be unable to function." Elena sighed. "It would be a relief to get our lives back to some sort of normality."

"You bet," added Georgina, as she gave a slight smile.

Elena considered. "If Mussolini was deposed, what would be his fate?"

"He could end up with a role in the Reichstag alongside Hitler."

Whilst Elena laughed, Georgina laid her glass on the table. Elena looked at her friend. "How is Stelios? I've not seen him recently."

"I haven't spoken to him for several weeks."

"He will have much on his mind."

"I did hear that a squad of German soldiers came to his mother's village and a shoot-out took place."

"They would be on the hunt for Manilos."

"Would he have been there?"

Elena nodded. "But he escaped. However, Alexandros, who is a friend of Stelios, was not so fortunate."

"What happened?"

"Shot in front of the villagers, a firing squad."

Georgina sighed, then looked at Elena in an inquisitive way.

"Dimitris told me."

"How did the Germans know where to look?"

"An informer."

Georgina leaned back. "Not a local!"

"People have little, or no food." Elena paused. "They will do anything to survive."

Once more, Georgina sighed. "War." She looked at her near-empty glass. "Any wine left?"

"Enough for another," Elena said, as she poured wine into Georgina's glass, then her own.

Georgina considered. "If the Italians did surrender, what would happen to their soldiers on Crete?"

"In what way?"

"Their weapons, they wouldn't require them." Georgina lifted her glass. "The Germans won't want the resistance to get their hands on them."

"That is true." Elena sipped her wine.

"If the Germans forced them to hand over weapons, maybe the Italians will put up a fight."

Elena raised her glass. "Let us drink to them killing each other."

Both ladies emptied their glasses.

After her final class of the day, Georgina left the school and ventured into Heraklion's town centre. She entered a cafe, went to an empty table and took a seat. A newspaper lay on a nearby table and Georgina leaned over. As she started to read, a waiter appeared and wrote down an order for a strong cup of coffee. When he departed, shouts could be heard from outside, close to the fountain monument. The waiter glanced out a window, then at Georgina. "With rumours of an Italian surrender, German patrols are being taunted." He grinned. "They may soon be on their own."

"What will happen to Italian soldiers if they surrender?"

"They may be shipped back to Italy."

A grey-bearded man at another table lowered his newspaper. "They are certain to be shot."

Georgina looked his way, remaining silent.

"Believe me, it will happen." The man put aside his newspaper. "However, I am sure Italians will try and put up a good fight."

"The Germans will want them to hand over their weapons," said the waiter.

The man nodded. "I have heard of dissent in and around Lassithi."

"If they do indeed fall out, I hope they destroy each other." The waiter went on. "Both have committed atrocities on the island."

"The Italians tend to plunder, rather than kill," added the man."

"I have heard of women being raped by them," said the waiter.

Georgina stared at the waiter.

"I'll get your coffee, madam."

As the waiter departed, the man lifted his glass, took a swig and looked across his table at Georgina.

"Are you from Lassithi?" asked Georgina.

The man nodded, and gave a slight grin. "What's an American lady doing here?"

"I'm a schoolteacher in the town. I came to Crete before the war started."

"Have the Germans asserted their indoctrination into your school?"

Georgina gave a faint smile. "Not yet."

The man finished his drink, put on a grey cap and then stood. Passing Georgina, he tipped his cap and left the cafe. The waiter returned with a coffee and laid it in front of Georgina. Minutes later, a German patrol burst into the café and an officer approached Georgina. She set her cup on the saucer.

"The man you spoke to, where did he go?" he asked sharply.

Georgina stared at the officer.

"I asked you a question."

"How should I know?"

"Come with me."

"I've done nothing wrong!"

"I will decide that," said the officer in his authoritative voice and flanked by armed soldiers. Georgina stared at them. "Where are you taking me?"

"Headquarters, it is near here."

Georgina drank some coffee, left money and then accompanied the officer and four soldiers to the Town Hall. The officer led her into a room and pulled one of two chairs forward. "Someone will be here to speak with you."

After the officer departed, he closed the door. Georgina sat and cast her gaze round the bare room. Then, she heard footsteps get louder and a different officer entered. As he sat down opposite, Georgina stared. The officer removed his cap and gave a faint smile. "I apologise for the inconvenience."

Georgina hesitated. "We met not long ago. Why have I been brought here? she said sharply."

"You talked to a man in the cafe."

"I also talked to you in a cafe."

The office gave a slight smile. "I am not the leader of Crete's resistance. You chatted with Manilos, the most wanted man in Crete."

"That depends of which side you're on."

Once more, the officer gave a slight smile.

"We didn't say much to each other."

"What did you discuss?"

"Italy's current situation."

The officer leaned back and reflected. "A situation, indeed."

"That officer who brought me here was abrupt and rude!"

"Your country drops bombs on our cities, therefore, an American accent is not a receptive one. Is that the correct term?"

"It will suffice. Originally, I'm from Britain where you have bombed cities."

The officer stood, and replaced his cap. "I apologise for the inconvenience, you can go."

Georgina rose. "I didn't get the chance to finish my coffee."

"Allow me to buy you one, later. To show our humane side."

Georgina considered. Should I?

"I am off duty on Sunday, and will be at the same location where we met."

"How did you know Manilos was in the cafe?"

"We have our sources."

The officer and Georgina left the room and then he escorted her to the building's exit. Turning to him, she stared. "It's Erich, isn't it?"

He nodded.

Following a quick walk, Georgina arrived home and after she entered, took off her jacket and hat. As she hung them up on a wooden stand, Elena appeared from the living room. "Were you delayed at school?"

"I was arrested by a German patrol."

"Arrested! Why?"

Georgina sighed. "After I left the school, went for a coffee and whilst there, spoke to a man at the next table. He left, then minutes later, a patrol came into the cafe and an officer confronted me."

Elena remained silent.

"They took me to their HQ, asked some questions and then let me go."

"Who was the man in the cafe you spoke to?"

"Someone called Manilos."

Elena put a hand to her mouth. "I can understand why they wanted to question you."

"If he is sought by the Germans, why would he visit a cafe in a busy public location? It doesn't make sense."

"Only a handful of people are aware of what he looks like, but no one in Heraklion."

"Why is that?"

"His hideaway is in the southern mountains."

"How would the German patrol have known it was him in the cafe?"

Elena shrugged her shoulders.

"Also, why appear in the midst of a hornet's nest?"

"Maybe to gather information for an attack on their headquarters and extract revenge for the recent atrocities by German soldiers." Elena sighed. "Twenty men from a village south of Heraklion were picked at random and then shot."

Georgina shook her head.

As tension grew between Italian and German forces on Crete, British secret service agents contacted the Italian Commander-in-charge in Agios Nikolaos. For safe passage of his troops to North Africa, all weapons would be handed over to the resistance. Secret service agents had also made contact with Janouski, who fronted Crete's communist resistance movement. At this stage, he and his non-communist counterpart, Manilos, acted alone in the island's conflict. However, Britain wanted both movements to act as one. This would result in a more effective and strategic guerrilla campaign against the German forces.

At a south-eastern mountain hideaway, British secret service agents met with Janouski, known as the 'devil' to his associates. He fought in the war against Turkey and distinguished himself in battle and was made an officer. He would command his troops not to take prisoners, hence his nickname. The three agents, John Murdoch, Vic Stampson and Alec Taylor, sat with the grey-bearded Janouski round a table. All three were well educated, well-spoken and well trained in the art of espionage. Each of them also had a taste for hard liquor, of the Scottish malt kind. However, on Crete, they had to settle for ouzo.

"We believe if you join forces with Manilos, it will hurt the Germans more," said John Murdoch.

"We can train your men to act as a formidable unit," added Vic Stampson.

"It is weapons that win battles, not training," said Janouski sharply.

"We may be able to assist you," said Alec Taylor.

Janouski pulled on his long beard. "How?"

"We're in negotiations to arrange a deal with the Italians," said Alec

Taylor.

"But they still need their weapons to fight the Germans," said Janouski.

"Not in Agios Nikolaos." Alec Taylor gave a wry smile.

"If they fight the Germans, I know who will win." Janouski laughed. "Italian men are too fond of food and women."

John Murdoch and Vic Stampson grinned.

"Over two years ago, we kicked them out of Greece." Janouski laughed louder.

"Will you form a partnership with Manilos?" asked Alec Taylor. "It is the best way forward for Crete."

Janouski scowled. "I do not trust him, he will betray us to the Germans."

"And if you had assurances he wouldn't?" asked Vic Stampson.

Janouski remained silent.

"Well?"

Janouski hesitated. "Only if I have an assurance."

"We will arrange a meeting between Manilos and yourself," said Alec Taylor.

Janouski glanced at each agent. "Okay."

After a celebratory toast, the three agents left Janouski's mountain hideaway and headed back to their remote southern base. Whilst they ventured through valleys and over steep hills, the three colleagues chatted.

"Will the two work together?" asked John Murdoch, as he glanced at his two colleagues.

Vic Stampson shook his head. "They don't trust each other."

"If we want to defeat the Germans, they must put their differences aside."

"I wish it could be that easy, Alec," said Vic Stampson.

"I heard that in the war with Turkey," said John Murdoch, "they fought side by side."

"Times have changed," said Alec Taylor.

"A common enemy can bring them together," said John Murdoch. "Albeit, on a temporary basis."

"The Germans will no doubt try to bring Turkey into the war and assist them in Greece," said Alec Taylor.

"With a possible Italian collapse, the Germans will need another ally," said John Murdoch.

"When this war comes to an end, I hate to envisage what will happen on the island," said Vic Stampson.

Alec Taylor looked his way. "Let's get this one out of the way first."

Vic Stampson gave a slight grin.

As they continued their trek through rocky terrain, the three colleagues continued to discuss the current situation. Minutes later, John Murdoch raised a hand.

"What's up?" asked Vic Stampson.

"Take cover," said John Murdoch.

The three agents hid behind a cluster of large boulders and John Murdoch pointed. All three peered at a German patrol down in the valley, then looked at each other.

"They've never been this far up a mountain," said Alec Taylor.

"And they are SS troops." Vic Stampson stared.

"Desperate indeed," said Alec Taylor."

"We'll have to find another way," said John Murdoch. "Let's take the hilly route."

"Is this not it?" asked Vic Stampson.

John Murdoch grinned. "I hope you're fit, Vic."

He laughed.

"Who would want to be a resistance fighter," said John Murdoch.

Alec Taylor and Vic Stampson laughed.

Next day, the agents met with Manilos, leader of Crete's non-communist resistance movement. Like Janouski, he fought the Turks and gained a reputation of being a brave fighter and respected leader of men. However, Manilos did not kill wounded Turks. As they entered the cottage concealed by trees and bushes, the sturdy frame of Manilos greeted them. "Have a seat, gentlemen," he said cheerily, giving each of the agents a firm handshake. "Would you like something to drink?"

"Do you have whisky?" asked John Murdoch.

"This is Crete, not Scotland." Once more, Manilos grinned. "Also, there is a war on."

The agents laughed and Manilos poured three glasses of ouzo for his guests, refilled his, then sat with them around a circular dark wooden table. After each agent took a swig, Manilos addressed them. "Soon, no Italians will be on the island."

"We have heard of skirmishes between them and German soldiers in various parts of the island," said John Murdoch.

"I hope the Italians are slaughtered." Manilos took a swig of his ouzo. "Especially, after what they did to our villages in the east of Crete." He shook his head. "Again, and again, their soldiers raped our women and stole our food."

As the three agents looked at each other, Manilos poured more ouzo into his glass and then took another swig. "Pigs!" He set his glass on the table.

Alec Taylor took a sip of his drink, then coughed.

"Can your men fight alongside those of Janouski?" asked John Murdoch.

Manilos hesitated. "If we want to rid Crete of Germans, we'll have to."

"So, you will commit to the cause?" asked Vic Stampson."

Manilos moved his head forward. "However." He wagged his finger. "If there is trouble between us and the communists, it will not be of our doing." Manilos finished his drink. "I don't trust them." He burped.

"Do you think they trust you?" asked Alec Taylor.

Manilos stared at him. "If so, I would be shocked."

Laughter ensued and when the four men finished off a bottle of ouzo, the meeting came to a close.

After the agents left Manilos's hideaway, they found it difficult to manoeuvre the steep a mountain pathway.

"Too much booze," said Alec Taylor.

"I agree," said John Murdoch, as he burped.

"At least our visit has been worthwhile," added Vic Stampson.

"Both parties will no doubt fight the Germans, but it's the aftermath" said John Murdoch.

"Hopefully, there won't be too much hostility and we can go home," said John Murdoch.

Vic Stampson glanced his way. "I hope that's the case, otherwise, we'll have to assist Manilos."

"This bloody path is full of obstacles," said Alec Taylor, as he tried to keep his footing.

"Vic Stampson grinned. "More will appear, it's a long way down."

The other two agents laughed.

After several men entered the cottage, they congregated round the table with their leader.

"What did the British agents have to say, Manilos?" asked the oldest.

"That we have to make an alliance with the communists." Manilos folded his bare arms.

"Easier said than done." The grey-haired man looked at his two dark-bearded fellow fighters.

Manilos faced all three. "If we are to beat the Germans, we need the communists to fight with us." He paused. "That is the reality of the situation."

"Will the British give us guns and ammunition?"

Manilos nodded.

"When we defeat the Germans, what then?"

"We take care of the communists in our own way," said Manilos, as he gave a wry smile.

Amidst laughter, Manilos poured four glasses of ouzo and then everyone drank a toast to the future.

CHAPTER 9

DISAFFILIATION

Major Neuberger joined General Muller in his office to discuss the Italian situation in Agios Nikolaos. Now that Italy had surrendered to America and Britain, the German army faced a dilemma of what to do with their former ally. Due to a temporary assignment in Athens, Captain Hoeness did not attend the crucial meeting.

Germany had given the Italian officers and soldiers a choice on their immediate future. They could join the Wehrmacht, work as forced labour in Crete, or be sent to Germany as prisoners of war.

"What was the outcome, General?"

"The majority wanted to work as forced labour on Crete."

"They may join the resistance."

"That is what I am afraid of." General Muller leaned back in his chair. "We will have to act fast."

"Upon meeting them at their garrison in Agios Nikolaos, I do not feel they can be trusted."

General Muller nodded. "That is the opinion of the hierarchy in Berlin."

At that moment, the telephone on General Muller's desk started to ring and he answered it. After a short conversation, he replaced the receiver and stared at Major Neuberger. "All Italian soldiers are to be rounded up and then shot." General Muller glanced at a clock. "It will begin on Corfu within the hour, therefore, head straight away for Agios Nikolaos."

Major Neuberger stood. "Officers as well, General?"

He nodded. "Also, ensure all their weapons are accounted for. We do not want the resistance to get their hands on them."

When German forces reached the town, they found that the Italians had anticipated their action and had taken up defensive positions. The Italian soldiers dug in and waited. A fellow officer approached Major Neuberger. "They must have received word from Corfu." The officer looked through his binoculars.

"It could be a long and bloody battle. There are eight thousand Italian soldiers on Corfu," said Major Neuberger.

"As for here, Stukas have been ordered to bomb those Italian positions." The officer pointed, then handed his binoculars to Major Neuberger, who took them and looked ahead.

When a field telephone rang the officer answered it. Moments later he replaced the receiver and glanced at Major Neuberger. "The Stukas are on their way from the airfield at Heraklion."

"It won't take them long to reach here."

Whilst German officers and soldiers waited, the drone of planes grew louder. Both sets of soldiers looked up into the cloudless blue sky. When each Stuka dived, their distinctive siren added to the fear of being hit by a bomb. After a prolonged attack, the Italian defences retreated into Agios Nikolaos town centre.

After the Stukas flew off, German troops moved forward. When they reached damaged buildings, the soldiers found many Italians dead, or wounded amongst rubble. As the German High Command had ordered no prisoners to be taken, the Italian wounded received a fatal bullet. Major Neuberger surveyed the route ahead and his fellow officer remarked. "I don't envisage another Stalingrad."

Major Neuberger nodded. "This lot won't put up a fight and if they do, the end will be swift."

German troops advanced in a cautious manner through the bombed-out perimeter. Close to the town centre, they came under fire from snipers on the top storeys. After they had shot at their targets, the sniper would take cover behind a stone wall. Using the explosive power of a shoulder rocket launcher, accurate German marksmen eliminated the sniper threat. As troops reached the town centre, they found their Italian counterparts had put together a barricade of carts and tables across the main street to block an advance. Major Neuberger looked at his colleague. "If only we had a Panzer."

His fellow officer nodded. "It would smash through."

Major Neuberger ordered his rocket launcher marksmen to fire at the barricade. Taking position, three marksmen fired as one and the barricade disintegrated. Shots came from Italian soldiers and the Germans returned fire. As exchange of gunfire continued, Major Neuberger ordered a number of his troops to make their way behind the Italian line of defence. Not long after, they encircled the Italians, however, some managed to flee. Demoralised captured Italian soldiers had their weapons taken from them and then transported to various secluded locations. In the meantime, squads of German troops searched for their enemy within the town. Major Neuberger's fellow officer commented, "The locals may hide them."

"Tell the troops that if a family has given refuge to an Italian, they will be shot," he said sharply.

With superior weapons and manpower, German troops soon took control of the town. Italian soldiers were rounded up and then led away to suffer their fate. At one location, they received a command to get out of the truck and stretch their legs. When they did so and started to chat, a cover on the rear of a second German truck was pulled aside to reveal a machine gun. Due to the enclosed area, Italian prisoners had nowhere to run. A hail of bullets rattled towards them until no one stood. A German officer went round the bodies and to ensure no survivors, fired his pistol at the head of anyone that moved, or groaned. After the slaughter, German personnel left the corpses to rot and then headed to the next area of execution.

Squads of German soldiers began to search properties in the town for Italians who had sought refuge with locals. When one squad burst into a property, an Italian escapee gave himself up. After being taken away, two German soldiers remained. A woman pleaded with them. "Please, don't shoot my daughter and son, kill me instead," she cried.

Both soldiers aimed and shot the three inhabitants. Then, crying could be heard from inside a cupboard. When a soldier opened the door, a young girl sobbed. Looking up at the soldiers, she wiped her eyes. The soldiers looked at each other, then left. Panic-stricken, the young girl stared at the bodies of her mother, sister and brother.

Rather than hide, some Italian soldiers made a final stand near Agios Nikolaos's harbour. With little ammunition or guns, they stood no chance and the Germans made them suffer a bloody end.

Two days after the carnage of Agios Nikolaos, Georgina comforted an inconsolable Elena. Having lost an aunt and two cousins who stayed in the town, it left her devastated. "I am going to join the resistance," she said, sniffing. "The Germans have to pay for what has happened in Crete."

At that moment, noises come from the rear entrance. Looking at each other, Elena and Georgina went into the kitchen and listened. As darkness had fallen, both women felt uneasy. Georgina picked up a broom and held her breath. When a knock on the door came, both women glanced at each other.

"Hello," said a man's voice.

Elena hesitated, opened the door and then popped her head out.

"Apologies, I need shelter." A man in a blue uniform held his side, then slumped to the ground.

As Elena and Georgina went outside, the soldier lay on a concrete step and groaned.

"He must have escaped from the Germans," said Georgina.

Both women assisted the injured soldier into the kitchen and then sat him on a chair. Dazed, he did not speak, then Georgina examined his side. "He hasn't been shot." She glanced at Elena. "Maybe he just had a bad fall."

"Falling onto the concrete step would not help," said Elena, as she gave a sympathetic smile. "In an attempt to escape, he may have jumped off a German truck."

"No doubt on its way to a place where prisoners would be executed."

Elena went to the sink, filled a glass of water and then put it to the soldier's lips. "Drink slowly."

The soldier took several sips, then a gulp. As he coughed, Elena handed the near-empty glass to Georgina, who refilled it. The soldier gazed at Elena, then smiled. "Are you an angel?"

Elena handed over the glass and several swallows later, the soldier sighed. Taking the empty glass, Elena asked, "Did you escape from Agios Nikolaos?"

The soldier shook his head.

"Then where?" asked Georgina.

The soldier looked at her with eyes about to close. "Lassithi." He drew breath.

"The battle ended a week ago," said Elena.

"I hid in ruins of various houses."

"Did you knock on their doors, too?" asked Georgina.

"None of the properties had a door!" The soldier looked at both women and said gravely, "I have not eaten for days." Once more, he sighed.

"Food is scarce, however, would some cold meat and vegetables suffice?" asked Elena.

"Yes," he said gratefully.

In a matter of minutes, Elena had put a plate in front of the soldier. After he cleared it, he leaned back on the chair.

"Tasty?" asked Elena.

Whilst he ate, the soldier nodded, thankful for any sort of food. Georgina looked at Elena who asked him his name. Still chewing, he looked at her. "Romano."

"Were all the Italians in Lassithi taken prisoner?"

The soldier stared at Elena, then shook his head.

"What happened to them?"

"All of our troops were executed."

"Every one of them!" said Georgina.

"The Germans do not take prisoners," said the soldier gravely.

"Now that you have escaped, what are your plans?" asked Elena.

"I have no regiment and if captured, the Germans will shoot me."

"Along with us," said Georgina, as she glanced at Elena.

The soldier looked at both women. "I do not want to get you into trouble, therefore, I will leave."

"Where will you go?" asked Elena.

The soldier hesitated. "Maybe find a small boat and sail from the island." He gave a faint smile. "I will have to watch out for the resistance, as well as Germans."

Georgina smiled.

"Heraklion is full of German patrols," said Elena.

"Also, all of the northern coastline," added Georgina.

The soldier sighed. "I have to try."

"You can rest here for a few hours," said Elena.

"Thank you," said the soldier gratefully, as he yawned and closed his eyes. Elena and Georgina left the kitchen and returned to the living room. Turning on the radio, they sat and listened to the late evening news broadcast.

A short while later, they heard the back door being closed. Elena got up off her chair and then went into the kitchen. She returned and stared at Georgina.

"Gone?"

Elena nodded. "No doubt he didn't want to get us into trouble." Hearing a loud bang on the front door, she looked towards it. "Open up," shouted a male voice.

When Elena opened the door, a German patrol stood and glared. Georgina came to the door and joined her. One of the patrol said sharply, "An Italian soldier was seen at this property."

"He forced his way in and we threw him out," said Georgina.

"You threw him out!" said the sergeant, staring.

"Both of us," said Elena.

"He had been injured," said Georgina. "It didn't take much effort."

Three of the patrol brushed past both women and searched every room. A short time later, they returned and shook their heads at the sergeant.

"You do not appear the forceful type," said the sergeant, as he studied both women.

"Appearances can be deceptive," said Georgina.

"Who informed you that he had been here?" asked Elena.

Ignoring her question, the sergeant joined his men and they marched off. After Elena closed the door, she sighed. "I hate those arrogant Germans."

"Let me sleep in your room tonight," said Georgina.

As both women lay, once more, a noise came from the back door. Elena turned to Georgina. "Did you hear that?"

"Yes, I did."

Elena lifted her head. "Someone is trying to open the door."

The two women got out of bed, put on robes and then went into the kitchen. Both stood behind the door, then looked at each other. Georgina pointed to the door handle and whispered, "Someone is picking the lock." She grabbed the broom again and held her breath. The door opened and Romano entered. Seeing both women, he smiled and closed the door.

"Why have you returned?" asked Elena.

"A German patrol had been on my trail." Romano gave a faint smile. "They will not be back."

"How did you know they had been here?" asked Georgina.

Romano pointed. "When they came, I hid over there in the bushes."

"You can't stay," said Elena. "It is too dangerous."

Romano paused. "Not even until tomorrow night? I promise to leave when it is dark. Then, I will be fit again." He held his side."

Elena glanced at the lock. "Where did you learn that skill?"

"Before the war, I robbed properties."

"Why didn't you knock, as you did before?" asked Georgina, intrigued.

"I did not want to wake you."

As Elena glanced at Georgina and gave a slight smile, Romano looked towards the floor. "I will lie here, if that it is suitable."

"Only until tomorrow night," said Elena.

"Thank you," said Romano gratefully.

Elena returned to the bedroom, went into a closet and took out a couple of blankets. Entering the kitchen, she handed them to Romano, who gave her a warm smile.

Georgina sighed. Maybe we can now get some sleep.

When she heard soldier's footsteps, Georgina opened her eyes. Lying still, she listened and hoped they would pass. When the footsteps became quieter, Georgina took a deep breath. Looking sideways, she observed Elena, still fast asleep.

Feeling thirsty, Georgina went into the kitchen for a glass of water. When she entered, a strange sight greeted her. Sketching a portrait, Romano looked up. "Good morning."

"If the German patrol had stopped outside, it would have been our last," said Georgina, staring.

Romano smiled. "They won't return."

"What makes you say that?"

"They have bigger fish to fry," he said cheerily.

"Such as?" From a tap, Georgina filled a glass of water then took a large swallow.

"One of our officers escaped and he is the son of Mussolini."

"A big fish, indeed."

"He went in the direction of the Heraklion countryside," said Romano, as he looked at the portrait and then stood back.

"If he has found refuge in one of the villages, it will be burned to the ground and its residents shot.' Georgina paused. "Is it true that your army carried out similar atrocities?"

"Not on Crete. I cannot speak for what may have happened in mainland Greece," he said, looking at Elena enter the kitchen. "It also happened on Crete," she added. "Your army massacred citizens and plundered villages."

"I took no part in such acts and can only apologise."

Georgina stared at the portrait and then Elena. Curious, she approached Romano, gazed at his work, then glanced at Georgina.

"It looks like you, Elena."

"It is not complete," said Romano. "I found a sheet of paper and a crayon."

"You did say that you worked as a thief," said Georgina.

"Only some of the time," said Romano, as a smile crept over his face.

Whilst Elena kept her eyes on the portrait, Georgina finished her glass of water and looked at the clock. "It will soon be time for the morning foreign broadcast."

"You have a radio?" Romano asked in amazement. "What is the latest news about Italy?"

Elena took a glass out of a cupboard and approached the sink. "On yesterday's broadcast, the Germans have retreated from Naples," she said, as she filled it with water.

"My family are from Naples." Romano laid his sheet of paper and crayon on the table.

"British and Italian armies have lost the battle for Leros." Elena took a large swallow.

Romano sighed. "That is not so good, our navy is based there. What is happening in the east?"

"The Russians have recaptured Kiev, in the Ukraine."

Romano beamed. "The Germans are now in full retreat and soon Stalin's Red Army will be at the Polish border."

Whilst Elena elected to stay in the house, Georgina ventured into Heraklion's town centre. A pale shadow of what it looked before the occupation, citizens as well as the buildings looked shabby. Orphan boys and girls ran around half-naked and beggars roamed the streets. Looking for an excuse to extract punishment, German soldiers prowled.

As Georgina walked around the market, she observed little or no food on display. An abundance of pottery and the odd rug existed, but that would not generate an income for the trader. Indeed, a once popular vibrant location had no atmosphere and only several people who browsed. A thin unshaven man approached Georgina and held out his wrinkled palm. "Could you give me money for something to eat?" he said humbly.

Georgina shook her head. "Sorry."

After the man moved on to another woman, a German officer on walkabout came over. "If you had given him money, others would have pestered you."

Georgina looked at the tall officer staring at the beggar, who made himself scarce. She cast her gaze around the vicinity. "This used to be an enjoyable place to frequent."

"The result of conflict," said the officer, as he looked at Georgina.

"Why remain, it's a hostile region?"

"You will have to ask Berlin."

Georgina gave a faint smile. "Would I get a reply?"

"Since our HQ cannot, I doubt it." The officer tipped his cap in a courteous manner, and rejoined a fellow officer.

Moments later, Georgina entered her favourite cafe and had the pick of its set tables. The usual waiter appeared and gave Georgina a welcome smile.

"Are you doing meals today?"

The waiter shook his head. "Afraid not."

"Coffee?"

"For our special customers, yes," the waiter said, smiling.

"Thanks," said Georgina gratefully.

As the waiter departed, from her window seat, Georgina observed a German patrol drag away a man. Pleading his innocence, cries fell on deaf German ears. The waiter brought Georgina her coffee, viewed the incident and shook his head. "Any excuse to arrest a Jew."

"There is now dissent directed at the Germans."

The waiter glanced at Georgina. "Their precious Reich gets smaller and weaker each month."

Georgina lifted her cup and took a sip. It's weak.

The waiter turned round. "How is your coffee?"

"Okay."

After the waiter left, Georgina watched a German soldier approach a group of local men. When a heated argument ensued, a German patrol appeared. At gunpoint, they ordered the locals into a lane and soon shots could be heard. The waiter dashed towards the window and stared.

"They took four men away and shot them!"

"What for?"

"The men argued with a soldier."

Soon an angry crowd confronted the German soldiers, who aimed their rifles at them. The crowd shouted abuse and then shots followed. Men and youths ran for cover to avoid injury, however, one of the youths fell to the ground. Moaning with pain, a German soldier aimed his rifle and finished him off. Georgina looked on with disbelief.

"Murderers!" said the waiter, shaking his head. "One day the war will end and when it does, we will extract revenge on them."

After Georgina got up and bid farewell, the waiter observed her near-full cup. As she walked out, tension filled the air. Locals directed their scowls at the German soldiers, but restrained themselves for fear of being fired upon.

Following a quick and pensive walk, Georgina arrived home and breathed a sigh of relief. As she entered, laughter came from the kitchen. As Georgina walked in, Elena and Romano looked her way. "Romano has almost finished, Georgina."

As he moved his black crayon to and fro on the sheet of white paper, Georgina gazed at it. "Superb." She glanced at Romano. "Is this the one you started?"

"That was a rough sketch."

Georgina glanced at Elena. "It's you."

She laughed. "Of course, it is."

"Please keep your head still, Elena," said Romano, as he drew.

Georgina studied the portrait. "Romano has captured your smile."

"Thank you." Romano glanced at Georgina.

Then, when synchronised footsteps became louder, Romano's hand ceased to move. Georgina went into the living room and watched through the net curtain. As the patrol passed, she returned to the kitchen. "Flexing their muscles."

Romano took a deep breath and when he applied the final touches, Georgina gazed at the portrait with admiration. Moments later, Romano laid his crayon on the kitchen table.

"Finished?" asked Elena.

Romano nodded and Elena left her chair. After an extended examination, gave Romano a warm hug. "You are indeed gifted." She stepped back, then dried her eyes.

"My farewell gift to you." He smiled. "You never know, it may be worth something one day."

When darkness fell, Romano stood in the kitchen, poised to leave. Elena had got in touch with a friend who would give Roman shelter until safe to escape the island. As Elena and Georgina waited with him, there came a distinctive knock on the back door. All three stared, then Elena moved forward and opened it. "Good evening, Nickolas."

"Evening, Elena." He stepped inside.

"Nickolas, this is Romano." Elena glanced at him

Nickolas shook Romano's hand.

"You have a strong grip." Romano grinned.

"We have to move fast, there is a German patrol not far from here."

Nickolas looked at Romano and Elena. "For safety, we will take the long route."

After a warm hug from Elena and Georgina, Romano departed. As the two men walked through thick bushes and trees, Nickolas broke the silence. "Which part of Italy are you from?"

"Naples. Where are you from?"

"Cyprus."

"Why did you come to Crete?"

"Unforeseen family circumstances."

"Did your wife accompany you?"

"I do not wish to discuss her, we should never have met."

Roman perceived a marriage not blessed in heaven, so remained silent. Following a trek through muddy man-made paths, they reached the outskirts of Heraklion.

"Will it not be dangerous to hide in the town?"

Nickolas shook his head. "They won't look for you here."

As the two men approached a block of apartments on three storeys, Nickolas cast his gaze around the vicinity. He and Roman entered the decayed building, then went up a narrow concrete staircase to the top floor. Inserting a key, Nickolas opened one of the two landing doors. Romano glanced at the opposite one. "Who stays in that apartment?"

"No one, it is empty."

After Romano entered, Nickolas closed the door and then went into a part-furnished room with bare floorboards. He had a quick look around, and went into the kitchen, accompanied by Romano.

"The apartment is small, but safe," said Nickolas.

As Romano stared at a cupboard, Nickolas opened it. "There is enough food to last a couple of days." He closed the cupboard and looked at Romano. "You will leave on Friday night."

Romano nodded. "What time?"

"I will contact a friend who has a fishing boat and get back to you."

"When?"

"At this time, tomorrow."

When Romano looked towards the bathroom, Nickolas grinned. "Don't worry, there is running water, however, no heating I'm afraid." Nickolas walked up to a closet and opened it. "There are a couple of blankets to wrap round yourself." Then he gave a bottle to Romano. "In case you have to relax."

"Why keep ouzo in there?"

"Safe-keeping." Nickolas grinned. "I will lock you in and see you tomorrow evening."

"What if someone knocks on the door?"

"No one will, but if they do, ignore them."

Romano nodded and then laid the half-empty bottle beside the cracked white ceramic sink. Nickolas departed, closed the door behind him and turned the key. Romano looked around his temporary habitat, then walked to the window. In the distance, he viewed Heraklion's harbour and a route to freedom. Feeling thirsty, Romano went into the kitchen and to his delight, found a clean glass. He turned on the tap and filled it with water. After a swig, he coughed and then spat into the sink. Grabbing the ouzo, he poured a large glass, took a couple of sips and sighed with relief. Opening the cupboard, he found meat on a plate and devoured it.

Following another glass of ouzo, Romano curled up on the couch with the two blankets wrapped around him. Outwith summer, even Crete could feel chilly. Then, he heard gunshots and raised his head. Shouts in German could be heard, Romano panicked. He got up, went over to the window and peered out. As more gunshots followed, Romano spotted two men in plain clothes running towards the harbour, then stagger and fall. A group of German soldiers approached the wounded men. An officer took out a pistol from his black holster and fired several fatal shots. As the patrol departed, Romano started to contemplate. As no mercy will be given, he had to avoid being captured. Returning to the couch, he made himself comfortable, then yawned several times.

Romano woke up to sunlight on his face, which shone through the bare window. He turned round, tried to get comfortable, but found it difficult. Beginning to feel hungry and parched, Romano got up, went to the cupboard and opened it. The food that remained would not fill a kitten's stomach, let alone his. He would have to venture outside and find something to eat. Then, Romano remembered that Nickolas had locked him in. He mulled his thoughts. Finding a nail, he approached the door and then used his expertise to pick the lock. Determined to eat, Romano opened the door and gave a relieved sigh. Entering the landing, he stared at an opposite door and walked over to it. Putting an ear against the door, he listened. Since Romano could not hear any activity, he elected to break into the apartment, hoping there may be some food. This being a safer option than to venture outside and be captured. After a number of attempts, his perseverance paid off and Romano entered. He searched in each of three rooms and then the kitchen. After he opened a cupboard, Romano beamed.

Several slices of bread and cheese lay on a plate. Given that they appeared fresh, perhaps someone could soon return. Taking the contents, Romano left and returned to his own temporary accommodation. Following a welcome snack and a glass of ouzo, he rested on the couch and contemplated his future. If he could reach his beloved Italy, what lay in store? There would be no sympathy from German troops, or British and American invaders. A dilemma, indeed. As his eyelids became heavy, Romano fell asleep.

Hearing loud voices from the apartment below, Romano awoke and listened. German shouts appeared to be directed at the inhabitants. Moments later, Romano could hear the inhabitants being taken outside and then ushered into a vehicle. As it moved off, he envisaged a cruel fate in store for them. Returning to his makeshift bed, Romano tried to relax, but to no avail.

When the daylight diminished, Romano longed for Nickolas to arrive. Although only a short stay, being confined to a deserted cold environment reminded him of a time in solitary confinement. If in a German prison camp, at least he would have fellow soldiers to chat with. Then came the sound of a key being inserted into the lock and Romano stared. As Nickolas entered, the apartment's resident sighed.

"Do not look distressed, it could only have been me."

"I heard German soldiers in the building."

"When?"

"Earlier. Several people appeared to have been arrested and then taken away."

"I heard, the Jewish family downstairs."

"How did you find out?"

"I have my sources." Nickolas spotted the bottle of ouzo.

"The tap water is undrinkable."

Nickolas grinned. "Come, let us go to the harbour, a boat will be due soon."

As both men walked down the staircase, Romano stared at an open door on the landing.

"They won't be back," said Nickolas.

After they left the building, Nickolas led Roman through a series of back alleys towards the harbour. Whilst they walked, Romano asked, "What about German sentries?"

"This is when there is a changeover, but we don't have much time to spare."

From a secluded building close to the harbour, Nickolas aimed a flashlight towards a small boat out at sea. After he repeated the action, a response followed. As the boat headed in his direction, Nickolas tapped Romano on the shoulder. "Let's go."

"Where to?"

Nickolas pointed and both men made their way to an unused part of the harbour, then waited. The fishing boat drew up alongside and its owner acknowledged Nickolas. When Romano stepped onto the boat, shots were fired from another part of the harbour. Nickolas ducked, looked round and ran off. As the boat sped off, Romano and several crewmen hit the deck. A barrage of gunfire followed, however, the boat received only minor damage. After it moved further away from the coastline and into total darkness, Romano breathed a sigh of relief. One of the crewmen looked his way. "You are safe now. When we reach Italy, what will you do?"

Romano shrugged his shoulders.

Italy had been humbled, surrendered and now faced an uncertain future. With their superior military resources, America with Britain's help would defeat the Germans and take control of Italy. What of his fellow countrymen who had been transported to Germany? No doubt they faced an existence of being forced to work in factories that produced weapons, or worse still, in a death camp. Rumours existed of Italian Jews being sent to German prisoner-of-war camps and then murdered. However, at this stage of the war, they remained unconfirmed.

CHAPTER 10

ABDUCTION

On a warm sunny evening in April 1944, leader of the non-communist resistance, Manilos, met with his three British contacts. As usual, the agents ventured up to Manilos's secluded mountain retreat and drank glasses of ouzo. Afterwards, Alec Taylor put forward a plan to capture a high-ranking German General.

"You want to abduct Friedrich-Hans Muller!" said Manilos.

"He is the highest Wehrmacht officer on Crete and the one who calls the shots," said John Murdoch.

"If you remove him from power, there will be a vacuum," added Alec Taylor.

Manilos frowned. "A vacuum?"

"A void, a missing link in the chain," said Alec Taylor.

Manilos nodded. "I understand. However, he will be well-guarded."

"We have devised a plan," said Vic Stampson.

"Tell me about it." Manilos looked at the three agents, then leaned back on his chair.

Vic Stampson put down his half-empty glass. "From his headquarters in Heraklion, Friedrich-Hans Muller is driven back to his mansion, Monday to Saturday at the same precise time. There is a blind spot on a bend five miles from Heraklion where a group of men can hide."

"I know it," said Manilos, nodding.

"When his limousine approaches the blind spot, we attack."

Manilos considered. "His vehicle has an escort and there will be at least four guards."

"Then we ensure that we have double the manpower to take care of them," said Alec Taylor.

"It could turn into a bloodbath," said Manilos. "If there are reprisals, the communists will blame us."

"We feel it would be a great humiliation for the Germans if we pull this off," added John Murdoch.

"I will discuss the plan with my men."

"We would prefer sooner rather than later," said John Murdoch, as he glanced at his two fellow agents.

"When you gentlemen return tomorrow night, I will give you my answer."

The three agents stood, shook hands with Manilos and left his retreat. Whilst they made their way down the steep pass, John Murdoch whispered to his two colleagues. When he deviated, the other two agents continued down the pass.

Several minute later, a cry and struggle could be heard. When Alec Taylor and Vic Stampson turned round, John Murdoch appeared with a grey-bearded stocky man and a gun aimed at his head.

"Who are you?" asked John Murdoch sharply.

"I am a peasant, I lost my way in the dark." The man stammered.

"Why did you follow us?" asked Alec Taylor, as he approached the man.

"I do not know what you mean."

"We're not stupid," said Alec Taylor sharply.

"Will I kill him?" asked John Murdoch. He pressed his pistol against the man's head, then glanced at his fellow agents.

"We'll take him to Manilos," said Alec Taylor.

The three agents escorted the man back to Manilos's retreat, to explain the situation to him.

"This is one of my men." Manilos looked at him, then the agents.

"He followed us," said Vic Stampson.

Manilos looked and approached the man. "Is this true?" Manilos looked at the agents. "Leave this with me, I will deal with him."

After the agents left, Manilos stared at the man and shook his head. Lifting a glass of ouzo from a table, he took a swig. "It would appear our stealth practices need more work."

The man grinned.

"Before being caught, did you overhear anything of interest?"

"Just small talk, Manilos."

The agents arrived back at their place of refuge in a disused monastery and then turned on a radio. The daily broadcast would give details about crucial events in Russia and the Far East. Due to poor reception, John Murdoch turned the knob to and fro.

"Don't lose the signal!" said Alec Taylor.

"I'm doing my best not to," replied John Murdoch, as he glanced over his shoulder.

"Keep it there," said Vic Stampson.

John Murdoch grinned. "Got it."

As they listened, the broadcaster announced that Russian forces had invaded Rumania. A hearty cheer ensued from the trio.

"That will cause concern in Berlin," said Alec Taylor. "The German supply of oil from Rumania will be in jeopardy."

Next came details of German cities being bombed by British and American aircraft which had caused severe damage. The agents grinned and continued to listen until the broadcast concluded. Vic Stampson looked at his two colleagues. "Preparations for the invasion of France will be underway."

"Is there any word on a proposed date?" asked Alec Taylor.

Vic Stampson shook his head. "Top secret, even I don't know."

"I would envisage June or July," said John Murdoch. "It's an ideal time."

"The channel will be calm," added Vic Stampson.

Alec Taylor deliberated. "Manilos didn't mention the recent massacres at Mesovouno and Pyrgoi."

"It could be that atrocities have become a way of life," said John Murdoch.

"They will get their revenge soon enough," said Alec Taylor.

"That's twice Mesovouno has been attacked," said Vic Stampson.

"What happened at Pyrgoi?" asked John Murdoch.

Alec Taylor sighed. "The SS arrived one morning and took around four hundred men, women and children from their homes." He hesitated. "Shot and burned alive."

"Bloody SS swines," said Vic Stampson, kicking a chair in disgust.

After a subdued day at school, Georgina took her usual route home through Heraklion's deserted streets. Atrocities by SS troops had taken its toll on not only the Cretan villages, but also citizens of the capital. Men, young and old, now afraid to venture outdoors in case of being picked upon by the occupiers. With German setbacks on all fronts and their cities bombed each day and night, their troops on Crete went out their way to extract revenge on innocent civilians.

As Georgina arrived home, she heard Elena sob in the kitchen. Without taking off her hat and jacket, Georgina entered and found her friend distraught. She had not seen Elena in such a stressful state. She wiped her eyes, then looked up at Georgina. "Now they have murdered my friend's brother and his three children," she said gravely.

Georgina removed her hat and coat, laid them aside, and sat down next to Elena.

"SS troops came to her village and massacred everyone." Elena sniffed. "No one stood a chance."

"They will get what they deserve."

Elena stared at Georgina. "But when? Crete is on its knees. The population cannot take much more." Elena's voice grew raspy. "People are either being murdered, or dying of starvation."

Georgina gave her friend a hug and then Elena looked at her gratefully. "I am glad you are here, someone so strong."

Georgina gave a forced smile. "Not always."

Once more, Elena wiped her eyes. "What do you mean?" She sniffed.

Georgina hesitated. "Before Eddie died, I went through hell."

Elena stared.

"I drank to try and forget his constant affairs with younger women and then came financial pressures." Georgina paused. "Eddie gambled away the mansion." She swallowed. We ended up being broke."

"Why did you not leave him?"

"I had nowhere to go." Georgina sighed. "Also, I hoped he would somehow mend his ways."

"You returned to New York?"

Georgina gave a faint smile. "I was arrested and then taken there."

"Arrested! Why?"

"The authorities in New York thought I had killed Dale, my husband." Georgina paused. "He was shot in a Manhattan street."

"Why did they suspect you?"

Georgina shrugged her shoulders. "They questioned me and let me go." She went on, "But not before a detective who dealt with the case made me sweat for several days." Georgina sighed.

"And all this time you have kept this to yourself." Elena tilted her head.

"My biggest secret." Once more, Georgina gave a forced smile.

"You come to Crete for a fresh start and now have to live in war zone." Elena shook her head.

"I felt worse in Los Angeles."

Elena also gave a forced smile.

"With my classes at the school, at least I'm self-sufficient."

"What about the German influence?"

"Other subjects have been affected, but not my music classes."

"No Wagner?"

Georgina gave a slight smile, then shook her head.

"I have heard he is Hitler's favourite composer."

"They leave my classes alone."

Elena stared down at the tabletop. "I wish they would leave the village alone."

Once more, Georgina comforted her friend. "Don't worry about food, I've found a source."

"Oh?" Elena raised her dark eyebrows.

Late that evening, Georgina met Captain Hoeness at a location just outside Heraklion. To avoid being seen, he had ensured that no German patrol would be in the area. Georgina, dressed in dark attire and a beret, brought along a schoolteacher she had known before he retired. When they entered a small empty building, Captain Hoeness greeted the two. The man stared at a number of boxes, which lay in a corner.

"That is all I could take without the storekeeper being suspicious," said Captain Hoeness, as he looked at Georgina and the man staring at brown cardboard boxes. "They contain tins of soup, meat and vegetables."

The man swallowed. "Most of our people are dying of starvation, this is a welcome gift." He looked at Captain Hoeness. "Why?" he asked in amazement.

"We are not all Nazis."

Georgina glanced at her companion. "This is Kai, he has come to give us a hand."

Captain Hoeness approached the man. "Let us get started."

"I'll help, too," said Georgina. "I'm stronger than you think."

"You take the smaller ones."

As all three lifted boxes and then put them into the truck, Captain Hoeness surveyed the vicinity. Once finished, he sat in the driver's seat. Georgina and the man sat in the rear.

"You know the way to the cottage?" asked Georgina.

Captain Hoeness glanced round. "I believe so."

After the truck moved off, Kai looked at Georgina and whispered, "What if he is stopped and searched?"

Georgina whispered, "He's a captain and will be able to bluff his way out of trouble. Have the British given you supplies?"

Kai nodded. "But it is not enough."

Georgina glanced at the boxes. "I hope these will help."

"Any food is a bonus." Once more, Kai whispered, "Although I am grateful to the captain, he is still a German soldier. His army has murdered friends and members of my family." Kai hesitated. "I am confused."

Georgina gave a slight smile. Surreal would be appropriate.

"However, he does not appear to be similar to the rest of his German scum."

As the truck headed towards a forest, Captain Hoeness glanced round at his two passengers. "Keep on this road, then turn right," said Kai.

"You're a fast driver!" said Georgina.

"I do not drive slow."

Georgina looked at Kai and going by his expression, still appeared baffled by the generous act. What could be behind it?

After the truck pulled up outside a secluded cottage with a white exterior, Captain Hoeness got out. A short grey-haired woman emerged from a doorway and scowled at him. Georgina and Kai appeared from the truck's rear.

"It is okay, Anna," said Kai.

"What is going on, Kai?" Anna stared.

"Food, Anna. Boxes of the stuff!" Kai grinned.

When the woman glanced at Captain Hoeness, Kai spoke, "He is here to help us."

"He is a German!"

As Captain Hoeness and Georgina started to empty the truck, Kai approached Anna to explain. After all the boxes had been taken into the cottage, Captain Hoeness returned to the truck. Before he drove off, Georgina approached the driver's window. "Thanks," she said gratefully.

"Same arrangement in two weeks. I do not blame the woman for being hostile."

"Family and friends have been murdered."

"Did you keep a box for yourself?"

Georgina nodded. "What if someone asks why you borrowed a truck?"

Captain Hoeness gave a wry smile. "I answer to a major and a general, who have more important issues to deal with."

After the truck departed, Georgina went into the cottage. The woman stood with a bemused expression. "Why is he doing this?"

"Because he has a conscience."

"I do not trust Germans, even if they bring us food." She looked at Kai. "There will be an ulterior motive, wait and see," Anna said sharply.

"Perhaps an apology for what has happened in Crete over the past three years."

"It is too late for apologies! He and the rest of them will suffer retribution for the atrocities they have committed."

Kai glanced at a clock. "I will take you home in about an hour."

"Thanks," said Georgina, as she adjusted her beret.

"By then, patrols are few and far-between."

"Would you like something to drink?" asked Anna. "I can only give you a glass of water."

"I am fine." Georgina gave a faint smile. "Maybe the captain will supply coffee next time."

Kai gave a slight grin and Anna remained silent.

When early evening came, Manilos and his men left their retreat and headed to where the ambush would take place. Given the intended victim, his men embraced this opportunity to kidnap the principal German officer on Crete who had caused extreme misery and hardship. However, Manilos stressed to his men that there would be no personal assaults on the general.

Following a trek, which lasted several hours, the resistance fighters met with John Murdoch and Vic Stampson. Manilos asked, "Where is the third agent?"

"He is on another mission," said John Murdoch, as he handed two German military police uniforms to Manilos. "Have two of your men to put them on." John Murdoch glanced around the group. "Hopefully, the uniforms will fit two of your men."

"To stop General Muller's limousine?"

John Murdoch nodded, then gave a slight grin. "The two who are clean-shaven."

Manilos gave a wry grin. "I understand."

John Murdoch then handed over a lantern. "When the driver spots this, he should slow down and stop."

Manilos stared. "And if he doesn't?"

"Aim for the tyres."

As two men changed into the uniforms, Manilos and other resistance fighters took up position along with the two British agents. John Murdoch checked his watch, then looked at Vic Stampson. "He should have left his office about now."

"Let us hope so," said Manilos. "We have walked miles to get here."

A short while later, the lookout made a distinctive whistle to signify a vehicle that approached, and the lantern was lit. Resistance fighters and both agents hid in secluded areas on each side of the road. When the sound of a vehicle's engine grew louder, everyone waited in anticipation. Vic Stampson glanced at his colleague. "That's a stroke of luck, no escort."

The two resistance fighters dressed as military policemen stood on the darkened road and one waved the lantern from side to side. As it shone, the limousine slowed down, then came to a halt. General Muller put down a document. "What is the problem?"

"Military police, General," said the chauffeur, as he glanced round."

At that moment, John Murdoch approached the limousine and pointed a gun at General Muller. Vic Stampson aimed his gun at the chauffeur.

General Muller wound down the window. "What is the meaning of this?"

"You're being kidnapped, General," said John Murdoch.

"You will pay for this." General Muller glared.

"Not half as much as you will," said John Murdoch, grinning.

Vic Stampson pointed his gun at the chauffeur. "Out of the vehicle," he said sharply.

"You too, General." John Murdoch waved his gun at him.

After he got out, General Muller cast his gaze around the vicinity, then at John Murdoch. "Who are you?"

"Two of us are connected to British Intelligence and the other gentlemen are resistance."

General Muller stared at the resistance fighters. "Who are you kidding?"

"Given the atrocities you've overseen, I would keep quiet," said Vic Stampson.

With stern expressions, the resistance fighters searched the general and his chauffeur. A handgun was found on the chauffeur and then handed over to Manilos. Taking the gun, he examined it and grinned. "This would not kill a rabbit."

The other fighters laughed.

"What do you intend to do with me?" General Muller looked at John Murdoch.

Manilos stepped forward. "You will be held responsible for many massacres on this island." He glared. "I should kill you here and now."

General Muller smirked. "Then you will also be a murderer."

"I do not kill innocent men, women and children." Manilos spat on the ground, then aimed his rifle at General Muller.

"We'll take it from here," said John Murdoch. "Get rid of the vehicle and we'll escort him south in our jeep."

Manilos nodded. "We will deal with the chauffeur." He grinned.

The two agents took General Muller to their vehicle. After the jeep moved off, two gunshots could be heard. With a gun aimed at General Muller, who sat in the rear seat, Vic Stampson asked, "What happened to your escort?"

Whilst General Muller remained silent, John Murdoch glanced round the immediate vicinity. "Can't get the staff these days, General?"

Vic Stampson laughed.

"Where are you taking me?"

Once more, John Murdoch glanced back. "To the coast and then Egypt."

"The war is over for you, General." Vic Stampson stared. "Be grateful you're not being transported to Russia, or handed over to the resistance."

"We will prevail in Russia, new weapons are being made ready."

"Your factories have been demolished," said John Murdoch. "British and American bombers have seen to that."

General Muller smirked. "You underestimate German expertise. Our factories are underground, bomb all you want."

Both agents remained silent.

General Muller looked at Vic Stampson. "You and the Americans are about to receive a shock."

"You're bluffing," said Vic Stampson.

"We do not need airplanes to bomb Britain."

"Can you expand?" John Murdoch glanced round.

General Muller sat back. "If you believe we will lose the war, you are mistaken."

Following a period of silence between both agents and their prisoner, the jeep arrived at a deserted part of Crete's southern coast. Its three occupants left the jeep and got into a small boat. As it left the shore, John Murdoch and Vic Stampson looked at each other, then General Muller.

"Tales of fantasy," said John Murdoch.

CHAPTER 11

GENOCIDE

As a consequence of victory in the war with Turkey in 1911, Italy laid claim to the historic island of Rhodes. In September 1938, the Italian government implemented anti-Jewish laws, which alarmed Rhodes' 4000 Jewish inhabitants. Fearing what had occurred in Germany, an exodus ensued. However, half of the Rhodes Jewish population remained and as a consequence, suffered hardship. With Italy being an ally of Germany and as German troops arrived on Rhodes, the Jewish community waited with apprehension.

From September 1943, Jewish people who lived on mainland Greece now faced being arrested and then dispersed, but on Rhodes this did not happen. Jewish citizens continued to live as best they could, but the situation would change later. Also, in September 1943 as a result of Italy's surrender to American and British forces, the German High Command wanted Italian troops on Rhodes to hand over their weapons. However, the Italian commanding officer on the island had not been given a direct order to surrender. Confusion reigned, therefore, Italian troops elected to fight the Germans. During the conflict, a particular group of them took shelter in a disused taverna on the outskirts of Rhodes Town. One soldier reflected. "I've enjoyed my stay here," he said, as he looked at his four colleagues.

"Me too," said a tall lean soldier.

"That's because of the women, Sergio," replied an older soldier.

Sergio grinned, then looked at a colleague. "What about you, Romano?"

He shook his head. "I should have gone back to Italy, rather than rejoin the fight."

The older soldier laughed. "If we are captured, you may get your wish."

"Another soldier commented, "We will no doubt be sent to a German labour camp."

Romano looked at him. "Is that where the Jews in occupied countries are being sent?"

"We go to a different type of camp," said the older soldier. "It's not in Germany."

"Where?" asked Romano, as he stared.

"I believe it is in Poland." The older man coughed.

"Quiet!" The tall lean soldier whispered, "I hear Germans."

The group stayed silent with hands on their rifles and looked at each nervously. Wanting to cough, the older man put a hand over his mouth and the others stared. As German accents approached the taverna, one of them stopped. "What about in there?" he asked.

A colleague looked towards the entrance, then shook his head. As the platoon passed, all of the Italians breathed a sigh of relief, except the older soldier. After a fit of coughing, he lay on the ground. A colleague went behind the taverna's bar and then returned with a bottle. Giving it to the older man, he grinned. "It's your lucky day."

The older man took a swig, then spat on the ground.

"What's up?" asked his fellow soldier.

He moaned. "It tastes like vinegar!"

The tall soldier grinned. "It may get rid of your cough."

Whilst the group laughed, a heavy mechanical vehicle could be heard on route towards the taverna. When the tall soldier peeked out a window, the vehicle stopped. He stared at his colleagues. "The tank commander may have spotted me."

Seconds later, a shot came from the tank. It hit the taverna wall and rubble fell onto three of the soldiers. Romano looked at the older soldier. "We have to leave."

"You go, I can't walk." Amidst the smoke, he started to cough and then drew breath. "Save yourself," he said, groaning.

As the tank's mechanism grew louder, Roman left through a rear exit. Moments later, another shot hit the taverna and its roof caved in.

Managing to evade capture, Romano found a disused cellar in which to hide. Resting, he lay against a wall and listened to gunfire a short distance away. With darkness about to fall, his eyelids became heavy.

When daylight shone through a cracked skylight window onto Romano's face, he woke up and then turned his head sideways. Putting up a hand to stifle the light, he gathered his thoughts. Romano looked around the cellar and observed a wooden chest in a corner. Getting to his feet, he walked towards it and opened the lid. Inside he found items of clothes, crayons and sheets of white paper. Romano's Italian uniform would be a hindrance, so he took it off and put on his acquired casual clothes. The grey trousers and white shirt had belonged to a man fond of hearty meals. Romano used his uniform belt to keep the trousers from being too loose and tucked in the shirt. Feeling thirsty and hungry, he went up a staircase, reached the door and put his ear against it. With no sign of activity, Romano turned the handle and peeked out. Looking around, the house had an empty feel, devoid of soul. Entering the kitchen, he found bread, cheese and two oranges. He lifted an empty glass tumbler, went to the cracked white ceramic sink and turned on a brass tap. After it spluttered, water came out and he filled the glass. Several swigs later, a sigh of relief followed. After he had devoured the bread and cheese, Romano entered a living room, which contained relevant furniture, an assortment of ornaments plus two portraits. Romano contemplated, then sighed. The Rabbi and his wife must have fled in order to avoid arrest.

After a period of reflection, Romano returned to the cellar. To take his mind off events, he used the paper and crayon to draw. Romano sat on the chest and rested a sheet of paper on a roof slate. A short while later, a woman's portrait had ensued. Picking up another piece of paper, Romano started to sketch a landscape of his home in Italy. Then, he heard voices from upstairs, and not of his native tongue. Romano put aside the crayon and pieces of paper, got up and stood behind the cellar door. As it burst open, Romano stood still, and held his breath. Three German soldiers and an officer surveyed the cellar, then stared at Romano. "Who are you?" barked the officer.

"I stay here, it's my home." He stammered.

"Why are you down here and not upstairs?"

"I come here to draw." Romano picked up his two drawings and showed them to the officer who examined them. Whilst Romano chewed on his lip, the officer stared at him. "Let me see your identification papers."

"I have lost them."

"You will come with us."

As soldiers led Romano away, the officer examined the crayon, lifted both portraits and left.

Sitting in an empty room inside Rhodes Town's German headquarters, Romano pondered about what lay in store. With no identification documents, the Germans could do as they please. A German soldier entered the room and glared at Romano. "Follow me."

"When do I get fed?" Romano gave a slight grin.

"Keep quiet!"

As Romano left the room, he observed a guard outside, also with a grim expression. Romano followed the soldier along a narrow corridor devoid of light and then found himself in a bright office. The soldier saluted an officer, departed and closed the door.

"Sit down," said the tall fair-haired German.

Romano sat on a hard-wooden chair and the officer went behind his desk. Sitting down, he opened a drawer, brought out Romano's two drawings and laid them in front of him. "Explain."

"What do you mean?"

"Who is the woman?"

Romano hesitated. "A past acquaintance."

"In Rhodes?"

Romano shook his head.

"And the landscape?"

"In Naples, where I grew up."

The officer leaned back on his black leather chair. "You are an Italian soldier on the run, are you not? You have no identification to verify you are Greek and also, we found your uniform."

"What now?"

"You will be sent to a labour camp," said the officer sharply.

"In Germany?"

"Eastern Poland."

Romano had heard rumours of camps in that part of Poland where men worked until they dropped.

"However, I can send you to another location." The officer went on. "Conditions are more favourable. For this leniency, I want you to paint a portrait of my family."

"Where will I work?"

"You will be given a room in the building for a couple of days."

"It may take longer."

"You will be allowed three at most." The officer opened another drawer, took out a photograph and placed it in front of Romano. He picked it up and then studied it. An attractive woman with long blonde hair and three girls also with blonde hair stood in a large landscaped garden. "That is my home in Dresden."

"A recent photograph?" Romano glanced at the officer.

"It was taken before the British and American bombers began their murderous indiscriminate attacks." The officer paused. "A quarter of the city is now in ruins," he said, staring into space. Seconds later, he looked at Romano. "I will have materials delivered to your quarters. If you require other items, then speak to the guard." The officer stood, went to the door and then opened it. "Guard."

A soldier entered, then escorted Romano to another part of the building. The soldier unbolted a door, then tilted his head. After Romano entered, the door was slammed shut and then bolted. Romano cast his gaze around his new temporary accommodation, which contained a single bed, metal closet and wooden table. He laid the photograph on the table, looked towards the bed and grinned. At least I'll get a proper sleep.

A short while later, Romano heard a key being inserted. When the door opened, the same soldier entered. Next to the photograph, he put materials on the table. Glaring at Romano, he barked. "Will these suffice?"

Romano approached the table and picked up a set of brushes. "Better quality would help."

"Use what is there." The brash soldier left and then locked the door behind him.

Romano replaced the brushes, then picked up the photograph and considered. German soldiers in occupied countries who would be concerned about their families back home. The twice-daily bombardment of German cities, food and medical shortages must play on soldier's minds. With continual setbacks, morale must be at an all-time low.

Following preparations, Romano started to paint. Whilst doing so, he let his mind wander and thought about life back in Italy. His mother, a widow from the First World War, had fallen out with Romano when he turned to crime. Francesca, Romano's older sister, until the start of the war in 1939 had kept in touch. Would she still live in Naples, safe and well? Also, had Romano's mother and sisters avoided being persecuted? The door being unlocked interrupted Roman's train of thought. A different soldier entered with a tray, laid it on the floor and departed. Romano put down his paintbrush, approached the tray and beamed.

After a bite to eat, Romano returned to his work and thoughts. How would the problems in Germany affect the officer's delectable wife and beautiful children? Perhaps he has had them relocated to the countryside? As Romano painted, once more the door was unlocked and this time the officer entered. With a brush in his hand, Romano stared. The officer approached his work and contemplated. "You said several days?"

Romano hesitated. "I could maybe manage it in two."

"Make it so," he said sharply.

Romano considered. One less day in a proper bed.

"Did you have your own studio in Italy?"

Romano shook his head.

"You worked for another artist?"

"For myself." Romano gave a faint smile. "I worked as a thief."

The officer raised his fair eyebrows.

"I robbed properties."

"When you have a talent such as this, why?"

"I mixed with the wrong type of people. I joined the army to atone for my past misdemeanours."

A smile flickered over the officer's face and he left the room. A guard followed, closed the door and locked it.

Next evening, Romano heard the key being turned again. He rose from his bed and waited. The officer entered, glanced at Romano and approached his work. Moments later, he turned to Romano. "Excellent. You can stay another day."

"Thank you, sir," said Romano gratefully.

As the contented officer returned his attention to the portrait, Romano took the opportunity to raise an important issue. "After I leave here, what will happen to me?"

"All Italian prisoners are being shipped to Athens."

"And then to Italy?"

The officer shook his head.

"Where, sir?"

"To Germany. New factories are being built and we need extra labour in order to complete them."

"Will I ever be allowed to return to Italy?"

"One day." The officer paused. "I have arranged that you will not be going to Poland and that is a blessing." The officer left and closed the door behind him.

Romano lay on the bed and once more, contemplated his future. When prisoners-of-war ended up in German factories, their fate had been sealed. Then, Romano looked at the door and thought for a moment. He got up, went over to it and listened. There is no night guard on duty. Romano turned the handle, pulled the door towards him and then closed it. Why had the officer not locked it and where was the guard?

A short while later, darkness fell and Romano made ready to escape. If caught, he could be shot. However, his imminent destination would be a fate worse than death. Opening the door, Romano popped his head out and looked down the dimly lit corridor. Being clear, he stepped out and closed the door. To escape, Romano would have to go down two flights of stairs and then get past guards at the main door. Reaching the stairs, he soft footed it down one flight and listened for any activity. Romano heard two soldiers in conversation at the ground level and stood still. After one moved off, Romano continued down the next flight. Before he reached the bottom, he could see a soldier on a chair with a newspaper in both hands. It would appear no officer had been assigned for duty this evening. Romano contemplated on how to get past him. Minutes later, the guard yawned. When it happened again, he lowered his newspaper and put it aside. As the guard started to snore, Romano with trepidation, moved down the stairs and then towards an exit door. When the soldier gave a loud abrupt snore, Romano stopped and held his breath. As dozing resumed, Romano made for the exit and slipped out. After he surveyed the vicinity for any Germans, Romano walked with quick strides towards the harbour. When a fishing boat's engine started, he dashed towards it. One of the crew spotted the escapee and helped him aboard. "You timed that well!"

Romano took a deep breath. "Where are you headed?"

"Somewhere safe."

Romano noticed a group of women and children huddled together near the cabin and looked at the crewmember. "They also had to flee the island," he said.

Unknown to islanders, the German High Command plotted to remove all Jewish residents of Rhodes to Poland. In the meantime, orders had been given for them to stay within the confines of Rhodes Town, or in the villages of Triamta, Kremasti and Paradisi.

On 18 July, a German officer accompanied by a squad of armed soldiers, arrived at the house of a prominent member of Rhodes Jewish community. The officer had received orders to gather all Jewish men over the age of 16 at the former Italian Air Force base. They had to report there the following morning with identity papers and a work permit. By doing this, they perceived that it meant being sent to a labour camp. When the men arrived at the base, their documents were taken from them and they ended up being herded into a basement. Next morning, women and children arrived, complete with belongings, as instructed. After valuables had been removed by force, families became reunited in a makeshift concentration camp. Unknown to them, German soldiers had plundered unoccupied properties and assets would be redistributed to the German High Command. Three days later, Jewish citizens would make their way to the port. Once there, they waited and no doubt contemplated their future. One family began to discuss what could happen next. "Where are we headed for, father?" asked Eli, the oldest son.

"I believe Athens," said Ezra.

"To work, mother?" asked Amos, the youngest son.

"We may get better accommodation," said Esther.

"Do you think so, mother?" asked Amos.

"It is possible."

Ezra looked at his wife, then loosened his tie. She gave a faint smile. "Too hot?"

As Ezra nodded, a boy arrived with a tray of sweets and went round the various groups of families. When he approached, Ezra stared at the tray. "How much for a small toffee?"

"Twenty Drachmas."

"What!" Ezra dipped into his jacket pocket and took out a bundle of coins. After a count, he looked at Eli. "Do you have five drachmas?"

"Hold on." Eli went into his pocket, took out a coin and gave it to his father.

Taking the coin, Ezra gave the boy twenty drachmas and then received a toffee. He pulled out a small knife and then cut the toffee into four pieces. As Esther watched, her husband handed a piece to each of his family. After a chew, Amos looked at his parents. "Will we get German, or Greek food on the boat?"

"I don't care. As long as it is substantial," said Esther, to the twelve-year old.

Fifteen-year-old Eli looked at his mother. "If I am sent to work in a German factory, how will I manage?" He glanced at his father. "I only speak our language."

His mother smiled. "You don't need to learn a language to repair furniture."

"I don't want to go back to school," said Amos. "I hate it."

"You have to learn about grammar, science and arithmetic," stated his father.

"Why can't I assist you to repair clothes, father?"

"Your mother and I want you to become a doctor and heal the sick. To do so you will have to attend school and then university."

Esther put a hand on her youngest son's arm. "Your father and I feel you have the ability," she said, smiling.

"You achieved top marks in your class," added his father.

Then, two German soldiers appeared and approached a man. After a short sharp discussion, they dragged him away through the startled crowd. As Eli turned to his father, a shrug of the shoulders followed.

"He must have stolen a sweet from the boy's tray," said Amos.

Eli looked at his parents. "What will happen to our house?"

"Upon our return, it will still be there," said his mother.

"When will that be, mother?" asked Amos.

"Hopefully, next year," said his father.

"I heard the British and American troops are near Paris," said Eli.

"And the Russian push towards Germany gathers momentum," said his father.

"I hope the war will end soon." Esther sighed.

Ezra put an arm around his wife. "It will and we can resume our lives." He grinned. "German troops are retreating on all fronts."

Esther gave a faint smile.

"And they failed to entice Turkey into the war," said Ezra.

A short while later, the families boarded three boats for an eight-day journey to Athens. Along the way, a hundred Jews from the island of Kos joined them. Due to a lack of food, water and overcrowded vessels, several people died on the horrendous voyage.

When the three boats docked at Athens, armed German soldiers with dogs that bared their teeth herded families towards the nearby railway siding and a waiting train.

"Where are we going, father?" asked Amos, as he stared at the train.

"I'm not sure." Ezra cast his gaze around the vicinity.

"Maybe Poland," said a grey-bearded man next to Ezra. He stared at the man. "Poland?"

The man nodded. "Work camps." He looked back over his shoulder, his eyes fixed on the mass. "There are many who couldn't lift a shovel."

His companion added, "After that journey, not many will be able." He coughed several times.

When a soldier walked up and down the line of people, an elderly man with a walking stick looked at him. "Can you tell us where we are going?"

"Get in line, or you will be beaten," the soldier cried.

When the soldier began to walk away, a man with white hair picked up a handful of dust. He spoke with a stammer. "Your Reich will soon be like this." The man let dust fall from his hand.

After the soldier took out a gun from his holster, an officer intervened. Surprised, the soldier looked at his superior, then replaced the gun and walked on. As the officer departed, another man in line commented, "He saved your life."

Whilst the white-haired man stayed silent, onlooker Amos pulled on his father's sleeve. He looked downwards. "What is wrong, Amos?"

"A soldier was about to shoot an old man and that officer stopped him." He pointed.

Ezra glanced behind. "He is an SS captain."

"I saw it as well," said Eli, as he looked at his younger brother.

Esther whispered to her husband, "Unusual behaviour for the SS."

Ezra nodded, then looked at her. "Are you okay?"

"Just tired."

"They treat us like cattle," said Ezra, as he sighed.

Esther stared at the train. "It is cattle trucks we are about to get on."

When each truck could take no more, a German soldier would slam the door shut and then lock it. Minutes later, a whistle blew, and the train departed. Several sick old men, who did not travel because they required medical treatment, received a bullet to the head.

As the train rolled along a single track, Eli peered out a small gap, then looked at his father who asked, "Can you see anything of interest?"

"Eli shook his head. "Barren wasteland, father."

Then, the drone of an aircraft became louder and Eli peered out. After it flew over the train, he turned to his father. "It's an American Mustang!"

"Why did it not fire at the engine?" asked a man who sat next to Ezra.

"It will be on a reconnaissance mission," said Ezra.

"Why do the Americans and British not prevent us from being persecuted?" Esther cast her gaze around the truck.

Despondent men and women stared at each other, or at the truck's wooden floor. Younger individuals remained silent comforted by their parents.

On the thirteen-day journey, a hundred men and women did not make it. A lack of sanitation, breathable air and infection ensured older people would suffer. When discovered at various stops, German guards threw dead bodies onto the side of the track.

When the train came to a halt, truck doors flew open to reveal a line of armed German soldiers. As the stale stench of air emerged from Ezra's truck, one soldier screwed up his face. Esther turned to her husband. "Now he is aware of what we have endured for many days."

As Ezra and his family left the train, welcome fresh air greeted them, plus an orchestra on a makeshift wooden stage which played a joyful tune.

"Where are we father?" asked Amos, as he cast his gaze around the wide-open area with five railway sidings.

"Auschwitz," said a railway worker who passed by.

A fellow traveller looked at Ezra. "Told you we were headed for Poland."

"With multiple railway lines, there must be many trains that terminate here." Ezra surveyed the setting.

The fellow traveller stared. "One of the lines leads straight to a building."

"Strange," added Ezra.

A stone-faced SS officer stood on a wooden box and then addresses the trains' occupants. "Men will line up in one row, women and children under fifteen in another."

Amos looked at Eli, then his father who gave a forced smile. "Do not worry, Amos, we will meet up later. Go with your mother."

As the orchestra played another melodic tune, two groups formed in the warm Polish sunshine. A different officer went down one line and tapped middle-aged men and the elderly on their shoulder. After they departed under guard, the officer looked at those who remained. "If you have a trade, raise your hand."

Those who did not meet the officer's quota were led away to join the older men. Then, a similar process took place with women.

Women not selected accompanied children away from the station. The chosen men and women did not suffer an imminent brutal fate, at least for a short time.

"Where do we go?" asked a curvaceous young woman to the officer.

"To a separate building."

She looked in the distance and shaded her eyes from the sun. "How far is it?"

"A twenty-minute stroll," said the officer.

"What about my son, he is only four and needs me."

"He is being taken care of and later you will be reunited."

As Ezra and Eli walked with other tradesmen to a building, they observed the older and infirm male contingent.

"Perhaps they are going to a place of care and rest," said Eli.

"Why is the building surrounded by barbed wire and a high fence?" asked Ezra, staring. "It's not as if they are capable of an escape attempt."

"What about Mother and Amos, father?"

"As soon as possible, I will try and find out their location."

"It is terrible that Amos had to witness that man and woman die in our truck."

Ezra remained silent, outraged at the squalid conditions he, his family and others had to endure to get here. He turned to Eli. "Maybe we can raise issues with someone."

"Cease talking," said a guard sharply.

Old weak men and women now faced a visit to a chamber for delousing. Men without a trade would be delegated to carry out laborious work in the nearby quarries and mines. Women would go on to suffer sexual misuse, sterilisation and experimentation, along with children.

Ezra and Eli entered a long narrow concrete building accompanied by a hundred other men. The guard instructed them on protocol and if anyone stepped out of line, they would be shot. After the guard slammed the door behind him, Eli looked at his father's long face. "Let us hope the Russians get here sooner rather than later."

Each of the new inhabitants made for an empty bunk and lay exhausted on it. Since they left Rhodes, it had been a long arduous two weeks.

Eli cast his gaze around the building. "Where are the men whose bunks are taken, father? There must be about two hundred."

"They will be doing their chores."

Ezra lay in his bunk for a while then got up and approached the solitary window. Concerned about Esther and Amos, he could not relax. In the distance, Ezra observed smoke which clouded the clear blue sky. As a fellow inhabitant joined him, Ezra turned round.

"What are they burning?" asked the man.

"Going by the amount of smoke, a great deal."

Ezra went outside to have a closer look and soon a guard approached with a large
Alsatian dog. "Get back to your quarters," he said, glaring. "Now!"

As the dog showed its teeth, Ezra retreated to the safety of his accommodation. He returned to his bunk and began to mull over his thoughts. There had been rumours of mass killings in this camp, but no one had any factual proof. If atrocities had occurred, the Americans and British governments would have intervened. Ezra closed his eyes and soon fell asleep.

Early morning, Ezra, Eli and the buildings' inhabitants were marched towards a lone railway siding near the camp where they joined others. One of the men looked at Ezra and joked. "Maybe we are going back to Athens."

"Keep quiet," said guard.

"Where are we going?" asked a young man.

"You will find out soon enough," said the guard sharply.

When the camp inmates reached a locomotive with trucks, they climbed on. Ezra contemplated. What lay in store? From the outside, a guard bolted all doors. A man observed uncertain expressions from the new arrivals. "This train is bound for a mine."

"A mine!" said Eli.

The man nodded. "Coal to power the camp and German industry."

"To make bombs and bullets," added another man.

"Just pretend to work," said Eli.

"Each group of workers has to achieve a target," said the man. "If not, punishment will follow."

"What type of punishment?" asked Ezra.

"Whippings and severe beatings."

"Is that why your face is bruised?" asked Ezra.

The man gave a slight nod. "You will work at least twelve hours each day, maybe more."

Ezra cast his gaze around the truck. "There are older men here who would struggle."

"If they can't keep pace, they are replaced."

"Do they not get lighter duties?" asked Eli.

The man shook his scarred bald head. "They are not seen again. You have much to learn about this camp." The man hung his head. "It is dreadful," he said gravely.

"Before coming here, what did you do?" asked Ezra.

The man hesitated. "A doctor."

Moments later, the train moved off and sped through the Polish countryside. Not long after, it stopped, and the doors were unbolted. As men piled out, armed guards with dogs ushered them towards their place of work.

In a cramped lift going down to the mine, Ezra observed faces of demoralised men who had suffered continuous hardship. How long would it take Eli and himself to wear the same expression? Ezra turned his thoughts to Esther and Amos. He had to discover their whereabouts and make contact.

The lift stopped, workers got out and armed guards directed them to their designated area. Whilst there, Ezra whispered to another worker, "When do we eat?"

"In six hours." He paused. "That is if the guards feel you have earned a meal."

"What if someone becomes ill?"

The man gave a faint smile. "Don't."

As work commenced, Ezra kept a close eye on Eli. His younger stronger body should cope with constant toil in dreary damp conditions. For those who tired, Ezra witnessed men receive a guard's whip. After an older man collapsed, he was dragged away. His replacement soon appeared and carried on the work. Coal production would remain intact, although at a cost to human life.

Whilst he worked alongside the replacement, Ezra discovered that he had fought against the Wehrmacht in Russia. Ezra whispered, "What is the latest on the eastern front?"

Soon, a guard appeared and Ezra distanced himself from the man. Gripping a whip, the guard approached Ezra with a stern expression. "What did you discuss?"

Ezra faced the guard. "I asked where he came from."

"Do not talk, you are here to work." The guard glared. "Is that understood?"

Ezra moved his head forward. "Yes."

"Resume your work.," said the guard, glaring.

After the guard strutted around the vicinity, Eli glanced at his father, who gave a faint smile.

After the shift ended, men headed for the lift, but several had to be assisted by their fellow workers. Because of strong late July sunshine, at the exit everyone put a hand above their eyes.

After he got on a truck, Ezra sat on the disjointed wooden floor and surveyed other workers. Little in the way of food and excessive labour would ensure a short life down the mine.

"What did the Russian say?" Eli sat down beside his father.

"The Red Army have taken back Belarus and most of the Baltic States."

"What about Poland?" asked a middle-aged man, as he took deep breaths.

"There is an uprising in Warsaw," said Ezra.

The man grinned. "The Polish resistance will give them hell."

"What of France?" asked another man with a relevant accent.

"The British and Americans are at the gates of Paris."

The man gave a sigh of relief. Apart from those who rested through extreme tiredness, Ezra now had the ears of everyone else in the truck.

"The Russian spoke about a new German fighter that is too fast for the Spitfire."

"How can that be?" asked another man in amazement.

"The Russian said it had a jet engine."

"It will be similar to the V2," said the Frenchman.

"What is that?" asked Eli.

"A flying bomb, a guided missile."

"No pilot!" said Ezra, staring.

The Frenchman nodded. "One went out of control and landed close to our village. Before we could retrieve it, the Germans arrived."

"If the Germans have a jet fighter, then it will shoot the allies out of the sky." stated Ezra.

"There is only one squadron," said a middle-aged man. "Before being sent here, I worked on the propulsion system." He cast his gaze around those who listened. "The Germans do not have enough resources to mass produce this fighter."

"How many do they have?" asked another man of similar age.

"Around twenty-five." The man grinned. "They have limited spare parts, so if one is shot down, it cannot be replaced."

Another man spoke, "My two brothers were part of the workforce who built a special factory for those jets."

"Special?" Ezra stared.

"It is underground."

"To prevent it from being bombed," said Eli.

The man nodded. Ezra cast his gaze around the truck. "Then for all our sakes, let us hope these German jets are somehow put out of action."

Everyone, who could, nodded.

Three days later and after another tiresome shift, Ezra lay in his bunk. Eli entered the building and approached his father with a glow. "Father, mother and Amos are safe."

Ezra got up. "Where are they?"

"In another block for women and boys."

"Amos is not a boy."

"He is now."

Ezra gave a slight smile. "Tell me more."

"They are at work on a farm. It is about a mile from here."

"Have you spoken to them?"

Eli shook his head. "A man who passed outside told me."

"Do you know his name?"

"Simon."

"I would like to speak with this person."

"I also learned that an attempt has been made to kill Hitler. It is true, father."

"With Germany in retreat on all fronts, it is not a surprise."

"Could the war be about to end and we can go home!"

"Time will tell, Eli." Ezra glanced at the window.

"More people arrived today."

"More people arrive every day."

"There must be other blocks to house them, they arrive in their hundreds."

Ezra deliberated. "Where is this Simon located?"

"Building E."

"I will go when it is dark."

"What if you are spotted?"

"The guards have a break just before eleven o'clock."

When darkness fell, Ezra made his way to building E. Looking around the vicinity, he knocked on the door. A lean middle-aged man answered.

"Can I speak with Simon?"

The man hesitated. "What about?"

"He spoke to my son, Eli, about my wife and younger son."

"You better come inside," he said, opening the door.

Ezra entered and observed a man younger than himself, but with less weight. He approached Ezra and held out his hand. After Ezra shook it, the man gave a faint smile. "Have a seat."

Before Ezra sat down, he glanced around the interior. "Where are the rest of the inhabitants?"

"They are with others, or dead. The empty bunks will be filled by tomorrow evening with new arrivals."

Ezra remained silent.

"You appear puzzled?"

"With others?"

"There is a particular place where men and women can socialise in the evening for a couple of hours."

"The Germans allow this!"

Simon nodded. "It is good for our morale. They feel it will aid us to work harder."

"Who attends?"

"It is by invitation, a rota."

"You mentioned people have died. In the mines?"

Simon glanced at the other man. "Gas chambers." He paused. "Have you not seen the smoke?"

"They are murdering our people!"

"As well as Russian prisoners, Slavs and gypsies."

Ezra hesitated. "How can you be calm and talk of this?"

Simon sighed. "The Germans are losing the war and until the camp is liberated, we can only do our best to survive."

"After the war, Germany will be held accountable for what has happened here," said the other man.

"As well as other camps," added Simon.

"Others!" said Ezra.

"There are another five camps."

"You look stunned," said the other man. "You did not know?"

Ezra shook his head.

"Come tomorrow evening at the same time and if there is any news about your wife and son, I will tell you."

Ezra got up. "Thank you," he said gratefully.

Simon accompanied him to the door, opened it and then looked outside. "See you tomorrow."

After Ezra departed, Simon closed the door. Looking at the other man, he shook his grey head of hair.

"Just as well you didn't mention the medical experiments and the whore houses."

"He's had enough trauma for one evening."

A short time later, a man with a wide grin entered and approached Simon. He took a couple of deep breaths.

"What is it, Yorgi?"

"The best news yet."

"Go on."

"Hitler is dead." A grin crept across Yorgi's scarred face.

Simon hesitated. "Who told you?"

"I overheard two guards."

Whilst they walked to the train, Ezra and Eli along with their fellow workers, had glum expressions. As Hitler had survived an assassination attempt, the celebration of his death had been short-lived. The struggle for each inhabitant of the camp to survive would continue. Even after only a week down the mine, Ezra had witnessed many deaths through severe beatings and exhaustion. Food and water shortages, plus long laborious hours without a break added to high casualty rates. Also, due to a lack of medical supplies, if a worker received an injury, treatment did not follow.

On the train, Ezra thought about Esther and Amos. He had tried to contact them, but his attempts proved fruitless. However, Eli being close at hand helped Ezra to remain sane.

Just as the shift began, Ezra noticed a high-ranking German officer in discussion with two subordinates. Eli whispered to his father, "Do you know who that is?"

Ezra made a discreet stare.

"It's the Armaments Minister."

"Why is he down in the mine?"

"Maybe ways to increase productivity."

A nearby worker groaned.

"Continue to dig," said Ezra. "They are headed this way."

Moments later, the Armaments Minister cast his gaze around the immediate area,

then approached Ezra. "Excuse me," he said politely.

Ezra rested his shovel, turned round and wiped his brow. "Yes?"

"I want you to answer me with honesty."

Ezra drew breath. "I will."

"Are you being fed in a sufficient manner? Do not be afraid to answer." The Minister glanced at his two subordinates. "No harm will come to you."

"The portions are insufficient, sir."

The Minister looked at Ezra's bare arm. "Does that gash hurt?"

When Ezra nodded, the Minister turned to one if his subordinates. "See that this man and any other with an injury receive urgent medical attention. Also, rations are to be increased."

After the three departed, a guard appeared and led Ezra to a room. After being attended to, he resumed his place of work. Eli whispered to his father, "A German who cares."

A fellow worker whispered, "It will be back to normal tomorrow."

"On with your work," shouted a guard, glaring.

Resuming his work, Ezra mulled his thoughts. For his family's sake, he had to survive and pray that the camp be liberated as soon as possible. With Russian, American and British troops on the move towards Germany, perhaps the nightmare will end soon and the family can be reunited. A guard walked towards Ezra and glared. "To get your extra rations, you will have to earn them."

CHAPTER 12

TURMOIL

With a small glass of wine clasped in their hands, Georgina and Elena sat in the kitchen. Four years of war had not only taken its toll on the island's landscape, but also on food and drink supplies. Whatever Crete produced, the Germans took and Cretans shared the scraps. The occupiers even had the island's police force doing work on their behalf. This angered the population and regular skirmishes with police officers occurred in small towns and main cities. Threats of retribution would be directed towards officers and no doubt played on their minds. However, as long as the German High Command controlled Crete, police officials had to abide by the surrender terms from 1941. To do otherwise, would result in officers being executed. Rather than be in conflict with their own people, some chose to join the resistance. Ironically, they ended up in conflict with former colleagues.

"How long must we endure?" Elena took a sip.

"With the attempt on Hitler's life, the Germans are also in turmoil," said Georgina, as she finished her wine and laid her glass on the table.

Elena looked towards the door. "Who can that be?"

"I'll get it." Georgina went to the rear door, then opened it. A police officer stood with a slight smile. "Is Elena at home?" He removed his hat.

"Faustus!" said Elena, as she approached the door.

"Good evening, Elena. I was on duty nearby, hope you don't mind."

"Come in," said Elena, smiling.

Elena glanced at Georgina. "This is an old friend, we studied together in Athens."

Faustus entered. "I cannot stay for long." He glanced at Georgina.

"Are you off duty?" Elena closed the door.

Faustus checked his watch. "Not yet."

"I am unable to offer you anything, we are on severe rations."

Faustus brought out a small jar of coffee from his jacket pocket. "It is not much, please accept this."

Elena raised her dark eyebrows and took it. "Thank you," she said gratefully.

"You don't by any chance have a bottle of wine as well?" asked Georgina.

Faustus gave a faint smile. "Sorry."

"When on patrol, it must be dangerous," said Elena.

"I have had a few scares." Faustus sighed. "As with all my colleagues."

"Why work for the Germans?" asked Georgina.

Faustus tilted his head. "It is my job and I need the money to feed my wife and two daughters."

"How is the war going for Germany? It can't be good," said Elena.

"From what I have heard, not good. They have retreated on all fronts."

"We heard about the attempt to kill Hitler," said Georgina.

Faustus smiled. "As me and my colleagues did with delight."

Both women laughed.

"I believe the Germans may soon leave Crete."

"When?" asked Elena.

"I am not certain. However, when they do, Crete may have another conflict."

"Both resistance movements," said Elena.

Once more, Faustus checked his watch. "I must go."

"Thanks for the coffee. Wine next time?" asked Georgina, as she smiled.

After he gave Georgina an extended look, Elena's guest departed. The two friends had a welcome cup of Greek coffee. Georgina set down her cup. "With the resistance in close proximity, he's lucky to still be alive."

"He appeared to recognise you."

"We've never met."

"Faustus is Greek for lucky."

"We may get our wine after all."

Elena laughed.

Several days later, Georgina headed for a small taverna outside Heraklion. She and her German officer friend, Erich, had arranged to meet there. As Georgina entered, Erich stood and welcomed her. "How was Athens?" she asked.

"Intimidating."

"You look normal without a uniform," said Georgina, as she gave a slight smile.

"I feel normal without a uniform."

Georgina laughed, and after the couple sat in a concealed area, a woman appeared with a bottle of wine and two glasses. As she left, Erich poured and Georgina cast her gaze around the establishment.

"Do not worry, no one will know you are here."

"It's deserted."

"That is why I asked you to come here."

Georgina picked up her glass, took a sip and then a large swallow. "Decent wine at last!" She turned to Erich. "What about the proprietor?"

"I have arranged for his family to receive several boxes of food."

"In return for his silence?"

"And the odd bottle of wine." Erich lifted his glass and took a swig.

"How much longer can you supply locals with food?"

"The next load may be the last. Given Germany's current situation, it will not surprise me if Berlin reduces supplies to us."

As Georgina finished her glass, Erich poured her another, then filled his. After a couple of sips, he set his glass on the circular oak table. "Some villages are going to be attacked and destroyed."

Georgina stared. "Which ones?"

"At this moment, I am unsure."

"Have the Germans not done enough damage?" Georgina sighed.

"It is a reprisal for an SS Major being murdered by the resistance."

"Did he not deserve his fate?"

"The High Command see otherwise and look for any excuse. I will try and find out where the attacks will take place and let you know as soon as possible."

"There have been too many atrocities on the island," said Georgina, staring.

Erich remained silent, sipping his wine. Georgina knew him well enough to perceive something was on his mind. "What's wrong, Erich."

"You do not want to know." He took a swig.

Georgina touched his arm. "You can tell me."

Erich hesitated. "When in Athens, I learned of preparations for all Jewish citizens to be sent to Poland."

"For resettlement?"

Erich shook his head.

"Then what?"

"Sent to a camp where they are given hard labour and also murdered. The most able would be used for work detail, but the rest would not be seen again," Erich said gravely.

"Shot?"

"No."

Georgina put down her glass. "I have heard rumours of people being gassed." She paused. "Is it true?"

Erich nodded, then finished his drink. "I would never have believed German soldiers could undertake such brutal acts."

Moments later, the proprietor approached Erich, who shook his head. He then looked at Georgina, who did likewise. After the proprietor departed, Georgina looked at Erich. "A few nights ago, a police officer came to the house."

"For what reason?"

"To see Elena, they are old friends." Georgina paused. "He appeared to recognise me."

"Maybe he has seen you in Heraklion."

Georgina lifted her glass.

"Suspicious?"

Georgina nodded. "I don't want you to get found out." She took a large swallow.

"What is his name?"

"Faustus, black hair and moustache. He's similar to you in height and build, but younger."

"How much younger?"

"He's in his mid-thirties."

"But not a captain," said Erich, as gave a slight smile. "I will investigate."

Georgina finished her drink. "I better get back, Elena will be concerned."

"I will take you home part of the way."

"Do any colleagues enquire where you go?"

"Their thoughts are on other issues." Erich paused. "They are concerned about the future. I give us six months."

Major Neuberger, Captain Hoeness and a Waffen SS officer sat round a table in their Heraklion headquarters. Since General Muller's abduction, Major Neuberger had taken command of German forces in Crete. With the Wehrmacht in full retreat from all fronts, SS troops became prominent to bolster morale. Enemies of the Third Reich due to their brutal methods had been feared throughout the war. Indeed, SS troops believed they were on a crusade to rid the world of anyone who did not fit into German culture. It was no secret in Nazi circles that Himmler had the ear of Hitler himself. Radical reforms since the start of the war meant radical measures and the SS duly obliged. Following a long discussion, the three men stopped for coffee. Major Neuberger sat back on his leather chair, then looked at the younger blond-haired SS officer. "What news from the eastern front."

"More troops are needed." The SS officer glanced at Captain Hoeness.

"The Russians now have air superiority, therefore, we have to increase production of our new jet fighters." He leaned back. "When that is done, they will smash the Russians out of the sky and our army can regroup."

"Why is production being held up?" asked Major Neuberger.

"Constant attacks by the British and American bombers."

"Do we not have an underground factory for this purpose?"

"There is also a shortage of oil."

"If the Russians take Rumania, then our main source is gone," remarked Captain Hoeness.

"We will ensure they do not," stated the SS officer, with an arrogance that befitted his rank and status. "The Russians will be crushed."

Major Neuberger picked up a printed sheet of paper. "Is it true that the resistance is about to take Athens?"

The SS officer shook his head. "We control the city."

Captain Hoeness stared at the SS officer. "Our source has told us otherwise."

The officer stared back at Captain Hoeness. "And who is this source?"

"That is confidential," said Major Neuberger. "This person also revealed that a meeting has been held by prominent Cretans with regard to the current situation."

The SS officer frowned. "Situation?"

"Mass killings in the villages by your men," said Captain Hoeness.

The SS officer turned to face him. "If they shelter and protect members of the resistance, killings will continue," he said sharply.

"You mean atrocities," said Captain Hoeness. "Why murder women and children?" He glanced at Major Neuberger. "Our army will suffer reprisals."

"Come now, Captain," said the SS officer, grinning. "Are you afraid of the natives?"

"On another matter, our source mentioned the British are about to land in Crete," said Major Neuberger."

"We will deal with them in the usual manner."

"They will have heavy armoury," said Captain Hoeness. "We do not."

"Members of the SS can handle any enemy of the Reich," said the SS officer, as he stared at both his colleagues.

"What about the Russians, they are about to enter Hungary," said Captain Hoeness.

The SS officer moved his head forward. "You strike me as a defeatist, Captain." He paused. "Are you?"

"Not a defeatist, a realist."

"Gentlemen, let us stick to our agenda," said Major Neuberger.

As the SS officer sat back on his chair, Major Neuberger looked towards him and revealed that killings would cease immediately. He turned to Captain Hoeness. "Prisoners of war on Crete are to be set free."

"But they will take up arms against us," remarked the SS officer.

"I am aware of that, however, those are my orders."

The SS officer stared in disbelief at Major Neuberger. He glanced at both men. "That is all for now."

Stone-faced, the SS officer got up and left the room. Captain Hoeness gave a wry smile to his colleague. "He did not appear pleased."

"We now have to think of the future, only the SS believe we can be victorious."

"There will be recriminations about our conduct."

"Hopefully, the SS will bear the brunt," said Major Neuberger, as he leaned back on his chair.

"How far are the Russians from the Oder?"

"I believe they will reach it within the next few weeks," he said gravely.

"And Poland?"

"We will soon have to withdraw." Major Neuberger could see the anguish in his fellow officer's face. "You have family who stay near Leipzig?"

Captain Hoeness nodded. "My mother."

"She should head west."

Due to consistent defeats on both fronts, the once-formidable army of the Reich had started to crumble. Hard- liners such as Major Neuberger now altered their stance towards the Cretan public. However, they would still expect severe punishment for all German soldiers and officers.

Alex Taylor, John Murdoch and Vic Stampson rested in their latest temporary mountain hideaway. Since SS troops had discovered their previous location, they had to make a quick exit. Manilos had found them a safe refuge, at least for the time being. John Murdoch cast his gaze around the room. "The previous one had sanitation."

"It won't be for long," said Vic Stampson.

"A landing is due in three days by the Royal Navy," added Alec Taylor. "We'll get decent food at last."

"Any food will suffice," said John Murdoch.

Alec Taylor grinned, then rubbed his ginger beard. "And some razor blades."

"The resistance has performed heroics to push the Germans out of mainland Greece," said Vic Stampson.

"Only Crete remains to be freed," said John Murdoch.

Alec Taylor sat back and rested against a concrete wall. "It's after the war I'm worried about. With the Germans gone, the resistance won't have an enemy to fight."

"Only one movement can be the dominant force on the island," said

Vic Stampson.

"And with their own ideology," said Alec Taylor.

"At least Turkey didn't enter the conflict," said John Murdoch. "That would have prolonged the situation."

Vic Stampson got to his feet, put a finger against his mouth, then walked to the door. He opened it and then grabbed a short dark bearded man. "Explain yourself," he said sharply.

"I do not know what you mean." The man stammered.

"Don't lie, you have been listening to our conversation," said Vic Stampson, as he glared at the man.

"I haven't, I'm not lying, he cried.

"Then why stand behind the door?" asked Alec Taylor.

"I was about to knock." Once more, the man stammered.

"Why have you come here?" asked John Murdoch.

The man went into his trouser pocket, took out a note and gave it to Alec Taylor, who read it. "Okay, you can go." He glanced at the man.

After he left, Alec Taylor watched him make his way down a hilly path. Closing the door, he looked at his two colleagues. "The resistance has control of the airports and the German supply route has now been cut off."

"Anything else in the note?" asked Vic Stampson.

"All Cretan prisoners have been freed from camps and the Germans have fallen back to Chania. And Manilos wants to meet with us."

"All goes well," said John Murdoch, as he smiled.

Vic Stampson nodded. "The beginning of the end."

A short time later, the agents headed to Manilos's place of refuge for the meeting. As they emerged from trees and bushes, a squad of SS troops confronted them. The agents stood and stared. Vic Stampson moved a hand towards a side pocket of his coat.

"Do not think about it," said an officer.

"What do you want with us?" asked John Murdoch.

"You are enemy agents and as spies you will be shot." The officer pointed his gun.

"You've got the wrong people," said Alec Taylor.

SS troops aimed their rifles at the three men. Out of nowhere, a group of men opened fire. After the last SS soldier fell, one of the men grinned. "Timing is everything."

"Who are you?" John Murdoch asked.

"We are from a local village and on our way to join up with Manilos."

"Where did you get rifles from?"

"We have a contact," said the man, as a grin crept across his face.

"Just as well," added Vic Stampson.

As the agents and seven villagers traversed through rugged terrain to Manilos's location, they chatted. The villagers revealed their experiences of horrific activities by SS troops.

"Then you had no hesitation in killing that squad," said Alec Taylor.

One villager nodded. "That is why we want to join Manilos."

"We will take revenge for what the SS did," said another. "The Germans are on the run and have retreated to Chania."

"So, we heard," said John Murdoch.

One of the villagers adjusted his black woollen hat. "That is where we will finish them." He looked at the agents. "Where are your rifles?"

John Murdoch pulled out a revolver from his coat pocket, then replaced it. "A representative of the communist resistance is due to meet with Manilos tonight."

The villagers looked at each other. To alleviate any concerns, John Murdoch gave a slight smile. "To join forces."

"The more the better," added Alec Taylor.

The villagers remained silent. Although both movements would be more formidable, deep divisions existed between the two movements.

As the party approached Manilos's hideaway, one of his lookouts entered the small building. "The British agents are here with a group of men."

Manilos frowned. "A group of men?"

"Villagers."

The lookout followed Manilos out of the building and both men looked down the hilly pathway.

"Perhaps it is the communists," said the lookout.

Manilos shook his head. "It's not them."

Moving towards the hideaway, Alec Taylor glanced at Vic Stampson and Alec Taylor. "Our guest has come to welcome us."

"He'll be unsure of who our companions are," said Alec Taylor.

John Murdoch cast his gaze around the vicinity. "No doubt the reason why several of his men have appeared with rifles."

The agents and villagers approached a stone-faced guard, who stood in front of Manilos. John Murdoch took a deep breath and then glanced over his shoulder. "These men have come to join you."

Manilos surveyed the group. "Can you kill Germans?"

One stepped forward and glanced behind. "Give us the chance and we'll prove it."

Manilos hugged him and then looked at the others. "Come inside and have a drink," he said cheerily.

Whilst the villagers mingled with resistance members, the agents accompanied Manilos into a room. "Take a seat, gentlemen." Manilos went to a cupboard, opened it and took out a bottle of ouzo. After he poured four drinks, handed each of the agents a full glass. "A toast to the eventual defeat of Germany." He grinned. "It will not be long now."

As each glass of ouzo was thrown back, the host refilled them and then sat opposite his guests. John Murdoch looked at a clock.

"Yes, Janouski is late," said Manilos. "Not a good way to start a collaboration." Manilos pulled on his grey beard. "He has the correct directions?"

"Yes," said John Murdoch.

"Maybe they have run into a German patrol," said Vic Stampson, as he looked at his two fellow agents.

"They can kill each other," said Manilos. "They will be doing Crete a favour."

The three agents glanced at each other in the knowledge that this would be an uneasy alliance. Then, a resistance member entered the room and went up to Manilos. "Boss, there are about a dozen men headed up the pathway."

Manilos finished his drink. "About time."

John Murdoch stood. "I'll meet Janouski and then bring him here."

After he left the room, Manilos nodded to the man, who then followed John Murdoch. Manilos filled a glass then set it on a table. When voices grew louder, John Murdoch entered, accompanied by a tall grey bearded individual who wore a stern expression. The scar on his left cheek added to a persona that would intimidate. John Murdoch stood between the two leaders, like a referee with two boxers ready to do battle. Turning to Manilos, he introduced Janouski. The two leaders squared up to each other, then Manilos grinned. "Let us drink." He handed Janouski a full glass. "To rid Crete of the Germans."

Aye!" said Janouski. He drank the ouzo, then handed the empty glass to Manilos.

As he refilled it, the three agents looked on and hoped that this would herald the start of a successful collaboration to end German occupation of the island. Manilos and Janouski sat down at a table, followed by the agents.

After a frank discussion, the two leaders stood and shook hands. Janouski looked at the agents. "We shall meet next week to discuss the guns and ammunition promised."

John Murdoch got up. "As soon as the shipment arrives, I'll be in touch."

"The sooner, the better." Janouski stared at Manilos. "We'll kick those Germans backsides so hard they'll never want to wage war on Crete again."

Manilos nodded his approval and then Janouski left the room, rejoined his men outside and they wandered down the hill. The agents sat and chatted to Manilos with relieved voices.

"He appears a good sort," said Vic Stampson.

Manilos grinned. "As did Mussolini and Hitler until they gained power." He paused. "The German people will by now have changed their viewpoint."

"Don't worry," said John Murdoch, "we won't give them too many arms, just enough for the battle."

"Before you go, let us have another drink." Manilos reached for the half-empty bottle and poured three glasses. "I am almost out of this precious commodity."

"We'll get you a supply," said John Murdoch.

"Ouzo is as important as bullets," said Manilos. "It raises the spirits."

The agents laughed and stayed for another glass. After a few more, they left.

Manilos turned to one of his men who entered. "Did you get any information from the communists?"

"No, boss, they revealed nothing."

"Similar to their leader." Manilos considered. "He talks a lot, but that is all."

"His men have new rifles."

"I will find out who the supplier is, but it could be the Russians." Manilos shook his head. "Janouski has the cheek to ask Britain for arms."

"Will the British give them guns?"

Manilos nodded. "The priority is to free Crete of Germans."

"And then?"

Manilos gave a wry smile.

After a less than ample portion of fish for dinner, Elena sat back and looked at Georgina, whose glass of water did not come close to be a substitute for wine. Elena stared at her plate. "It is just as well we enjoy fish."

Georgina set down her glass. "But for how long." She sighed. "Oh, for a large juicy steak, medium rare."

"Do you miss America?"

Georgina leaned back. "There would be no war-torn cities or food shortages."

"Do not forget the wine."

Georgina laughed, then looked at the clock.

"Did you plan to meet Erich, tonight?"

Georgina nodded. "It could be our last."

"Since Chania fell to the resistance and British, Heraklion is their last line of defence. I hope the conflict will end soon. Everyone has suffered and most are scarred for life," said Elena gravely.

"War with the Germans will end, but what about after they've gone?"

"Diplomacy will prevail between the two resistance movements."

"Let's hope so." Georgina glanced at the clock and got up. "I won't be long."

"Are you sure it is safe to venture out?"

"New York in 1929 was more dangerous," said Georgina with a slight smile. She went into the bedroom and made ready. After leaving, Elena watched her friend walk along the deserted dark street.

A brisk walk later, Georgina reached the taverna where she and Erich had agreed to meet. When she entered, the proprietor welcomed her with a warm smile. "Good to see you again." He wiped the wooden bar top.

"Did you get a supply of food?" Georgina took a seat at a nearby table.

"Enough to feed my family." The proprietor sighed. "Desperate times."

"You have some wine?"

"Only a single case left."

"I only require one," said Georgina, as she smiled.

The proprietor laughed, opened a bottle and then poured a glass. Leaving the counter, he laid the full glass in front of Georgina. As she took a sip, the door opened and a police officer entered. Georgina set her glass down and stared at the officer.

"Why are you here? There is a curfew," said the officer sharply, as he looked at Georgina, then the proprietor.

"I am about to close," said the proprietor, wary of the officer.

"Then why does this woman have a full glass?" The officer glanced at Georgina.

"She is a slow drinker."

The officer glared. "Do not mess with me, I can close you down."

At that moment, a person entered the bar and its three occupants turned round and stared. "What is going on?"

"They have broken the curfew, sir."

"I will deal with this."

The police officer glanced at Georgina and the proprietor, then departed. After the German officer closed the door, he took off his cap. "I do not know who is worse, them or the SS."

Georgina laughed and the proprietor grinned. "A schnapps?" The proprietor put an empty glass on the counter. Erich nodded, and sat down beside Georgina. She kissed him. "You came just in time."

The proprietor brought over a full glass and set it in front of Erich, who looked up. "Thanks."

"Why are you in uniform and what if that police officer tells someone?"

"I found out that the police had orders to patrol this sector. If asked, I will say that I wanted to investigate the establishment," said Erich, as he took a sip of his drink.

"Why this sector?"

"A tip-off that two members of the resistance had been seen."

"Who would reveal their whereabouts?"

"I believe a local woman, but do not know her identity."

"A collaborator!" The proprietor stared.

Erich set his drink down. "I will try and find out." He looked at the proprietor, shaking his head. "Cretan citizens should not betray their countrymen." The proprietor approached and topped up Erich's glass. "What news from the east?"

Erich lifted his glass. "The Russians will soon be at our border," he said gravely.

Georgina touched Erich's hand. "Be glad you're in Crete."

"Not really, Georgina. After the atrocities that have been committed, revenge will no doubt follow." Erich went on. "It is only a matter of time until we run out of food and ammunition. We no longer control the airfields, or seaports." Erich finished his drink.

"Your troops still occupy Heraklion's airfield, do they not?" asked the proprietor.

"Not enough supplies are being flown in."

"Why is that?" asked Georgina.

"No spare fuel for the planes."

"Because you have lost the oil fields in Rumania?" asked the proprietor.

Erich nodded. "Our main source." He paused. "Forces in Crete can be supplied from Austria, but Berlin will see it as not worthwhile."

After Georgina finished her drink, Erich held her hand. "It is going to be difficult for us to meet again."

"Let's wait and see."

Erich gave a forced smile. The proprietor came over and then filled Georgina and Erich's glasses. He returned to the bar, poured himself an ouzo, then proposed a toast. "To the end of hostilities and a peaceful Crete."

All three emptied their glasses. Erich and Georgina said farewell to the proprietor and then left the taverna. As they stood outside, distant gunfire broke the evening silence. Erich sighed. "It is a firing squad."

"Resistance fighters?"

Erich nodded, then looked at Georgina. "I will walk you home."

"I'll be fine."

"Are you sure?"

Georgina nodded, then kissed Erich. "See you here a week from now at the same time."

"Goodnight." He hugged her.

Making her way through dark dingy streets, Georgina soon arrived home. As she entered, two men stood beside Elena with grim expressions. Elena glanced at them. "They are resistance, Georgina, and believe you are a spy."

Georgina removed her black beret, then stared at them. One spoke sharply, "Why have you been seeing a German officer?"

"I've tried to find out information which could assist you."
"There, I told you," said Elena, as she looked at both men.
"What have you found out?" asked the other man."
"The Germans no longer control the seaports around Crete. Also, Heraklion is the only airfield they can use."
"We are aware of that."
"That is my up-to-date information."
"When will you next see the officer?"
"I'm not sure. He wouldn't commit to a specific date."
"When you do, we require information on reinforcements and when supplies will be flown into Heraklion."
After the two men left, Georgina took off dark her dark coat and stared at Elena. "Me, a spy!"
"Someone must have spotted you with Erich."
"He isn't a Nazi."
"To the resistance, they all are. You are a foreigner, therefore, under suspicion."
Georgina considered. Maybe they think I'm the woman collaborator Erich mentioned.
"Are you okay?"
Georgina nodded.
"The resistance will now monitor you, so be careful."
Once more, Georgina nodded. That lets the collaborator off the hook, whoever she is.

On a dull Monday morning, Major Neuberger met with Captain Hoeness in his office. The two resistance movements had kicked the Germans out of Chania and with ammunition and food scarce, the German situation in Crete had become desperate.
"How long do we have?" asked Captain Hoenesss.
"Days." Major Neuberger sighed.
"Does Berlin know the full extent?"
"Yes, however, they have more urgent matters to contend with."
"I believe the city is being bombed on a regular basis."
Major Neuberger stared out the window. "The Red Army are on the outskirts ready to launch their offensive." He turned to Captain Hoeness. "We will have to plan for a surrender of the island."
"Right away?"
"In a few days."
"To the British?"
Major Neuberger nodded. "Otherwise, the resistance will slaughter us." He considered. "Who is worse, the Russians, or the Cretans?"
"We will soon find out."

As Major Neuberger gave a forced smile, Captain Hoeness got up. "I will contact the British."

Major Neuberger lifted his black telephone. "When I inform Berlin, there will no doubt be an order to stand firm and not to surrender."

"Fight to the last man."

"What if he had been killed last July? Our men would not be in the position that they have to catch fish to survive." Major Neuberger continued, "Now with all the fruit produce and meat stock finished."

After Captain Hoeness left the room, Major Neuberger opened a drawer and took out a gun. Staring at it, he contemplated his future.

CHAPTER 13

SURRENDER

After the Germans ammunition ran out, they had no choice but to lay down their arms. Due to withdrawals from strategic bases in the Mediterranean and lack of fuel, soldiers on Crete had been left to fend for themselves. Two years earlier in Stalingrad, a similar situation had existed, which resulted in the largest number of German soldiers to surrender. The numbers on Crete did not compare, but Berlin would view it as a humiliation. However, with Cretans eager to get revenge for four years of atrocities committed by German soldiers, being humiliated would be the least of their worries. General Harry Hainsworth and John Murdoch met with Major Neuberger at British Headquarters in Heraklion, which used to be inhabited by the Germans.

"Major Neuberger, we have a problem," said General Hainsworth, as he leaned back on his chair. "We haven't got a camp large enough to hold all German prisoners."

"But there are a number of camps scattered around the island," replied Major Neuberger. "We imprisoned many Cretans in them."

"The problem is, Major," said John Murdoch, "we don't have the manpower to run those camps."

"Do not have the manpower!"

"I'm afraid that is the position we find ourselves in."

"We could ask the Cretan resistance to help, but that would be unwise," said General Hainsworth.

"They would kill us."

John Murdoch gave a faint smile. "Our view, also."

Major Neuberger looked at General Hainsworth. "My men have to be protected. The Geneva Convention is clear on that issue."

John Murdoch stared. "You didn't adhere to the Geneva Convention when your men committed village massacres," he said sharply.

"I did not command any squad to carry out atrocities, the SS make up their own rules."

John Murdoch glanced at General Hainsworth, knowing how the British Government viewed SS activity, not only in Crete, but elsewhere. "Nevertheless, Major, atrocities are attributed to soldiers of the Wehrmacht," stated General Hainsworth.

Major Neuberger sighed. "General, we no longer have an army," he said gravely.

At that moment, a member of staff entered the office with a tray and three cups of coffee. After he left, Major Neuberger lifted his cup, took a drink, then another. He looked at John Murdoch. "We ran out of coffee, sixteen days ago."

Once more, John Murdoch glanced at General Hainsworth. The General lifted his cup. "As for your men, we will have to come up with some sort of a solution."

John Murdoch looked at General Hainsworth. "And fast, sir." He lifted his cup and took a sip.

General Hainsworth nodded, then drank his coffee. Setting his cup on the tray, he looked at General Neuberger. "We'll get back to you."

"When, General? A solution has to be found now."

John Murdoch finished his coffee, then set his empty cup down. "Your army, or what is left of it, will have to vacate their barracks."

"Soon?"

John Murdoch nodded. "The government want you out of the buildings and properties that officers and men took over in 1941."

"We are being taunted and shouted at by those who gather outside our locations."

"Major, be thankful it is not bullets directed at you," quipped John Murdoch.

"Can you put on extra guards?" Major Neuberger glanced at both men.

General Hainsworth stood. "I'll see what I can do."

Major Neuberger got up. "Thank you."

"I'll see you out, Major," said John Murdoch, as he stood.

Minutes later, he returned and sat down opposite General Hainsworth, who lit his pipe and leaned back.

"I wouldn't want to be a German on Crete, sir."

"Self-inflicted, John, it's their own doing." He puffed.

"Where can we put them until they are shipped back to Germany?"

"No point in them being sent back yet, the country is a pile of rubble, especially Berlin." Once more, the General puffed on his pipe. "The Red

Army are pounding it with heavy guns."

"And more, from what I hear."

"Women will no doubt suffer, young and old."

"Red Army soldiers will extract revenge for German atrocities in their country, and the same will happen here."

"I don't blame them."

As darkness fell, Georgina walked with caution through the subdued Heraklion streets. Erich had managed to contact her amidst upheaval within the Wehrmacht.

After Georgina entered the taverna, she observed Erich with two drinks on the table. Sitting down, Georgina kissed him and then lifted her glass. "Why the urgency?" She took a welcome sip.

"The British have ordered us to head for a camp on the outskirts."

"Heraklion?"

Erich nodded.

"There is no camp there."

"It is going to be a makeshift one with barbed wire for a perimeter."

Georgina laughed. "That won't keep prisoners in."

Erich gave a faint smile. "We cannot go anywhere, Crete is surrounded by water."

"The war in Europe will soon be over, therefore, you won't be in captivity for long," said Georgina, as she sipped her wine.

"Make that glass last, Georgina, there is no more."

"What!"

"The stock is finished." Erich lifted his glass and stared at it. "My final schnapps before I go into captivity."

"When it ends, what will happen to you?"

"Be sent back to Germany and help to rebuild it."

"On the radio, it mentioned Russian soldiers have entered Berlin."

"Our Leader will not be pleased, it will soon be his birthday."

"Will he allow himself to be taken prisoner?"

"He believes that Germany can still win." Erich shook his head. "Instead of being in Berlin, he should witness what happened here and beyond."

"The crumbling Reich."

Erich nodded. It had all gone well for Germany until the fateful decision by Hitler to invade Russia.

"Will there be reparations as in the previous war?"

Erich shrugged his shoulders. "If so, Germany is in ruins and broke, therefore, cannot pay."

Georgina held Erich's hand. "We will somehow keep in touch."

He gripped it. With the other hand Georgina pulled a piece of paper out of her coat pocket and gave it to Erich. "My address, write to me as soon as you can."

He took the piece of paper and put it into his inside coat pocket. "My men and I just want the war to end."

"As we all do." Georgina finished her wine and set the empty glass down. "Then I can have my usual intake."

Erich smiled, then finished his drink. As both customers left, they acknowledged a farewell gesture from the proprietor. Outside, Georgina and Erich hugged and kissed. Hearing distant footsteps, the couple hid in an alley until they diminished. "Greek police on their rounds," said Erich.

"What will happen to them?"

"Perhaps the British will employ them to keep order."

Once more, Georgina hugged Erich. "Why did we have to meet in this damn war."

"At least we met."

Georgina looked at Erich and smiled. He kissed her. "Goodbye for now, Georgina."

"Goodbye, Erich." Georgina's voice grew raspy. "Write to me," she said, wiping a tear from her cheek.

"I do not have a napkin this time."

Georgina sniffed, then smiled.

"I promise to write." Erich departed, and a few moments later, looked back at Georgina, who waved.

The proprietor lifted two empty glasses and returned to the bar. Whilst he washed them, his wife appeared. "Will we see them again?"

The proprietor shrugged his shoulders.

"They make a nice couple."

The proprietor nodded. "I will miss the food and wine he gave us."

"He is a good German. I hope that he will not be faced with repercussions."

"If he doesn't, it will be a miracle!" The proprietor dried the glasses. "I have heard all Germans will remain on the island until an official surrender."

"It cannot be far off."

"We may have another conflict to contend with."

"Between the partisans?"

"There is much hostility between the two."

The proprietor's wife sighed. "Is there no end to conflict on our island?"

"It could have been worse if the Turks had joined forces with Germany. Who knows what would have happened?"

"I hate to imagine."

"At least one conflict will conclude."

"The police officers will still be hated."

"They will soon come under Athens jurisdiction."

"People will not forget whom they worked for and their behaviour," said the proprietor's wife sharply.

"Maria, we must put the past behind us and rebuild Crete."

"What will we do for food now that Erich cannot supply us?"

"There is a rumour that the British will provide rations."

"For all of the island?"

The proprietor nodded. "As a thank you for our help to defeat the Germans."

"Many people we know who helped have been murdered by those Nazi thugs."

"We met one who acted in a humane manner."

On 10 May, the German Army in Crete surrendered to British forces on the war-ravaged island. From Heraklion where they had massed, a despondent trek followed to a camp several miles along the coastline.

When they arrived, officers and non-commissioned personnel surveyed a fortified barb wire perimeter fence with a solitary outhouse for latrines. A junior officer looked at Captain Hoeness. "Escape will not be a problem, sir, wire-cutters are all we require."

Captain Hoeness stared. "Where would we go?" he asked sharply.

"We can steal a boat and take to the sea."

"And then?" Captain Hoeness looked out to sea. "British ships now come and go as they please." He glanced at the junior officer. "You would be picked up, tired and hungry." Captain Hoeness went on. "At least here we will be fed."

"I have been on rations for eight months," said the junior officer.

Captain Hoeness put his arm on the junior officer's shoulder. "We all have. As for an escape, our best chance is when we are shipped off the island and arrive at our destination."

"Make a break inland, sir? Or, we could take over the ship and then sail to a safe place."

"Let us wait and see what happens."

Then, a crowd of Cretan men and women with stern expressions approached the fence. One grey-haired woman scowled at a group of German soldiers and spat. "Nazi pigs, you are going to pay for atrocities committed over the last four years."

A younger dark-haired woman spat, then shouted. "This camp will not protect you."

The junior officer glanced at Captain Hoeness. "And that is the women!"

When he gave a forced smile, the junior officer cast his gaze around the perimeter. "If it rains, there is no cover."

"The British will do their utmost to make our stay as unpleasant as possible."

"How long are we here for, sir?"

"At least a couple of weeks."

"Where is Major Neuberger, sir?"

"This morning he did not appear and when I asked, received a blunt reply."

"I do not trust the British."

Captain Hoeness stared at the perimeter fence. "It is them that concern me."

A few moments later, two other Wehrmacht officers approached Captain Hoeness and the junior officer. "Erich, we have heard rumours that our Leader has committed suicide."

"I doubt it, Mannfred. Who told you?"

"A guard. In such a situation, who would take charge of the Armed Forces? Reich-Marshal Goring?"

"I believe Admiral Donitz is next in command."

"Where is Major Neuberger?"

Captain Hoeness shrugged his shoulders. "He did not appear this morning."

"Is it true that the Hitler Youth fought the Red Army in Berlin?" The fellow captain asked in amazement.

Captain Hoeness sighed. "Given the state of our forces, I would not be surprised."

The fellow captain shook his head. "If true, it signals the end for us."

Unknown to the officers and German personnel on Crete, the final weeks and days of Hitler's Reich resulted in a torrid time for not only troops who defended German soil, but also its inhabitants. Entering Germany, Russian soldiers showed no mercy as women, young and old, were raped and men murdered. When word reached the Berliners about these savage acts, many took their own lives rather than endure terror.

As the four officers continued to chat, more locals converged around the outside perimeter. The junior officer looked at his colleagues. "Let us hope the British give us protection."

Then, rocks hurtled by youths, landed close to a group of German soldiers. As they stared, obscene shouts followed in quick succession.

"Where are the British guards?" asked Captain Hoeness.

"No doubt drinking cups of tea," said the fellow captain.

Captain Hoeness gave a slight smile.

"However, not for long." The officer looked towards the Cretan mob. "Once we have gone, they will fight among themselves."

"As in Eastern Europe and the Balkans, communists will want to impose their ideology in Greece," said Captain Hoeness.

"I have heard from a reputable source of divisions between members of the government in Athens on how their country should be run."

"It does not make for a harmonious future," added Captain Hoeness.

A local youth picked up a small rock, stared at the four officers and then threw it in their direction. As they ducked, Captain Hoeness remarked. "Wherever we end up, it will not be as bad as this!"

As daylight filtered away and with no proper shelter, groups of soldiers huddled together and chatted to pass time. A corporal looked at Captain Hoeness. "What did you do before the war, sir?"

"A schoolteacher."

"What did you teach, sir?" asked a private.

"Languages, but wanted to teach history."

"Why didn't you, sir?"

"I was better at languages," said Captain Hoeness, as a smile flickered over his face.

"What do you think historians will say about this war, sir?" asked the corporal.

"That we had conquered most of Europe and let it slip from our grasp."

"How did it happen, sir?" asked another private.

"Bad decisions from those in charge."

"Our Leader?" asked the corporal.

Captain Hoeness hesitated. "It could have been certain generals who imparted wrong advice."

"It doesn't matter now, we've lost the war," said the corporal.

"Will you return to teaching, sir?" asked a private.

"I hope so, but it depends on what the British decide." Captain Hoeness cast his gaze around the group. "If the Russians had captured us, we would be on our way to a Siberian labour camp by now."

"I just want to return home," said the corporal.

"Where is that?" asked Captain Hoeness.

"Essen." The corporal stared at the ground. "Since being bombed two years ago, it resembles a pile of rubble."

"As with most of our towns and cities," added Captain Hoeness.

"Why did the British and Americans continue to drop bombs?" asked a private. "There will be nothing habitable left. Indeed, no home to get back to."

"Revenge for their cities being bombed in 1941," said another private.

"Murderers!" said the corporal.

"The British no doubt made similar comments," said Captain Hoeness.

The corporal looked his way and remained silent, bitter that his country lost the war and was obliterated by the allies.

"I would like to be sent to somewhere sunny and warm with a beach," said a private.

"That is where you are now," said a fellow private.

The group laughed.

"But without the barbed wire and violent locals."

Captain Hoeness gave a slight smile.

"Perhaps Turkey," said the corporal.

"It's only across the water," added a private.

"We could highjack a boat," said another private.

The corporal looked at Captain Hoeness, "What do you think, sir?"

"It would give the British a reason to shoot us."

Whilst murmurs followed, several Cretan men threw large stones at some German prisoners. However, the stones were picked up and returned. When the Cretans ran off, German prisoners cheered.

"That will teach them," said the corporal.

"They will soon be back," said Captain Hoeness.

"And when they fight with each other," said the corporal, "let us hope the communists are licked."

"Britain and America will back the non-communists," added Captain Hoeness. "Dr Goebbels believed the allies would join us to fight Russia."

"Then we would have stood a chance," said the corporal.

Then, elevated chatter came from another group of prisoners and Captain Hoeness looked across at them. One approached with an expression of shock. "A British guard has told us that our Leader has committed suicide."

"He is lying," said the corporal. "Our Leader would fight till the end."

"The guard said also Dr Goebbels."

"It is propaganda," said the corporal sharply.

Captain Hoeness pondered. That's ironic.

"Who occupies the Chancellery?" asked the corporal.

"The Russians," said the fellow prisoner.

The corporal shook his head. "I hoped it would be the British or Americans." He stared at Captain Hoeness. "The Russians will not give up Berlin."

"Or Germany," said Captain Hoeness.

The corporal sighed. "The future looks bleak," he said gravely.

Captain Hoeness turned to him. "Do not lose heart." He glanced around the group. "Winston Churchill will ensure the Russians play fair."

Whilst the discussion on a Russian occupation continued, two British soldiers approached Captain Hoeness. "Please come with us."

"Where to?"

"General Hainsworth's office."

"What for?"

"You will find out when we get there."

"Mention our inadequate accommodation, sir," said the corporal.

A short while later, Captain Hoeness and his two escorts arrived at British Headquarters. After they took him into General Hainsworth's office, one of them departed, whilst his colleague closed the door and stood.

"Take a seat, Captain," said General Hainsworth.

"Thank you."

General Hainsworth leaned back on his chair. "You are being transferred to another location."

"All of the prisoners?"

"No, just you."

"Why?" Erich asked in amazement.

"For being associated with the SS."

"I am not an SS officer."

"According to our sources, you acted with them."

"Your sources are mistaken, General."

He cleared his throat. "You will be transferred tomorrow morning to a place where other German SS officers are being held."

"Can you reveal where it is?"

"Scotland." General Hainsworth paused. "At least you will have a roof over your head."

"That is a vast improvement," said Erich, as he looked at the guard who had a slight grin.

"It's a scenic place near a village and better than the ruins of Crete."

"How long will I be held there?"

"I'm not sure."

When Erich stood, so did General Hainsworth. "Be glad you're not in Russian captivity," he said, giving a wry smile.

"Is Major Neuberger at the Scottish camp?"

General Hainsworth shook his head.

"Where is he?"

"He's vanished. We'll find him sooner or later."

Erich returned to the camp and began to reflect. Leaving Crete would prevent he and Georgina from being reunited. Also, when searched, soldiers removed the note that she had given to him with her address. Georgina would be unaware of Erich's departure and if she asked of his whereabouts, would be met with a strong rebuff. Erich recalled that Georgina told him that before going to stay in America, she lived in a Scottish village. Could there be a connection? On another matter, being tarred with the SS could mean harsher treatment at the Scottish camp It may be a scenic location, but what penalties lay in store? Once more, Erich's thoughts turned to Georgina, and that they may never be together again.

CHAPTER 14

CULTYBRAGGAN

Following an arduous sea journey from Crete to Scotland, Captain Erich Hoeness along with other German prisoners-of-war, disembarked at the port of Leith. After the necessary documentation process, they would be transferred to several secure Scottish locations. One fellow German officer approached Erich. "Where are you going to?"

"Comrie. I have been told it is in Perthshire."

"My location is a place in the far north which I cannot pronounce."

Erich gave a faint smile. "Good luck."

Armed soldiers ushered the prisoners to their respective lorries for transport out of Leith Docks. Erich walked up to a stone-faced guard. "Does this take us to Comrie?"

He glared. "I will be in the lorry along with another guard. Any trouble and you'll be shot," he said sharply.

Erich observed a broken nose on the soldier. I know how he got that. He climbed inside and sat with other subdued prisoners. Downbeat not just for being defeated, but the turmoil faced by their families back in Germany. As the guards got on and sat down, one prisoner looked at them. "How long will the journey take?"

"Too long for me," said the guard with a broken nose.

Murmurs followed amongst several prisoners and when the guard stared at them, silence ensued. Both guards sat at the rear and displayed contempt for their prisoners dressed in shabby clothes. Erich looked at them and reflected. Less than four years earlier, these officers had been part of an army, which conquered most of Europe. Each foe had been defeated with speed, precision and effective battle strategies. Now, Germany was in ruins and occupied by Russian, American and British forces. Also, would reparations have to be paid, as at the end of WW1? A prisoner seated next to Erich pulled back a dark curtain to peek out the window.

"Replace that bloody curtain," shouted the second guard.

As the prisoner did so, Erich glanced his way. The prisoner moved his head towards Erich. "This will be a long journey."

"Did you observe anything of interest?" whispered Erich.

The fellow prisoner shook his head.

On the ninety-minute journey, both guards remained silent, and thus set the scene. If a prisoner started to chat, one of the guards would give him a less than courteous reprimand.

When the lorry came to a halt, both got out and looked inside the vehicle. "Move," they shouted.

After the twenty prisoners left the lorry, each cast their gaze around the vicinity. In front, stood four rows of huts on a large field. One prisoner looked at Erich. "At least it is better than Crete."

"Welcome to Cultybraggan," said one of the guards. "For those who can't pronounce it, camp number 21."

Watched by established inmates, the prisoners were escorted to a distant hut. Whilst they walked, Erich spotted an officer from his time in Athens and waved. As the officer walked towards Erich, a guard intervened. "Get back to your hut." The twenty prisoners entered their designated quarters, then each made for a bunk. After they settled, a guard stood at the entrance and pointed to a notice on the wall. "Adhere to those rules or face the consequences." He shut the door behind him.

Moments later, one inmate shouted, "Who said the Russians were the worst."

All inmates laughed, then several approached the notice typed in German. As Erich joined them, an inmate looked at him. "Given what we had on Crete, two meals a day is luxury itself."

Another inmate added, "Our families in Germany will be lucky to get one meal per day."

A hush followed, then inmates returned to their bunks and no doubt reflected on what lay in store for their loved ones.

Next morning, Erich and his fellow inmates found out they had been deemed 'grey', as opposed to white, or black. White meant inmates could work on the nearby farm, join a local choir or orchestra and even attend English classes. Inmates classed as black were confined to camp, but their grey counterparts received limited exposure to the outside. One inmate raised an issue amongst the group. "I am not a Nazi thug. I joined through conscription less than two years ago."

Another commented, "As with the rest of us." He looked at Erich.

"Can you speak to someone?"

"I will try, but the British will not alter their decision." Erich glanced around the group. "They are stubborn and stick to their principles."

"They have assigned Polish guards to our hut," said another inmate.

"As in all the huts," added Erich.

"The British have enlisted them for a reason," said the inmate. "Extract revenge for their country invaded by us six years ago."

Erich addressed the group. "Do not give them a reason to bully us. We do not want to play into their hands." He went on, "If there is any aggressive behaviour by them, the British will ignore our claims."

"We can't just take it," said a young inmate.

"If there is a problem, come to me. Do not retaliate."

"I trust we do not attempt to escape, Erich?" asked another inmate.

"It is not worth it."

"The camp is surrounded by hills," said the young inmate. "If one of us escapes, there must be many opportunities in which to hide."

"And then what?" asked Erich sharply. "If you speak to anyone, they will recognise your accent."

After several of the group laughed, the young inmate acknowledged his weakness through a nod and grin.

"Let us bide our time and soon we will return to our homeland." Erich gave a faint smile. "At least what is left of it."

The group looked at each other and agreed. As they ventured outside into the warm May sunshine, Polish guards who stood nearby glared. Erich hoped his group would keep their cool. When a Polish guard passed by, Erich approached him. "Could I speak with the person in charge of the camp?"

"Why?"

"About recreation facilities."

"You have plenty of grass." The guard cast his gaze around the site. "What more do you want?" He stared. "This is not a holiday camp," he said sharply.

"A football would be a start."

The guard grinned. "To practice for the next World Cup."

"To keep the men occupied." Erich paused. "Perhaps we could arrange a match between guards and prisoners?"

The guard smirked. "Similar to your army, you would be disgraced."

Erich paused. "We have an international player in our hut."

"Who?" The guard stared at the nearby piece of grass.

Erich glanced behind. "Leopold Neumar."

Leopold raised his hand and the guard looked towards him, then Erich. "We also have an international player, Edward Madejski. He alone could beat you on his own," said the guard, grinning.

"Let us put him to the test."

"I will talk to my senior officer."

Erich left the guard and returned to his group of men lying at ease on the grass. Those who looked up shaded their eyes. "We may have a game of football against the Poles."

"We will murder them," said Leopold Neumar.

Erich gave a faint smile. "It should diminish friction between us."

"Not if we beat them, Erich," quipped Leopold.

The group laughed.

The prisoners settled into a routine of daily exercise, relaxation and Nazi ideology removal. In most cases, inmates at Cultybraggan had been ordinary German officers conscripted to fight for their country. Once a week, those in two huts would have the opportunity of a walk through the countryside accompanied by armed guards. In the summer months with picturesque scenery, Erich and fellow inmates looked forward to this privilege. However, on this particular day, one of the other hut's occupants elected to try his luck and escape. As prisoners stopped for a break, some leaned against a stone dyke, which separated the road and a field. When guards chatted amongst themselves, the opportunist fell backwards into the field and hid behind the dyke. Being nearby, Erich had watched with interest and Leopold commented. "I wager he will not participate in the football game."

Erich looked towards the guards and whispered, "They are unaware."

Leopold glanced round and gave a slight grin. "Too busy chatting."

After each guard threw away his cigarette butt, they resumed their positions at the front, middle and rear of the prisoners. As guards and prisoners moved off, Erich glanced back. Several minutes later, the escapee ran across the field towards a forest and refuge. Two women who appeared in the field to cut hay viewed with open mouths.

"We have to alert the soldiers, Jenny," said one.

"Right away."

Both women ran towards the road and shouted to attract the soldier's attention. Quick-thinking German prisoners turned round, shouted and waved back to them with wide grins. One guard shook his head and muttered. "Some women don't care
who they flirt with."

Prisoners and guards returned to Cultybraggan and following a role count, the penny dropped. As the escapee was not from Erich's hut, he hoped no penalties would ensue. A Polish guard came to the hut and wanted Erich to accompany him to the camp's officer-in-charge.

"Why does he want to see me? Is it to do with someone who escaped?"

"Come with me and you will find out," said the guard sharply.

Erich followed him to a building at the camp's far end. He walked up several wooden steps and then entered an office with a large desk, brown leather chair and table. On it stood a bottle of whisky and two crystal glasses.

"Colonel Stoddart will be here soon," said the guard, as he departed.

Whilst Erich cast his gaze around the room, a tall grey-haired officer with a moustache entered. Going by the ribbons on his uniform jacket, he had been victorious in battle. "Please sit down, Captain," said the Colonel politely, as he sat behind his desk.

"Thank you," said Erich, as he took a seat.

"Would you care for a whisky?"

"I only drink schnapps, or white wine."

Colonel Stoddart gave a wry smile. "Of course. How is your accommodation?"

"Adequate, Colonel, but the men are bored. They would like to work on the local farm or help the villagers in some way."

"The problem being that men in your hut are classed as dangerous prisoners."

"We are not Nazis, Colonel, just German soldiers who fought for our country, as you did."

Colonel Stoddart leaned back on his chair. "A local church is being renovated and need men to remove rubble and help with other manual tasks."

"We would be delighted to assist," said Erich, as a smile flickered over his face.

Colonel Stoddart stood. "I'll be in touch."

Erich got up and Colonel Stoddart led him to the door, then opened it. "We captured the inmate who escaped."

Erich shook his head. "A pointless act."

After Erich left, Colonel Stoddart returned to his desk, picked up the telephone and a woman's voice answered. "Yes, can I help?"

"Comrie Parish Church, please."

"I'll connect you, sir," said the switchboard telephonist.

Several days later, two armed guards escorted Erich and four prisoners from the camp to Comrie. Following a brisk march, they made the one and a half miles in less than thirty minutes. Their eagerness to visit the village ensured a consistent pace.

At the church, both guards spoke with a man dressed in clothes appropriate for demolition work. He looked at Erich and his fellow prisoners, then the guards. "What if they try to escape, or take me hostage?"

"We'll be in close attendance," said a guard.

The builder glanced at the prisoners. "Do they speak English?"

"One does," said the guard, as he glanced at the group.

As the builder sighed, the guard looked at Erich and signalled for him to come over. When he did so, the guard introduced him to the builder. "How good is your English?"

"Adequate, how is your German?"

The builder grinned. "Who else speaks English?"

"Two of us. I will act as an interpreter for those who do not speak English."

After he gave instructions through Erich, the prisoners went to work. Being seventy years old, the steeple required overdue maintenance and as good fortune would have it, certain prisoners did not fear heights. At ground level, Erich spoke to the builder. "How long will we be here?"

"After the steeple, there is internal work which also needs urgent attention." The builder took Erich into the church and pointed. "Water has seeped through that wall."

"From where?"

"There is a river which runs behind the church."

"Idyllic."

"Maybe so, but it has caused much damage."

At that moment, a man in black attire and white hair appeared from a room and then approached both men. "How are the repairs coming along, Mr Robb?"

"We'll get there, Reverend."

He looked at Erich. "My thanks to you and your men for their assistance."

"It is good to enjoy the village atmosphere."

The church representative smiled. "Is there anything we can do for you?" He went on, "We have a garden fete in two weeks and you are welcome to attend."

"During our break, would it be possible to have a kick-about?"

"In the church grounds?"

Erich nodded. "We won't damage the grass."

"You only get a fifteen-minute break," said the builder.

The church representative nodded. "Since it is for a short time."

Erich gave a faint smile. "Do you have a football?"

"You can use my grandson's."

"Thank you."

When Erich imparted his news to the men, work on the steeple progressed in a positive manner. Soon, the lunchbreak arrived and a good-natured kick-about followed. Whilst the builder watched with a mug of tea in his hand, the ball came his way. As Erich retrieved it, the builder glanced at a prisoner. "Who is the guy in a red shirt?"

"Leopold." Erich glanced at him. "He has played for Germany."

After the kick-about resumed, the builder remained transfixed on the artistry provided with makeshift prisoner footwear. Opposite the church, a woman looked on, left her cottage and approached the builder. Sipping his tea, he turned to face the grey-haired woman, smiling. "Could one of them help me shift an ornament in my garden?" She looked at a ladder, which led up to the roof. "Before they resume work."

The builder agreed and signalled to Erich, who then came across. The woman viewed him with a sheepish expression.

"Could you give this lady a hand to shift an ornament?" asked the builder.

Erich frowned. "A table ornament?"

The woman smiled. "A garden ornament, a bird bath. Come, I'll show you."

Whilst his colleagues continued their kick-a-bout, Erich followed the woman to her cottage. She glanced at Erich. "Round the back."

Eric walked along a narrow gravel path at the gable end, then entered an area with a trimmed lawn surrounded by hedges and small plants. "This is similar to what my mother's garden used to look like."

"In what part of Germany did she stay?"

"Not far from Dresden." Erich paused. "A bomb exploded nearby and damaged the property." He glanced at the woman. "My mother was injured in the blast."

"I'm sorry to hear that."

Erich cast his gaze around the garden and spotted a grey object three feet high in a corner. The woman shook her head. "The garden firm put it there, but it's too heavy for me to move."

Erich gave a slight smile. It is more than half her height.

"Could you put it in the centre?"

Erich approached the object, lifted it and then walked across the lawn. He manoeuvred it into position, then looked at the woman. "How is this?"

"Perfect," said the woman, smiling.

Erich walked towards her and then looked over his shoulder. "With this hot sunny weather, the birds will be grateful."

The woman laughed. "Would you like a cup of tea?"

"Thank you, but I should resume my work duties."

"Have a cup of tea, you deserve it. If the builder isn't pleased, refer him to me."

Following two cups of tea and several plain digestive biscuits, Erich returned to the church. Under supervision from the builder and another inmate who spoke broken English, work continued. The builder looked at Erich. "You took your time!"

"Agnes insisted that I had a cup of tea and a chat."

Due to the camp commander being one to promote harmony, a football match had been arranged between guards and inmates. The Polish guards believed their German opposition would crumble under pressure from their dynamic forward strikers. Also, the guards were better prepared for the match in terms of facilities in which to train and footwear. When Erich asked for the same, a negative reply came forthwith. The Poles had the camp commander's ear. The game would take place on a piece of unused land near Cultybraggan. To add authenticity, white lines had been painted, as in a proper football pitch. The camp commander had managed to get a qualified referee, but no linesmen. John Valentine, a local grocer and part-time Grade 1 official referee until called up to fight in North Africa, welcomed the opportunity to referee again. However, as he fought against the Germans, would borderline decisions favour the Poles? To add glamour, the match could be classed as a prestigious 'international friendly' between two countries that competed in the 1938 World Cup.

When the final Saturday in August arrived, the match had received vast publicity. So much so, locals' requests to attend had been granted. A donation towards the Cultybraggan Festive Dinner being the admission price. Football strips were borrowed from local amateur teams whose games had been suspended until the following season. The guards played in red shirts and the inmates wore white. John Valentine was the man in black.

As the game got underway, the guards attacked the inmate's goal in a relentless manner, like the German blitzkrieg attack on their country six years earlier. The ball was now on the other foot, but the inmates survived early pressure. On a solitary first-half attack, the inmates almost scored. Leopold Neumar's 'long-ranger' came back of the bar and cleared to safety.

The second half commenced with another guard's onslaught, but the inmates, once more, weathered the storm. With less than one minute left, Leopold Neumar went on a mazy run, which took him into the penalty box. As he prepared to shoot, an ill-timed tackle from a guard floored him. The German players looked towards John Valentine in anticipation of a blatant penalty award. As both sets of players and spectators held their breath, John Valentine's finger pointed to the penalty spot. Every outfield guard and also their goalkeeper surrounded him and protested. One member of the public grinned. "It's just as well the referee doesn't speak Polish."

When the turmoil had died down, Leopold Neumar placed the brown leather ball on a white painted spot. To distract him, the goalkeeper stood on his line, jumped up and down then waved his arms. Unperturbed, Leopold ran forward and as the goalkeeper anticipated a shot to his left, the ball went in the opposite direction. When it hit the back of the net, John Valentine blew his whistle for full-time. Guards stared at each other in disbelief, then walked off the pitch. The inmates took the applause of locals and then showed their appreciation with a similar gesture. One onlooker said to another, "They soaked up the pressure and then hit on the break."

"An awareness of tactics."

"If Germany has players similar to the goalscorer, they will do well in years to come."

"Maybe, but they'll never win anything."

"As the Poles buy from John's grocer shop in the village, they may boycott it!"

Joyful inmates entered a hut in which to change into their everyday attire. Leopold Neumar turned to them. "A cheer for our coach."

The players cheered as one and Erich took the acclaim in a gracious manner. Whilst he changed, Leopold looked at Erich. "Have you coached before?"

Erich shook his head.

"How did you know which tactics to deploy?"

"I set out the team to soak up the pressure, then break forward. I knew our robust defenders could cope with the Poles forward prowess. We only attacked several times, but got the penalty."

Leopold grinned. "That is twice we have beaten them in recent times."

The players laughed and cheered. Erich gave a faint smile. At least on this occasion, war will not break out.

The eleven players left the changing hut to cheers from other inmates who waited outside. Polish guards glared at the victors. Colonel Stoddart gazed at the scene from his office window, then turned to a fellow officer. "I hope the German victory doesn't sour relations between them and the guards."

"We'll soon find out."

"I expected the guards to hammer them."

"They had ninety-five per cent of the play, the German manager is a shrewd one."

"I note that they use 'coach' instead of manager." The colonel considered. "This challenge match has whetted my appetite for the resumption of a football season."

"I believe it won't be till next year."

Colonel Stoddart gave a wry smile. "Until then, perhaps a rematch between guards and inmates?"

"And an acceptable admission fee?"

"You bet," said the colonel, as he grinned.

Erich had received word that he must report to Colonel Stoddart within the hour. As he entered, the colonel greeted him. "Have a seat, Erich.

"A rematch, Colonel?" Erich sat opposite.

"Heavy rain has scuppered that for the time being."

"The guards will use any excuse."

Colonel Stoddart gave a slight smile. "The reason why I wanted to see you is that one of the local families wish to repay you for doing jobs at their property."

"Opposite the church."

Colonel Stoddart nodded.

"They do not have to, it is my pleasure."

"Nevertheless, I've agreed. I believe it is your birthday soon."

"Next month."

"Then it is appropriate."

Erich stood, walked to the door, then turned round. "Colonel?"

"Yes?"

"The men are concerned about what is going on in Germany. It would help morale if I could tell them."

"Only if it is good news."

"Is it all bad? Any news is beneficial."

"Germany is being split into four zones. The French will control south-west, we, north-west, and United States, the south."

"What about the east?"

The colonel hesitated. "That part of Germany will be controlled by the Russians."

"That will affect half of the men in our hut." Erich went on. "They have families in Dresden and Leipzig. My mother lives near Dresden."

"Also, territories gained after 1937 will be taken from Germany."

"The guards will be happy."

Colonel Stoddart gave a slight smile.

"I take it our Armed Forces have disbanded?"

"And the factories which produced weapons will only be allowed to work at 50% capacity."

"Are there to be reparations? If so, how can Germany pay with a reduced manufacturing output?"

Colonel Stoddart leaned back on his chair. "That is a good question."

"The French demands will be high, as in 1919."

"It's the Russians you have to fear."

Erich sighed. "Thank you for the latest news," he said gratefully.

"There is a German newspaper that is in operation. I can't remember the name but will find out." Colonel Stoddart stood, went to the door and opened it. "Maybe we can obtain copies."

"That would be good, Colonel, and appreciated by the prisoners."

After Erich departed, Colonel Stoddart returned to his desk and opened a drawer. He took out a newspaper, Suddeutsche Zeitung, and browsed through it.

With winter on its way, Erich left the camp and walked in a brisk manner to

Agnes's cottage. The snow had so far stayed away, but a nip in the air existed. As Erich went along the dark single road, the heavy coat given to him by an inmate kept out some of the cold chill. Erich had been allowed the afternoon away from camp, he looked forward to seeing Agnes again.

When he arrived at the cottage, Erich gave his usual three knocks. Moments later, Agnes answered. "Come in, Erich," she said cheerily.

He wiped his feet on the doormat, and rubbed his hands. After Agnes closed the door, she glanced at Erich's worn black shoes. "Did you keep your feet?" Unaware of a term used in villages and towns during a traditional Scottish winter, Erich remained silent. "Was the road icy?"

Erich shook his head. "I kept my feet." He paused. "I must remember that one."

Agnes smiled. "There is someone I want you to meet." She led Erich into the warm cosy living room, where a young woman with long auburn hair stood near the fireplace. "This is my daughter, Fiona. She will give us a lift to the cinema in Crieff."

Erich approached the young woman and as he shook her hand, she pulled it back. "My apologies, I should have warmed my hands," said Erich, as he glanced at the fire.

"I'll knit you a pair of gloves, Erich," said Agnes. "Does the camp supply headwear in winter?"

"Only if you are in the British army."

Fiona laughed.

"Did you come here on your own?"

"They trust me, Agnes." Erich gave a faint smile.

When she glanced at her daughter, Fiona looked at the clock on the dark wooden sideboard. "We better leave now to catch the start of the film."

Both women put on their hats and coats, then all three left the cottage. Erich entered the black saloon and sat in its rear leather seat. After both women got in, Fiona started the engine, then drove off. She glanced at her mother. "At least the roads appear okay."

Whilst Erich studied the interior, Fiona looked at his image in the front mirror. "Are there similar cars in Germany, Erich?"

"Yes. Who is the manufacturer?"

"Company called Austin."

Agnes looked round. "Do you drive, Erich?"

He nodded. "The army taught me." Erich paused. "They will no longer have need for vehicles."

As Agnes glanced at Fiona, Erich looked out the window. "Why do some houses have a Christmas tree and not others?"

Agnes looked round. "They put their tree up early."

"Is there a stipulated time?"

"Twelve days before Christmas Day."

"When do German families put up their trees, Erich?" asked Fiona.

"We have not celebrated Christmas for a number of years."

Glancing at her mother, Fiona gave a slight smile. Once more, Agnes looked round. "The film we are going to see is about a man and woman who meet by chance."

"The critics have given it good reviews," added Fiona.

"Is it set in Britain?" asked Erich.

"Yes," said Agnes, "in England."

"What is it called?"

"Brief Encounter," said Fiona, as she looked in the mirror. "Have you heard of Celia Johnson, or Trevor Howard, Erich?"

"The only person allowed to watch British films in Germany was Adolf Hitler."

Agnes smiled, then turned round. "Well, tonight you're in for a treat!"

After the film, a subdued Erich walked with Agnes and Fiona back to the car. As they headed back to Comrie, Erich stared into the dark countryside. Agnes looked round. "Did you enjoy the film, Erich?"

"The actors played their parts well."

Fiona glanced at her mother. "The sign of a good film is when people leave the cinema and chat about it."

"In the foyer, you could hear many," added Agnes, as she straightened her hat.

"The film reminded me of someone."

Agnes glanced round. "Who, Erich?"

"A lady I met in Crete."

Fiona looked at Erich in the front mirror, intrigued.

"She came from Scotland."

Agnes turned round to face Erich. "Where about?"

"A place called Argyll.""

"Why did she move to Crete?"

"I am not sure, but she taught music at a school in Heraklion." Erich paused. "We have lost touch with each other."

"What happened?"

"Before we could meet again, I was imprisoned on Crete and then shipped to here."

"She may have contacted the authorities on Crete of your whereabouts," said Fiona.

Eric sighed. "They will not give out information about German soldiers."

"Did you plan to reunite?" asked Agnes.

"Yes."

"After being released from the camp, you could return to Crete and meet up again."

"But when will that be? For all I know, Georgina may have left the island. I have heard there is now a civil war going on."

The car soon arrived at Cultybraggan Camp and Erich got out. He thanked Fiona and Agnes for their kindness. After the car drove towards Comrie, Fiona glanced at her mother. "He liked her. How long will Erich be at the camp?"

"Until they deem him not to be a Nazi."

"Erich isn't a Nazi."

"They are all tarred with the same brush, Fiona."

"If the woman he met has left Crete, she could be anywhere."

"A brief encounter, indeed."

As 1946 arrived, the inmates of Cultybraggan did not have much to celebrate or look forward to. With no sign of being released and dire times in Germany, they endured low morale. Due to the winter snow and ice, even a rematch against the guards would not take place until spring. A guard entered Erich's hut and looked his way. "Report to Colonel Stoddart," he said sharply.

"Now?"

The guard nodded.

Erich put on his coat and followed the guard through several inches of snow to Colonel Stoddart's office. Before he entered, Erich wiped his feet. "You wanted to see me, Colonel."

"I have received word from headquarters that you must return to Germany."

"Am I being released?"

"Have a seat." The colonel cleared his throat.

After Erich sat down, Colonel Stoddart went to his desk and then picked up a document. "This states that you are to be tried for war crimes."

"War crimes! Against whom?" Erich asked in amazement.

"Were you based in Heraklion along with a Major Neuberger?"

"Yes, but I did not commit any crimes." Eric paused. "In fact, I supplied local villages with food. I removed supplies from our store and delivered through a contact."

"Who was the contact?"

"A woman who stayed in Heraklion."

"A member of the resistance?"

"She had links to them."

"Then this woman can verify your story."

"If she can be traced. Because of the civil war, Georgina may have left Crete."

"That's not a Cretan name."

"She is from Scotland, moved to America and then Crete.

"What about the atrocities committed there?"

"Not by my squad, Colonel."

Colonel Stoddart read the document, then looked at Erich. "In Athens, you supervised at a work camp?"

"Only for a short time, a temporary transfer from my duties on Crete."

"Prisoners had little food and no medical treatment."

"I raised this issue with my commanding officer."

"Any witnesses?"

"My commanding officer."

"If he is still alive and can be traced. If not dead, many German officers are in hiding."

"A group of prisoners would be aware."

Colonel Stoddart paused. "I am aware of your character and you do not strike me as someone who has committed war crimes. Nevertheless, Erich, you will have to go before a court of law. If you can find someone to substantiate what you have told me, you have nothing to fear."

"Where am I being sent to?"

"Nuremberg."

"Why there?"

"A series of trials will take place which involve leading members of your military. These will be in the public domain."

"In public?"

Colonel Stoddart nodded. "However, your trial will be a low-key affair behind closed doors."

"It will not be only me?"

"There are many of your rank, and higher."

"From this camp?"

"You are the first. Headquarters will no doubt contact me about further officers to go on trial."

"When do I leave, Colonel?"

"Tomorrow morning at first light."

As Erich stood, Colonel Stoddart left his desk and then led him to the door. After he opened it, a warm handshake followed. "Good luck, Erich."

"Thank you, Colonel."

Subdued, Erich walked back to his hut and raised his head. Within seconds, the sky had turned from blue to black. An inmate from a nearby hut approached and as he passed, shook his head. "Another storm is imminent."

CHAPTER 15

INTERNAL CONFLICT

Taking a deep breath, Georgina entered from the rear door and as she closed it, looked at Elena with her nose in a newspaper. "There are men being fired upon in the town centre!" Once more, she drew breath.

Elena lowered her newspaper. "Government, or communist?"

Georgina stared. "Does it matter?" She took off her coat then hung it on a hook. "This is worse than the German occupation."

"There could be more incidents to follow."

"Why do you say that?" Georgina removed her hat and shook her hair.

"There is an anti-government demonstration organised for next week."

"If in Heraklion, blood will spill."

"Twenty-eight people lost their lives as a result of a recent demonstration in Athens and many more received injuries. Government troops just opened fire!"

"They would be under orders."

Elena glared at Georgina. "Similar to the German soldiers? We have substituted one tyrannical regime for another." She threw aside her newspaper on the kitchen table. "There is no excuse for what happened in Athens," said Elena sharply.

Taken aback by her friend's reaction, Georgina sat down. "Are you going to the demonstration?"

"It is my duty. We have to show solidarity against the new government."

"Don't, Elena, it will be dangerous."

"I believe in a democratic Greece, it is the way forward for our country," said Elena, as she thumped the table.

To change the topic of conversation, Georgina got up, walked to her coat and took out a jar of instant coffee. Elena raised her dark eyebrows. "Where did you get that from?"

"An American officer visited our school last week and being a teacher by profession, he wanted to know about the pupil's welfare. Several days later, the school received a box full of gifts."

"What sort of gifts?" Elena asked in amazement.

"Writing books, pencils and crayons for the pupils. I asked him if he could also be generous to the teachers," said Georgina, as a smile flickered over her face.

"Did they all get a jar?"

Georgina nodded.

Elena considered. "With American and British finance, the Greek government will no doubt prevail."

"Would you rather have the communists in power? Look what transpired in Russia." Georgina set the jar down in front of Elena. "Hardship and food shortages, not to mention persecution and purges." Georgina went on. "The countries that Russia accumulated on their way to Germany will have to endure a similar fate. Also, millions of ordinary Russians died from starvation before the war against Germany."

"Finished? It cannot be worse than it is at present in Crete," said Elena sharply.

"The Germans caused our current situation, not the government. America will introduce a system whereby our economy can flourish."

"Flourish?" Elena had a puzzled expression.

Georgina gave a faint smile. "Grow." She paused. "Let's have some of that coffee."

As Elena prepared two cups, Georgina mulled her thoughts. Due to political differences, and previous heated discussions, a wedge had been inserted between them. With the political unrest in Greece, opposite viewpoints began to surface. Elena set two cups on the table. "I have got used to black coffee."

"I have it on good authority that the Americans will ensure milk is supplied to Crete."

When Elena lifted her coffee and took a sip, Georgina did likewise and considered. I feel this could be another one of those difficult evenings.

Alex Taylor, John Murdoch and Vic Stampson sat and waited in Manilos's hideaway for him to appear. The resistance leader had remained loyal to Britain and America. In the aftermath of WW2, his communist counterpart, Janouski, had now sided with Yugoslavia, Albania and Bulgaria. Although the two resistance leaders did not trust each other, both pooled their resources to help defeat their German occupier. Soon, they would confront each other and commence a brutal civil war in Crete. Then, the sound of voices could be heard and four men entered the room. Manilos grinned at the three agents. "Now we have another foe to rid our island of." After he exchanged a warm handshake with each agent, everyone sat round a wooden table. Manilos looked at one of his men. "Bring a bottle and four glasses."

"Okay, boss," said the resistance member.

John Murdoch glanced at the other two men who stood with grim expressions at the entrance door. "Can we have some privacy, Manilos?"

"Of course, my friend." Manilos looked at the men and tilted his head.

As they left, a bottle of ouzo and four glasses arrived on a wooden tray. After the resistance member set it down, Manilos filled four glasses.

"Anything else, Manilos?" asked the resistance member.

"Not for now."

The member departed, then closed the door behind him. Manilos raised his near-full glass. "To our new collaboration, gentlemen." He looked at the agents who in turn raised their glass and toasted the new partnership. After they each took a swig, Manilos refilled everyone's glass. He stared at the bottle and grinned. "This kept me going through the previous war, and for this new one, it will do the same."

When Vic Stampson laughed, John Murdoch glanced at Alex Taylor, who appeared pensive. A new series of bad hangovers would no doubt ensue. Vic Stampson took a swig, then set his glass on the table. "Why four guards, Manilos?"

"The same number accompany Janouski. If our paths cross, I will not be outnumbered."

"You may not meet him. We've been told he is in a different mountain hideaway from his previous one and on the other side of Crete."

"I am aware of that." Manilos took a swig, then put his glass down. "Let us talk business."

"Yugoslavia is a problem," said John Murdoch. "Tito is hell-bent on a confrontation."

Manilos filled up his glass. "As they are allied to Russia, an endless supply of weapons will be at their disposal."

Alex Taylor looked at Manilos and gave a wry smile. "We have it on good authority that Stalin is not keen on this particular conflict. An agreement has been made between Stalin and Churchill that Greece will not become a Russian satellite." Alex Taylor sipped his drink.

"That is good news," said Manilos, nodding.

Vic Stampson glanced at his two colleagues. "I don't get why Janouski has sided with Bulgaria." He finished his drink. "For four years, they have been common enemies."

"Thanks to Russia, Bulgaria is now communist," added Alex Taylor."

"Even though," said Vic Stampson, as he pondered.

"All for one," said Alec Taylor.

"We are going to need more weapons," said Manilos. "If so, I can recruit extra men and women for the fight."

"Women?" asked John Murdoch.

Manilos nodded. "They are more ferocious than some of my men! Remember what our women did to the German soldiers." Manilos paused. "They rushed to get off the island."

Laughter followed and so did more ouzo. The seeds had been sown for both resistance movements to compete for control of Crete. Due to the occupation and conflict between Italian and German troops, the island had become a barren wasteland. Its impoverished residents would have to endure more misery.

Elena and Georgina listened with interest to the radio on a chilly February evening. Due to not only severe cold weather, but also despondency, islanders ventured out only on the odd occasion. When they did, it was to chop trees for firewood to heat their home. In some cases, a wooden door had to be sacrificed and as a consequence, left a draft.

After the broadcast, both women sat in the kitchen and held a cup of American coffee to feel its warmth. With the jar nearly empty, strong coffee would have to wait for a refill. Georgina looked at the jar, then Elena. "The officer will be at the school next week." As Elena gave a forced smile, Georgina pondered. I'll change the subject. "How is your uncle?

"He is fine."

"And his business?"

"He survives."

Georgina paused to consider a question that Elena would react to. "At least he won't have to hand over most of his haul of fish to an occupier." Following another negative response, Georgina sipped her coffee. "Are you going out later?"

Elena shook her head. "Perhaps tomorrow evening."

Georgina had her suspicions that Elena may have joined the anti-government movement on the island. A source at the school revealed that meetings took place on a particular evening at various secret locations. Conversations between the two women now focused on external, rather than internal matters. If Georgina mentioned the latter, silence tended to follow. She chose a topical subject. "I hope the new organisation will bring future world peace."

Elena sat back. "The League of Nations failed, why would the United Nations succeed?"

"More members and a determination to avoid atrocities similar to the holocaust and here."

"Why has there been no intervention by the United Nations in Vietnam? French troops have marched in and taken over."

"Before the war, it belonged to them."

"Britain may face the same hostility from India, Singapore and Burma."

Georgina nodded. "It's a possibility." She considered. More probable than possible.

"I am glad the SS officer and his men received punishment for what they did to
civilians in Lithuania," said Elena, as she sipped her coffee. "Why have public trials in Nuremberg, just hang them all," she said sharply. Elena finished her coffee, then laid the cup aside.

"Some may be innocent."

"Not on Crete," she said abruptly.

Georgina reflected. One German was. He put his own life at stake to help locals. "It's the Russians who people have to be wary of. They will attempt to spread their ideology."

"Did Canada have to expel twenty Russian diplomats?"

"The broadcast said all of them had been found guilty of spying. What else could they do?"

"The accused diplomats believed in a cause."

"But was it the correct one?"

Elena stared, rose and left the kitchen. Georgina sighed, then recalled the harmonious relationship between her and Elena, but now politics had driven a wedge between them. One piece of radio news that interested Georgina came in the form of a transatlantic commercial service from France to New York. Then, a knock on the kitchen door. As Georgina got up to answer it, Elena appeared. "It could be for me."

When Georgina sat down, Elena opened the door and there stood a man in a dark coat and beret. "Could we speak in private?"

Elena nodded. "I will get my coat."

After Elena left the kitchen, Georgina looked at the man, who acknowledged with a forced smile. She shivered. "Come inside, if you wish."

The man remained silent and turned up his coat collar. Soon, Elena returned and glanced at Georgina. "Be back later."

"Tonight?"

Elena did not reply, departed the kitchen and closed the door behind her. Georgina leaned back and gave a slight smile. It reminded her of how she behaved when meeting Erich. However, Georgina feared this could prove a dangerous liaison, rather than a romantic one.

Four days later as Georgina left school, a man wearing a drab coat and in short supply of razor blades approached. She stopped, then stared at him.

He coughed. "Excuse me, can I have a few minutes of your time?" asked the man politely.

"I've no money to spare," said Georgina sharply.

"I apologise for my shabby appearance," said the man, as he gave a slight smile. "I'm an undercover secret service agent and work for British Intelligence on Crete."

"Is this some sort of a joke?"

"Do I sound British?"

"I would say Scottish."

The man nodded. "Born in Dundee."

"What do you want with me?"

"Give me five minutes and I'll explain."

"You said a few."

"I'll buy you a coffee, it's a scarce commodity around here."

Georgina hesitated. "Okay, a few minutes."

The man led Georgina to a nearby restaurant and both took a seat. He cast his gaze around the establishment and soon a waiter appeared.

"Two coffees, please," said the man.

"We are short of milk," said the waiter.

"Black is fine," said Georgina.

"Me too," said the man, as he unbuttoned his long grey coat, frayed at both lapels.

After the waiter departed, Georgina removed her hat, placed it on the table and looked at the man. "Do you have a name?"

"John Murdoch, and you are Georgina Rhodes. That is your real name, is it not?"

Georgina stared. "How do you know my surname?"

"I told you, I'm with British Intelligence, it's my business to know."

"What else do you know about me?"

"A teacher of music in a Heraklion school and not charged with her husband's murder. Don't worry, Mrs Rhodes, I'm not here to dig up your past."

"Well then, what?"

"You share a house with a woman."

"Yes."

"Have you seen a change in her?"

Georgina hesitated. "Recent events can make people act in a differently."

"Did she change when the Germans occupied her country? My organisation suspects her of being a spy for the communists."

"You mean the democrats?"

"No, Mrs Rhodes, I mean the communists, led by Janouski." John Murdoch paused. "My instinct tells me that you may have been aware that something isn't right."

"I can't imagine her being a spy."

"We do."

"Why have you approached me?"

"I would like you to monitor her movements."

"Movements?"

"Who and when she meets someone."

"She is my friend," said Georgina sharply.

"If our information is accurate, she will be discovered and suffer the consequences of her actions." John Murdoch paused. "I'm trying to help."

"Elena, or the government?"

"Both."

"I'm not at home all the time."

"In the evening you are."

"Are you spying on me as well!"

John Murdoch whispered, "Please, keep your voice down." He glanced around the vicinity.

"Elena is my friend, I can't spy on her."

"Give it some thought and if you change your mind, get in touch."

"How?"

"Contact the waiter who served us. He is one of our contacts in Heraklion." John Murdoch glanced at the counter. "His name is Basil."

"Is that his real name?"

John Murdoch shrugged his shoulders. "That's the name he uses."

Georgina looked up. "Here comes Basil with our cups of black coffee."

John Murdoch looked over his shoulder, then at Georgina. "I'll get him some milk by Friday."

"Can you get me a jar of coffee?"

John Murdoch gave a faint smile. "Once you've made contact."

"I need some evidence of who you are."

"Working as an undercover intelligence officer, it's not advisable to carry identity papers. After all, I may get captured."

"That could prove fatal, I suppose."

As the waiter approached, John Murdoch looked up. "Basil, what am I? John Murdoch glanced at Georgina. "The lady needs evidence."

"You are a British secret agent," whispered Basil, as he set both cups on the wooden table.

John Murdoch looked across the table. "Satisfied?"

As Georgina gave a slight nod, the waiter departed. A short while later, she left the restaurant and walked home through deserted war-torn streets. With German troops gone, the citizens of Heraklion had looked forward to a fresh start and to rebuild their lives. Now, another war loomed and for how long this time?

After two weeks, John Murdoch waited a short distance from the school. Then, he spotted Georgina and approached her. "Hello, again."

She jumped.

"My apologies, I didn't mean to startle you."

"Well, you did!" Georgina paused. "I don't have any information for you."

"Has your friend ever gone out late at night?"

"Several times, why?"

"Where did she go?"

"I didn't ask. It could have been to visit a friend."

"Does she not tell you?"

"We're not on good terms, just now."

John Murdoch took out a jar from his coat pocket, then handed it to Georgina. "Maybe this will help. As soon as you are aware of anything, contact Basil. We believe the communists are going to launch an attack, but unsure of the location."

"How do you know?"

"Another source." John Murdoch glanced at the jar. "Enjoy."

"Thanks."

"Put the jar in your bag, someone may try to steal it."

As Georgina did so, John Murdoch departed. Moments after they went their separate ways, the agent looked back and observed a man who walked behind Georgina. Suspicious, John Murdoch followed too and watched as he approached and then spoke to Georgina. When she reacted in a negative manner, the agent intervened and pulled a gun out of his inside coat pocket. "Turn round," he said sharply.

The man stared, ran off and Georgina sighed. "He wanted my bag."

The agent replaced his gun. "In future, don't walk with a bag."

Georgina cast her gaze around the vicinity. "Thank goodness you're here, there's no one else around," she said gratefully.

"That's why he tried his luck."

"During the war, a local man would not steal from a woman."

"People are more desperate than before. Also, a common enemy existed to vent anger at."

"And since that enemy has gone, the conflict is within."

John Murdoch nodded. "The sooner it ends, the better for Crete and its people."

"I'll keep my ears open."

"And your bag hidden."

Georgina nodded.

"Will you be okay?"

"I've not far to go."

"I would walk you home, but your friend will spot me and may ask questions."

"I'll be fine."

"We'll chat later."

Gripping her bag, Georgina continued her walk home. Due to what had happened, her steps quickened. Sooner than usual, she opened the front door, closed it and took a deep breath. Once composed, Georgina went into her bedroom and took off her hat and coat. When she entered the kitchen for a glass of water, Georgina expected to find Elena with her nose in a book. Elena was not there. However, she did observe a piece of paper, which had fallen onto the floor beside a table leg. Georgina picked up the hand-written note and put it on the table. After a welcome glass of water, Georgina sat down and stared at the note. Should she read it? Being curious, Georgina cast her eyes over the note then put it aside. She had to contact John Murdoch right away. Georgina put on her hat and coat and headed for the restaurant. Given her recent experience, quick steps would now be the norm.

As Georgina entered, Basil served a couple at a nearby table. She approached the counter and waited. Moments later, Basil appeared with a tray of used cups and plates.

"I need to speak with John Murdoch."

"One minute, please." Tray in hand, Basil entered the kitchen.

Georgina adjusted her hat and looked out the window. Squads of government troops marched past watched by locals.

"A show of strength to the people of Heraklion."

Georgina turned round.

"You wanted to see me."

When Georgina nodded, John Murdoch looked at an empty table in the far corner of the restaurant. "Let's have a seat."

After he and Georgina sat down, shots could be heard, followed by screams. Georgina and several customers stared out the window. John Murdoch glanced at Georgina. "Another clash between troops and protestors."

"Not the communists?"

John Murdoch shook his head. "If it had been, there would be more than a few shots." He leaned forward. "What's up?"

Georgina handed over the note she had found and then John Murdoch read it. Be at the pre-arranged location within the hour. The assault goes ahead. GS.

"I found it under the kitchen table."

John Murdoch laid the note aside. "It doesn't mention where the attack will occur."

"If she has to meet others within the hour, it can't be far."

"Does she have transport?"

Georgina shook her head. "Unless someone picks her up."

"I'll wager it's at the police station."

"Why?"

"They collaborated with the Germans and now work for the government." John Murdoch got up and gave Georgina the note. "Put it back where you found it."

"Where are you going?"

"To try and prevent a police station from being blown up," said John Murdoch sharply.

Georgina left the restaurant and feared for Elena's safety. Also, not being a violent individual, why would she participate in such a brutal action? Although her political views leaned towards the communist regime, Georgina still found it difficult to comprehend. Walking through the streets, an uneasy tension filled the air. Who sided with which resistance movement?

As she entered the house, Georgina gave a sigh of relief, then removed her hat and coat. She went into the kitchen then jumped. Two men with stern expressions stood.

"Who are you? How did you get in?"

"You met with a British secret agent," said the older of the two.

Georgina raised her eyebrows. "Did I?"

"Do not deny it, you were spotted with him outside the school," said one man sharply.

"Someone did approach me."

"What did you discuss?" asked the same man.

Georgina stared at both men. "Who are you?"

"We ask the questions," said the younger of the two.

"Not in this house." Georgina paused. "I'll contact the authorities."

"If you do, Elena will disapprove."

"Where is she? What have you done with her?"

"She is safe," said the older man. "I will ask again, what did you and the British agent talk about?"

"Why do you want to know?"

The younger man pulled a knife out of his inside jacket pocket and Georgina glanced at its shiny blade. "He invited me out to dinner. However, I told him he wasn't my type."

The younger man gave a slight grin.

"You spoke for some time," said the older man.

"He wouldn't take "no" for an answer."

Both men looked at each other, then the youngest replaced his knife. Georgina stared at both. "When will I see Elena?"

They turned and left, closing the door behind them. Georgina examined the undamaged lock. It had been picked.

Whilst they walked away from the house, the younger man glanced at his older colleague. "Do you believe her?"

"I do not trust foreigners." He paused. "My instinct tells me that there is something afoot."

"Elena would not have told her about our operation."

"The other movement suspected her of collaborating with the Germans."

"Maybe she is a mercenary."

The older man remained silent.

The three British agents met at their headquarters in Heraklion to discuss the current situation. Whilst the destruction of one police station had been averted, another suffered heavy damage. "How many dead?" asked Vic Stampson.

"Three," said John Murdoch, "and three injured."

"Murderers," remarked Alex Taylor.

"The communists don't discriminate," said John Murdoch.

"What is the latest on the northern villages?" asked Alex Taylor.

"They embrace the communists," said John Murdoch.

"All the villages can't be sympathetic." Alec Taylor frowned.

John Murdoch gave a faint smile. "Communist guerrillas are ex-partisans who fought the Germans are thus given food. When government troops on their tails reach a village, people are arrested for being receptive to the enemy."

"Don't they understand what is going on?" Alec Taylor shook his head.

"I hear that more American military advisers are being sent to mainland Greece," said Vic Stampson.

"For bankrolling the Greek government, they are entitled," added John Murdoch. "Since 1944, we've ploughed in £85m."

"At least government forces are now better equipped to deal with the communists," said Vic Stampson.

"And better trained, Vic," said John Murdoch, grinning.

"No doubt the Americans will take the credit," added Alec Taylor.

"With the communist camps being in Albania, the Americans may have to invade the country," said Vic Stampson.

Alec Taylor looked his way. "We don't want WW3, Vic, Stalin would react."

"He isn't interested in this war," said John Murdoch. "The Eastern Bloc is his."

Vic Stampson leaned back on his wooden chair. "At least both sides have agreed to ensure children are away from the conflict. I believe 30,000 are being relocated to the Eastern Bloc."

"What about other children?" asked Alec Taylor.

"Camps are being set up by the government and will have indoctrinating classes," said John Murdoch.

"Similar to Western Germany," added Vic Stampson.

John Murdoch got up, went to a cupboard and opened it. Taking out a bottle of whisky and three glasses, he filled them to the brim. Alec Taylor proposed a toast. "To the future Greek government."

"And the commencement of a new English football season," said Vic Stampson, as he grinned.

"In Scotland as well," added John Murdoch.

The three agents clinked their glasses, took a swig and then emptied them. Alec Taylor looked at John Murdoch. "By the way, where did you obtain the whisky?" he asked, surprised, but delighted.

"Same place as the coffee, my American contact." He refilled each glass, then sat down.

"I hear you've recruited an assistant, John," said Vic Stampson.

"A blonde American lady," added Alec Taylor.

"Is she your American contact?" asked Vic Stampson.

John Murdoch gave a slight grin. "She is not my assistant, nor my American contact." He took a sip. "However, the person that she shares a house with has links to the communists."

"Will she tell on this person?" asked Vic Stampson, as he sipped his whisky.

"Georgina Rhodes is a capitalist and an anti-communist, it's good to have her on board."

"But is she reliable, John?" asked Alec Taylor.

"I believe so. Our friends in America's National Intelligence Authority gave me information."

"Anything of interest?" Alec Taylor raised his eyebrows.

"When she lived in New York, her husband was murdered and the NYPD thought she may have been involved. She later met an actor and moved to California."

"I would like to meet this woman," said Alec Taylor.

"The actor died not long after they met."

Alec Taylor sighed. "Perhaps not."

As John Murdoch grinned, Vic Stampson took a swig and put his empty glass on the table. "On another note, it can't be a harmonious atmosphere with a capitalist and a communist under the same roof."

"Throughout the country most towns and villages will be similar," added John Murdoch.

Alec Taylor looked at John Murdoch. "Did your American friends tell you any other snippets of interest?"

"Albania is about to declare itself as a republic, also Hungary." John

Murdoch finished his whisky and set it on the table. "The recent United Nations event in London went well. Churchill gave a speech on the potential threat of Russia and their desire to engulf other nations."

"You mean the Soviet Union, John," said Vic Stampson.

"My contact also spoke about a threat to peace in Asia."

"The Chinese," said Alec Taylor.

John Murdoch shook his head. "North Vietnam. They have just appointed a leader called Ho Chi Minh, who seeks recognition for his country."

"Being in control of Indo-China, the French will not be receptive," said Alec Taylor.

"He won't be as bad as Stalin," quipped Vic Stampson.

Alec Taylor laughed.

Vic Stampson looked at John Murdoch. "Are you saving the whisky for a special occasion?"

All three glasses received a refill.

Georgina finished her music class and departed the school. Since the civil war began, pupil attendance had fallen and as a consequence, she only taught on two afternoons per week. With Elena gone and also her father's subsidence, Georgina faced hardship. The majority of people on Crete endured similar problems, however, American aid had been injected and this prevented Cretan citizens from starvation.

Georgina reached a depressed Heraklion town centre, where men mingled around the concrete fountain. Hands in pockets, their shabby appearance and glum expressions epitomised this difficult period. Georgina reflected on her time in New York during the Depression of 1929, where a similar sense of hopelessness existed. With time on her hands, Georgina walked through the market to browse, but only half of the stalls remained open for business. Traders had also joined the despair that engulfed Heraklion. A stocky man with a white beard approached Georgina. "Come to my stall pretty lady, I have many good gifts," said the trader cheerily.

"I'm just having a look."

"Then come and see my selection. You won't be disappointed."

Georgina glanced sideways. "I passed your stall a few minutes ago."

"I will give you a good price for any item."

"I've no money with me."

"Come back tomorrow?" The trader grinned.

"Perhaps."

Returning to his stall, the trader shouted at a youth lifting a trinket. Not being able to catch the thief, he stopped and took deep breaths. Georgina watched. He won't vacate his stall again.

Leaving the market, Georgina heard footsteps behind her and glanced round. A man in a grey cap and jacket walked behind in close proximity. Georgina crossed the deserted street and the man followed. She stopped and faced him. His inability to shave and a prominent cheek scar made Georgina held her breath. "Hand over your bag," said the man sharply, as he glared.

Georgina hesitated. "I don't have any money."

"What is in the bag?"

"Only what a woman would use." Georgina drew breath.

"Give me the bag, I have a knife." The man went into his coat pocket.

Georgina noticed another man cross the street put a hand into his coat side-pocket, which created a bulge. The man's footsteps made the robber turn round. "Beat it, or I will shoot."

After he fled, the gallant individual produced a bare hand from his pocket. As Georgina stared, he grinned. "It works every time."

Georgina sighed. "Thanks."

"You should not walk the streets alone, it is dangerous."

Georgina drew breath. "I'm grateful."

"Someone asked me to keep an eye on you."

"Who?"

"A British agent."

"John Murdoch?"

The man nodded. "I work for the Greek government."

"Are you also an agent?"

The man nodded. "When out, ensure you are with someone." He looked at where the man ran off. "Opportunists will then think twice."

"Give my thanks to the British agent," said Georgina gratefully.

"He would like to see you about a security matter. He will be at the restaurant tomorrow at three o'clock."

"I'll be there."

The man glanced at Georgina's bag.

"I won't carry one again."

The following day, Georgina left her house and headed for the appointed restaurant. After her scare from yesterday, she walked through the streets minus a bag and with a tinge of apprehension.

Soon, Georgina reached her destination and entered. She spotted John Murdoch at a table with his nose in a book. As Georgina approached, he looked up and laid the book aside. She sat down, removed her hat and then placed it on the table.

"Good to see you again."

Georgina glanced at the book. "Brave New World by Aldous Huxley."

"It's set in the future where society is genetically engineered."

"Did the Germans not attempt to carry out this type of experiment?"

John Murdoch hesitated. "Who told you that?"

"A German officer based on the island."

"It's not standard knowledge."

Georgina gave a wry smile. "I'm good at getting people to talk."

"You would have made a good SS officer."

Georgina laughed.

"Since you can get people to reveal information, perhaps you can help us to find out where Janouski is located?"

"Janouski?"

John Murdoch nodded.

"I don't know of anyone who is a member of the communist party."

"Oh yes you do."

"I haven't seen Elena for days."

"There is someone at your school who is an activist."

"In the school!"

Once more, John Murdoch nodded.

"Who?"

"The history teacher."

"Are you positive?" Georgina paused. "He is the last person that I would suspect."

"Why?"

"He's an introvert."

John Murdoch gave a wry smile. "They make effective spies."

"What evidence do you have?"

"Before Draco followed you…"

Georgina interrupted. "Draco is the man who confronted the robber?"

John Murdoch nodded. "A man left the school and dropped a file, which Draco retrieved. It contained communist propaganda material."

"I take it Draco didn't hand the file into our school?"

"Correct. However, Greek historical tutorial material was also in the file."

Georgina gave a slight smile. "That's a comfort."

"Draco kept the several sheets of propaganda and discarded the file." John Murdoch paused. "Are you on good terms with this teacher?"

"We say hello to each other."

"Be more chatty."

"He may not want to talk."

"Use your charm, ask to meet later."

"He may have a partner."

"He hasn't, I've checked."

"Maybe I'm not his type. Also, he's younger."

"There's a war on and men need to be comforted."

"I will only go on a date, Mr Murdoch."

"That is what I meant, Mrs Rhodes."

Georgina hesitated. "I'm not a spy, this isn't my thing."

"I'll get you more coffee and other American essentials. We have German wine looted from a garrison in Chania."

"Okay." Georgina glanced towards the counter. "Basil rings the till, but there is no transaction carried out. That's the third time I've seen him do it."

"The ring signals a stranger has entered the restaurant."

Once more, Georgina glanced towards the counter.

"Draco will escort you home."

"Where is he?"

John Murdoch glanced to a table in the corner. "Behind you."

After Georgina turned round, a dark-haired man with a droopy moustache gave a slight nod. She rose and then looked downwards. "When can you get the wine to me?"

"As soon as I can." John Murdoch gave a faint smile. "Information on Janouski will speed up the process. Almost forgot."

Georgina put on her hat. "Yes?"

"You dated a man called Stelios?"

"I haven't seen him for several years."

"He was taken prisoner by the Germans and then shot. His girlfriend turned out to be a German spy."

"Two members of the resistance confronted me and claimed I was a German spy."

"It would appear she tried to 'stitch you up'."

Georgina pondered. Jealous bitch.

CHAPTER 16

THE ASSIGNMENT

After her music session had finished, Georgina went to the school office and handed in the classroom key. As she approached the exit door. Georgina stopped. Damn, forgot my umbrella. Returning to the office, she retrieved it and then departed. Whilst she walked toward the school exit door, Georgina heard footsteps on the stone floor from behind. Anxious, Georgina stopped, looked round and faced a tall slim individual with short black wavy hair. "Hello," he said.

"Are you finished for the day?"

"Yes, at last." The man gave a slight smile.

When both schoolteachers left the building, Georgina dropped her umbrella and the man picked it up. After he handed the umbrella to Georgina, the man glanced upwards. "A sensible choice to bring one."

As the rain started to pour, Georgina put up her umbrella and the man his raincoat collar. He looked at Georgina. "I must dash."

"Do you have far to go?"

"I will be fine."

"Let's go for a coffee and by then the rain may have gone off."

The man hesitated, then nodded. Under a small umbrella, the two colleagues walked to the centre of Heraklion. A short time later, they arrived at a restaurant open for business.

"Phew!" said Georgina, as she put down the umbrella and gave it a shake. The man put down his collar. When they entered, only one other customer could be seen. Georgina looked towards a far corner. "How about over there?"

"Okay," said the man, smiling.

After they sat down, a waiter appeared with two menus in his hand. Georgina looked at his cheerful expression. "A meal for two?" The waiter laid two menus on the white tablecloth.

"Two coffees, please," said the man politely.

The waiter stared, picked up the menus and departed, along with his cheery expression. Georgina leaned across the table. "I don't suppose he'll serve many meals in this horrible climate."

"Indeed, the weather is grim."

A smile flickered over Georgina's face. "I meant the war." She paused. "I should introduce myself, my name is Georgina."

"I am Emilio."

"Given that we teach in the same school, it's strange that our paths haven't crossed." Georgina considered. His name and looks are that of an Italian. "Are you from Italy?"

"My mother left after the First World War ended. Father was killed in 1917 and she brought me to Crete for a fresh start."

"Did your mother have relatives on the island?"

Emilio nodded. "An aunt and uncle in Hersonissos."

"Greece and Italy have suffered over the last six years."

"Especially, Greece, with a civil war now to endure."

Whilst the waiter prepared two coffees, Georgina glanced towards the counter, then unbuttoned her coat.

"Why did you come to Crete?"

"Similar to your mother, a fresh start."

"Why leave a prosperous country such as America?"

"Personal circumstances."

Emilio sat back on his chair. "It is indeed strange that our paths have never crossed."

"I only teach part-time and in a different part of the school." He doesn't appear the introvert I took him for.

Emilio looked up. "At last, coffee." He glanced at Georgina. "I will pay."

Georgina smiled. Good, I'm skint.

Before she left to meet Emilio for a dinner date, Georgina took a final look in the mirror. What would Elena be doing and is she well? The mountain terrain of Crete won't be a hospitable place at this time of year. Georgina put on her hat, adjusted it and then left the house.

A winter chill in the air still existed, therefore, Georgina walked in a brisk manner. Wary of strangers, she kept her eyes open and her wits intact. Emilio had offered to call at the house, but since Georgina had to extract information from him, she wanted to keep her distance. To become familiar would make Georgina's task more difficult than it appeared. After all, if she did not succeed, no luxuries would come her way. Several minutes later, Georgina could not feel the house keys in her coat pocket. After a few moments of reflection, she retraced her steps. Outside the house, she spotted her keys beside the door. She shook her head and cursed. Picking them up, Georgina placed the keys deep into her coat pocket. Now, she would not be at the restaurant on time. Once more, Georgina cursed.

Making her way to the town centre, Georgina heard a loud bang. Residents emerged from properties with bewildered expressions onto the street. One young woman with no make-up went up to Georgina. "Did you see what happened?"

"An explosion, I think."

A middle-aged man looked at both women. "It will be another bomb attack by the communists."

As a murmur followed between residents, Georgina walked with apprehension to her rendezvous with Emilio.

Upon her arrival several minutes later, Georgina observed police and soldiers in attendance. A medical crew had been quick on the scene and Georgina watched them lift a bloodstained body onto a stretcher. The injured person taken into an ambulance appeared devoid of life. Horrified onlookers conversed with each other. Georgina approached a police officer. "What happened?"

"An attack on the restaurant." He glanced at the damaged exterior.

Sunned, Georgina stared, then looked at the police officer. "I had arranged to meet someone here."

The police officer stared. "A man or woman?"

"A male colleague from work."

"Five male casualties have been reported."

The ambulance crew returned with a stretcher to the bomb-blast establishment and brought out a body covered with a sheet. Georgina glanced at the police officer. "A fatality."

He nodded. "I'm afraid so."

Georgina cast her gaze around the vicinity for any trace of Emilio. When the bomb exploded, had he been inside? The police officer looked at Georgina with a concerned expression. "This is the third in a week."

"Why would this restaurant be targeted?"

"Government staff are known to dine here."

"I would have been here earlier, but was delayed."

"Just as well, otherwise, we would not be having this conversation."

Once more, Georgina cast her gaze around the vicinity. "I can't see my colleague."

"I suggest you return home. Injured personnel will be revealed tomorrow."

As she walked home, Georgina reflected. New York appeared a

paradise compared to Heraklion. Also, she thought about Emilio and hoped he had not been a victim. A brutal conflict now existed between two rival ideologies in Crete. Additional misery for the public and what would the outcome be? Given the situation with Crete's economy, there would be no winners in this civil war.

The following day, Georgina took her afternoon class and when it finished, went to the school office. The female administrator with tied back grey hair sitting behind a desk looked up over her spectacles.

"Was there a history class today?" Georgina put her classroom key on a hook.

The administrator nodded. "This morning, but the pupils had a different teacher. Why do you ask?"

"I haven't seen Emilio today."

As the administrator started to use a typewriter, Georgina left the office. Leaving the building, she walked for several minutes and then someone appeared from a secluded doorway. Georgina jumped. "Do you have to do that?"

John Murdoch grinned. "My apologies."

"I don't have any information for you."

"Did you meet up with him?"

"We went for coffee and arranged to meet last night at a restaurant in the town. However, when I got there, a bomb had destroyed it." Georgina paused. "If I had been there on time, a hospital visit could have been on the cards."

"Indeed."

"He missed his class today."

"Oh?" John Murdoch raised his dark eyebrows.

"What do you want me to do?"

"When is your next class?"

"In two days."

"Are you on your way home?"

"Yes, why?"

"There is someone I would like you to meet."

"Who?"

"One of my colleagues. I am being moved to mainland Greece, therefore, he will be your new contact."

"Is it necessary for us to meet just now?"

"He has access to coffee and wine," said John Murdoch, as he gave a wry smile.

"Where are the goods that you promised me the last time we met?"

"They are at Basil's restaurant. Don't worry, I didn't forget."

The amiable British agent and Georgina went to the restaurant and a short while later, entered. A man, who sat by himself in a corner, looked up. His dark blue overcoat and scarf being protection from the current Cretan winter. As John Murdoch led Georgina towards his table, the man stood.

"Vic, this is Georgina."

"Pleased to meet you," said Vic politely, as he shook Georgina's hand.

When she and the two agents sat down, a waiter came over to take their order. Vic looked up at him. "Three coffees, please, Leo."

The waiter nodded and then departed. Georgina glanced at both men. "Is it Basil's day off?"

"He has gone to collect supplies for the restaurant," said Vic Stampson.

"Coffee and wine?" Georgina gave a slight smile.

Vic Stampson pulled out a small jar of coffee from his coat pocket and as Georgina stared, laid it in on the table in front of her. She looked at John Murdoch. "A small jar?"

"There is a war on, you know." He glanced at his colleague.

"Thanks," said Georgina, as she put the jar in her coat pocket.

Three coffees arrived on a silver tray and after the waiter set them down, Vic Stampson gave him cash. The waiter thanked him and left. Whilst Georgina sipped a welcome cup, John Murdoch glanced at his colleague. "The person that you arranged to meet had been tipped-off about the attack," said Vic Stampson.

"How do you know?"

"A contact in their organisation."

"Can this person not reveal where Janouski is?" Georgina looked at both agents.

"They don't know," said John Murdoch.

"Hence why we need your assistance," added Vic Stampson.

"What makes you think Emilio will want to meet again?"

John Murdoch gave a wry smile. "Your looks."

Vic Stampson grinned, lifted his cup and took a swig. After he set it down, stood. "Good to meet you, Georgina, I'll be in touch."

Georgina looked up. That was sudden. After Vic Stampson departed, she began to contemplate.

"What's up?" John Murdoch took a swig of his coffee.

"Is your colleague going to confront me near the school as well?"

"I'm not sure, but at least you'll know who it is," said John Murdoch, as he gave a slight smile. When the history teacher returns to work, make another arrangement."

"Where?" Georgina paused. "I don't want to get blown up."

"A quiet taverna will do the trick. Do you know of one in the town?"

"Yes."

John Murdoch stood. "Good luck, and thanks for what you're doing. I understand that this isn't your thing."

"I'd appreciate a favour."

"More coffee?"

Georgina gave a faint smile. "No, information."

"What about?"

"A German officer taken prisoner when the war ended."

"On Crete?"

"His name is Captain Erich Hoeness."

"He could be back in Germany, but if something turns up, I'll let Vic know." John Murdoch paused. "I trust he wasn't a Nazi?"

"He removed food from German stores and supplied Cretan families."

"Doesn't sound like one."

"He wasn't."

"I'll walk you home."

"It's okay, I don't carry a bag anymore."

John Murdoch gave a slight grin and following a farewell to the waiter, left the restaurant. Georgina finished her coffee and thought about Erich. The waiter approached with his distinctive tray, lifted two empty cups and saucers, then looked at Georgina. "Another coffee, madam?"

Georgina looked up.

"It's on the house."

She smiled.

Georgina finished her Tuesday class then went to the school office. As she handed in the door key, Emilio appeared and Georgina stared. "Can we talk?"

Georgina nodded and Emilio gave his classroom key to the administrator, then both schoolteachers left her office. In the corridor, Emilio gave a forced smile. "I apologise for last week."

"You blew up the restaurant?"

Emilio smiled, then stared. "I am relieved you were not injured."

"I looked for you." Georgina paused. "What happened?"

Emilio hesitated. "Something urgent came up. Let us make a new arrangement."

"Where shall we meet?"

"I know a quiet establishment."

"In Heraklion?"

"I can assure you there will be no trouble."

"Is it a restaurant?"

"A taverna."

"What is it called?"

"Sergios. It is owned by a relative of mine."

"When?"

"Let us say Friday evening, around 7.30?"

"Okay."

"See you then," said Emilio, smiling.

"Have you finished for the day?"

Emilio shook his head. "I have to see the Principal about a personal matter."

Georgina left the school and shivered. Putting up her coat collar, she walked in a hurried manner and as the wind blew, held onto her hat. As Georgina turned a corner, a man wearing a dark hat and long grey coat stepped out of a doorway. She jumped. "What is it with you guys and creepy doorways."

Vic Stampson tipped his hat. "My sincere apologies," he said politely.

"What do you want?"

"Have you made contact with the schoolteacher?"

"As a matter of fact, he contacted me."

"When do you plan to meet?"

"Are you going to spy on us?"

Vic Stampson shook his head. "Just curious."

"We've arranged to meet on Friday evening at a local taverna."

"What is it called?"

"Sergios."

"There won't be any bombs going off at that establishment."

"What makes you say that?"

"It is run by one of Heraklion's most popular citizens."

A male and female teacher from the school came into view and as they passed Georgina, they gave an acknowledgement. Moments later, Vic Stampson looked their way, then at Georgina. "They will think that I'm a friend."

Georgina stared. I hope not. "Has John Murdoch been in touch?"

"Why do you ask?"

"I asked him if he could discover the whereabouts of someone."

"Who?"

"An Erich Hoeness."

"A German!"

"Yes, a German," said Georgina sharply.

"He hasn't contacted me." Unshaven Vic Stampson turned up his coat collar. "See you next week."

"Bring the wine, Vic," cried Georgina.

He grinned and departed.

Whilst Georgina got ready to meet Emilio, she thought about Elena. Would she be in the mountainous north region of Crete where a communist camp is reputed to be? If so, their primitive facilities would not endear Elena, who enjoyed her comforts. Georgina stared into the mirror and observed another facial line, followed by a sigh. These wars will be the death of me. She put on her hat and coat, then left the house.

Walking towards the town centre, Georgina noticed two scruffy men near an alleyway. On the opposite side of a street, Georgina could feel the weight of their stares. Are they opportunist thieves, and which group in the civil war do they have an allegiance to? If desperate, it would not matter who they steal from. Grateful that she did not have her handbag, Georgina quickened her steps.

As she approached the taverna, Georgina heard laughter emanate from it. A quiet drink would not ensue this evening with Emilio. Inside, she observed men and women at tables full of glasses. Then, Emilio approached from behind. "Georgina."

She turned round.

"I hope I did not startle you," said Emilio, as he gave a slight smile.

"I'm just a bit tense."

"In a climate of war it is understandable."

Georgina cast her gaze around the bar. "It doesn't appear so."

"People here forget about their troubles and enjoy themselves."

Georgina stared. "Indeed, they do."

"Let us sit down." Emilio led Georgina to a vacant table in the far corner.

Georgina removed her hat and placed it on an empty chair beside her. As she unbuttoned her dark coat, Emilio tried not to stare at Georgina's cleavage. A waiter came over and did his utmost to remain professional. Emilio glanced at Georgina. "What would you like to drink?"

Georgina looked up at the waiter. "A glass of white wine."

"A large glass, madam?"

Georgina gave a slight nod and then the waiter looked at Emilio.

"My usual."

After the waiter departed, Georgina watched people consume glasses of wine and spirits with total disregard of the consequences. "No shortage of alcohol here."

The owner has his contacts." Emilio gave a wry smile.

"Must be a good contact." Once more, Georgina cast her gaze around the bar. "Is it like this every night?"

Emilio shook his head. "Monday is quiet."

"Only Monday?"

"Here, people forget the war." He looked at a group of jovial customers. "Most of them will have relatives or friends who see action."

"They are doing a good job." Georgina paused. "Which side?"

"Does it matter? Who do you believe fights for a just cause, Georgina?"

"I'm an American, therefore, neutral."

"The Americans as well as the British support the government. More so the Americans, as they make a larger contribution."

"I don't get involved in politics."

Emilio looked up. "Here come our drinks."

Georgina glanced round. Well timed.

From his wooden tray, the waiter placed a drink in front of Georgina and then Emilio. Picking up her glass, Georgina took a large swallow and set it down. I needed that.

"How long have you lived on Crete?" asked Emilio, as he sipped his glass of ouzo.

"Since before the Italians invaded."

"We kicked their backsides," said Emilio, smiling.

A well-built middle-aged man entered, spotted Emilio and came over to the table. He stared at Georgina's dark blue dress and then faced Emilio. "Can we speak later?"

Emilio nodded. "Of course."

Before the man departed, he looked at Georgina, gave a faint smile and then headed for the bar. Georgina picked up her glass and looked across the table. "A relative."

"No." Emilio took a swig. After he set his glass down, the waiter reappeared with two drinks. "Courtesy of Sergio," he said cheerily, then departed.

Georgina emptied her glass, set it down and picked up the full one. "I like your relative."

"He is a generous individual." Emilio picked up his half-empty glass and finished it. "He killed many Germans."

Georgina glanced round. "Is that why he is popular?"

"A friend to most Cretans."

"Most?"

"Crete is split between two directions in which to progress."

"What is Sergio's viewpoint?"

Emilio leaned back. "Similar to mine."

"And that is?" asked Georgina, as she sipped her wine.

"Equality for all."

Georgina pondered. He's not a government supporter that's for sure.

"And what about you, Georgina?"

She stared at her glass. "As long as certain comforts are available at all times, I've no preference."

When Emilio laughed, Georgina gave a slight smile. Then, he moved forward and stared. "Your friend had a preference."

Georgina looked at him, surprised. "Elena? How do you know?"

"I cannot say," said Emilio, as he leaned backwards.

"How is she?"

"I believe she is well."

"Do you know where she is?"

"I am unsure of her location."

"She'll miss her wine," said Georgina, as she looked at her glass.

At that moment, the waiter came across and whispered into Emilio's ear. He nodded and looked at Georgina. "I have to speak with Sergio." He stood.

Georgina looked up. "I'm going soon, I've an early start tomorrow."

"I will no doubt see you at some point."

As Emilio followed the waiter, Georgina finished her wine and left the taverna, watched by Sergio.

Walking home, Georgina reflected on her evening in the company of Emilio. Good looks and charm would not influence him to reveal the whereabouts of Janouski. Vic Stampson would have to come up with another solution.

Emilio sat with Sergio and another man. The waiter came over with three drinks, set them on the table and left. After the three men lifted their glasses, Sergio looked across at Emilio. "An attractive woman."

"She teaches music at the school."

"Has she been there long?"

Emilio nodded.

Sergio glanced at the other man. "Nikos spotted her with a man near the school who we believe is a British agent."

"They chatted for a short time," said Nikos.

Emilio looked at Sergio. "She does not give me the impression of being a spy."

"What is her stance on politics?" asked Sergio.

"She does not have one."

Sergio picked up his glass. "Did she say that?"

"As long as she has enough wine to drink."

When Nikos laughed, Sergio stared at him, then finished his drink.

Alex Taylor and Vic Stampson sat in their furnished Heraklion town centre government office and chatted. Given their previous makeshift places in which to operate, this was luxury. Then, a knock on the door and both agents looked up. A tall bronzed man in a regular British uniform entered. "Excuse me, sir." The sergeant glanced at each agent. "Would you care for a cup of tea?"

When both men nodded, he departed and closed the door. Vic Stampson looked at his colleague. "A warm drink is welcome today."

Alex Taylor got up and gazed out the window. "It's cold for April."

Vic Stampson looked towards it. "Anything of interest?"

Alex Taylor shook his head, then stared. "Wait a minute."

"What is it?"

"Two Greek soldiers have approached a man and are carrying out a search. He's not pleased." Alex Taylor glanced at his colleague. "One of the soldiers has found a gun on him."

Vic Stampson got up and approached the window just in time to see the man run off. After he ignored a soldier's command to stop, shots rang out. The man held his leg, then limped off down an alleyway. Alex Taylor commented, "I'll wager there will be a reprisal tonight.

Following a knock, the door opened and a junior soldier entered with two white mugs of tea. Each agent took a mug, thanked the young man, and as he left returned to their seats. Vic Stampson took a sip. "Pity there is a shortage of sugar."

"Little point complaining to Winston, he's no longer in charge."

"He would have made sure we received a supply." Vic Stampson reflected. "I still find it difficult to believe Atlee won the election. After all, Winston kept us going throughout 1941."

"When we stood alone."

"So why did he lose?"

Alec Taylor shrugged his shoulders. "Perhaps the British public wanted a fresh start. On another matter, how is our pretty associate faring? Has she met with the schoolteacher?"

"She contacted Basil to pass on a message," said Vic Stampson, as he grinned. "She asked about the wine I promised her."

Alec Taylor laughed and as both men sipped their cups of tea, there came another knock on the door and a young woman in uniform entered. She laid a piece of folded paper on the table. "Sorry to interrupt, sir, we just received this message for you."

After the soldier departed, both agents looked at each other and grinned. Vic Stampson set his cup down, picked up the note and started to read.

"Important news?" asked Alec Taylor, as he sipped his tea.

"It's from John."

"Bad news?"

"Our pretty associate asked him to find out what happened to a Captain Erich Hoeness based in Heraklion during the German occupation."

"Oh?"

"From what I've heard, this SS officer gave supplies of food to the local community."

"Sounds far-fetched."

Vic Stampson glanced at his colleague. "I've heard this from a number of sources."

"What does John say?"

"Captain Hoeness was taken to a camp in Scotland, along with other SS personnel."

"The surroundings will be a distinct contrast to here," said Alec Taylor, as a grin crept across his face. "Are you going to tell her?"

Vic Stampson picked up his mug. "If there has been a romance, she may head straight for Scotland. I need her to be here."

"If she asks, say John hasn't been in touch. Did he mention the situation in mainland Greece?"

Vic Stampson shook his head. "It would not be good news. The partisans appear to have the upper hand."

"Yugoslavia's Tito is the driving force with his troops, supplies and guerrilla tactics."

Vic Stampson finished his tea, then put the mug beside the note. "This war is not cricket."

"More like rugby," said Alec Taylor, grinning, "A game for ruffians, but played by gentlemen."

"Not on this occasion."

After a further interruption, the junior soldier returned and looked at each agent. "A refill, sir?"

Both nodded.

On another bitter cold morning, complete with hat, coat and scarf, Georgina walked to school. Although class numbers had fallen, it still provided an income. Essentials came courtesy of her liaison with British Intelligence, but for how long? As for Emilio, Georgina had not seen him and he had made no effort to contact her.

Doing her best to keep warm, Georgina walked quickly and arrived at the school in good time. As she entered the office to collect her class register, the stern grey-haired administrator looked over her spectacles. "You may not have a full class today."

Georgina loosened her light blue woollen scarf. "Why not?"

"Since Monday, a sickness bug has affected most of the classes." The administrator sat back on her chair. "Several teachers have reported in sick."

"Which subjects are affected?"

"Geography, mathematics and history."

Georgina picked up her register from a table. That could explain why Emilio hasn't been in touch. "Did you manage to find replacement teachers?"

"The classes have been cancelled," said the administrator, as she sighed. "Hopefully, they will resume soon."

Georgina left the office and walked to her class. When she entered, only three pupils had turned up. She put the register on her desk and gave a forced smile to attendees. "Glad you could make it." Otherwise, no payment for me.

One pupil raised his hand.

"Yes, Eros?"

"Miss, can we learn about the recent war instead of music today?"

"Mr Gabris is off sick and he was going to discuss it," said another pupil.

Georgina looked at them. "Don't you enjoy being taught music?"

"With the civil war in progress, it would be relevant, said the third teenager."

Georgina gave a wry smile. Smart. "Okay, we will have a history lesson and a double period of music on Thursday."

Each of the pupils gave a slight smile. Georgina sat at her desk, ticked three names in the register, then laid it aside. "What do you want to know about the Second World War?"

After a pupil raised their hand, Georgina acknowledged them. "Yes, Carin."

"Did Germany start it?"

"They invaded Poland, and because of this unprovoked attack, Britain and France declared war on them."

Another raised a hand and Georgina looked their way. "Yes, Eros. "Why did they invade Poland?"

"To expand German territory. Prior to Poland, they entered Austria and then Czechoslovakia."

"Is entered the same as invaded, miss?" asked Alexa.

"The occupation of Austria and part of Czechoslovakia came by means of diplomacy."

"Is that another word for a bribe, miss?" asked Carin.

Georgina smiled. "It has been known."

Another pupil raised his hand.

"Yes, Eros.

"Why did they attack us?"

"To bail out Italy when Greece made them withdraw back to Albania."

"Are the Italians poor fighters?" asked Carin.

"It would appear so," said Georgina, as she gave a slight smile.

"They drank and ate all the time," said Eros sharply.

Once more, Georgina smiled.

"Why did Turkey not enter the war, miss?"

Carin looked at her fellow pupil. "In case they were beaten by our army."

"Can you tell us about the First World War, miss," said Alexa.

"Before it started, some of the countries involved had monarchs, who ruled Austria, Germany and Russia. When those countries faced defeat, their monarchs were overthrown."

"For the better?" asked Eros.

"In the case of Germany, a dictator emerged, which resulted in a war where Germany suffered high casualties."

"And the country's self-respect," added Carin.

Georgina nodded.

"Can you tell us about your home in America, miss?" asked Alexa.

"How long did you live there?" asked Carin.

"I stayed in New York for twenty years and then moved to California."

"In New York, did you stay near Wall Street?" asked Alexa.

"No, a place called Upper Manhattan. Wall Street is in Lower Manhattan. Upper Manhattan had bars, restaurants and theatres. Also, a railway which ran under and over the city."

The pupils stared at each other, no doubt their young imaginations stirred at the thought of one of the world's largest cities. Carina asked, "How many people live in New York?"

"When I lived there, about six million of various nationalities. A lot of people emigrated from Europe and beyond for a better life. However, we had a depression in 1929, which caused hardship for families."

"Similar to Heraklion?" asked Eros.

Georgina nodded.

"Please tell us about California, miss," said Carin. "I would like to visit there someday."

"Did you meet Charlie Chaplin?" asked Eros.

"No, but I sat near to him in a restaurant."

Both teenage girls stared in awe, made an emotional 'wow' and gave a wide smile.

"And he bought me a drink."

"Why did you leave California?" asked Carin.

"I had heard so many good things about Crete, I wanted to live here."

All three teenagers giggled.

"Did you meet any other famous film stars, miss?" asked Alexa.

"A few."

Alexa looked at her two fellow pupils. "I am going to be an actress one day."

"Me too!" said Carin.

"What about you, Eros?" asked Georgina.

"I want to go into politics, miss."

"Is there any particular reason?"

"To represent Crete and help our people in any way I can," said Eros.

"What happened to the German soldiers who surrendered on Crete, miss?" asked Alexa.

"I presume they went back to Germany and rebuild their lives."

"What about the SS guards who committed crimes in our towns and villages?" asked Carin.

"They will be tried in a court of law." Georgina's train of thought turned to Erich. As an SS officer on Crete, would he be prosecuted? Given he helped locals, surely not.

Miss," said Eros.

Georgina reflected.

"Miss."

Georgina looked at him.

"Why did the civil war start?"

"Different ideologies between two resistance movements."

"Which side do you support, miss?" asked Alexa.

Georgina hesitated. "Whoever is best for Greece."

"How long will the war last, miss?" asked Carin.

"It should end as soon as possible."

Carin looked at her two fellow pupils. "I cannot get my favourite cheese."

"And chocolate," added Alexa.

As the three teenagers giggled, Georgina glanced at the circular wall clock. "Let us leave it there. When Mr Gabris returns, he can answer any other history questions you may have."

After the pupils departed, Georgina again began to reflect. Did Erich stand trial? Has he returned to Germany and his job as a schoolteacher? I must ask Vic Stampson if he has any news.

CHAPTER 17

THE RECKONING

After a late morning cup of coffee, Georgina turned on the radio for the twelve o'clock news. The civil war showed no sign of an end and hardship in Crete became a routine existence. With a definite split in ideology, the population of Heraklion became more wary of each other and as a consequence most withdrew from public view. Only young men and other brave individuals dared to venture out after dark.

A recent impromptu history discussion with her music class had made Georgina think about the past. Her cultured Manhattan and lavish Californian lifestyles had become a distant memory. Her sister, Elizabeth, had mentioned in her letters to visit whenever it suited. As she stayed in the south of France, Elizabeth's invitation had appeal. However, as with most people who had left Scotland for pastures new, Georgina thought about a return. Since she left Argyll as an ambitious young woman for New York, three eventful decades had come and gone. Her late husband and former partner had both gambled: not only on a card table with her money, but also with her affection and patience.

When the international news broadcaster spoke, Georgina listened in the hope of an exclusive. As a sign of the times in war-torn Heraklion, radio is the main form of entertainment. Apart from Japanese women being allowed to vote for the first time and Syria's independence from France, the news did not expand. Due to threats of it being bombed by partisans, the radio station in Athens had closed; thus, local news had ceased. Also, since newspapers on the island remained scarce, gossip became Crete's main source of communication. Depending on whom it came from depicted the reliability. Georgina turned the radio off, and went to a closet. She picked out a book, sat down and opened it. After a short read, she put it aside and contemplated. To heck with this mundane humdrum day, I'm going out to the town centre and take my chances. Georgina went into her bedroom, opened the wardrobe and then put on a jacket and hat. Before she left, Georgina checked herself in the mirror.

As she suspected, apart from young males, the streets remained deserted. Not only because of partisan bomb threats, also robbers.

When Georgina arrived at the town centre, a group of youths had congregated at the fountain in Lions Square. As a government patrol marched past, one youth taunted them. After he repeated the act, several police officers appeared and confronted him. A struggle followed, and other youths joined in. A melee ensued; one police officer took out his pistol from a holster and fired several shots. After the youths ran off, the officer replaced his gun. A bloodstained youth lay near the fountain surrounded by officers. People in the vicinity, stood in silence and stared.

Minutes later, an ambulance arrived on the scene. A crewmember got out, lifted the body and took it into the vehicle. After it moved off, a murmur ensued between the crowd of bystanders. A white-haired man supported by a walking stick who stood next to Georgina shook his head. "When the Germans left, I looked forward to a new beginning." He sighed. "Will I ever see peace in our town again."

George looked at him. "Perhaps in the near future, this can't go on forever."

The man shook his head. "The communist representatives did not bother to turn up for last month's government elections." He stared. "It could be a long drawn-out conflict."

After the man departed, Georgina headed for the market, but when she got there found the shutters up. A stocky individual passing shook his head. "No trade, therefore, no traders." He went on, "However, it's open on a Monday and Friday morning," said the man.

"Do you have a stall?"

"My younger brother has, I'm glad it's not me."

Georgina sighed. "There isn't much to do in Heraklion these days."

The man glanced towards a building. "The church is open and it costs nothing to enter," he said, with a slight grin.

As he walked on, Georgina returned to the square and spotted Emilio with two men. Moments later, they went into an establishment where Georgina and he had visited. Should she enter? Whilst Georgina stood and considered, Emilio left the taverna and got into a car. After it moved off, Georgina elected to return home. With dark clouds on the horizon, it appeared the right choice.

Following a light evening meal, which was all Georgina's budget allowed, she sat on the couch with a book. Being a cheap form of entertainment, to read became a regular occurrence. Several minutes later, Georgina put down her book and mulled her thoughts. Should she remain here and if so, what does the future hold? The money earned from teaching kept her head above water, but only just. Also, would she see Elena again? Living on her own did not suit Georgina. She compared her depressed situation to before Eddie appeared on the scene. However, afterwards, a life of luxury came about, albeit for a short time. Eddie's gambling addiction soon shattered Georgina's affluent Californian lifestyle. Georgina sighed, then picked up the book again. Then, she heard knocks on the rear door. Georgina hesitated. Who could that be? Once more, she laid down her book and listened. Hearing a faint cry, Georgina got up and then went into the kitchen. "Who is it?" she cried.

"It, it is Elena," said a raspy woman's voice.

"Elena!"

"Please let me in." She coughed.

Georgina unlocked the door and after she opened it, Elena slumped inside. Georgina helped her get to her feet and onto a chair. Taking several deep breaths, Elena sniffed, then looked up. "I need water."

Georgina took a glass out of a cupboard, went to the sink and turned the tap. She gave the glass to Elena, who grabbed it. Seconds later, she handed back the empty glass.

"Another?"

When Elena nodded, then drew breath, Georgina refilled the glass and handed it to her. Noticing Elena shiver, Georgina left the kitchen and returned with a blanket. Elena put down the half-empty glass, took the blanket and wrapped it around herself. Georgina stared at a bedraggled Elena reaching for the glass and taking a large swallow. "I had to flee the camp." Once more, Elena drew breath.

Georgina sat down opposite her. "Where was the camp?"

Elena hesitated. "In the western mountains."

"You have walked all that distance!"

"I hitched a lift most of the way."

"What made you leave?"

Elena finished her glass of water, then stared at Georgina. "They killed my father," she said, sniffing. "It happened two weeks ago." Elena paused. "I only found out yesterday." She burst into tears.

Georgina got up, left the kitchen and returned with a handkerchief. Elena took it and wiped her eyes. "Murderers."

"Why did they kill your father, Elena?"

"He spoke out against their attacks on innocent civilians." Once more, Elena wiped her eyes.

"Will they come after you?"

Elena shook her head.

"Are you sure?"

Elena gave a forced smile. "They have bigger fish to go after."

"It must have been horrendous in those mountains."

"I would not recommend it."

"I'll get you a change of clothes." Georgina stared. "You can discard those togs."

Once more, Elena gave a forced smile. After Georgina left the kitchen, Elena cast her gaze around the kitchen, glad to be home. Georgina returned and looked at her friend. "I've put the clothes in your room. Do you want something to eat or a hot drink?"

Elena shook her head. "Just to sleep in a proper bed," she said, yawning.

Georgina focused her attention at Elena's head. "You don't suit a ponytail."

Elena gave a faint smile. "Or, being a terrorist."

"I can't wait to hear about it."

Elena's eyes started to close and the soiled handkerchief fell from her grasp onto the floor. Georgina assisted her to stand, then to her bedroom. After soiled clothes had been discarded, Elena got into bed and fell asleep. Georgina turned off the light. She'll sleep well tonight.

Next morning, Georgina entered Elena's bedroom with a cup of coffee. As the occupier remained fast asleep, Georgina tapped Elena's shoulder. She screamed, then sat up. Georgina stared. "That bad?"

Elena nodded.

"This may help."

Elena took the cup. "Where did you obtain coffee?"

"I have a story to tell," said Georgina, as she sat on the side of Elena's bed.

"You have dated an American soldier?"

"An undercover British agent supplies me with a jar now and then. I'll tell you about it later."

Elena took a couple of sips.

"Are you hungry?"

"I am fine."

"When did you last eat?"

"Yesterday morning."

"You're not hungry!"

"In the camp, you learn to go without."

"That's why you've lost weight."

"Also, long treks over hills." Elena finished her coffee and handed the empty cup to Georgina. Still taken aback by Elena's sudden appearance, she asked, "How did you manage to escape?"

"I waited until dark and then slipped away."

"Did no one spot you?"

"I was on guard duty." Elena yawned. "By the time anyone would have noticed, an hour would have passed. I walked over the hilly terrain towards the road and a truck approached." Once more, Elena yawned. "The driver dropped me off not far from Heraklion."

"Did he ask why you happened to be stranded in the middle of nowhere?"

Elena nodded. "Told him I had left my jealous abusive boyfriend and was going back to stay with my parents."

"He would have felt obliged to give you a lift," said Georgina, as she gave a slight smile.

"How have you coped being here on your own?"

"It has been okay." Georgina sighed. "I've managed."

"Have you had to go without food at any time?"

Georgina shook her head. "The money from the school has been a blessing." She hesitated. "However, now there is two mouths to feed."

"My father left money in a trust for me and I will go to the bank tomorrow." Elena yawned. As both eyes closed and her head fell onto the pillow, Georgina rose and left the bedroom.

Whilst in the kitchen, Georgina glanced at the clock. Soon it would be twelve o'clock and time for the mid-day news. She went through to the living room and turned on the radio.

A few minutes later, Elena appeared in a white gown and sat on the couch. She looked up at Georgina, who had her ear to the radio. "The sound of someone speaking woke me. What is the latest?"

"World news leads with the formation of the United Nations, an organisation formed to keep peace."

"Why have they not intervened in Greece?"

Georgina shrugged her shoulders.

"Are there any newsworthy items?"

"Do you know that Greece has a new Prime Minister?"

Elena stared. "Who?"

"Tsaldaris, a right-winger."

"That will not please Janouski."

"As soon as the result became known, members of his organisation stormed out of the municipal building. Did you not hear about the election?"

"We are only told positive news about our cause to defeat the government." Elena paused. "However, it is not my cause anymore."

Georgina pondered. "Elena?"

She yawned. "Yes?"

"Was Janouski at your camp?"
"That is his base. Why?"
"Just curious."
Eyes half-shut, Elena got up from the couch and looked towards Georgina. "I'm going back to bed, I could sleep for a day."
"See you tomorrow morning," said Georgina, smiling.

After her Thursday class, Georgina locked up and then went to the administrator's office. "Have a good weekend," said Georgina, as she handed in the key.
"You too." The administrator put the key onto its hook.
Georgina left the school and took her usual route home. Soon, she heard footsteps behind and looked round. "I may have a lead."
Vic Stampson grinned. "Let us go to Basil's place."
A short while later, Georgina and Vic Stampson reached the restaurant. As they entered, the usual waiter looked their way. The British agent acknowledged him and not long after they sat down, two coffees arrived. The waiter gave his usual courteous smile, then left. As Georgina removed her hat and laid it on a chair, Vic Stamps looked at her. "What news do you have?"
Georgina lifted her cup. "My friend turned up out of the blue."
"The one who joined the communists?
"She knows the whereabouts of the person you seek."
Excited, Vic Stampson moved forward. "Where?"
Georgina set her cup down. "In the western mountains, but she isn't sure of the exact location."
Vic Stampson leaned back. "Then how are we to find it? The western mountains are a large and remote area."
"My friend has a rough idea and will take us there."
"Us?" Vic Stampson frowned.
"She won't go back unless I accompany her."
"Why?"
"She's afraid."
"We will give her all the protection she needs." Vic Stampson lifted his cup and took a couple of sips.
"I believe my friend may have been mistreated in the guerrilla camp and that's why she wants my presence."
"How do you feel about a trek over dangerous terrain? Not to mention the mission itself."
"They killed her father and she wants revenge. She won't help unless I'm there."
"Does your friend realise you and she may get killed in the process?"
Whilst Georgina mulled her thoughts, Vic Stampson took a swig and

set the empty cup down. To signify a solution, Georgina put her hand on the table. "Once the location is discovered, my friend and I will head back. We'll keep a safe distance."

"Does your friend have a name?"

"Elena."

"Tell Elena not to worry. Once we find the location, one of our soldiers will escort both of you back to Heraklion." Vic Stampson gave a slight grin. "For the capture of Janouski, it is the least we can do."

"What about the wine you promised?"

From his coat pocket, the agent brought out a small jar of American coffee and laid it on the table in front of Georgina. "The wine will follow later."

She put it into her jacket pocket. "Thanks."

"Our American source is in mainland Greece just now, so future luxuries have been put on hold."

"Where in the mainland?"

"Athens."

"Is there a particular reason?"

"To prepare Greek defences against a communist attack through Albania."

"Given what happened in 1939 when Italy invaded, the Greeks will be aware of what to expect."

"Let us hope so."

Georgina rose. "Thanks for the coffee."

Vic Stampson got up. "When can Elena and you be ready."

"She is still not herself, so perhaps a few days. Janouski ordered her father's murder."

"Retribution?"

"An eye for an eye, as the Cretans would say."

"The sooner we rid Crete of Janouski and his gang the better. People have suffered enough."

Georgina put on her hat. "Has John Murdoch been in touch about an Erich Hoeness? He said he would."

"I will try to contact him and find out. Because of the situation in Athens, it may take some time."

"I'd be grateful for any information." Georgina looked towards the counter, then at Vic Stampson. "No strangers today."

"So far," he said with a slight grin.

After Georgina left the restaurant, Vic Stampson sat and contemplated an attack on Janouski's base. The waiter appeared and lifted the empty cups, then looked at the agent, who nodded. "But stronger this time."

The waiter gave a wry smile.

On a dull, humid Sunday afternoon, Georgina and Elena got ready for the task to trace Crete's communist leader, Janouski. If British Intelligence agents succeeded in being able to eliminate him, his followers would lose heart and disband, or leave the island. This would in turn allow government troops to concentrate on mainland Greece and save their hard-pressed resources. Vic Stampson had once said to Georgina that 'to get rid of the problem, you have to cut off the snake's head.'

Before they left the house, both women looked at each other. Georgina gave a faint smile. "No make-up today."

Elena gave a nervous laugh and then Georgina looked at her and nodded. Elena drew breath. "Revenge for my father's death."

The two women walked through empty streets to the centre of Heraklion and its government building. Waiting outside to meet them, Vic looked at Georgina. "I see you have dressed in an appropriate manner," he said with a slight grin. "Come this way, please."

Alec Taylor emerged from the building and both British agents led Georgina and Elena to a parked truck. As the two women climbed on board, four men in dark attire on each side greeted them with a cheer and whistle. Vic Stampson sat down and glanced at the commandos. "Now, now chaps, respect for the ladies."

Muttered apologies came forthwith and the truck moved off. Sitting next to Vic Stampson, Georgina leaned towards him. "You're going to take on Janouski and his fighters with only eight men!"

"And the driver. We will use guerrilla tactics against the guerrillas." He grinned. "Give them a taste of their own medicine."

"The art of surprise," added Alec Taylor, sitting across from his colleague.

"Will you be able to find Janouski?" asked Georgina.

"With Elena's help, it is possible."

Georgina looked across at a subdued Elena who sat next to Alec Taylor, gave her a warm smile and then turned to Vic Stampson. "How far will the truck take us?"

"About seventy miles."

"It will be dark by then," said Georgina.

"Ideal for a surprise attack."

"But will that not make it more difficult to find the camp?"

Vic Stampson glanced across at Elena. "She found her way to the road in darkness.

As the truck drove over frequent potholes in the road and other minor obstacles, Vic Stampson turned to Georgina. "When this war ends, I hope the government do their utmost to fix this damn road."

His colleague looked over. "It won't be a priority."

Georgina smiled, then turned to Vic Stampson. "What is the latest on the civil war in mainland Greece?"

"The communists don't have as many men and arms, but do have knowledge of the terrain. Most communist troops fought the Italians and Germans in those locations."

"Do they have the edge?"

"At present, yes."

"What happens if they are victorious?" asked Georgina, as she stared.

"A new order for Greece, similar to Rumania, Czechoslovakia and Poland."

Alec Taylor looked at Georgina. "Let us hope the Americans keep their promise to back us and Greece until Tito's army is defeated."

Once more, Georgina turned to Vic Stampson. "Is Yugoslavia the driving force?"

He nodded. "However, from our source in Yugoslavia, he and Stalin don't see eye to eye."

"In the future, Yugoslavia will have their own problems to deal with," added Alec Taylor. "The country is made up of different ethnic races and that will lead to tension."

"Look what happened in Germany," said Vic Stampson.

"That happened because of Hitler," said Georgina.

"Who is to say another lunatic won't emerge in Yugoslavia?"

Georgina remained silent. Moments later, the truck jolted and its passengers were thrown to and fro. Alec Taylor looked across at his colleague. "Could have been worse, it may have been a mine."

Vic Stampson grinned and Georgina observed a tense, stone-faced Elena.

Vic Stampson whispered to Georgina, "Will she be okay?"

"I hope so," she whispered.

At dusk, the truck reached the point where Elena thought she had hitched a lift days earlier. After everyone got out, the driver parked in a discreet location nearby. Alec Taylor viewed the vicinity. "They won't spot the truck in a hurry."

"The trees and growth make an ideal camouflage," added Vic Stampson. He turned at Elena. "You're sure this is where a truck picked you up?"

She stared. "I recall those rows of trees on either side of the road." Elena pointed. "From here, I could see those peaks.

Both agents and Georgina looked into the distance. "Which direction should we take, Elena?" asked Vic Stampson.

Once more, Elena pointed. "Up that gorge."

When Georgina sighed, Vic Stampson glanced her way and made an effort to reassure her. "It will appear worse than it is."

"Let's go," said Alec Taylor. "It will be dark soon."

Vic Stampson looked at both women. "Keep close to me."

As the commandos headed up the gorge, both agents and women followed close behind. After a lengthy period through growth, slippery rocks and mosquitoes, Vic Stampson turned to Elena. "I'll wager it must have been easier to come down."

She gave a forced smile. Then, Georgina stumbled and Alec Taylor caught her. She composed herself. "I hate to imagine if I'd worn high heels."

Faint laughter followed, and the party continued on a slow weary incline. Georgina moved closer to Elena. "How far now?" She drew breath.

"At least another two hours."

Georgina cast her gaze upwards. The lead commando stopped, then raised his arm. When each member stood still, he moved forward with rifle at the ready. From the undergrowth came a rustle and a small animal darted off. Sighs of relief ensued and Vic Stampson remarked. "A common occurrence with this type of terrain."

"Not good for my stress levels," said Georgina.

Vic Stampson grinned. "Or mine."

After a tiresome period, Georgina observed Elena, she hadn't shown any signs of fatigue. Vic Stampson glanced at Georgina. "Her guerrilla training has paid dividends. Are you okay?"

Georgina took a deep breath. "Put it this way, I'll stick to teaching."

A short while later, Elena stopped. As Georgina, Vic Stampson and Alec Taylor approached, she pointed. "The camp is below that ridge of mountains."

Whilst Alec Taylor looked through his binoculars, Vic Stampson moved closer to him. "Anything of interest?"

"Difficult to see in the dark," said Alec Taylor, as he lowered his binoculars. "I would say another hour's trek."

Georgina raised her eyebrows, then sat on a rock. Vic Stampson looked towards her. "Rather than continue, you could remain here."

Georgina stood. "I'm not staying here on my own," she said sharply.

Both British agents and women caught up with the commandos and continued through heavier vegetation. To survey the scene, Alec Taylor looked through his binoculars. "I can see faint lights in the distance, but not much else."

"There will only be a single guard on duty," said Elena.

"Since your departure, they may have taken more precautions." Alec Taylor stared at the senior commando.

"I'll take a couple of men and have a closer look," he said.

After three commandos moved forward and disappeared into the undergrowth, Elena looked at Alec Taylor. "What time is it?"

He checked his watch. "Almost 10.40. Why?"

"Most of the camp will be asleep." Elena glanced at Vic Stampson and Georgina. "Their ouzo consumption."

"Their fondness for it may cost them," said Vic Stampson.

A short time later, the senior commando returned with his two men and approached Alec Taylor. "There is only the one guard."

"Any activity within the camp?" asked Vic Stampson.

The sergeant shook his head. "All appears quiet."

Vic Stampson turned to both women. "You stay put, we'll take it from here."

"I want to continue," said Elena.

"Why?"

"To make sure you get Janouski."

"Don't worry, we will."

Georgina looked at Vic Stampson. "What if we're attacked?"

"That means we have failed," said Alec Taylor, gravely.

Vic Stampson pulled out a small gun from his inside jacket pocket and gave it to Georgina. "A precaution."

She hesitated, then took it. "How does it work?"

Muted laughter came from the commandos, then Vic Stampson gave her a quick demonstration. "Got it?"

"Got it." Georgina put the gun into her coat pocket.

"See you later," said Alec Taylor, as he observed Georgina and a pensive Elena.

After the two agents and commandos left, Georgina sat on a nearby boulder and Elena joined her. "I am sorry to have dragged you into this."

"Forget it, I enjoy a piece of the action." Georgina removed one of her shoes, then rubbed her foot. "Mind you, if I had known it would be this bad I'd have worn different footwear."

Elena smiled. Although both women wore berets and coats, being stationary in darkness on a high level ensured cold conditions. To keep warm, they huddled together and Georgina put up her collar. "At least the climb up here kept me warm. I hope they complete their mission soon."

For what appeared a lengthy spell, Georgina and Elena chatted to keep their minds active. They stared at stars in the sky and pinpointed the brightest. "Do you think man will ever reach one of them?"

"I doubt it, they will want to fight with each other instead."

"Then perhaps a woman may go to the stars one day."

"I don't think men would let her. Society would require a dramatic change."

At that moment, Elena looked round and Georgina stared. "What's up?"

"I heard something."

"They've returned, thank goodness," said Georgina gratefully.

"I do not think it is them."

"What makes you say that?"

"My guerrilla training." Elena whispered, "There, I heard it again."

Georgina glanced over her shoulder. "Let's hide in those bushes behind us."

The two women made themselves scarce and took cover. As they remained still, a man in dark grey attire with a rifle appeared. Georgina peered between ferns and whispered, "He's not one of ours."

The man cast his gaze around the vicinity, looked down and then picked up a handkerchief. As Georgina cursed, Elena whispered, "It must have fallen out of your pocket."

As the man examined it, Georgina stared at him, then whispered, "I know him."

"I know you are here," said the man. "Come out and you will not be harmed." He paused. "You have my word."

"He is a teacher at my school," whispered Georgina.

Elena stared at her. The man laid his rifle on the ground, then looked around the vicinity. "There, I am no longer armed." He paused. "The two British agents and the commandos have been taken prisoner."

Elena whispered, "Give the gun to me, I know how to use it." After Georgina handed it over, both women stood and emerged from behind bushes. The man stared at them.

"We meet again," said Georgina.

After a grin crept across the man's face, Elena pointed the gun at him. He stared at her. "No need for that."

"Why are you here, Emilio?" asked Georgina in amazement.

"To ensure your safety, and I do not believe in taking women prisoner. When the agents and commandos were captured, Janouski wanted several men
to go after you, but I volunteered."

"How did they get captured?" asked Elena sharply.

"We have look-outs at various points in proximity to the camp. After you left, security was stepped up."

"What will happen to them?" asked Georgina.

"A prisoner exchange."

"How do you know about us?" asked Elena.

"One of our men overheard two commandos mention you."

"So, what now?" asked Georgina, as she tilted her head.

"Make it look that you overpowered me and then return to the truck."

"How do you know there is a truck?" asked Elena.

"Because you would not walk from Heraklion," said Emilio, as he stared at both women. "Now, one of you will have to knock me out." He paused. "To make it look real."

Elena handed the gun to Georgina and she stared. "I can't do it, we work in the same school!"

Emilio moved towards Elena and turned round. "It will look as if I had been caught by surprise." He glanced behind. "Be quick, another will be on his way to ensure your capture."

Elena thumped the gun handle down on Emilio's head, and he slumped to the ground. Georgina stared. "That looked professional" She paused. "Don't tell me, your training."

Elena nodded.

"Did they train you to drive as well? How are we going to get back to Heraklion?"

"My father taught me." Elena smiled.

After an easier downward trek to the road, the two women found the truck. Georgina looked at Elena. "We don't have the keys." She sighed.

"Do you have a safety pin?"

Georgina hesitated. "Yes, why?"

"Give it to me." Georgina handed it over and Elena went to the driver's door. After she inserted it into the lock, Elena moved the pin in a circular motion. Soon, the door opened and Elena looked at Georgina. "Now comes the difficult part."

"You're doing well, so far."

Elena got into the cab, then tinkered with wires under the dashboard. As Georgina looked on, the engine started and she cheered. As Elena sat in the driver's seat, Georgina got in and closed the door. "You're full of surprises."

Elena manoeuvred the truck onto the road and as it gathered speed, she glanced at Georgina. "My first steady boyfriend worked as a vehicle mechanic and taught me a few things."

"He sure did." Georgina paused. "Did he teach you to drive a truck?"

Elena shook her head. "A car." She glanced at Georgina. "I should be okay."

After several scary sharp bends and a series of difficult gear changes, Elena's competence grew. Georgina started to relax. "How will the agents and commandos be treated?"

"Since some of the commandos are from Crete, everyone should be okay."

"Don't think I'll see Emilio at school again."

"It would appear he has a new role."

"Our lucky charm."

Elena nodded.

"If taken prisoner, what would have been your fate?"

"You do not want to know," said Elena, as she glanced at Georgina.

A few miles on, a jeep approached and flashed its lights. Georgina looked at Elena, who shrugged her shoulders. Moments later, Elena glanced in the side mirror and put her foot on the accelerator. Georgina stared at her. "What's up?"

"The jeep that passed us is on our trail." Once more, Elena glanced out the side mirror. "They may be guerrilla fighters."

"You should not have flashed the headlights, it's made them suspicious."

As the jeep got closer, shots were fired at the truck. Elena drove faster and pulled away. She looked in the mirror. "They have given up."

"I'll be glad to get home."

Halfway to Heraklion, the truck began to slow down. Elena changed gears, but it made no difference. When the truck came to a halt, Georgina sighed. "I spoke to soon."

"We may be out of petrol."

"Surely our driver filled the tank for a return trip," said Georgina, as she shook her head.

Elena tried to start the truck, however, no joy. She sat back and tilted her head towards Georgina.

"What now?"

"We will have to walk."

"My feet will not be pleased."

Elena turned off the headlights and both women got out. Elena spotted liquid beside the truck and moved closer. "The bullets hit the petrol tank."

Georgina approached and stared. "Swines."

"Let us carry on along the road, we know where it leads to."

"It must be about four," said Georgina, as she yawned.

"At least it is not too cold."

"At this time of the morning there won't be many vehicles on the road to give us a lift."

"If we spot one, move off the road and find somewhere to hide. It may be the enemy."

"After our efforts to get this far, I don't want to end up a prisoner," said Georgina, as she gave a faint smile. "Besides, I have a class on Tuesday."

Amidst an eerie silence and darkness, the two women started to walk along the side of the road. After a continuous period, Elena glanced at Georgina. "How are your feet?"

"I'll survive." She paused. "Elena?"

"Yes?"

"Did every person who joined the communists receive training?"

"Some in a certain speciality."

"Speciality?"

"How to blow up a building and not cause much damage. Also, stealth tactics."

"If you are going to blow up a building, why would you be concerned about how much damage is caused?"

"Less damage equates to less Cretan civilians being killed."

"And stealth?"

"Merge with the environment and use it to your advantage."

"Hence why the agents and commandos are now in captivity." Georgina glanced sideways. "Let's rest for a short while."

"Best to keep the momentum going."

"Your training?"

"No, I want to get home as soon as possible."

As Georgina laughed, Elena stopped. Georgina did so likewise and stared. "What is it?"

"I hear a vehicle." Elena pointed. "Hide behind those bushes."

"It may be one of ours."

"Do you want to take that chance."

The two women went behind a bush and waited. As the vehicle approached, it slowed down. Elena whispered, "It is a jeep."

"Ours?"

"Not sure."

After the jeep came to a halt, one man got out and headed for a tree. Georgina glanced at Elena and whispered, "Too much to drink."

"I think that is Janouski!"

"Are you sure?"

"He is similar in appearance." Elena went into her coat pocket, then pulled out the gun."

"Are you going to shoot him?"

"He had my father killed."

"It would be better to take him prisoner." Georgina watched as the driver sat and then lit a cigarette. "What should we do?"

As Elena contemplated, Georgina stood and walked towards the jeep. The driver stared at her. "Do you have a cigarette?"

"Where did you come from!"

"Does it matter?" Georgina smiled.

Whilst the driver grinned and then chatted with her, Elena encircled the jeep and pointed the gun. "Hands in the air," she said sharply.

The driver looked round and stared at a second woman. "Now!" When he raised them, Elena said sharply, "Give me your gun."

After the driver did so, a shot was fired from behind a tree. Georgina and Elena ducked and then the driver slumped forward. Georgina stared.

"He's not much of a shot." From behind the jeep, Elena peered and then a second shot followed. "What now?" Georgina looked at Elena.

"I hear another vehicle." Elena listened. "It is another jeep."

"If it belongs to them, we won't be going home for the foreseeable future," quipped Georgina.

When the noise grew louder, the two women waited. The jeep came to a halt and three men got out. Elena stared. "They are wearing uniforms."

Georgina stood. "Janouski is over at the trees," she shouted, as she pointed.

A shot came forthwith and the soldiers sheltered behind their vehicle. When Janouski ran off, the three soldiers pursued. A short while later, the communist leader returned in handcuffs. Elena approached him and aimed her gun. "You swine, you murdered my father."

"Lower your gun, he is worth more to us alive," said a soldier.

Elena stared at Janouski; the gun aimed at his chest. The soldier approached her. "I said lower the gun." He aimed his at Elena.

She threw the gun aside and Janouski sighed. After he was handcuffed and taken away, another soldier approached Georgina. "We received word of what happened and came to look for you." He picked up the gun.

"Received word?"

The soldier nodded, then glanced at the jeep with a dead guerrilla slumped forward. "One of us will take you back to Heraklion." When the soldier glanced at Elena, Georgina gave a slight smile. "She'll be okay."

The following week, Georgina left the school building and headed home. When she turned a nearby corner, she stopped. "They let you go!"

"All of us." Vic Stampson handed over a jar of coffee.

Georgina took it. "What about the wine?"

"Finished for the week?"

"Finished for good. Music classes have ceased."

"Why?"

Georgina tilted her head. "To save paying a music teacher."

"Can you not stand in for the former history teacher?"

"Someone else has."

"How is Elena?"

"She is moving to Salonika."

"Oh?" Vic Stampson raised his eyebrows.

"To look after her aunt. She was close to Elena's father and his death hit her hard."

"Are you also going to Salonika?"

Georgina shook her head. "With no job and the war, I've made up my mind to leave Crete."

"Back to America?"

"Scotland. I left as a young woman and now feel that it's time to return." Georgina paused. "Maybe I'm just homesick."

"When you get there, you can look up a Captain Erich Hoeness."

Georgina stared.

"That is the information I have on him."

"Why taken to Scotland?"

"There is a camp where former SS officers are put through a process of denazification and democratisation, then sent back to Germany."

"He wasn't a Nazi. Where in Scotland is the camp?"

"Near a village called Combie."

"You mean Comrie?"

"Do you know it?"

"I believe it's near Perth."

Vic Stampson held out his hand. "Good luck, Georgina, and thanks for your assistance."

She shook it. "Glad you got Janouski, no doubt a prize capture."

"It wasn't Janouski."

"Elena recognised him."

"The captured man is similar in appearance and an important member of the guerrillas, hence why we were all exchanged for him. When Janouski goes anywhere, he is accompanied by an entourage, not a solitary driver."

"Elena was going to shoot him."

"Just as well she didn't, or we wouldn't be having this conversation, said Vic Stampson, as he gave a slight grin."

"At least you know where his camp is."

"By now it will be in another remote location."

Georgina put the coffee jar into her pocket, then smiled at the agent. "Thanks for those," she said gratefully.

"My pleasure."

"One of the soldiers who found us told me that they had received word of what had happened. How did they know, and where we would be?"

"Perhaps a government secret operative in Janouski's camp managed to contact them."

"A double agent!"

As Vic Stampson departed with a wry smile, Georgina continued her walk home and reflected. Espionage and being a schoolteacher? She shook her head.

CHAPTER 18

THE HOMECOMING

As the ship left war-ravaged Heraklion, Georgina looked back and reflected. With the brutality of Italian and German occupation, plus a civil war, how much more would Crete have to endure? Then again, Georgina learned that the people could take as much as an army threw at them and remain steadfast. However, the current situation had not been the result of an invasion from another country, but internal conflict. Crete itself would be the loser. A voice broke Georgina's train of thought. "Reminiscing?" A woman wearing a cream coat matching her large floppy hat, smiled and when she did so, wrinkles portraying a long life appeared.

Georgina looked to her right. "I lived here for sixteen years."

"You still have an American accent. Which part are you from?"

"New York, what about you?"

"Washington. My husband is a diplomat on the island, hence my visit."

"Are you going back to Washington?"

The woman shook her head. "London. We've stayed at an elegant apartment in Islington for two years. When the war ended, I thought we would be going home, but then this damn conflict began." She gave a slight smile. "My husband's skills are in demand."

Georgina considered. Could it be the gentleman who visited the school? "How long has your husband been on the island?"

"Not long after the German surrender. There is much unrest in Crete, thus the American presence."

"And a subsidy to the Greek government?"

The woman nodded. "The communists must not be allowed to win the civil war." She paused. "Why have you to chosen to leave now?" The woman glanced towards the Heraklion coastline. "It must have been tough during the German occupation."

"I'm homesick."

"It won't be long till you're across the Atlantic."

"I'm not going to America."

The woman stared. "Oh, where?"

"Scotland."

"Why there?"

"I was born there, then went to America."

"My father came from Greenock. He moved to Liverpool, then Canada and worked on the Canadian Pacific Railway."

Georgina gave a slight smile. "Far travelled."

"Then he moved to Chicago, met my mother and that's where I grew up."

"I'm headed for a place called Comrie, a village in Central Scotland. I met someone in Heraklion and just found out that's where he went."

"Did he not let you know?"

Georgina hesitated. "He was a German officer and when the war ended, sent to a camp there. He syphoned supplies of food to locals."

"From German stores?"

Georgina nodded.

The woman gave a slight smile. "Before my mother's family emigrated to America, they came from Germany."

"What part?"

"Essen." The woman paused. "It's just as well she left, the British flattened it."

Just then, a sudden gust of wind ensued and both passengers held onto their hats. The woman looked up at the grey sky and then Georgina. "Better go inside, I feel a storm on the horizon."

"Yes, lets."

Two days later, the ship docked at Leith and passengers disembarked. Georgina looked at the woman. "How do you get to London from here, Mary?"

"I'll catch a train from Edinburgh Waverley to London Kings Cross. Our apartment isn't far from the station."

"That's good."

"What about you, Georgina?"

"An overnight stay, and tomorrow morning I'll head for Comrie."

"Do you know of somewhere?"

"One of the officers on board mentioned a hotel located nearby."

Mary looked towards a taxi stance. "I'll get one to Princes Street." She turned to Georgina. "Can I give you a lift?"

"The hotel isn't far."

Mary gave Georgina a warm hug. "Hope you find Erich." She picked up her suitcase and then approached a stationary taxi. The driver got out and assisted his passenger. Once inside, Mary sat back and as the taxi moved off, waved. Georgina picked up her suitcase and walked towards another stationary taxi, whose middle-aged driver wound down a window. "How far is the Links Hotel from here?" asked Georgina.

"I'll take you to it."

"I'm going to walk, someone told me it's not far."

The driver glanced at Georgina's suitcase. "It will be a struggle with that to carry," he said sharply.

Georgina gave a slight smile. "Okay."

The driver got out, opened the passenger door and assisted Georgina. She held her beige hat and entered. Suitcase at her side, she leaned back on the brown leather seat.

Several minutes after the taxi moved off, it came to a halt outside a terraced building. Opposite, Georgina gazed at the well-maintained flat expanses of grass bordered by trees. The driver glanced over his shoulder. "Here we are."

Georgina got out, viewed a pristine white exterior and put her suitcase on the ground. After she paid her fare, the driver gave a kind acknowledgement and drove off. Picking up her up her suitcase, Georgina walked down a short gravel path and then entered a reception area. A young woman with long dark hair looked up from behind a wooden desk. "Can I help you, madam?" She gave Georgina a wide smile.

"A single room, please." Georgina laid her suitcase on the polished wooden floor.

The receptionist checked a black register book. "Just one night?" She glanced up.

When Georgina nodded, the receptionist turned the book around and handed over a dark blue fountain pen. After Georgina signed in, she returned the pen. The receptionist looked at the book. "You haven't given an address, madam."

"I'm in limbo," said Georgina, as she gave a slight smile.

The receptionist gave her guest a key. "First floor and turn left, madam. Breakfast is from 7.30 till 8.30am."

Georgina took the key. "Thanks." Pity there isn't a porter. She lifted her suitcase and went upstairs. When she entered the room, Georgina put her case on the brown carpet flooring and looked around. Laying her suitcase on the bed, she unpacked and then counted the money Elena had given her as a parting gift. Georgina considered. Tomorrow I'll have to find a bank, I doubt the hotel will accept drachmas. As she put the thick wad of notes into her black leather bag, there came a knock on the door. When she answered it, the receptionist greeted her. "Are you having dinner, madam?"

Georgina nodded.

"It's from 7.30 till 9pm. Forgot to mention it."

"That's okay. Where is the nearest bank?"

"About five minutes' walk from here, a street called Leith Walk."

"I've travelled from Crete and only have drachmas, so I'll have to go tomorrow morning. Will the bank be open?""

"Yes. In the meantime, dinner and any drinks can be put on a tab."

"Terrific."

After the receptionist departed, Georgina closed the door, then yawned. She removed her shoes, lay flat on the soft bed and reflected. Glad the taxi driver didn't pay close attention to the note I gave him. Moments later, Georgina's eyes closed.

Following a traditional Scottish breakfast, Georgina walked to the bank situated near the foot of Leith Walk. She entered and then approached a polished wooden counter where a grey-suited male employee gave a courteous smile. Georgina went into her bag and pulled out a bundle of notes. "I would like to exchange them for pound sterling, please." She gave them to the dark-haired spectacled employee.

He took them. "Hold on, please," he said politely.

Georgina cast her gaze around the vicinity and admired a dust-free tiled black and white floor and unblemished magnolia coloured walls. Then, the employee returned, smiling. "Here you are, madam." He handed Georgina a bundle of notes and a form. "Please sign this."

Georgina wrote her name, returned the form and then put the cash into her bag. The employee took the form and laid it aside. "Anything else, madam?"

"I noticed a railway station nearby."

"Leith Central."

"Can I get a train to Comrie from there?"

The employee shook his head. "You will get a train to Comrie from Princes Street Station."

"Is the station far from here?"

The employee gave directions and then Georgina left the bank. Another male employee approached his colleague and grinned. "Not from around here."

"She had an American accent." The man paused. "She is off to Comrie."

"What's there? I would expect her to hit the high spots of Edinburgh," he said, grinning to his colleague.

Walking back to the hotel, Georgina became aware of stares from not only men, but also women. Her light bright attire contrasted with grey or dark worn by Leithers. An out-of-summer tan added to their intrigue, the result of a sixteen-year stay in the Mediterranean.

When she entered the hotel, its receptionist looked up from her desk. Georgina approached and handed over what she owed. The receptionist counted the notes, then gave Georgina a receipt. "Where are you off to, madam?"

"Comrie. How do I get to Princes Street Station? Someone in the bank gave me directions, but I can't remember."

"You could take a tram, there is a stop near the bank. Or, I can call for a taxi."

"The taxi sounds better," said Georgina, as she stared at her suitcase.

Minutes later, a black taxi appeared outside the hotel. As Georgina left the building, its driver got out and opened the rear passenger door. After Georgina stepped inside, she sat next to the window. The driver got in, sat and looked round. "Where to?"

"Princes Street Station, please."

The taxi soon reached Leith Walk, headed up towards Princes Street and then straight along. After it entered the station from Lothian Road, it came to a halt. The driver looked round. "No drachmas, only sterling," he said with a slight grin.

"How much for both fares?"

"£1."

After Georgina handed the driver three notes, he examined them, got out and opened the passenger door. Delighted to receive a good tip, he assisted Georgina with her suitcase and bid her farewell. She lifted it and spotted an information sign. Entering a room with a high ceiling, Georgina approached a desk staffed by a middle-aged bald male clerk. "How do I get to Comrie?" Georgina put her suitcase on the marble floor.

"Take a train to Gleneagles, and from there you will catch a connection to Comrie, madam," he said politely, looking over his horn-rimmed spectacles.

"When is the next train to Gleneagles?"

The clerk glanced at a large clock. "In twelve minutes, platform 6."

"Do I buy a ticket here?"

"Under normal circumstances you could, but my machine is out of order. You can buy one from a conductor on the train."

"Thanks."

"My pleasure, madam," said the clerk, as he straightened his dark sober tie.

Georgina lifted her suitcase, went to the appropriate platform and got on her train. When she sat down, a sigh followed. Whilst Georgina waited for the black locomotive and five maroon carriages to depart, she looked out her compartment window. Men and women passengers, who left an arrival, wore smart formal attire. Georgina reflected. Bustling conservative Edinburgh, with its elegant buildings and Capital infrastructure, is far removed from war-ravaged downtrodden Heraklion.

Following a long delay due to a signal malfunction, frustrated Georgina reached Comrie. Stepping onto the platform, she cast her gaze around the tranquil rural surroundings. When a stocky man in a dark blue uniform blew his whistle, the train moved off and left a trail of steam. As Georgina turned to face the railway man, he put the silver whistle into his jacket pocket. "Can I help, miss?"

"Do you know a good place to stay?"

"I would recommend the Royal Hotel."

Georgina lifted her suitcase. "Is it far?" I hope not.

"Five minutes walk, and that is with your case," he said cheerily.

Georgina gave a slight smile. Fascinated by the idyllic and charming Scottish setting she asked, "Do many trains come through here?"

The railway man removed his uniform cap and rubbed his thinning grey hair. "Four passenger trains and a couple of goods trains per day." He replaced the cap.

"Are you the stationmaster?"

"Also, the guard, porter and landscape gardener." He glanced at a row of flowerpots.

"It's a fabulous location," said Georgina, as she glanced around the vicinity.

"Have you come all the way from America?"

Georgina took off her hat and gave her long blonde hair a shake. "I've travelled from Greece." She replaced her hat.

"To visit someone in the village?"

Georgina nodded.

"I now have paperwork duties to carry out," said the railway man, as he approached a door of the small station building. Before he opened it, looked over his shoulder. "Enjoy your stay, miss."

"Bye." As Georgina lifted her suitcase and headed for the station exit, the railway man spoke, "Oh, miss?"

Georgina looked round. "Yes?"

"Tell the owner Bert sent you, they'll give a discount."

"Will do," said Georgina, smiling.

As he went into an office, Georgina left the station and soon reached the hotel. She entered and observed the tartan carpet, which covered the reception area. A well-groomed woman who sat behind the desk looked up. "Yes, madam?"

"A single room, please." Georgina put her case on the carpet.

"Please sign the register book," said the receptionist politely.

When Georgina did so, a key was laid a key in front of her. Putting down the fountain pen, she then picked up her key. The receptionist smiled. "First floor, madam, next to a bathroom."

Georgina lifted her suitcase. "What time is dinner?"

"From 6.30 till 8.30." The receptionist glanced at a clock. "You will have to be quick."

Georgina went up a varnished wooden staircase and along a short brown carpeted landing, which led to her room. She did a quick unpack, went downstairs to the dining room and sat at a set table. Not long after, a waitress in sober black attire approached and took her order. When she left, Georgina observed that only three out of twenty tables had a guest. The waitress returned with a large glass of white wine and set it on the white tablecloth.

"Thanks," said Georgina gratefully.

"Be back soon with your starter."

Georgina lifted the glass, took a couple of sips and then a large swallow. She set the near-empty glass down, then stared at it. I should have ordered a bottle.

Minutes later, the waitress returned with Georgina's starter and soon after, another large glass of wine. She smiled. "If you require anything else, just let me know."

"Thanks."

Events of this long day ensured a healthy appetite and Georgina devoured her evening meal. As she reflected, the waitress approached and glanced at a clock. "Have you finished, madam?"

"Perhaps another glass of wine?"

"The dining room is about to close, but we have an excellent lounge bar," said the waitress, as she pointed. "Through that door and turn right."

Georgina left the dining room and entered a small, but charming lounge bar. Its roaring coal fire, dark wooden furniture and tartan rugs on a polished wooden floor made for an appealing habitat. A claymore hanging on a wall above the fireplace caught Georgina's eye. Chatting with drinks in their hands, two white-haired women sat at a circular table near the bar counter. The barman with wavy brown hair dressed in a white shirt, tartan bowtie and black trousers looked Georgina's way. "Yes, madam, what can I get you?"

"A large glass of white wine, please?"

"House white, okay? That's what we serve in the dining room."

Georgina nodded. As the barman poured, the two women looked up. He put the glass on the bar in front of Georgina. "You are a guest, madam?"

"Yes."

"Do you want me to add the amount onto your bill?"

"Room 8."

Whilst the barman wrote on a notepad, Georgina picked up her glass and glanced at the two women. One of them smiled. "Would you like to join us?"

Georgina sat down and set her glass on the table. "I'm Georgina."

"This is Jane and I am Agnes. Are you Canadian?"

"American. I'm originally from Scotland, then moved to New York."

"Are you on holiday?" asked Jane.

"I'm here to find someone."

Both women looked at each other and the barman stopped drying a glass he had just washed. Georgina sipped her wine. "We met in Crete."

"How long ago?" asked Agnes.

"During the German occupation."

Agnes gave a wry smile. "Was he by any chance a captain in the SS?"

Georgina stared. "Do you know him?"

Agnes nodded, then picked up her glass and took a sip. Georgina set her glass down. "Where can I find him?"

"He has returned to Germany."

"Gone home?"

Agnes shook her head. "Taken to Nuremberg for trial."

Georgina hesitated. "He is not a Nazi. Erich supplied food to the local community in Heraklion at risk to himself."

As a glass fell out of the barman's hand and smashed, all three customers looked towards the bar. "Sorry," said the barman, as he gave a slight grin and then started to pick up pieces of broken glass.

Agnes looked at Georgina. "That does not surprise me. Erich visited on a number of occasions and I got to know him."

"I received information that he was a prisoner here."

"The government allowed prisoners time out to integrate with our community," said Jane.

"My daughter and I took Erich to a cinema in Crieff," said Agnes, "to see a film called Brief Encounter."

"It's a terrific film," added Jane, smiling.

"What is it about?" Georgina lifted her glass.

"Two people meet by accident and a romance ensues." Agnes paused. "Erich enjoyed the film as it reminded him of someone."

Whilst Georgina remained silent, the barman dried another glass and once more, tried to appear disinterested. Georgina took a large swallow. "Don't suppose I'll see him again."

"If he has done what you say, Erich will not be found guilty of the publicised atrocities on Crete."

"Atrocities!" Georgina sat back. "I know him, he isn't capable."

"Then all will be well," said Agnes, as she finished her drink.

"How would I find out?" Georgina set her empty glass in front of her.

"You could go into the camp and ask whoever is in charge," said Jane. "All prisoners have gone, but the camp may keep records of judicial proceedings and outcomes."

"Explain who you are and give him a wide smile," added Agnes.

"Is it far from here?"

"At the bottom of the road." Agnes looked at the barman. "Sandy, can you give me a pencil and piece of paper?"

He nodded, searched around the bar and moments later, came over to the table. Agnes took them, wrote down the address and then gave the piece of paper to Georgina. "Once you've been to the camp, let me know how you got on. You can sample my home-made scones with a cup of tea," said Agnes cheerily.

Next morning, Georgina left the hotel and made her way to the camp. With no suitcase to carry, a walk would be a pleasant experience in the beautiful lush green

Scottish countryside. Being the month of April, birds were in good voice amidst the spring sunshine. The scene was a stark contrast to barren, battle-weary Heraklion and its surrounds.

When Georgina reached the camp perimeter entrance, no guard could be seen. She pushed the gate, and to her surprise it had not been locked. Georgina observed two rows of huts with no windows in a large grass field. However, one hut further on had windows and she considered. That would appear to be the office. Georgina approached it and knocked on the wooden door. She stood, looked around the vicinity and knocked again. A tall man in a uniform opened the door and stared.

"Good morning," said Georgina, smiling.

The soldier grinned. "It is now."

"I'm trying to trace someone who was based here."

"Please, come in," he said politely.

Georgina entered a room comprised of dark green filing cabinets, a wooden table and two chairs. The soldier closed the door. "Please, take a seat."

After Georgina sat down, she unbuttoned her beige coat. The soldier sat opposite and cleared his throat. "I am Lieutenant Reid, how can I help?"

"I would like to know the whereabouts of a former prisoner."

"You are American?"

Georgina nodded.

"Why do you want to trace a German prisoner?"

"We met in Crete."

The officer leaned back. "Why were you in Crete?"

"I moved from New York during the depression and worked as a music teacher, then came the war."

"And now there is another one in progress." The office paused. "The person you want to trace, what was his name?"

"Erich Hoeness, a captain in the SS."

The officer reflected. "I remember him, he organised a football game between prisoners and guards."

"Would it be possible to get in touch with him?"

The officer got up and then went to a filing cabinet. He opened it, took out a file and returned to his desk. As the officer read a document, Georgina looked on and chewed her lip. He looked up. "Erich was taken to Nuremberg and put on trial for crimes against the Cretan population." The officer stared at Georgina.

"And?"

"That is the last piece of information we have."

"Is there any way I can make contact?"

"You could try the German authorities, but they are in disarray just now." The officer went on. "The country is trying to get back on its feet and that will take some time. A request such as yours would be at the bottom of an exceptionally large pile."

"What if I went to Germany?"

"I wouldn't recommend it. Because of the turmoil, crime is rife and people are being attacked for a packet of cigarettes."

"I could visit his apartment in Hamburg."

"With the city destroyed by bombs, most people would be relocated. We had an officer here whose family stayed in Leipzig and relocated to a small town many miles away. Also, you have to be prepared that he may have been found guilty, and for that crime the punishment is death."

Georgina stared at the officer.

"I'm sorry." The officer paused. "If any news comes my way about Erich, I will get in touch."

"I'm only here for a short time, then moving on."

"Where are you off to?"

"I'm not sure."

"Back to Crete?"

Georgina shook her head.

The officer went into a drawer, pulled out a notepad and wrote on it. Tearing off the top sheet, he handed it to Georgina. "That is the camp telephone number. Call anytime."

Georgina looked at the officer and gave a forced smile. The officer stood, as did Georgina and he led her to the door. After he opened it, she stepped out, then viewed the camp.

"The majority of prisoners here weren't a bad bunch. By the way, what is your name?"

"Georgina Rhodes."

"Good luck, Georgina."

When she departed, the officer closed the door and returned to his desk. Picking up the file, he replaced it into the filing cabinet and shook his head.

Walking back to the village, a downhearted Georgina took out a piece of paper that Agnes had given her. She showed it to a passer-by and they gave her directions.

Not long after, Georgina found the small tidy cottage, walked up a garden path and then knocked on the door. When it opened, she was greeted warmly. "Come in," Agnes said cheerily.

"Thanks."

Agnes closed the door and took her guest into a small living room. "Have a seat, Georgina. Did you find out about Erich?"

Georgina sat on a two-seater floral patterned couch, shaking her head. Agnes sighed. "That is a pity. What do you intend to do now?"

"I may take a trip to the West Highlands."

"Why there?" Agnes raised her eyebrows.

"A fellow passenger on the train assured me that the experience would be unforgettable," said Georgina, as she gave a faint smile. "It may cheer me up."

"Good idea."

"How would I get there?"

Agnes contemplated. "A train from here to Gleneagles, then one headed for Glasgow, and from there, the West Highland Express."

"It sounds like a long trek."

"Or, I could ask my daughter if she would drive you to Crianlarich."

"Why there?"

"It is a stop on the line from Glasgow, and not too long a drive."

"That would be terrific, Agnes," said Georgina, smiling.

"Before I call my daughter, we'll have a cup of tea and some of my home-made scones." Agnes paused. "Erich loved them."

As Georgina got out the car and closed the passenger door, Fiona retrieved her suitcase from the boot. Taking it from her, Georgina smiled. "Thanks for the lift."

"My pleasure, enjoy the West Highlands."

"I'll try my best."

"Have you decided which part you are going to visit?"

"The train terminates at Mallaig, so I'll settle for there."

Fiona got into her car, closed the door and then wound down the window. Georgina looked her way.

"I have heard views from the train are fantastic," said Fiona, smiling.

Following a courteous wave to Fiona as she drove off, Georgina walked under an archway then up a concrete staircase to the platform. On either side lay a single railway line surrounded by trees and bushes. On the platform stood a white painted stone building with 3 signs, which stated a ticket office, waiting room and cafeteria.

After she bought a ticket to Mallaig, Georgina returned to the platform and put her suitcase on the grey tarmac surface. Moments later, she looked at her watch. Fifteen minutes until the train arrives. Georgina glanced at the cafeteria entrance, picked up her suitcase and went inside. A sturdy grey-haired woman behind the counter greeted her. "Yes, madam, can I help you?"

"A coffee, please."

"Black or white?"

"Black."

From a silver metallic jug, the woman poured coffee into a white ceramic cup and then set it on the counter in front of Georgina.

"How much?" Georgina put her suitcase down.

"Theepence, please," said the woman politely.

Georgina took a threepenny coin out of her coat pocket, gave it to the woman who rang it up on the cash register behind her. As Georgina took a sip, the woman turned round. "Is it the northbound train you are getting?"

"Yes, I'm off to Mallaig."

The woman looked at a circular clock on the wall. "It will be here soon."

Georgina picked up her cup and took a couple of sips. Being piping hot, she laid it down on the counter.

"Which part of America are you from?"

"New York."

"Are you here to visit someone?"

Georgina shook her head. "A vacation."

The woman smiled. "Anywhere in the West Highlands is picturesque at this time of year."

"It's mild for April."

"Long may it continue." The woman stared out a window, which overlooked the platform. "Your train is early."

Georgina drank some coffee, placed the half-empty cup on the counter and picked up her suitcase. "See you." She hurried out the door, boarded a carriage and then entered a compartment. Georgina closed the door and struggled to put to put her suitcase on a rack above. She drew breath, then took a window seat. Where is a gentleman when you need him? Moments later, a guard's whistle blew and smoke accompanied by chugging from the train's locomotive announced the departure.

Soon, the black steam engine with six shiny maroon carriages crossed a viaduct and as it did so, Georgina gazed at Crianlarich village below. The train then rolled through valleys with lochs on either side. At times, branches from trees, which bordered the single track, swished against Georgina's window. When a man with combed-back grey hair dressed in a dark blue uniform entered the compartment, Georgina looked his way.

"Ticket, please."

After Georgina handed her ticket over, the ticket inspector gave it a thorough examination. "Thank you, madam," he said, handing it back.

"When does the train reach Mallaig?"

The ticket inspector pulled out a gold pocket watch from his waistcoat. "In three hours and sixteen minutes." He gave a slight grin. "Providing there are no delays."

"That's a long haul."

"Being a route through hostile countryside, the locomotive can only travel at a certain speed. Besides, if the driver went fast, you would miss unforgettable scenic views," said the ticket inspector, as he grinned. "Enjoy the journey, madam." He departed and closed the brown wooden framed glass door behind him.

Following a stop at Roy Bridge, a tall dark-haired man with a newspaper in his hand entered the compartment. He closed the door, sat down diagonally opposite Georgina and then opened his broadsheet edition. As Georgina stared out the window, she could hear pages being turned every few seconds. Georgina glanced towards the tweed-suited individual with a deerstalker hat to match. He must be a fast reader, she thought. After the man laid his newspaper aside, he looked at Georgina. "Excuse me, would you mind if I smoked my pipe?"

"Then would you open the door?" asked Georgina sharply.

"Certainly." The man pushed it open, then looked at Georgina. "Have you travelled far?"

"From Crianlarich."

"You are from America, are you not?"

Georgina gave a slight smile. "I thought you meant today. I'm from New York."

"Are you going all the way?" The man took out a brown pipe from his jacket side-pocket. "To Mallaig?" asked the man, as he lit his pipe.

"Yes."

"Have you booked accommodation?" He puffed on his pipe.

"Not yet, why?"

"A relative owns a rather nice place not far from the station."

"What is it called?"

"The West Highland Hotel."

"An appropriate name." Georgina paused. "Any item of interest in your newspaper?"

The man removed his pipe. "In the international section, it stated that Chinese communists are at war with the nationalists." He shook his head. "After a world war, countries should rebuild, not cause further carnage."

Georgina reflected. Not just China, also Greece. When the man sat back and puffed on his pipe, Georgina looked towards him. "Was there any mention of the trials in Germany?"

As the man shook his head, the train arrived at Spean Bridge. Soon, Fort William came into view and Georgina's fellow passenger stood and tipped his hat. "Enjoy your stay."

"Thanks."

After passengers departed and others boarded, the train left for its ultimate Mallaig destination. On this part of the journey, Georgina marvelled at a range of stunning views. A long viaduct that stretched across a valley near Glenfinnan station, plus silver sands at a beach close to Morar, being the highlights.

When a contented Georgina got off the train, she could smell the sea air. As she left the station, a harbour full of fishing boats greeted her. Georgina put down her suitcase and stared. Situated on the coast, Mallaig was an ideal location to have a fishing port to serve near and afar. Lifting the suitcase, Georgina followed instructions given by her fellow passenger to a hotel. After she ventured halfway up a brae, Georgina stopped for a breather. After she put her suitcase down, footsteps could be heard from behind. When Georgina turned round, an older teenager dressed in a white T-shirt and blue jeans smiled. "I'm going that way, can I give you a hand?"

"Thanks," said Georgina gratefully.

The teenager lifted her suitcase with ease and as he walked alongside Georgina, glanced. "We don't get many tourists here."

"Why not? The village has scenic views and a fantastic train journey."

"There is no promotion of the area by the Local Authority."

"Perhaps someone in the village should take charge."

Several moments later, the teenager glanced at Georgina. "I'm off to college in September."

"Near here?"

He shook his head of brown hair. "Paisley."

"What are you going to study?"

"Business Management."

"When you finish your studies, contact the Local Authority and sow the seeds of promotion. They can apply business techniques to enhance the area." Georgina continued, "Now that the war is over, people will want to enjoy themselves." From near the top of the brae, she gazed at the sea view." This location is stunning."

"That's what I'll do for my main project," said the teenager, as he beamed.

Not long after, Georgina and the teenager reached a large stone building within its own landscaped grounds. Georgina drew breath. "Thanks, I'm not used to hills. Are you a local?" His accent isn't Scottish.

"I am staying with a family in the village." The teenager paused. "I lost my parents and older brother in the war," he said gravely.

"I'm sorry to hear that." Georgina frowned.

"My parents wanted me to have a good education and that is what I intend to do."

"I suspect you will fulfil that. What is your name?"

"Amos." The teenager glanced at the hotel entrance. "Do you want me to carry your suitcase up the steps?"

"I'll manage from here."

After Georgina thanked the teenager, he walked on. She lifted her suitcase and went up half a dozen concrete steps. When she approached the reception desk, a man with a high hairline got up from his seat. "Yes, madam?"

"Do you have a single room?"

"For how long?"

"A week."

The man checked the hotel register. "Yes, we do, please sign in." He turned the register around and gave Georgina a dark fountain pen. "Did you come by train?"

"Yes, lovely journey," said Georgina, as she signed the register. After she returned the pen and received a key, the man left his desk and picked up her suitcase. "This way, madam."

Georgina followed him up two flights of white painted wooden stairs with a burgundy carpet. When they approached a room, the man opened the door, entered and placed Georgina's suitcase next to a wardrobe. "Just let me know if there is anything you require," he said politely.

"Are you the manager?"

"The owner," he said with a slight smile.

"What about mealtimes?"

"Breakfast is 7.30 to 8.30am and dinner 7 till 9pm. We don't do lunch, as guests prefer to eat in the village at that time of day."

"Is there a school in the village?"

"Yes, why?"

"I may decide to stay and apply for a position."

"What do you teach?"

"Music."

"My sister is a teacher at the school and will ask her if there is a vacancy."

"Thanks," said Georgina gratefully.

After the owner left and closed the door behind him, Georgina cast her gaze around the room. A single bed with wooden side cabinet, wardrobe and dressing table appeared adequate for her short stay. She opened the door, then peeked into the corridor. Good, the bathroom is in close proximity.

CHAPTER 19

SERENITY

On a sunny Monday morning in May, Georgina left for her first music class of the week. Although not a full-time post, the income allowed her to rent a modest cottage, which overlooked the bay. Once more, Georgina entered a chapter in her eventful life. This time, however, no devious partner or a war would get in the way of a joyful stress-free existence.

Since she arrived in the scenic village of Mallaig three years ago, memories of her time in Crete still lingered. At present, the civil war continued to bedevil Greece, although a BBC radio bulletin suggested that due to ammunition and manpower shortages, a communist surrender could be imminent. 'God bless regular American capital injections to the military' would be the Greek Government's cry.

Not far from the cottage, Georgina's walk took her round Mallaig's bay, through its main street and then along a road opposite the harbour. As dark clouds formed and stifled the bright sunshine, she sighed. It can't be perfect every morning.

"Good morning, Miss Rhodes," said a girl politely, as she joined Georgina and walked alongside.

"How are you today, Kirsty?"

"Fine."

"Did you have a good weekend?"

Kirsty nodded. "Did you?"

"Yes, thank you."

"What did you do?"

"I went to a ceilidh at the West Highland Hotel."

"Did you meet anyone?"

Georgina gave a slight smile. "I met many people, all from around the local area." She considered. Not so young.

Soon, teacher and pupil arrived at the school gate, entered and made their way to the classroom. While Georgina sat at her desk, other pupils filtered into the room. When nine o'clock came, Georgina took the class register, however, one pupil had not turned up. She addressed the eleven pupils. "Does anyone know where Mhairi is?" Georgina spotted a raised hand. "Yes, Donald?"

"Mhairi couldn't attend this morning, miss. She has to finish a short story."

"How do you know?"

"Mhairi told me."

At that moment, giggles resounded amongst the pupils and Georgina gave a faint smile. "Because she doesn't enjoy learning about music is no excuse," she said sharply.

"The short story has to be handed in by lunchtime, miss."

"Why?"

"A competition in the Oban Times."

"Mhairi wants to become a writer, miss," said a girl pupil.

"She has written several short stories, miss," said another girl.

"One appeared in the Oban Times six months ago," added Donald, as he glanced around pupils near him. "But I didn't like it."

"What was it about?" asked Georgina.

Donald moaned. "The ferry from Kyle of Lochalsh to Kyleakin."

"I've been on it," said a boy, as he grinned.

"Me too," said a girl. "Since I can't swim, I didn't want to go on it."

"How long has Mhairi been writing short stories?" asked Georgina, now curious.

"Almost a year, miss," said Kirsty.

"Then I must buy the next edition of the Oban Times to see how good a writer she is," said Georgina, as she glanced at the pupils. "Especially, since she missed my class."

Muffled giggles followed and the music lesson commenced, minus a potential writer.

The following week, Georgina went into the local newsagent and bought a copy of the Oban Times. With no class that afternoon, Georgina went for a stroll along the harbour to view the varied selection of colourful boats. Later, she found an empty bench, sat down and opened her newspaper. Amidst a clear blue sky and warm sunshine, Georgina browsed through it. There's not any mention of Mhairi in this edition. As a seagull landed nearby, Georgina stared. It wandered around for a few moments, then looked her way. Georgina smiled. "Sorry, no sandwiches with me today."

After it flew off, she returned to the newspaper and noticed an article on clothes. Ah, rationing has ceased, however, not many will have cash to spend on a new outfit. Turning the page, Georgina came across international affairs. Since Crete, she had retained an interest in what happened overseas. Britain has joined a North Atlantic Treaty Organisation. If it keeps the peace, fine, but the League of Nations failed. Further down, an article that related to the Republic of Ireland. It had separated from the United Kingdom. Georgina sighed. That could create trade barriers. On the next page, another article caught her interest. East Germany was now known as the Federal Republic of Germany. Georgina put down the newspaper. What happened to Erich? Is he in Germany and if so, where?

After a period of reflection, Georgina rose and headed home. Although content with her new life in a picturesque Scottish village, her memory of a lost love remained. A tall man with a short white beard and brown walking stick approached, grinning. "A beautiful day, is it not? The world being at peace also helps." He went on, "I was a naval officer in WW1 and all I've known is conflict after conflict between European countries."

"Enjoying a welcome retirement?"

"So far," said the man, as he coughed. "How do you like our village?"

"I've settled in."

"But do you enjoy the tranquil way of life?"

"I've never been as relaxed as I am now."

"You came here from Crete?"

Georgina nodded. "There's a conflict still in progress."

"Where in America did you live?"

"New York." He's an inquisitive one.

The man cast his gaze around the vicinity. "It's not for everyone, you have to be a certain type of individual." He raised his navy-blue cap. "See you around."

Georgina watched the man head for a small boat and when he reached it, shook hands with two men of similar age. She resumed her stroll and arrived at one of the village's three tearooms. Georgina entered, sat down at a window table and took off her cream jacket. A slim waitress dressed in dark attire, which matched her long hair, appeared and gave a courteous smile. "Yes, madam?"

"A white coffee, please."

"Be right back."

Georgina gazed out the window at a panoramic view of the bay. Even the sound of an exit doorbell failed to distract her tranquil state of mind. The waitress returned with a white saucer and full cup. "Would you like a scone or piece of cake?"

"I'm fine just now, thanks."

"If you change your mind, just let me know," said the waitress cheerily.

"With this fine weather, why not have tables and chairs outside? Customers could have a tea or coffee and also enjoy the sunshine."

"Here, it can be sunny one minute, then it pours," said the waitress, as she glanced out the window. "We don't have the climate that Heraklion has." She gave a wry smile.

"How do you know I came here from Heraklion?"

"This is a village, madam." The waitress departed with a smile and Georgina sat back to savour her afternoon cup of coffee.

A short time later and wanting to soak up the sun, Georgina finished her coffee and then paid the amiable waitress.

After a relaxing stroll, she approached the cottage. When Georgina opened the door, she observed a folded piece of paper inside her letterbox. Taking it out, she unfolded the note and read it.

That evening, Georgina walked around the bay and then up a brae to the West Highland Hotel. Once inside, she went into the well-furnished cocktail bar. A bald grey suited man stared at her, stubbed out a cigarette on the bar counter ashtray and then emptied his glass. Georgina spotted him and approached the bar. The man coughed. "Glad you got my note. I'm in Mallaig on business." He stammered.

"How long for?"

"I leave tomorrow morning."

"Are you a resident here?"

"Yes." The man blinked like an owl. "What would you like to drink?"

"A whisky, just a small one." Going by his breath, he's had a few large ones.

As the man went to the bar, Georgina sat down at a circular oak table. She unbuttoned her jacket, then glanced downwards. Tartan carpets are indeed popular. The man returned with two drinks and after he laid them on the table, sat close to Georgina. After she moved further away, the man took out a packet of cigarettes and a silver lighter from his jacket pocket. Georgina stared. "I thought you didn't smoke," she said sharply.

The man hesitated. "Only some of the time." He replaced the packet and lighter, lifted his glass and took a swig.

Georgina lifted her glass. When I've finished this, I'm off.

"I enjoy a good malt." The man held up his half-empty glass and studied it, then drank the remainder.

Georgina gave a slight smile. I don't doubt it.

"Would you like another drink?"

"No thanks, I have a full glass, said Georgina, as she glanced at the table."

The man got up, went to the bar and soon returned with another full glass. He sat, took a swig, then set the glass down. "Have you been to many ceilidhs?" The man licked his lips.

Georgina shook her head. "Only the one we met at in this hotel." She took a sip. "What is it that you do?"

"A sales representative for a whisky company."

Georgina glanced at the man's near empty glass. "That brand?"

A grin crept across the man's face. "No, and I hope no one finds out, or I'll be in hot water." He paused. "I've reserved a table for 7.45, I trust you don't have other plans?"

"I have to mark exam papers tonight," said Georgina, as she set her glass on the table. "I can't put it off." She tilted her head. "Sorry."

The man finished his malt. "I could come through at the weekend."

"Two friends and I are going hill-walking. Hopefully, the current gorgeous weather will continue." Sounds plausible.

Following a period of silence, Georgina rose. "Thanks for the drink, Roy."

He stood, staggered, but steadied himself by holding onto a chair. As Roy drew breath, Georgina held his arm. "Are you okay?"

"Just about."

"Better not have any more, you may give yourself a nasty injury."

As red-cheeked Roy gave a forced grin, Georgina said goodbye and left with one thought. Later on, he won't be able to stand.

A week later following a busy day at school, Georgina arrived home. After closing the front door, she checked the letterbox. Inside lay one letter plus a folded piece of paper. Georgina sighed. Sorry, chum, you're not my type. Lifting both out, Georgina went into the kitchen and dropped the piece of paper into a waste bin. She laid her letter on the table, made a cup of coffee and then sat down. After she took a couple of sips, Georgina opened the letter.

Dear Georgina, I hope you are still enjoying life in Mallaig and that the teacher position is still to your satisfaction. Since your last letter, six months have passed, so I presume much has changed. However, I have news that will interest you. Two days ago, I had a visit from someone who you will be delighted to learn is alive and well. Erich revealed that due to being in captivity and the family in turmoil in East Germany, he could not contact me. Erich asked about you and told him everything I knew. As you don't have a telephone, I am sure you won't mind that I gave Erich your address. I also supplied him with details of how to reach Mallaig, so you may receive a visit in the near future. Given what he has been through in the past three years, his charm and pleasant manner remain unaltered.
Agnes

Georgina put Agnes's letter aside, then stared at the bin. She retrieved the piece of paper, unfolded it and started to read.

Moments later, Georgina went into the bedroom and sat in front of her dressing table. Meticulous make-up complete, she put on her favourite pale blue jacket, grabbed her black leather handbag and left the cottage.

Following a brisk walk in the late May warm sunshine, Georgina arrived at the West Highland Hotel. As butterflies fluttered, she drew breath and walked into the cocktail bar. The sole customer, a gentleman who wore a white shirt, dark blue suit and tie that matched, looked out the window at Mallaig's coastline. Georgina approached him. "Do you like the view?"

The gentleman turned round, stared and smiled. "Always."

When Georgina and Erich embraced, the barman dried a glass and did his best not to appear interested. Erich stood back. "You look as lovely as ever."

Georgina forced a smile, then wiped a tear from her eye. Her voice grew raspy. "And so, do you."

"Let us sit down."

When they did so, Georgina took a handkerchief out of her handbag, then dabbed her eyes. As she replaced it, Erich quipped, "At least here you can carry a handbag."

Georgina laughed, then sniffed. Erich signalled to the barman who brought over a silver tray, which contained a bottle of champagne and two crystal glasses. When he departed, Georgina stared at the bottle.

"I thought it appropriate since we have not shared a drink in what feels like an eternity," said Erich, as he poured two glasses, then handed one to Georgina.

"What happened after you had been taken back to Germany?"

"I was investigated by the allies and then put on trial. However, witnesses came forward to testify about the food I made available to local families."

"Many families."

"Also, an ex-Jewish prisoner-of-war testified about my conduct whilst on duty in Athens."

"I told people you weren't a Nazi, but a gallant officer."

"After being released, I visited my mother at her home in a village just outside Leipzig." Erich paused. "I found her malnourished, therefore, I stayed until she recovered." He sighed. "Then I came up against restrictions on being allowed to leave the eastern sector."

"What did you do?"

"I arranged for someone to smuggle me out."

"What about your mother?"

"She wanted to stay and be with her friends in the village." Erich raised his glass. "To our future."

Georgina did likewise. "Long and prosperous."

The reunited couple clinked glasses, then sipped their champagne.

Following another, Erich looked at Georgina. "I do not think prosperous is appropriate. I have little money and no job."

"My school requires a foreign languages teacher for the start of next term. Also, you have somewhere to stay." Georgina took Erich's hand. "It's small, but cosy."

"My instinct tells me that I am going to enjoy Scotland."

Georgina smiled. Me too.

ABOUT THE AUTHOR

David Munro was born in Edinburgh and lived there until the age of 27. He was employed by a major brewery within the capital and relocated to Aberdeen, then Glasgow. David attended university and college to attain Chartered Marketer status. As an arts professional and with experience of different cultures, this lends itself to creative literature.

David's love of history allows him the opportunity to delve into past cultures and pinnacle events. His latest novel, Georgina, has a Second World War theme, telling a story of heartache, romance and espionage.

As a writer, David's ambition is to give his readers enjoyment through interesting stories with compelling characters. Georgina has one male and two female characters that readers will embrace. To achieve recognition in the form of a best-seller is a goal.

For details of other novels by David Munro: www.timejigsaw.com

Printed in Great Britain
by Amazon

62911385R00156